# ANYONE WHO HAD A HEART

# ANYONE WHO HAD A HEART

*by*

Mia Dolan

**Magna Large Print Books**
Long Preston, North Yorkshire,
BD23 4ND, England.

British Library Cataloguing in Publication Data.

Dolan, Mia
    Anyone who had a heart.

    A catalogue record of this book is
    available from the British Library

    ISBN   978-0-7505-3219-8

First published in Great Britain in 2009 by Ebury Press,
an imprint of Ebury Publishing
A Random House Group Company

Published in Large Print 2010 by arrangement with
Ebury Publishing, one of the publishers in the Random House Group

Magna Large Print is an imprint of Library Magna Books Ltd.

Printed and bound in Great Britain by
T.J. (International) Ltd., Cornwall, PL28 8RW

## Acknowledgements

I have been so lucky to have a great team behind these books, the success of a book is reliant on many people all working towards the same goal. I am very aware that without the dedication of the team from Ebury we wouldn't have had the success with *Rock A Bye Baby*, and be continuing that success with *Anyone Who Had a Heart*.

In particular I would like to thank: Hannah Telfer and Mel Yarker from Sales; Alex Young, Zeb Dare and Di Riley from Marketing; Hannah Robinson, Sarah Bennie and Ed Griffiths from Publicity. I am also very grateful to Publishing Director, Hannah MacDonald, for having such vision and to my editor Gillian Green for having the patience of a saint.

A special thanks as always to my family, who never seem surprised when I start doing something new.

Thanks also to Jeannie Johnson, who is my rock with these books.

And, last but so not least, a special thanks to the man in my life, Craig Darrock who never wavers, never complains, and always manages to lift me up when I fall down.

For my daughter, Tanya Dolan, who is so much more than just a daughter.

## Chapter One

**1967**

The first thing Marcie Brooks had noticed about Father Justin O'Flanagan was his eyes. They bulged slightly and his pale pupils were fringed with yellow like watery egg yolks. On that first meeting she'd been only eleven years old and still under the impression that only devils had yellow in their eyes. The fact that a priest owned such eyes was worrying and made her suspicious that hell and all its wickedness had infiltrated the Holy Church. From that moment on she'd tried to avoid looking at him, always hanging her head rather than facing him head on.

She knew he was coming today. Her grandmother had informed her as such and although she told herself she was a big girl now, the memory of those eyes had stayed with her.

'There's nothing to be afraid of. He's just a man,' she whispered to her baby daughter. Joanna was lying pink and sleeping, dark lashes flickering as she dreamed her innocent dreams. Looking at her Marcie was reminded of Johnnie, her baby's father. Their love had been short lived but very sweet, cut short by an accident on the North Circular when Johnnie's motorcycle had collided with a lorry. If he'd lived they would have married and Joanna would have had a father. As it was

Marcie had been left an unmarried mother and had to return home to Sheppey to live with her grandmother. Not that Father Justin was aware of that fact; her grandmother had lied on her behalf saying that Marcie's husband had been killed. 'I'm sure the Holy Mother will forgive me,' she exclaimed after crossing herself. 'And Father Justin is not the sort to indulge in idle gossip.'

Marcie hoped she was right.

She was having this baptism done for her grandmother's sake. Her days of churchgoing had stopped years before and the thought of going to confession in the sure knowledge that Father Justin was on the other side of the screen filled her with horror. Some day she might feel differently, but not now.

'Just to please your great-grandmother,' she said to the sleeping child. Marcie had been through a lot in the last year. At times since Johnnie's death she'd even found herself questioning what sort of God would have taken her baby's daddy away from her. 'But we won't say a word to Granny will we. We'll do this just for her.'

She smiled lovingly at the baby at the same time as a pain tightened in her chest. 'And you are like your father,' she said, softly stroking the pretty pink cheek of the child she so loved.

Thinking of Johnnie brought other memories flooding back. One above all others she tried to block from her mind. She'd been foolish enough to trust her friend's father as a shoulder to cry on. Her trust had turned out to be ill judged. He'd taken advantage of her naivety and inexperience. For a while she'd even feared that the child might

14

be his – he'd certainly been convinced of it. There was no longer any doubt about that in her heart. Joanna was the spit of her father.

She'd never pressed charges against Alan Taylor, her friend's father. It was her word against his after all. And she did have something to be grateful to Alan for – if he hadn't come and collected her from the home for unmarried mothers, Joanna would have been given up for adoption. So far since coming back to Sheppey she'd managed to avoid him.

However, this particular meeting could not be avoided. Her grandmother, Rosa Brooks, had been born on a Mediterranean island where the Catholic Church was as necessary to life as the air itself. Following her marriage to a handsome, though slightly irresponsible, sailor in the British Royal Navy, Rosa Brooks had exchanged the Mediterranean island of Malta for the island of Sheppey. Her visits to the confessional and the mass were reduced to once a week. She'd never forced Marcie or the rest of the family to attend if they didn't want to. Marcie didn't want to, but special occasions could not be avoided.

'Joanna must be baptised,' exclaimed her grandmother.

Marcie couldn't argue with that. She didn't want her darling daughter to bear any of the sin she herself felt responsible for. Dislike for the priest faded the moment she looked down at her sleeping daughter. Her cheeks were pink and blue veins, as fine as cobwebs, showed in her eyelids. Marcie couldn't resist gently touching the sleeping child's fingers.

15

The sound of the garden gate opening heralded the priest's arrival. Glancing out she saw him sweep up the garden path, his black robe skirting over heavy black boots, the sort that a docker might wear.

Before going downstairs, she stood in front of the mirror, checked that there was no trace of make-up on her face and that her hair was tidy. She also rehearsed her answer to the number one question he was likely to ask.

*Why have I not seen you at confession, child?*

'I went away to work in London which is where I married Johnnie, Joanna's father.'

Her grandmother calling for her to come down was the signal for her to take her 'wedding ring' from the small tin box that held her less than extensive jewellery collection.

The curtain ring was a bright and brassy alternative for the real thing and at quick glance would fool anyone. Eyeing it too closely would betray what it really was, but being a mother and widowed was preferable to being a mother and unmarried.

Father Justin O'Flanagan was sitting on the settee in the front room balancing a plate on his lap and holding a cup and saucer with both hands.

The front room was rarely used so was chilly compared to the rest of the cottage known as number ten Endeavour Terrace. The old gas fire spluttered intermittently with small blue flames amongst the amber.

'Take a seat, Marcie,' said her grandmother indicating the armchair on the opposite side of the fireplace to her own.

Father Justin had an oblong face and a wide mouth that seemed to stretch from one side of his pallid countenance to the other. When he smiled his mouth resembled a letterbox, so straight it was and gaping as if ready to devour the morning post.

'Ah, Marcie. I'm glad to see you, child.' His Irish brogue grated from his throat as though he were forcing his words over a layer of gravel.

'Good morning, Father Justin.'

She gave a curt nod of her head, which was useful seeing as it meant she could avoid looking into his yellow eyes and instead turn her attention to the teapot.

''Tis nice to see you, Marcie, but I was sad to hear about your husband.'

Marcie thanked him for his sympathy. Father Justin had not visited the house so much as he used to, not approving of her father's divorce and remarriage. She wondered what he'd thought of her real mother. It crossed her mind that she could ask him what she was like, but the thought of having to take tea with him put her off. Those eyes would be boring into her. She couldn't cope with that.

Her grandmother, perhaps sensing what was on her granddaughter's mind, took the conversation in the right direction.

'As you know, Marcie, Father Justin has come to discuss having Joanna baptised.'

Her grandmother's jet-black eyes scuttled between her granddaughter and priest. Although she'd been in England some years, her obeisance to a priest and all things Catholic had never quite

17

gone away.

Nevertheless, she said it all with some pride, almost as though no other grandchild in all the wide world had ever been so privileged.

'Of course,' said Marcie.

'Your grandmother tells me your husband died in a road accident before the child was born. That's very sad indeed.'

Seeing as she was supposed to be a poor young widow, it was easy to get away with hanging her head and not looking at him this time. She nodded accordingly, 'That's right, Father. He was riding his motorbike.'

'Ah yes,' said the priest nodding his head in understanding. 'It would be a motorbike. Dangerous things they are!'

He took a big mouthful of cake and swigged back some tea. Seeing as both plate and cup were empty, her grandmother took them and asked if he required a refill. Of course he did! Father Justin had a big appetite and an insatiable desire for fruitcake, especially of the home-made variety that her grandmother produced.

'Never mind, child,' he said, leaning across and patting her hand.

She instinctively placed her right hand over her left so the ring was hidden, just in case he chanced to notice how cheap looking it was.

Father Justin sprayed crumbs as he ate his second slice of cake. Throughout the munching he outlined the ceremony in between regular repetitions of how sad it was that the father of the baby would not be there.

'So how about the grandparents – the father's

parents I'm meaning?' he added. 'Was Joanna's father of the faith?'

Marcie felt her face colouring up beneath the intensity of his eyes. It always seemed to matter so much to Catholics that everyone around them was Catholic too.

'No,' she said shaking her head. 'They were not.'

'Are you sure about that? Did you ask them? You know how it is in this day and age, Mrs Brooks,' he said to Rosa. 'People are reluctant to give any outer sign of their faith for fear of attracting mockery. Tis sad it is, but unless you ask you may never know. So think about it, Marcie,' he said, turning his egg-yolk eyes back to Rosa Brooks' granddaughter. 'I'm usually right about these matters.'

In a way it was hard not to laugh and tell the smug priest to his face that on this occasion he was very, very wrong. Johnnie's father – or adopted father as it had turned out – was a vicar; a Church of England, Protestant vicar!

'Will you take another piece of cake, Father Justin?'

The priest, whose girth had got steadily wider over the years, had barely wolfed down the second piece and now pounced on a third.

'Lovely cake, Mrs Brooks.'

He took her smile at face value, thinking it merely a response to his flattery rather than an intention to terminate his awkward enquiries.

Two more cups of tea were needed to wash down the cake before the good father rolled forwards in an effort to get up off his broad backside and prepare to leave.

'Oh, Mrs Brooks. You most definitely took me into the paths of temptation,' he said while patting his bulging midriff. 'And a very pleasant experience it was too. That fruitcake was the best I have ever tasted.'

Rosa Brooks threw her granddaughter a look behind the priest's broad back. 'The fourteenth of September it is then,' she said to him as she showed him to the door.

'Indeed,' he said while placing his broad-brimmed hat on his head. 'I look forward to it.'

Marcie stood behind her grandmother and watched him leave. He hung on the open gate a while bending down to fix his bicycle clips around his ankles. By the time he'd finished that and was reaching around the hedge for his bicycle, his face was flushed.

Rosa Brooks raised her hand to bid him goodbye. Surely he was going now.

The priest stepped out onto the cracked pavement outside the cottage gate. He stood with his back to them looking this way and that, as though something was wrong, as though something had caused him alarm.

Rosa ventured halfway along the garden path looking puzzled. 'Is something wrong, Father?'

The expression on his face was one of absolute disbelief. 'Some snot-nosed little toerag has stolen my bike!'

Rosa Brooks made the sign of the cross over her chest. Behind her Marcie stuffed her fist into her mouth to stop herself from laughing out loud. The priest's consternation detracted from his devilish eyes and also stopped her worrying about him finding out the truth about her un-married state. It was a well known fact that for a Catholic, Father O'Flanagan was more than a bit touched with the fire and brimstone eulogy more common with Baptists and Methodists. He did not approve of original sin – '...because he hasn't tried it himself,' according to her father.

'Call the police, Mrs Brooks! Call the police if you will!' exclaimed the red-faced priest waving his arms around like an out-of-control windmill.

'I have no phone,' Rosa pronounced. She pointed in the direction of the red telephone box at the end of the road. 'There is a public tele-phone.'

'Pennies! I need pennies!' Hitching up his robe, Father Justin O'Flanagan proceeded to rummage in his trouser pockets.

Marcie found herself wondering why he wore a robe when he wore trousers underneath. It must be awful on a hot day she concluded.

Out of common courtesy, her grandmother proceeded to escort the fuming priest along the pavement to the telephone box at the end of the terrace. Feeling it safe to poke her nose out, Marcie ventured to the halfway mark where her grandmother had stood. She paused briefly, and once sure that they'd reached the telephone she proceeded further.

Standing by the gate she looked up and down the road just as the priest had done. There was no sign of a bicycle. It could be anywhere if the kids hereabouts had anything to do with it.

Fancying she heard Joanna crying, she went

back into the house and went immediately to the kitchen. No doubt Joanna wanted a bottle.

The bright sunlight momentarily blinded her so the interior of the cottage seemed even darker than usual.

First she ladled three spoonfuls of Cow and Gate powdered baby milk into a Pyrex jug. Filling the kettle from the tap beneath the kitchen window, she chanced to look out to a sunlit back garden. Sometimes she could imagine the tree that used to be there and the woman on whose lap she'd sat while she stroked her hair.

On turning off the tap she once again chanced to look out along the straight path that cut through a lawn on one side and a vegetable patch on the other. The bushes at the end of the garden had yellowish leaves. The sunlight gilded them with flame-like brightness, yet it was not this that caught her eye. A dark figure moved just beyond the fence, pushed open the rickety old gate. He was pushing a bike in front of him.

'Garth!'

Plonking the kettle down on the draining board, she darted out the back door and up the path not sure whether to be angry or amused.

'Garth! What are you doing with that bike?'

Physically Garth had the body of a young man in his twenties. Due to an accident at birth he had the mind of an eight-year-old.

At first he looked surprised to see her, before a sunburst of merriment swept from his mouth to his eyes and all over his face.

'Some boys were going to take it,' he explained. 'I wouldn't let them. I knew it was yours because

22

it was outside your gate.'

She took the bike from him. 'Oh, Garth.'

'Did I do right, Marcie? I didn't let them take it. Did I do right?'

Garth was easily confused and likely to get upset if she told him he'd done wrong.

She smiled into the vacant blue eyes. His hair was awry and his face looked like a war zone. It was sprinkled with scraps of blood-stained tissue paper. He'd obviously been trying to shave himself and, as usual, had not made a good job of it.

'You did right, Garth, but it isn't mine. Tell you what, how about you go in and put the kettle on. I'll be in shortly to give Joanna her feed. I won't be long.'

She could imagine Joanna was getting irksome that she hadn't yet come with her bottle, but she had to put this right before the police came. Garth would be terrified if they started asking him questions.

Rather than be slowed down with the bike, she ran along the back lane and was just in time to stop Father O'Flanagan from dialling.

'It's alright,' she gasped on hauling open the heavy door. 'We've found your bike. Garth put it round the back because some young scallywags were about to make off with it.'

She was breathless and in the rush to stop the pennies from dropping into the box, her neatly brushed hair was wild and the top button of her dress had sprung loose exposing an inch or so of cleavage.

She told herself that Father O'Flanagan wasn't looking at her with surprise, only misgiving, that the sudden change from demure to wanton had merely shocked him, but she felt distinctly uncomfortable under his gaze.

'Have you noticed Father Justin's eyes?' she asked her grandmother, later that evening.

Rosa Brooks was hemming a tablecloth with a bright green silk cross stitch. Without raising her head, she looked at her granddaughter with hooded eyes and waited for her to continue.

'I think they're devilish eyes. I caught him looking down my cleavage.'

Her grandmother's gaze stayed steady. 'Is that so?'

'When I took his bike to him.' She went on to explain the rest of it. 'Maybe I just took him by surprise.'

Her grandmother's eyes went back to what she was doing. Her lips were pursed and she was stabbing the needle in and out of the material with more force than before.

At the back of her mind Rosa Brooks was remembering another priest, another place and another time.

In future she would ensure she was always present whenever Father O'Flanagan called. He was supposed to be celibate, but she knew that what was supposed to be and what actually was were often two very different things.

## Chapter Two

It wasn't in Alan Taylor's make-up to be a churchgoer. He prided himself on being the big businessman with second-hand car dealerships in Sheerness and also down in Deal. In this respect he considered himself something of a benefactor to the community – especially the Brooks family over the years

'I gave Tony Brooks a job. You'd think he'd be more grateful,' he oft repeated to his daughter Rita or anyone else who would listen. 'And I treated Marcie Brooks as if she was my own daughter!'

He was always careful to stop there. From the time she first blossomed into puberty, Alan Taylor had developed an unhealthy obsession with Marcie Brooks. The fact was she was beginning to look as gorgeous as her mother. He had been obsessed with Mary Brooks too. Unknown to Tony, her old man, he'd pursued her and got rebuffed every time. I mean, who did she think she was anyway? Just a tart, if local gossip could be believed! A tart no different to any of the others around the London nightclub scene.

A churchgoer he definitely was not, but these were special circumstances. Anyway, he wasn't actually entering the church, he was merely observing.

There was a handy little parking space close by where he could watch without being observed.

He'd heard from a friend of a friend that the christening – baptism – call it what you will, was scheduled for eleven o'clock this morning. The event wasn't secret, of course, but even if it had been Babs – Barbara Brooks, Tony's second wife and Marcie's stepmother, would still have blabbed it from here to bloody Sheerness and back again. She had a big trap that one. No wonder his old pal Tony had slapped her about a bit in the past. He might have done the same himself, if he had been married to her. Though Alan considered himself more of a lover than a fighter. Women were made to be taken to bed and loved. As far as he was concerned, they wanted it as much as men did, though sometimes they said they didn't. But that was all it was. They often said no when what they really meant was yes.

Dressed in their best, the Brooks family plus a few friends were making their way towards the church door. He saw Marcie with the baby in her arms. She was wearing a pretty, short dress with matching jacket. That was when he wondered whether he shouldn't get on in there and sort everything all out, point out that the kid was his. It was, wasn't it?

He saw Tony with Babs and the kids. Babs was done up like a dog's dinner, her skirt way above her dimpled knees. Chance was that if she bent down she'd be showing her knickers. Silly cow! She'd been a good-looking bird when she was younger and she made the effort to keep hold of her looks. The trouble was now she was trying too hard. There was a time to stop dressing like a seventeen-year-old and start acting your age. The rule didn't apply to men of course as far as Alan was concerned. They were different than women. Younger women liked older men; father figures. Sugar daddies.

The awkward lad was there too. He couldn't remember his name and wasn't entirely sure he even had one. Not that he cared. The lad spent a lot of time round at the Brooks' old cottage in Endeavour Terrace. His mother chose to think he didn't exist half the time and probably wished he didn't. Given half the chance she'd be off with the milkman or some other bloke who gave her the time of day. Now here the idiot was at Joanna's christening, Marcie's kid. Bloody nerve. Him going into the church as bold as you like, whereas him, the kid's probable father...

Suddenly he burned with anger. The ungrateful bitch! Marcie's baby would have been adopted if it hadn't been for him. She should be thankful. She should have married him instead of telling him to get lost and insisting that her rocker sweetheart had been Joanna's father. He still chose not to believe it. He always would.

Once the little group had disappeared inside the church, he got out of his car. Not wishing to be seen stalking them, he'd left the Jag at home and borrowed his daughter's mini. It was a mustard colour and bog standard and suited the occasion. The Jag was flash and would have been instantly recognised. He hadn't wanted that. He was hoping for a moment when Marcie was away from the rest of the family. So far it hadn't occurred.

'Right, old son. Get on in there and sort them all out.'

He crossed the road swiftly, legged it up the path to the church and reached for the door. On second thoughts he decided to take a look-see in one of the side windows just to make sure that nobody too handy – one of the family's rough relatives – was attending. Tony had told him to stay away from Marcie and made it clear what he'd do to him if he didn't. In the past Alan would have laughed the threat off. Who was Tony Brooks but a small-time thief with attitude though not necessarily the right muscle to back it? Alan was a man of means, as bent as Tony but a bit more subtle about it. OK, not all his operations were legit, but at least he kept up the façade of being legal if nothing else. Tony had crime written all over him and even trusted the people he worked for. Silly sod! Didn't he know there was no honesty among crooks? That was the trouble with Tony: he was so trusting. Give him a good reason for what you were doing and he'd swallow it hook, line and sinker.

However he'd heard that Tony Brooks was now working for some heavyweight Sicilian gangsters in the East End. Alan chewed his lip nervously at the thought of it. Perhaps one of Tony's new contacts might be among the invited guests.

Furrowed by many feet, a track had been worn through the rough grass sprouting around the church's stout stone foundations. Careful not to muddy his slip-on Italian shoes or the hems of his Levis, he picked his way along carefully. There were puddles in places and he did a quick sidestep, nimbly avoiding a dog turd.

Once he felt he was on safe ground, he placed his

hands on the sloping stone window ledges and pulled himself up, the toes of his shoes jammed into gaps where the mortar had fallen out.

The effort proved fruitless. Thick plates of stained glass made up the majority of the windows. Those that weren't stained glass were protected with sheets of stiff wire. There was nothing to be seen.

That made his mind up. If he couldn't see in then he was going to go in.

He jumped down, dusted his hands on his jeans and made ready to put in an appearance and stake his claim. What the fuck could any of that lot do anyway?

He smirked at the thought of their faces; them in all their finery acting as though they'd never broken a commandment in their lives. Christ, at some point that bloody family had broken them all. Not that he couldn't own up to a few sins himself, but that was beside the point; he wanted to stake his claim. Most of all, he wanted Marcie. He'd had her once, but once was not enough. She hadn't exactly been responsive. In fact she'd been blotto following the drinks he'd given her. Next time he had her she'd want it as much as he did, and nobody was going to stop him.

Stumbling back onto the path that led back round to the front of the church, he thought he heard someone call him. He looked round but couldn't see anyone.

He told himself he was imagining things.

Taking a deep breath, he prepared to grab the church door and yank it back. The plan was that at the same time as doing that, he'd shout out that the baptism had to stop. He didn't want Joanna baptised; not here in a church of left-footers. And seeing he was the baby's father, what he said was law. Wasn't it?

The truth was that he didn't have a clue about the lawful bit and whether a father could justifiably prevent a baptism taking place. He had no proof that he was even a contender to be Joanna's dad though he still couldn't accept that the 'greaser' Marcie had been going out with was the kid's father. And wasn't he the one who'd fetched her back from the place where she'd given birth to the kid? He'd even offered to marry her and the little cow had turned him down. Just as her mother had turned him down.

The people in the church were in for a nasty surprise. But did he care? Sod it, he did not!

He didn't get far.

'Oi! What are you doing with my bloody car? I had to get the bus here thanks to you. What's the matter with you, Dad? Getting senile are you?'

His daughter Rita was presently sporting a pudding-basin hairstyle. Apparently she'd seen some pop star with the same style on TV. The pop star had been skinny and had long legs. Rita was more substantially built and the kindest thing that could be said about her legs was that they were strong. In fact they were chunky and the girl was not suited to wearing miniskirts.

Her eyes glimmered from amidst coal-black eyeliner and mascara. She'd drawn extra eyelashes beneath her bottom eyelids – the latest fashion for the hip chick of today. The effect made her look as though her eyes were stranded at the bottom of two deep dark wells. Her lips were plastered with the same foundation as the rest of her face. He believed it was called American Tan. She always wore it.

Her hair was pale brown and, teased out with the wire tail of her comb, curving into the nape of her neck. Her dress had big green spots and her shoes were white and had ankle straps and chunky two-inch heels.

Rita had once been the apple of her father's eye. She wasn't too sure she was now. Her father had changed since Marcie had come home with Joanna. He didn't dote on her as he once had, in fact it seemed he'd become obsessed with the girl who had once been her friend. As of yet she still hadn't worked out why.

Puzzled, she frowned at her father. 'Did you hear what I said? What are you doing here?'

The last thing he wanted was for Rita to know the truth. Deciding to make light of it, he shoved his hands in his jeans and laughed.

'Just thought I'd come along for the crack. Old Tony being a grandfather now and all that. Thought I'd go in and pull his leg a bit.'

Rita was selfish and spoilt but no fool. Her father had allowed her greater freedom than most girls of her age had, and doing that had made her streetwise. She eyed him with suspicion.

'I don't think we're invited, Dad.'

Still smiling he shrugged casually as though it were all a huge joke. 'That don't matter. We're old mates, me and Tony. We go way back...'

Rita was getting impatient. 'I don't care about you and Tony. I want my car.'

Alan got the keys from out of his pocket. 'There you are.'

'And I want some money.'

Her father raised his eyebrows. 'I gave you some earlier this week.'

'I've spent it. Come on. I need a new dress and some shoes. I've seen a super white pair and a dress to match.'

'What's wrong with the white shoes you're wearing?'

Rita threw him a disparaging look and held out her hand.

Alan delved into his pockets and brought out a pound note, a ten-shilling note and two half-crowns.

Rita eyed the handful of money with contempt. 'That's not enough!'

Alan sighed. When money had been plentiful he'd showered his little girl with presents and gifts of money. Anything and everything she'd wanted he'd given her. But the used car game wasn't as good as it had been – not when you had to play things straight it wasn't, and just of late he'd been playing it straight.

'I'll have to go to the bank.'

'I'll drive you there.'

Her heels clip-clopped back along the concrete path from the church to where he'd parked the car. He told himself he should have parked further from the church then she wouldn't have noticed him and decided she needed more money for shopping. As it was the day for him had been ruined; it had taken some courage to show his face at the church – not that he'd actually done that thanks to Rita. In a way he was glad; Marcie's old man had threatened to chop his balls off if he didn't stay away from her. Tony Brooks was a rough diamond, but not known for violence towards his mates. However, this was about his daughter. There could always be a first time, so perhaps Rita had done him a favour turning up when she did. On this occasion he'd been prevented from making a fool of himself, but another time, another place, things might be different.

## Chapter Three

There was no celebratory spread in a local hostelry following Joanna's baptism. Instead Rosa, Marcie and Babs had made ham and cheese rolls spread out on the table in the kitchen at number 10 Endeavour Terrace. Here and there a bowl of pickled onions and beetroot interspersed the plates of white bread and the fruitcake Rosa had made especially for the occasion.

Only the family attended plus a few neighbours. Garth gorged on the leftovers and said it was the best party he'd ever been to. Everyone knew it was the *only* party he'd ever been to, but didn't have the heart to correct him.

The day had been fine but by five o'clock storm clouds had blown in from the sea and rain was hammering against the windows. Although a fire glowed red and yellow in the grate and the lights were lit, the old cottage held on to its gloomy corners.

Marcie watched as her father bent over the cooing baby telling her crazy stories that she was far too young to follow. Marcie smiled. It didn't matter that Joanna didn't understand. She was enjoying being spoken to and her father enjoyed telling stories to his first grandchild.

A small figure in black appeared at her side. 'Your father is very proud.'

Marcie agreed with her grandmother. For all his faults her dad loved kids. 'I think he firmly believes that she's the most beautiful baby in the world and that nothing bad can possibly happen to her because he's around.'

'He will do all in his power,' her grandmother said softly.

There was something about her grandmother's tone of voice that made Marcie look at her. The olive-skinned face was difficult to read at the best of times and even though her guard was down on this most auspicious of days, she was still hard to interpret.

Knowing that asking what was on her mind wouldn't bring forth an answer, Marcie turned her mind to other things. The future was doubly important to her now she had a child to take care of. Johnnie, Joanna's father was dead so there was no income forthcoming from that quarter. Neither would his parents – or, as she had found out, his adoptive parents – support her financially. There was some money likely from National Assistance, but that was tiny and would provide little towards their daily costs.

Until recently, there had been another option; Alan Taylor had asked her to marry him. His daughter, Rita, had once been her best friend, but things had cooled between them for more than one reason. Marcie accepted that they'd grown out of each other and to her mind it was all for the best. At one time she'd desperately wanted her dad to be like Alan Taylor. He'd been so 'with it', so understanding of young girls out to have fun. She hadn't seen through the friendliness to what he'd really wanted. She'd trusted him enough to spend an evening with him, to accept a drink or two. She didn't remember much about that night. The alcohol he had plied her with had caused her to pass out, and it was only the morning after that she realised what had happened. Her knickers had been on inside out and back to front and she had felt raw and bruised 'down there'. There was no getting away from the horrible fact: Alan Taylor had raped her. So it was for the best that her friendship with Rita was over along with any contact with Rita's father.

Her grandmother was allowing her to live in the old cottage for free and her father helped where he could. However, she had made some money towards her keep from dressmaking, though it would never be enough to fully support her. Basically she needed a job and only the day before she'd seen exactly the sort of job she needed.

She told her grandmother about it. 'It's advertised as full time, but only from eight till four. I thought I'd try and get them to take me on part time...' She paused, looked at her grandmother and tried to gauge her initial reaction. 'It wouldn't be so much money part time, but I was wondering...'

Rosa Brooks was typical of women born on the islands and countries scattered or surrounding the Mediterranean. Her hair was still jet black, her skin paled from tawny to olive by the lack of sunshine, and her eyes were quick and dark. She wore her hair in a bun at the nape of her neck and as a widow always wore black. Her mind was still quick and her family meant everything to her. Her family was who she lived for.

'You wish me to look after Joanna.'

It was a statement rather than a question. Marcie nodded. 'Well. Yes.'

She felt her stomach turning inwards and wished she hadn't asked. It was much too big a burden for her grandmother. How could she have even suggested it?

'Of course I will look after Joanna.' Rosa's smile brightened her face and sent a sparkle to her eyes. 'It's wonderful to have a baby in this house again. Your grandfather warned me you would ask. Your grandfather had such insight you know. I miss him.'

The last three words sounded tacked on and a little sadder than everything else. Though Marcie's granddad had long since died, Rosa gift was such that she maintained that she talked to him regularly since his passing. Her grandmother's words also touched a chord in Marcie that she hadn't known was there. What would things have been like if Johnnie had lived? Would she still be in London? Would they have a little place of their own where the boards were bare, the furnishings old and battered? Poor as it might have been, they would have been happy. Of that she was sure.

'It's a sewing room serving the hospital, making nurses uniforms, sewing hems around sheets and making pillowcases. I thought three days and on the other days I could do my own sewing.'

She wasn't sure about the uniforms, but hoped that the sewing wouldn't be confined to sheets and pillowcases. If it was, well, she would have the consolation that she'd be doing her own sewing on the other days.

'Mrs Spontini is very pleased with her funeral dress,' said her grandmother.

Mrs Spontini was one of her grandmother's closest friends. They went to church together and drank tea with the priest on those days when he met with the more senior members of his congregation.

Marcie said she was glad. In her heart of hearts she never wanted to make Mrs Spontini a funeral dress ever again. The old trout had criticised the whole project from beginning to end so it came as something as a surprise to hear that she'd intimated to her grandmother that she was pleased with the end result.

Like her grandmother, Mrs Spontini was a widow who had married an Englishman back in the 1920s. Originally from Italy, she had crooked legs and black eyes either side of a hooked nose. As was the habit of Mediterranean widows, she only wore black but had different black dresses for different occasions.

The very next day Marcie took her application

37

form into the hospital sewing department that maintained and made the various items needed on the wards. The interview was for ten o'clock. She also took a sample of her sewing: a very pretty blouse she'd made for herself, the front of which was covered in pin-tucks.

She didn't bother with her fake wedding ring. She had heard it was still difficult for married women to get jobs. Single girls always got priority.

Miss Gardner, the workroom supervisor, had black kiss curls and a bouffant hairstyle. She wore a tight skirt and a black polo-neck jumper and big gypsy-style earrings jangled from her lobes.

She read the application form in quick bursts, glancing up intermittently. It made Marcie think she was trying to catch her doing something she shouldn't.

Marcie felt as though a wire-wool brush was scouring her insides. She put her nerves down to the fact that this wasn't just for herself, this job was for Joanna too and their future together. She badly needed the money.

At last Miss Gardner put down the form and picked up the blouse, examining the pin-tucks one by one.

'Not bad,' she said at last. 'Well, Miss Brooks, it seems you have a number of things in your favour. Number one, you can sew. That fact is very evident.' Her fingers lightly touched the blouse. 'Number two you're very young and not married. That means we'll have a few years' work out of you before you get yourself hitched to a man and proceed to produce a family. It is both the hospital's and this section's policy that we employ single women with no family ties. Once you get married we expect you to leave. That is why I am still a Miss not a Mrs,' she said with a short, sharp smile.

Marcie deduced there was bitterness behind that smile and imagined that at some point in her career, Miss Gardner had been forced to choose between her work and a man. She thanked her lucky stars that she'd chosen to go along as Miss Brooks and not to admit that she had a child. She sensed that being an unmarried mother would be regarded as a far worse crime than marrying.

'You don't mind working only three days?'

'I look after my grandmother on the other two days. She's getting on a bit,' Marcie lied.

She crossed her fingers beneath the desk as she said it. Her grandmother had advised her that it was the best thing to say. 'And what's more, I *am* old,' she had added, with one of her rare wry smiles.

'You can start on Monday,' said Miss Gardner without giving her the option of whether she could make it or not. The workroom, explained Miss Gardner, was run on disciplined lines similar to that of the wards. A ward sister was in charge in the hospital. Miss Gardner ruled the sewing rooms, alternating her supervision with a Miss Pope. Miss Gardner explained what wage Marcie could expect, when time and a half was paid and when double time, plus piecework rates.

Marcie was walking on air when she left. She gladly ran for the bus home, needing to spend her energy before getting on and sitting down because she just wouldn't have been able to keep still.

'You look happy,' said the middle-aged woman sitting next to her on the bus.

It was true. She just couldn't stop smiling. 'I am,' she said exuberantly. 'I've just got a job.'

'Best of luck to you, darling and may you be happy in your work.'

Marcie said that she would be. It was just the kind of job she'd been looking for: three days a week.

Yet again she thanked her lucky stars that she'd opted not to mention having a baby. She suspected that should they ever hear of it they'd fire her right away and no way must that happen.

## Chapter Four

Babs had left her job at Woolworths following the move into a council house, but had managed to get two days' cleaning a week. On those days she brought her youngest, Anne, round for Rosa to look after, with Marcie's help of course,

Marcie's half-sister was now walking well and, although Marcie didn't mind looking after her, she was beginning to get into mischief. The fact was that Marcie was still working on her two days off. She'd started designing and making dresses. The patterns were based on the pictures she saw in magazines. Seeing as they were basically what was termed a 'shift' dress, that is straight up and down, very short and with few darts, she found them easy to make. If she included working on

40

weekends, she managed to make two and a half dresses a week, sometimes three.

Her father, being a cheeky bugger at the best of times, had acted as her salesman and managed to coerce Sheppey's first and one and only boutique to sell what she made.

'You've just got to go along and see the woman in charge. Her name's Angela. I said you were as good as that Mary Quick woman...'

'Mary Quant,' Marcie corrected.

'That's the one. Anyway, get yourself along there and show her what you've got.'

In the past Marcie would have curled up inside at the thought of doing something like that, but that was in the days when she only had herself to think about. The fact that she was doing this for Joanna made a big difference.

Her grandmother helped her put the dresses on silk-covered hangers inside a full-length polythene cover. Her quick hands smoothed out the wrinkles, patted the sleeves straight and lay the whole package over Marcie's arm.

She did this silently. At times like these Marcie felt the old guilt descend about getting pregnant before Johnnie had married her. Her grandmother was old-fashioned. She'd been brought up in a different world. Marcie wondered...

'Gran, I'm sorry to have been so much trouble...' Her grandmother looked at her. The olive-skinned face was composed: neither condemning nor implying that everything was in order.

'God made it happen.' Her hand patted her granddaughter's shoulder and she smiled. 'You have blossomed from a rosebud into full flower.

41

Who are we to question?'

Marcie noticed that the jet-black eyes were moist and there was a proud jut to her grandmother's chin. A lump came to her throat. She could say nothing in response, but she knew what her grandmother meant. First she'd procured the job at the hospital and now there was this. In a small town on a small island this counted as success.

'I'll see you later,' she said, her lips brushing her grandmother's cheek. The skin was very soft and also very thin. It struck Marcie that her grandmother was getting old. She'd never thought of her as old before now. But Marcie was older too, no longer the innocent little girl not long out of school. In the space of a year she'd grown up considerably.

It would have been difficult to carry three dresses on the bus into Sheppey, but her father had offered her a lift. By hook or by crook most probably the latter – Tony Brooks had acquired a car. Marcie couldn't recall whether her father actually had passed a driving test, but didn't question his right to be cruising down the road with the window open. Every so often he flicked a cloud of cigarette ash from a smoking Woodbine. He was in a good mood, his spirits at an all-time high.

'The Brooks' are going places,' he exclaimed with pride and patted his daughter's knee. 'You're a clever girl, our Marcie. I always knew you were. OK, you made a little mistake – not that it was your fault,' he added before she had chance to remind him that Johnnie had died. His motorcycle had been crushed by an oncoming lorry. They would have married. She knew they would have married. 'And we got Joanna out of it. Wouldn't wish her away for the world,' he said proudly.

'Looks as though you're going places too, Dad. I didn't know you could drive.'

He made a huffing sound. 'There's a lot of things you don't know your father can do, our Marcie. Driving's only one of them. Not that it's that difficult mind you. It's like riding a bicycle, once done never forgotten.'

'Don't you have to have a licence?'

'Not if you don't want to or if you were driving before the war when licences weren't needed.'

Marcie wasn't sure what he was saying here and was wise enough not to push the matter. She preferred riding along in ignorance rather than worrying about being stopped by the law. The police and her father were past bedmates. So was prison.

She tried studying her father's face to glean some semblance of the truth, but without success. He was whistling and smiling as though he hadn't a care in the world.

'So what do you think of the car,' he asked suddenly.

'It's lovely. Where did you get it?'

'A mate of mine in London lent it me. I did a few jobs for him when I was up there last. "Tony," he said. "You're a right diamond and that's a fact. You've done me proud. Here's your moolah. Now get off down and see that family of yours. Family is dead important," he said to me. More important even than dosh, except that you get to spend it on your family.'

Marcie laughed. It wasn't what her father was

saying that made her laugh, but the way he was saying it. He'd picked up a lot of cockney idioms during his sojourn 'working' in London.

Her father laughed too. 'It's great. Bloody great,' he exclaimed with overblown exuberance.

The boutique was named 'Angie's'. The window display consisted of black and white dresses, black and white shoes, black and white sweaters, hats, feather boas and tights.

Her father promised to wait for her outside. 'Now go on,' he muttered, shooing her towards the shop door.

Heaving the dresses over her arm, she headed in that direction and pushed open the door.

An old-fashioned brass bell jangled above her head. Multicoloured spotlights picked out the clothes hanging on the rails and pinned to the walls. A huge poster of the Rolling Stones, a fairly new group with an R and B beat and an impertinent attitude dominated one wall.

'Can I help you?' The speaker was a tall, slim girl with long black hair and a square-cut fringe hanging low over sharp blue eyes. Marcie was reminded of Cathy McGowan on the TV show *Ready Steady Go!* Her clothes were spot on too. She was wearing a pale-mauve dress with a mandarin collar and a zip up the front. Her tights were white and her shoes patent burgundy that changed colour dependent on which spotlight she was standing under.

Marcie went straight into her pitch. 'I'm Marcie Brooks and I believe the shop owner, Angela Babbington, expressed interest in my dresses.'

'I'm Angela. How do you do.'

44

They shook hands, Marcie almost dropping her samples when she did so.

'I've brought three along to show you.'

The welcoming smile tightened a little. 'Look, I know I did say I would take a look, but you have to understand–'

'You can have them on sale or return,' blurted Marcie. She'd heard the term somewhere and it did sound self-explanatory. If the dresses got sold, she got paid. If they didn't sell then she would not.

Angela Babbington seemed to pause for breath, her pink lips slightly parted. 'Well...'

Marcie jumped in again, unzipping the dust cover and taking each dress by turn, holding it against herself for effect.

The first one was made of a pink woollen material with speckles of blue and green interwoven into the fabric. The sleeves were gathered into a tight cuff and it had four buttons and the collar had elongated points.

'Winter, spring or autumn wear – even summer given our English summers,' Marcie added with a laugh.

To her delight, Angela took the dress from her and began to study it.

Marcie went straight on to the next one, which was a soft peppermint green and had an A-line skirt. The material was fairly silky and swirled slightly at the hem.

'Great for the weekend,' Marcie exclaimed.

Silently, Angie took that one too. Marcie could tell by her expression that she was hooked on both dresses. Now for the third. She'd purposely left the

45

one she regarded as her best dress until last.

'This is definitely for dancing.' She held the black all-wool dress against her. It was plainly cut, the sleeves long, the neck round and a cavalcade of small brass buttons down the front. It also had red inserts over the shoulders and the hem ended way above the knees.

'Great with black or red tights,' said Marcie.

Judging by the look on Angela's face, she thought the same.

Marcie's heart seemed to burst into song when Angela said, yes, she would take them.

'Can you make more by next weekend?'

'Which one?'

'All three.'

A creeping fear seeped down Marcie's spine. She was a one-man band and couldn't make any more than three in a week. Four would be a push and she couldn't possibly make three of each design in a week. She pointed this out to the boutique's highly impressed owner.

'That's just it,' said Angela. 'I don't want to be the same as the big chain stores in the high street. I want to be more exclusive, so if you could make me one of each of these for next week, we'll see how things go. I think I'll sell these this week, though I've got a suspicion that the black dress will be in great demand. I might have to ask you for three of the black for the following week in different sizes. Would that be alright?'

*Would that be alright?*

Marcie could almost have skipped with delight.

'Yes! Yes! Of course it would.'

'Shall we say a split of sixty–forty?'

Sixty and forty made one hundred. That was what sale or return would mean. Whatever Angela sold the dresses for, she, as the manufacturer would get sixty per cent.

'That depends...'

'I'm thinking of seven pounds ten shillings and sixpence. They're each worth that.'

Marcie made no comment but kept her gaze fixed on the dresses. It was worth doing.

Thinking that Marcie was in two minds whether to leave the dresses – and the opportunity – with her, Angela bounced back again.

'OK. How about seventy–thirty?'

Out of necessity, Marcie hid her delight. The material had been given to her by a friend of her grandmother's. The price of cotton and buttons was neither here nor there. Basically it meant that she would earn somewhere around five pounds per dress after expenses.

'Done,' she said, offering her hand. She promised she'd call into the shop on the following Monday.

She grinned like a Cheshire cat all the way back to the car.

'Hey! You looks like the cat that got the bloody cream, girl,' her father crowed. His face beamed with delight.

'I have,' said Marcie as she slid into the passenger seat, hunched her shoulders and sighed with satisfaction. 'She wants me to make some more.'

'I guessed it,' he said, smacking the dashboard with his hand. 'I just knew she'd pay you handsomely for them frocks. How much did she give you?'

'Nothing yet. She's bought them on sale or return.'

Her father frowned. 'What's that mean when it's at home?'

She began to explain. He stopped her.

'I know what sale or return means, girl. I weren't born under the bloody gooseberry bush. What I mean is why didn't she pay you out then and there? What's wrong with handing over the readies?'

'Dad, I'm happy with that. It means I'll make fifteen pounds in total on those "frocks" as you call them. And she wants more!' Exhaling a deep sigh, she sat back against the sun-warmed leather and closed her eyes. 'I can't believe it. I can't believe I've been so lucky!'

Her father was looking at her, his face a mix of emotions. He was glad for her but also concerned about the dresses being left there until they were sold. He only handed something over in exchange for cash. That's the way you did things in his world.

'Well, if it's fine with you, then it's fine with me,' he said and turned the car keys.

A green Jaguar overtook them, squeezing by in a place where there wasn't really that much room to squeeze by. The faces of father and daughter tensed as their eyes followed its rear lights.

A pregnant silence followed before her father asked whether Alan Taylor was still following her around.

'I don't think so,' said Marcie. The truth was that she wasn't really sure. She'd sometimes had a feeling she was being followed, but couldn't believe that Alan was so stupid as to upset her father further. They'd been good mates, but Alan's behaviour had soured their friendship. Her father had threatened to punch his lights out and worse – and he would. She didn't want that to happen and her father end up in prison again, but if Alan did keep on, it could happen.

Alan frightened her.

Certain that he was Joanna's father, he'd asked her to marry him. Although responsible for stopping the adoption of Joanna and bringing her back from the home for unmarried mothers, the fact remained that he had raped her in the first place.

She had worried at first whether it was possible Joanna was his daughter, but one look at the child, especially now she was growing, and it was obvious who her father was. She had Johnnie's eyes and the half-smile that lifted one side of her mouth. Oh yes, she was relieved to know that she was Johnnie's alright.

Her father looked around him at the flat marshes and the glow of a ship's light in the distance. He shook his head. 'You can do better than this, Marcie. You can do better than that shop. Sheppey is too small for somebody as clever as you. London! That's where it's all happening.'

His daughter's trips to London had been sporadic, short and not necessarily very happy.

'This is my home,' she said stubbornly.

'It's all happening in London. It's the fashion capital of the world. That's what I was told recently.'

Marcie began to giggle. 'What do you know

49

about fashion, Dad?'

It was true. Her father's dress sense was pretty basic, consisting of jeans and a leather jacket. As far as women were concerned, he liked short skirts but the clothes didn't really matter. It was the body inside the trappings that appealed to him. He told her all this as he drove along.

For her part she took advantage of his chattiness, explaining how she felt. 'I like fashion, but I'm not sure about moving away from Sheerness. There's Joanna to think of. And Gran.'

When he looked at her, she held her head on one side and smiled.

The sight of her seemed to do something to him, the same reaction as an electric shock might have done. Looking stunned, he turned his gaze back to the road ahead. For a while he said nothing and then, 'Your mother liked fashion. She could sew too.'

Marcie jerked her head to stare at him. It was the first time *ever* that he'd mentioned her mother unbidden and in such a regretful manner. It left her with a funny feeling flickering inside – like a trapped butterfly beating its wings against a window pane.

If she hadn't been so taken by surprise, she might have urged him to explain things further. Her throat had turned dry, perhaps because she wanted to ask so much and the words tumbled over each other in the effort to come out of her mouth. At last all she managed to say was, 'I didn't know that.'

She'd taken too long to comment. She realised that by the sudden setting of his features back to the hard man he liked to project, the man he liked everyone to think he was. The moment had passed.

'Never mind. That's the past. This is now. Wait till I tell Babs how much you're going to make on them frocks!' His tone had turned sharp and snappy.

'I'd rather you didn't tell Babs yet,' she blurted.

He asked her why that was.

'I want Gran to know first. It's Gran that brought me up. It's Gran that looks after Joanna when I'm sewing. She deserves to be first.'

Her father kept his word and didn't mention anything at all to his wife.

Marcie waited until her father, plus her step-mother and baby Anne, had left before telling her grandmother just how successful she'd been.

'Fifteen pounds! Isn't that wonderful? And she wants me to make more.'

Her grandmother agreed with her that it was indeed wonderful and said that when she next went to mass she'd light a candle to the saint who took care of seamstresses.

'A letter has come for you.'

The letter had been placed on the dark oak table of her old treadle sewing machine. It was white and looked quite expensive. She studied the post-mark. London W1. The handwriting was rounded, vaguely familiar and written with a blue fountain pen. Whoever it was from, this was personal.

Joanna began crying just as she was about to open it. Marcie picked her up from her pushchair, the same one they'd used for her half-sister, Annie. Babs had handed it over willingly saying

51

she had no plans whatsoever to have any more kids. 'I'm taking the pill and I don't care who knows it. No more prams and pushchairs for me!'

Rosa had not spoken to her for days after she said that. The reason was clear. Babs was taking the birth control pill. The Pope did not approve so Rosa did not approve and had not resumed speaking until her son, Marcie's father and Babs' husband, informed her they were getting too old for all that nonsense. Rosa chose to believe him. Marcie did not.

Between turning down the gas and laying the table, her grandmother glanced out of the kitchen window.

'Is something wrong, Gran?'

Her grandmother seemed to come to, her eyes blinking as though Marcie had awoken her.

'I thought I saw someone at the back gate.'

A pang of fear clutched at Marcie's heart. She prayed it wasn't Alan Taylor.

Rosa Brooks noticed her concerned expression. 'I do not think it is anyone to worry about. It is just that Garth has not been around since Joanna's baptism. I was hoping it was him. Did you know his mother died?'

'No!' Marcie was genuinely surprised, but perhaps that was because she had been so bound up in her own world. So many things were going on at the present time. She was happier than she'd been for a while because things were going in the right direction, but now she felt guilty she hadn't known about Garth's mother.

Her grandmother explained that following his mother's death the landlord had thrown him out of the old flat above the hardware store. 'No one has seen him. No one knows where he has gone.'

'Have you heard from his mother?' Marcie asked.

Her grandmother was famed in certain quarters as a woman with a direct line to the spirit world. On mention of Garth's mother, her expression soured. 'I do not wish to speak to her. She should have made better provision for her son. I worry about him.'

Garth's mother, Edith Davies, had never had much time for him, preferring to entertain a never-ending procession of men friends. Apparently Garth was the result of a wartime liaison with a Polish flier, though that might only be hearsay. Edith had served as a land girl at a time when men in uniform were as plentiful as parsnips.

Rosa Brooks had pitied Edith in life despite her morals. Edith not providing for Garth had upset Rosa. Subsequently, in death she wanted nothing to do with her.

Joanna chuckled as Marcie sang to her and whirled her around in a haphazard waltz.

She became so busy what with feeding Joanna, getting her ready for bed then talking to her grandmother about the dress shop and the job at the hospital that it wasn't until she was undressed and about to get into bed that she remembered the letter.

Marcie fingered the paper. In her world the height of writing pad luxury was Basildon Bond. But this paper was far superior to that. It was as thick as parchment and the return address was printed at the top of the paper – actually printed!

Now how posh was that?

Before reading, her eyes swept to the signature. Allegra Montillado.

Montillado! Such an exotic name.

She read on:

*Dear Marcie,*

*It's been a while since Sally and I wrote to you after you left Pilemarsh in such fairy-tale circumstances.*

*I don't know whether you realised it at the time, but you left us with such mixed feelings that day and far from dry eyes.*

*We cried because we were so happy for you. Out of the three of us you were the one brave enough to keep your baby, although, of course, circumstances always dictate what you have to do in life.*

*How we envied you being able to do that, so although we cried with happiness for you, we also cried for ourselves.*

*The past is past; I hope you are happy and that Joanna is growing rapidly. I would love to see her.*

*If you should ever be in London, do look me up. The address and telephone number are at the top of this paper. I would love to see you again and also to see Joanna.*

*Much love and best wishes,*
*Allegra Montillado*

Marcie placed the letter back in its envelope and sat on the side of the bed. Had it really been only a year since she'd arrived at the forbidding entrance of Pilemarsh Abbey, a home for unmarried mothers?

It was on the bus travelling there that she'd met

54

Sally and actually inside the home that she'd met Allegra. Allegra had arrived in her mother's chauffeur-driven car. Unlike Sally, Allegra had never disclosed the identity of her child's father. Strangely enough Sally and Marcie had respected her privacy on that score.

Her bedroom was very dark once she turned out the light. Joanna snuffling in her sleep accompanied the creaking of old beams as the cottage settled down for the night.

Rumour had it that the cottage had once been home to a carpenter working on one of Nelson's warships. Marcie didn't know whether it was true, but as far as she knew the old beams certainly creaked like those on a wooden ship.

What with Joanna's snuffling plus the darkness, she could quite easily imagine that she was back at Pilemarsh Abbey, waiting for somebody to come along and snatch her child away.

Drifting into sleep also meant drifting between the past and the present. Old fears threatened to come back and haunt her. Unable to fall asleep properly, she drew back the curtains. There was no moon, but enough light from street lamps to keep her thoughts fixed in the present and to drive the dreams away.

The past was dead. There was a lot happening in her life and she had bright hopes for the future. Everything would be wonderful.

Outside the salt-laden breeze rustled the tough grass and the brittle leaves still hanging on the hedgerows from last autumn. A cat slunk around the rubbish put out for next day's collection and yowled on meeting another cat halfway round. A quick scrap and then both went their own way.

The shadow of a man fell over where they had been fighting, keeping close against the hedge surrounding the small front garden. The figure loitered as though half expecting the front door to open and Marcie to invite them in. Once it was obvious that this was not going to happen, the figure slunk away like a fox in the night.

## *Chapter Five*

Rita frowned at her father. He was drinking heavily, a freshly opened bottle of whisky already half empty, and it was making her angry.

'Why don't you fill the bath up with that stuff, get in it and drown your bloody self?' Her tone was scathing.

'Oi!' he said, pointing an accusing though shaky finger at her. 'Less of that lip. And no bad language. I won't have that bloody swearing in my house!'

Rita rolled her eyes heavenwards. The fact that he'd been swearing himself seemed to roll over his head.

Despite the fact that she appeared selfish in her demands on her father, deep down she loved him – not altogether affectionately but in a possessive way. After all, without him she couldn't have the nice things he always bought her. The thought of not being able to buy whatever she wanted sent a shiver down her back. It wouldn't be long before he would be the one making demands on her! He was getting older, wasn't he?

'Dad! Pull yourself together.' She put her arms around him, steeling herself as she breathed in the smell of strong spirits and stale aftershave. He wasn't taking care of himself like he used to do. More's the pity, she thought with a grimace.

'It's all her fault,' he exclaimed between mannish blubbering.

Rita presumed he was referring to her stepmother, who'd shot off with a rent collector from Shoreham.

'That cow, Steph. I'll scratch her eyes out if I ever run into her.'

'Not Steph! Her! Marcie. It's my kid, Rita. It's my kid!'

Rita froze. She could hardly believe what she was hearing.

'You? You and Marcie?'

'Yeah. Marcie.'

His words scorched into Rita's brain like a red-hot branding iron. Marcie Brooks with her high and mighty ways...! To think that they'd once been close friends. Rita scowled on recalling Marcie's usual air of condemnation when she'd gone off with a bloke for the night. She'd never admitted it, but Marcie had made her feel a right slut. And who was Marcie to point the finger? After all, Marcie was the one who'd 'copped out' and got lumbered with a kid. Marcie Brooks not Rita Taylor! Rita Taylor knew how to take care of herself. She'd started taking birth control pills at the earliest opportunity.

57

Rita was smug with self-righteousness at being so clever as to prevent getting pregnant. She felt no guilt at the fact that she'd sold Marcie aspirins disguised as birth pills. It had started out as a cruel joke and a way of getting back at Marcie for being so prim and proper. And pretty. There was always that. Marcie was very pretty.

She'd been quite amused – but far from surprised given what she'd done – to hear that her one-time best friend had got pregnant. But that was before her father had confessed to having an affair with Marcie. An affair! She tried not to think of her old dad with a girl the same age as she was. It was disgusting really. Far more important to Rita were the implications as far as she was concerned. Her dad's affection for first Marcie and now her daughter meant that she was no longer the apple of her father's eye. She had rivals!

## Chapter Six

Marcie's first day at the hospital consisted of hemming sheets on an industrial electric sewing machine. Although making nurses' uniforms was not as exciting as designing and making something fashionable, they were more challenging than hemming bed sheets.

'You're new. I have to be sure about the quality of your work before allowing you to make uniforms,' Miss Gardner had stated. 'If you're good enough we might even ask you to work full time.'

Working full time was the last thing she wanted, but she didn't say so. The work was mind-numbing but she kept her head down and got on with it. Besides Miss Gardner and Miss Pope, eight seamstresses were employed; two were close to her own age, two just entering their twenties. The other women were older. Like the other girls they were all unmarried.

Marcie was wary of becoming too friendly with any of them. No one on Sheppey was that much of a stranger, but luckily there was no one there who knew her. Most of them lived closer to the hospital than she did, but one person did recognise her.

Mary Durban was about forty-five with iron-grey hair and pink-rimmed glasses. Just a few hours into the job and she caught Marcie in the ladies' cloakroom washing her hands.

'Here. Am I right in thinking that you're Tony Brooks' girl?'

Marcie went cold inside but couldn't deny it. 'That's right. He's my dad.'

Mary beamed and the pale eyes behind the pink glasses twinkled. 'We were at school together, me and your dad. Well, not exactly together. He was in the secondary boys and I was in the girls. But we boys and girls used to get together after school. You know how it is. I had a crush on your dad. My, but he was a good-looking bloke back then. Best in the school with his dark Mediterranean looks. Not that he would have given me a second glance. He could have any girl he wanted. And he did!'

'Is that right.' Marcie smiled nervously. She didn't know quite what else to say. On the one hand she didn't want to appear unfriendly; on the other she was loathe to become too close and have Mary asking her questions. Miss Gardner had been very specific about not employing married women whether they had children or not. She needed this job. She couldn't afford to lose it.

The hospital had a canteen. All the girls and women employed in the sewing room went there. Marcie made the decision not to, afraid that she might inadvertently let something slip and her secret would be discovered once everyone was away from the strict discipline imposed by Miss Gardner and Miss Pope. Instead she went out of the hospital and round to the shops. She found a small park where she could sit and eat the sandwiches her grandmother had prepared for her. That was OK on fine days, but in bad weather it wasn't so good. She sat shivering beneath an umbrella, the rain dripping in silvery drops from the ends of the spokes. The pigeons came scrounging around her feet come rain or shine.

It was on one such day when she was watching a group of pigeons scrambling for the pieces of crust that someone discovered her. The pigeons scattered as a cigarette end landed on the ground. The steel-capped toe of a black work boot stubbed it into the tarmac path.

'Well, I never. It's Marcie Brooks. What you doing 'ere then?'

Bully Price was younger than her. She estimated he was probably fifteen though he had the body and height of someone far older. He was looking down at her with what passed for a smile on his face.

'Eating my lunch,' she said warily. She'd crossed Bully's path before and the experience had been far from pleasant. Bully's real name was Billy but the nickname suited him down to the ground. He'd always been a gang leader and intimidator of small fry – young boys like her brothers and the vulnerable like Garth Davies. She'd given him a good talking to, on more than one occasion, not that it had done any good. Although he was younger than she was, Bully had a thing about her. She'd much prefer to avoid him if possible.

He didn't ask whether he could sit beside her on the park bench; Bully never asked to do anything. He just did it.

He smelled of oil.

'Left school now. Got meself a job in a garage. An apprenticeship, like.'

'I guessed.'

He laughed. 'Yeah. Great boots. Great overalls.'

She didn't look at him but sensed by the tone of his voice that he was beaming broadly.

One of the boots kicked out when a pigeon came looking to retrieve a piece of bread. It fluttered off in a flurry of feathers.

'Not doing too bad for money now. I don't get much on the apprentice front, but the boss lets me do a bit of overtime and pays me full rate for that. He's not supposed to really, but a bloke's got to have a few shillings for nights out, know what I mean?'

Suddenly she knew where this was going and was ready to laugh in his face at the thought of it.

'So how's the youngster?'

The question took her off guard. This was not the one she'd been expecting.

She decided to play ignorant. 'Youngster?'

'Your kid. I heard you had a kid. Heard the father got smashed up on the North Circular. That right?'

Marcie exhaled a deep breath and said in a small voice, that yes, Johnnie had been killed in a road accident.

She felt him glance down at her left hand.

'Didn't get round to marrying you then?'

She curled her fingers into her palm wishing she'd brought the pretend wedding ring in her pocket for use in moments like these. Lying was not second nature to her but under the circumstances the lie was preferable to leaving Bully to make his own conclusion.

'I don't mind if a girl's made a mistake. I'd still take her out.'

There it was; the question she'd sensed was coming.

'How about coming with me to the pictures? There's a good one on at the minute. *Bonnie and Clyde*. There's a lot of blood in it. How about it?'

Marcie had heard about the film. There was a lot of controversy about the violence in it.

'It's an eighteen certificate,' she said matter-of-factly.

'Yeah. I know it is. I only go to over eighteen or X-rated films. I don't like soppy stuff.'

Marcie was under no illusion that if she consented to go with him she'd spend most of the film fighting him off. In the darkness his hands would be everywhere. The thought of him trying to kiss her made her feel sick.

She felt his arm sliding along the back of the bench, his hand heading for her shoulder.

'You have to be an adult to watch X–rated films,' she muttered, meaning to say that he was still a child.

He bent his head, ducked beneath the umbrella and looked up into her face. 'Now come on, Marcie. Do I look like a little kid?'

He smirked at the thought of anyone thinking his overlarge frame was below eighteen years of age. He definitely had a point, but it altered nothing for Marcie. There was no way she wished to accompany Bully Price anywhere.

'No, thank you.'

He looked surprised at her rejection, the smirk sliding into a sneer.

'Washing your hair or something?'

Marcie made an instant decision. She'd stood up to him in the past, and she'd damn well stand up to him now.

She sprang to her feet, her half-eaten sandwiches falling to the ground. 'No. I just don't want to go out with you.'

'Just because you're older than me? That don't make no difference. No difference at all.'

The sun was coming out. She shook her head at the same time as shaking the rain from her umbrella. 'That isn't the reason, Billy. The fact is I don't like you. I don't like you at all.'

To her great surprise he laughed at that. 'What's that got to do with anything? Fact is, Marcie Brooks, who else is going to bother with soiled goods? Granted you're a tasty-looking bird, but you've been broken in.'

'Broken in!' Marcie recoiled with horror. 'I am not a bloody horse, Billy Price! You're disgusting ... a disgusting little boy!'

That sickly grin returned to his face. 'No I'm not,' he said, towering above her now and clutching his crotch. 'I'm a big boy. I can show you if you like.'

Marcie didn't give him chance. Swinging the closed umbrella in a wide arc, she brought it smashing across the side of his head. Only the fact that his boots were heavy stopped him from falling over.

Feeling elated, she stalked off with her head in the air. The fact that he was shouting after her made no difference to the lightness of her footsteps. She imagined that if she cared to look down her feet would be floating four inches off the ground.

'You just wait, Marcie Brooks. I'll bring you down a peg. You'll come running then when no other man wants you. You just see if you don't.'

## Chapter Seven

London was grey and it was raining. So much for April.

Tony Brooks was uncomfortable with what his new employer was asking him to do. I must have mellowed with age, he thought to himself.

'I just want them to understand that I am not a

64

fucking charity. They owe me nearly a fiver in back rent. Sort the dough out or chuck them out. That's the terms of my contract.'

Victor Camilleri leaned back in his leather swivel chair and placed his feet on the desk, crossing them at the ankles. His footwear was shiny and begged attention though Tony knew better than to stare at them. Victor wore a made-up boot on his right foot. Rumour had it that he'd suffered polio as a child. But nobody was so stupid as to ask why the built-up boot and the limp; nobody would dare.

Tony knew that Victor did not give the tenants of his rotten properties the kind of written contracts like the sort he'd signed with the council. They were told verbally what the terms were: you pay the rent or piss off.

Some of the punters who rented flats and bedsits from Victor deserved to get a bit of aggro. Most paid up pretty promptly once Tony and another bloke, Bernie, went calling round. The majority were immigrants and were having trouble finding jobs let along paying the rent. Colour prejudice meant what jobs there were – mainly with London Transport and British Rail – were fought over. The same prejudice also prevailed in the private renting sector. That's why Victor could charge what he did for property in the East End of London, most of it earmarked for demolition and redevelopment. In the meantime people lived in buildings where the brickwork was mouldering as a result of age, neglect and bomb damage. One of Victor's flats was better than no flat at all.

'Right,' said Victor at last. 'Go to it, boys.'

Bernie followed Tony out of Victor's office, leaving their employer lighting up yet another King Edward, his expensive suede shoes resting on the desk.

Bernie offered Tony a Woodbine.

Tony eyed it ruefully. 'Christ! How can you smoke that crap after getting a sniff of that cigar?'

Bernie laughed. 'Victor's the business, and that's a fact.'

Tony opted to drive. That way he didn't *have* to smoke. The fact was that sometimes this job turned his stomach. It wasn't that he was afraid of the people he had to face; on the contrary, he felt sorry for some of them, hence the terrible taste in his mouth. A cigarette would have tasted pretty grim, hence refusing one.

He'd been cock-a-hoop when he'd first got the job with Victor Camilleri. His reputation had been carried by word of mouth straight to the big Sicilian's front door. There were no takers for the job besides him. He chose to believe that this was because everyone knew he was the best man for the job and nobody wanted to cross him. He chose to blot out the fact that the previous incumbent had got knifed in the guts by a West Indian pimp who hadn't quite got the lay of the land just yet – the criminal land that is.

The 'tenant' today lived on the ground floor of a Victorian tenement.

Tony looked up at the dirty brickwork. 'I bet you can see all the way to Battersea Bridge from the top of this place.'

Bernie giggled. 'Yeah. The last view a punter's likely to get before they spin down to the ground like a bleeding Sputnik.'

He got no response from Tony, who liked to think he was hard but fair. He also liked to think he had more of a brain than Bernie. All Bernie had were big meaty hands and a temper that was the wrong side of normal.

Six stone steps led up to a wide front door. The door had chipped paint and a huge knocker with a big black knob underneath. Not that they needed to knock. They had keys, not that they needed them; the door was already ajar.

The hallway smelled of stale cabbage and chip fat. A pram was parked against the right wall, another a bit further along against the left. On glancing into the pram Tony saw a pair of small brown fists like blobs of chocolate against the pure white of a knitted blanket.

Bernie got in front of Tony, fist already bunched to hammer on the door.

Tony eased him out of the way. 'My job I think.'

He was right. It was his job to give out the official line – the demand for payment. A Mrs Ella Reynolds lived here. She owed three weeks rent at ten and six a week running to a total of one pound eleven shillings and sixpence. As far as Victor was concerned, it was a fair deal even though it did not include electricity and gas which was paid for by slot meters.

He caught a glimpse of a door opening further along the passage and a pair of frightened eyes peering out. One glance at the visitors and the door closed again. Everyone knew who they were – or at least, the tenants of this place certainly did.

A young and pretty black woman came to the

door. She had a toddler clinging to her skirts and her dark eyes flickered nervously. For a moment Tony half expected her to shut the door in his face. It wouldn't be the first time.

'Well now, Mrs Reynolds. What appears to be the problem?'

He heard Bernie giggling behind him. Bernie thought he handled matters too politely and sounded like a copper. He didn't care. Bernie would give the woman a clumping without a second thought. He wouldn't. That was the difference between him and Bernie. He knew when to go for it and when not to.

Mrs Reynolds wrapped her hand around the small child's head, clamping her to her skirt. It was as though there was strength in melding them both together. There wasn't, but Mrs Reynolds was frightened.

'My husband, Joe, he's gone down the National Assistance,' she said in a thick Jamaican accent. 'Joe pay when he get back.'

Her voice was stridently brave. Tony found himself admiring her and the gutsy way she was protecting her kid. He thought about Marcie. Unlike Mrs Reynolds she had no man to put the bread on the table. He knew how he would feel if anyone went around demanding money she couldn't pay from his daughter. He'd fucking kill 'em!

'Look, love,' he said, lowering his face so they were eye to eye. 'Mr Camilleri let you have this place out of the goodness of his heart when nobody else would give you house room being as you're of a coloured persuasion. Know what I mean?'

She nodded slowly.

'But he didn't let you have it for free. That was not the intention,' Tony went on. 'He let you have this place out of the kindness of his heart and ten shillings and sixpence a week. Right?'

Mrs Reynolds nodded her head very slowly, her eyes round with fear. Sensing her mother's discomfort, the toddler began to cry.

'Joe pay you,' said Mrs Reynolds.

'And when might that be?'

'When he comes home. He pay you then.'

Tony shook his head. 'I'm afraid that's not possible Mrs Reynolds. Either I get paid now or take goods to the value of – got it?'

'Like this pram.'

Tony turned round. Bernie was jiggling the pram so violently that the baby was rolling from side to side, bouncing off the inside padding.

'Ain't much of a pram though. Might improve it a bit if I push it down the steps and out in the road. Maybe a bus might run it down and make it look better. Bit squashed though.'

Mrs Reynolds screamed, 'No!'

Tony grabbed the handle of the battered pram, which was worth practically nothing. The baby had started to cry.

'Leave it out, Bernie.'

He gave the big bruiser a warning look. Though Bernie was an ape in a suit, he had respect for the geezers who gave the orders. Tony was the man, so Bernie obeyed, though he did point at Mrs Reynolds and tell her the boss would not be pleased.

No, thought Tony. The boss wouldn't be pleased and even if he let Mrs Reynolds off, Bernie would spin a tale. The fact was that Tony was beginning to feel sorry for her. He kept thinking of his Marcie. He couldn't shift the similarities from his mind.

'Let's go inside and discuss this further, shall we, Mrs Reynolds?'

He picked the baby up and told Bernie to stay where he was.

'Mrs Reynolds and I will go inside to discuss business. No point in upsetting the kids now is there.'

Looking hesitantly up at him – no doubt worried she was letting someone in who was going to rough her and the kids up a bit – she let him in anyway.

'Shut the door, Mrs Reynolds.'

Tony handed over the baby.

'I haven't got any money. Not yet.'

Tony's eyes swept the cramped room the family lived in. The kitchen was in a small aperture behind a green chenille curtain.

Mrs Reynolds was rocking the crying infant in her arms. The toddler was crying at her skirt.

Tony looked deeply into her eyes. 'You have to pay, Mrs Reynolds. You know that, don't you?'

She nodded, her big eyes seeming to fill her face.

It was alien in this game, but he couldn't help being sympathetic. Tony, my old son, you're losing it, he thought to himself. You must be getting old.

'Look. An old mate of mine works for the bus company. Get your old man to go along there. Ask for Jim Collins and tell him that Tony Brooks sent him along. Got that?'

She stared at him a second then her bottom lip began to tremble. 'I don't know... I might forget ... me memory...'

'Got a pencil? A piece of paper?'

She grabbed a child's crayon from the table. Tony tore a scrap of paper from the back of her rent book and wrote the details down.

'Get him to see Jim. He might be able to help.'

The face that had been so taut with fear now relaxed a little. Mrs Reynolds gave a small smile.

'My Joe! He bin trying to get a job on the buses.'

Tony nodded. He was sticking his neck out and neither he nor Mrs Reynolds was out of the woods yet.

'There's still the matter of the outstanding rent,' Tony said to her.

She shrugged helplessly. 'I do have a ten bob note in me purse. I was keeping it to buy my groceries. Milk for the baby ... and Theresa. I don't mind going without meself...'

Tony held up his hand. 'This time we skip it. Just make sure you pay the next time the collector comes round.'

He knew it was foolish, but when he turned for the door he got a fiver out of his pocket and entered it in the record book. He also recorded it in her rent book.

'You owe me now,' he told her.

She stared at him in disbelief.

'Just one thing,' he added. 'You tell no one. Right? Not even your old man. If anyone goes shooting off their mouth, we're all up the Swanee. Right?'

71

The rest of the rent collecting went as per normal. At the end of the day Tony went for a drink at his favourite East End pub. Around about eight o'clock he phoned the phone box at the end of Grafton Street where he, Babs and their three kids rented a council house. There were always kids playing out in the street so no problem it going on ringing indefinitely.

A kid answered. 'Yeah? Who's that?'

'Tony Brooks.'

'Dad!'

It was Arnold, one of his boys.

'Arnold, mate. How the devil are you my son?'

'I'm alright, Dad. We've chucked a rope over a lamppost and made it into a swing.'

'Is that so?'

'Yeah. Our Archie's on it at the minute. Do you want me to get him?'

'No. I just want you to tell your mother and your grandmother that I'm home this weekend. Can you do that?'

'Yeah. Mum's down at the chippie at the minute. Our Annie's round with Gran.'

'Great. I'll leave you to take care of it, son. OK?'

'OK, Dad.'

Tony was thoughtful as he replaced the phone. He loved his kids and of course he wanted to see them again. Even little Annie. He'd never been quite sure whether she was his or not. Babs had put it about a bit in her time. But even that didn't matter now. The problem was Mrs Reynolds – Ella. He wanted to see her again too.

## Chapter Eight

Marcie told no one about her run in with Bully Price. The fact was that not only was she worried he might blab her circumstances where hospital staff hung around, she had been mortified by his terminology. He'd disgusted her with the words he'd used when applied to her, just a girl who'd got pregnant without being married. Would it always be like this? she wondered. Would she always be thought of as a girl who was easy, bestowing her favours on anyone who wanted them?

The thought of it made her sick. Only the fact that she loved Joanna so much prevented her from regretting what she had done.

Deep in thought over her sewing, she didn't immediately hear her grandmother speaking.

'Marcie! You are not listening to me?'

'Sorry.' She jerked her head up. Her cool blue eyes met the jet-black ones of her grandmother.

'I said your father is coming home this weekend. The boys came round to tell me.'

Marcie was pleased to hear it. 'This dress will be finished by then,' she said as she lovingly caressed the peacock-green material. 'I'm hoping Angie will have sold the other two.'

Her happiness was infectious. Her grandmother smiled at the same time as rubbing the heated iron over a pure linen sheet. 'You will be like Coco Chanel in no time.'

'I'd prefer to be like Mary Quant,' said Marcie. 'Or Biba.'

Her grandmother shook her head. 'I do not know these people I only know that there is no chic like French chic.'

Marcie had no ambition to be plain chic or French chic. She wanted to be fabulously fashionable in a young person's way. For the younger generation, the biggest name of all was Mary Quant. That was who she wanted to be.

Joanna had settled down to sleep. Marcie was tired but determined to finish what she was doing even though her eyes were sore.

She fancied her grandmother was watching her.

'The hospital job will not last. You know that, don't you?' her grandmother said softly.

There were very logical reasons why the job wouldn't last, though Marcie had not voiced them. She nodded. 'I know. It's very boring work in any case. If I could succeed in the world of fashion...'

'It will happen.'

Her grandmother sounded very sure about it and when Marcie looked up into her weathered face, she saw there what seemed like strength. She knew that look, knew what it meant. Her grandmother was willing her to succeed. Somehow the old woman was reaching out to her, offering her own strength to bolster her granddaughter's. Either that or she knew what would happen in the future. She did that sometimes, seeing what people could not see for themselves.

There was a big party when Tony Brooks came

back to Sheppey. That was the way it was with the Brooks family. He had money to spend and what was money for if not for spending? The music was loud, the voices were raucous and those neighbours that did complain were invited to join in.

He came home on a Saturday and, much to his wife's annoyance, went round to see his mother before going home to see her.

'Had to see my favourite girls,' he said kissing mother, daughter and granddaughter in turn.

Marcie had just finished pressing the second dress she'd made that week for Angie's Boutique. It had been two weeks since she'd taken the first two round and they'd sold within that time. Now there were two more ready to be delivered. Her father said he was proud of her.

'Were you going on the bus with them?' he asked.

She told him that had been her intention.

'I've got the car outside. Hop in,' he said, straightening his tie, a half-smoked cigarette dangling from the corner of his mouth. 'You coming too, Ma?' he said. 'Bring the kid. After the frocks are delivered, I'll get my old lady to make us a cuppa. How does that grab you?'

It grabbed them right enough, though how it would grab Babs to have everyone descend on her at Tony's invitation was another matter. Especially seeing as he hadn't reported home first.

Marcie could forgive him for that. Her step-mother was hardly top of the pops on her personal chart. They tolerated each other and that was it.

Angie was over the moon with the new dresses.

She paid Marcie her share of the dresses she'd already sold. She also put in an order for what she wanted next.

'I'd like some geometric ones,' she informed Marcie. 'The dress divided into four quarters: black on the right chest, white on the left, black from the waist down on the left and white on the right. They're all the rage in London at the moment.'

Marcie didn't need to be told that. She read every fashion magazine she could get her hands on. She promised she'd have two dresses of that style ready by the end of the following week.

The two dresses had sold for three pounds nineteen shillings and eleven pence each. Angie gave her seventy per cent of the sale as promised.

Marcie was over the moon. What with her wages of four pounds ten shillings and sixpence a week from the hospital, plus the extra from her freelance work, she wasn't flush but was doing well enough.

Her father questioned the amount when she told him.

'I thought you were going to get more than that.'

It was true. They had discussed her ending up with around fifteen pounds per week – a wonderful sum. Unfortunately Angie hadn't been able to sell the dresses for as much as she'd initially hoped. They had to face hard facts.

'This isn't London. People aren't going to pay that much for a dress here. In London I could make that easily. I could make even more if all I was doing was designing and running up dresses.

As it is I can only do it in my spare time. I have Joanna to think about.'

Her father turned thoughtful as they headed for the council house he shared with Babs, the two boys and little Annie.

Babs wasn't at home.

'She's having her hair set round Doreen's,' young Archie pronounced. 'I expect she'll come back with it in one of them bouffers or something.'

They all knew he meant bouffant but didn't bother to correct him. Archie was almost eleven and swiftly growing into a know-all and hated being told he was wrong.

'Better get round and tell her I'm home and we're all parched for a cuppa.'

He gave Archie sixpence. His younger brother Arnold held out his hand too so he had to give him the same.

Marcie put the kettle on and got out Babs' best tea service of yellow cups and saucers with white spots all over them.

Babs came running round with her hair still in curlers and a fag hanging from the corner of her mouth. A multi-striped towel flapped around her shoulders.

'You didn't tell me you was bringing the family over!' she snapped at Tony.

Marcie's grandmother fixed her with black button eyes. 'Are we welcome or are we not?'

Eyes outlined in black pencil and caked mascara flickered nervously and Babs managed a tight smile. 'Course you are, Ma. It's just that I'd made arrangements to have me hair done. If he'd said he was bringing you over, the kettle would have been on. But that's my old man. Never tells me anything,' she added, throwing a look in his direction.

Tony ignored both her look and the accusation in her tone. He slid his hand into his coat pocket.

'Here. Have a tenner. Buy yourself something nice.'

Marcie poured the tea, but didn't miss a thing. If there was one way to get to her stepmother's heart, a ten pound note would do very nicely.

The boys had been given sixpence each to fetch their mother, but their father added a further half a crown. 'Get yourself some fish and chips.'

They didn't need telling twice.

'Like greyhounds at the White City,' their father observed as they ran off, knees grubby beneath short flannel trousers and long grey socks at half mast.

Marcie felt her stepmother's eyes on her as she gave Joanna and Annie, her half-sister, a biscuit each.

'That's a nice dress. I saw one a bit like it in that shop that's opened – a boutique they call it.'

'Angie's,' Marcie pronounced smugly. So! Even Babs had noticed the shop that was selling the dresses she made.

'Marcie made it,' her grandmother said, pride shining in her eyes. 'And the one you saw in the shop was also made by her.'

Babs folded her arms and looked disbelieving. 'Go on! That was one of yours? It wasn't a home-made dress I saw. It was modern.'

'Just because I made it doesn't mean that it's

not modern. I made the pattern myself and measured it all out properly,' Marcie said hotly. 'And she's sold them. And I've been paid my cut of the deal. Ask my dad.'

It never failed to surprise Marcie how much her father kept from her stepmother, almost as though he maintained an invisible partition between the two different sections of his family.

Despite her heavy foundation, Babs visibly reddened. There was a portion of hurt and a portion of anger in her eyes when she turned to her husband.

'You didn't tell me that. Well, isn't that typical! Leave me to make a fool of meself!'

Tony Brooks had a temper threshold. 'Shut it,' he snapped, pointing his finger between her eyes. 'Marcie makes frocks for the frock shop. Now you know. Now you can let the subject drop, right?'

'Must be making a fortune,' Babs muttered defiantly.

'Shut it,' Tony said again.

On the drive back to Endeavour Terrace, Tony was unusually quiet. Marcie was pretty certain that this wasn't about Babs. Their marriage was a series of arguments, misunderstandings and making up under the bedcovers on a regular basis. Something else was worrying him.

Marcie looked out of the window.

'It's going to rain,' said her grandmother.

Marcie nodded.

A flock of sheep were grazing on the tough grass. At first the scene was peaceful, but then the sheep began to run and flock together for safety.

Marcie strained to see what had panicked them and thought she saw a shadow alternately loping and creeping along by the hedge.

For a moment she thought she recognised the figure, but the glimpse was so fleeting and the car was moving quickly.

Back at number ten, Endeavour Terrace, Tony knew better than to refuse his mother's invitation to come in. More tea was consumed along with buttered crumpets. Rosa Brooks was of the unshakable opinion that her daughter in law did not feed Tony properly. That was why his cheeks were so gaunt and he'd lost weight. She refused to put it down to dividing his time between the job in London and his family on the Isle of Sheppey.

He followed Marcie up to her room when she went up to put Joanna down. The little girl had enjoyed her day out and was now quite spent. Her father looked down on the sleeping child with her.

'Does she look like me, do you think?' Marcie asked him.

The question seemed to take him unawares. He took some time thinking about it.

'Well, yeah. I think so. It's a shame though ain't it?'

She frowned and looked at him. 'What are you talking about, Dad?'

'You having Joanna. Now don't get me wrong, I'm not condemning you for having her. The little tike didn't ask to be born and I know we wouldn't unwish her for the world but I do wonder how far you'd have got up in the smoke without having a kiddy, what with these frocks and all that.'

His terminology was getting irritating. Marcie rolled her eyes. 'Dresses, Dad! Dresses!'

'That's what I said, didn't I?'

She sighed. Her dad was of a certain age and old names stuck. Like the steel needle on a wind-up gramophone, he was stuck in a groove and couldn't get out unless he was pushed. She determined to do the pushing.

'They're called dresses nowadays. Mini-dresses.'

'Well, they are that,' he exclaimed, a wicked glint in his eyes. Like everyone else he had seen hemlines rise further and further away from the knees until they were little more than tunics. Thank goodness somebody had invented tights to wear with them!

'Well, Dad,' said Marcie, 'that's fashion for you, and fashion is all about moving with the times.'

His smile was genuine enough but his face crumpled ever so slightly. 'Your old man's getting old. Christ! Never thought I would. Thought I'd stay twenty-one for ever.'

They both smiled, but his comment about Joanna still grated on Marcie's mind. What had he meant by it? They both fell into an uncomfortable silence. He broke it first, the awkwardness nudging him into explaining.

'All I meant was, it's like you were saying, that a frock ... sorry ... dress shop in London would pay you shedloads of money, well, beyond what a local little place here would pay.'

'But I've got Joanna,' Marcie said abruptly.

It was obvious that he would have said more, but her abrupt intervention had brought him up short.

'That's right,' he said, his voice soft and full of affection. 'You've got Joanna and nobody and nothing is ever going to alter that.'

## Chapter Nine

Rita Taylor was livid to think that her friend – her former best friend – Marcie Brooks had been having it off with her dad. Christ, what a little tart she turned out to be, and wasn't she glad that they weren't best friends any more.

It occurred to her to spread the word around that Marcie had got pregnant by her father. A warning voice in her head told her that wouldn't be wise. People might blame her father seeing as he was a lot older than Marcie. Besides, she didn't want to besmirch either his good name or her own. They had a position in the community. They had a nice house, a nice car and her father, although he hadn't been so interested in business just lately, brought in a good income.

She was sitting in front of the telly watching *Coronation Street* with a chip butty for company. The people she considered friends hadn't called for a few days because she'd been in such a foul temper. When she was in a bad temper she always resorted to food.

Her father was the only one who had phoned to

say he was sleeping over at the car dealership he owned down in Deal. Deal was too far to travel if he'd been drinking, and she was in no doubt that he had. His consumption of alcohol had increased drastically over the past year. At first she'd put it down to her stepmother leaving, but now she knew the truth and the truth made her angry. She was set on exposing Marcie for the slut she considered her to be. Best of all she'd like to get her to leave Sheerness and Sheppey too. Trash like her didn't belong here. That was her opinion anyway. But how could she get her own back at her? How could she do that without damaging either her or her father's reputation?

The answer came just a few days later. She'd undertaken a secretarial course at the local college and through that had got herself a job as a clerk/typist in the offices of a local solicitor. Not for her the old job she'd used to have with Marcie selling candy floss to day trippers along the seafront at Sheerness. She'd made the decision to better herself so mornings and afternoons were spent buried up to her armpits in paperwork and typing. Lunch times were a welcome break when she could stroll along the high street, stuffing her face with a hot pie and chips bought from the local chippie.

It was during one of these lunch breaks that she bumped into Bully Price, though almost treading on him might have been a better description.

A pair of large black working boots was sticking out from beneath a broken-down car. Occupied with her thoughts, Rita tripped over them and fell against the side of the car. The car rolled slightly.

A face smeared in oil came out from beneath the car. 'Rita Taylor! That's my feet you're treading on!'

'Bully Price! You've got the biggest feet in Sheerness. No. Come to think of it, you've got the biggest feet in the whole of Sheppey.'

'And you're hardly bloody Tinkerbell the fairy, are you? And stuck-up with it, just like yer mate Marcie Brooks. Gets herself a job at the hospital and she's all airs and graces.'

Rita had been going to walk on, but what Bully had said stopped her in her tracks. 'She's got a job as a nurse! Are you kidding?'

'Nah,' he said, sliding out from beneath the vehicle and getting to his feet. 'She weren't wearing a uniform or anything.'

So Marcie had a job at the hospital. Rita fingered her lip. One of the girls working in the solicitor's office had once worked at the hospital. The girl's name was Wendy Heale and she'd been sacked once she'd set the wedding date.

'It's hospital policy,' she'd explained. 'They prefer to employ single women in the support services like the canteen, the sewing room and such like.'

Rita almost whooped with joy at this. Marcie was good with a needle. She used to make a lot of her clothes. Poor cow had to. She couldn't afford to buy straight off the rack like Rita could – thanks to her father.

She decided there and then that she'd find out exactly where Marcie was working. After that...

## Chapter Ten

Marcie felt a sharp jab in the small of her back. 'Hey! You!'

Jane Gale had started picking on her only days after she'd first started work in the hospital sewing room. When the first jab had occurred she'd smiled weakly and took it as a joke.

'That hurt,' she'd said, but had kept her smile as she said it.

To turn the other cheek was the wrong thing to do when it came to Jane Gale. Retaliation and exchanging like with like was the only thing she truly understood. Marcie badly wanted to bash her one, but held back. Jane Gale was also something of a sneak. It didn't help that she was Miss Pope's niece and as such attracted some degree of protection.

'Hey! You!'

The jabs were always accompanied with the same exclamation. Sometimes Marcie considered that Jane Gale practised those same words every night in front of the mirror. She wasn't the brightest girl she'd ever met and her vocabulary echoed the fact. Being a bully was Jane Gale's way of communicating that she really was better than Marcie, even if she could barely string two words together.

The turning point came when she jabbed at Marcie just as she was leaning over the sink washing her face.

Joanna had been poorly for a few days and so had kept her awake the night before. Sleep had been intermittent, punctuated with the wails of a red-faced child who wouldn't settle. Marcie couldn't wait for Wednesday and her day off, not that she'd be resting much. Angela Babbington had popped round to Endeavour Terrace with an urgent order for two more dresses in the geometric black and white style. Marcie felt obliged to fill the order as quickly as possible even though her grandmother told her to slow down, that there was no need to rush at things as though her wages might be cut short at any time. But that was exactly how Marcie felt about both her present and her future. She had to have financial security for herself, but mostly for her child. At the back of her mind was the nagging guilt about bringing Joanna into the world. She hadn't asked to come, and it was her fault she was here, therefore she had to do everything she could to do her best by the child.

Tired and not in the best of tempers, this time she reacted to Jane's bullying.

Jane gasped as Marcie grabbed her by the throat, her eyes popping out of her head.

'Just leave me alone, you stupid bitch! Do you hear me? Just leave me alone!'

She suddenly realised that she was holding the collar of Jane's overall so tightly the girl's face was turning pink.

Marcie came quickly to her senses, instantly regretful of what she had done. She released the stiff collar, flattening it with both hands – as if that was going to make any difference to someone like Jane Gale. Neither did her apology.

'I'm sorry,' she said, quickly coming to. 'You took me unawares.' The sound of running water took her attention back to the sink where she'd swilled her face. She'd left the tap running and the water was beginning to spill over the edge.

Before she had chance to spring for the tap, Jane bounced back, her face contorted with a sickly grin. 'Poke, poke, poke!' Each word was accompanied with a jab of her finger.

This was too much! Marcie reached for the tap with one hand; with the other she grabbed Jane by the nape of the neck and ducked her head in the water.

Just seconds – that was all it was – but Jane came up dripping.

Marcie left her there.

'You wait, Marcie Brooks!' Jane shouted after her. 'I'll tell on you. You just wait. I'll tell on you.'

Marcie shook her head and couldn't help smiling because Jane sounded so juvenile, just like a schoolgirl threatening to tell teacher. The problem was this was more serious. Marcie hadn't meant to lose her temper but she was tired and she'd had enough of Jane's bullying. She consoled herself with the thought that Jane was really the one at fault. She had as much right to complain about Jane as Jane had to complain about her. All she hoped was it wouldn't come to that, after all, Miss Pope was bound to side with her niece.

For the rest of that day she kept her nose to the sewing machine. Watching the stitching grow down each boring seam was monotonous but also strangely mesmerising. Jane was put out of her mind, at least for now.

Miss Pope did not ask to see her. Nobody mentioned anything having happened in the ladies' cloakroom. Nobody even seemed to notice that Jane's thick fringe was wet or that her eye make-up was smudged into a murky sludge colour.

The day ended as it always did, with the day's work being folded and put away, and the machines switched off. All is well, Marcie told herself.

The next morning Marcie walked past Jane with a spring in her step, confident that nothing had been said and nothing would be said.

Jane didn't say a word and Marcie said nothing either. Nose in the air she collected some work and went straight to her machine.

It wasn't until mid morning that a sudden cloud appeared. Miss Pope said she wanted to have a word with her.

That bitch Jane Gale! Had she done for her after all!

She looked in Jane's direction. Her machine was standing idle, her seat empty, a pillowcase clamped in place ready for sewing.

She could be in the ladies' cloakroom. Or she might already be with Miss Pope making good her story.

It was difficult not to be nervous, but she determined to stick up for herself. Jane had kept on and on until she'd retaliated. What else was she supposed to do?

Neatly folding her work, she noted where her stitching had got to so she could easily return to it and switched off the power supply.

They wouldn't sack her for dipping Jane's face

in the water surely? She couldn't have been immersed for more than three seconds – not long enough to drown her.

If all else fails I'll have to apologise again, she said to herself. It wouldn't be easy but she'd do it if she had to.

She walked to the door, certain she could feel the eyes of the other seamstresses burning into her back. She knew the other girls whispered that she was a bit standoffish but she couldn't help that. Keeping slightly aloof was the strategy she'd adopted for keeping her unmarried mother state a secret. They'd understand that if they knew, but they didn't know.

A nervous feeling knotted and bent and twisted itself around in her stomach.

Mouth dry, tongue cleaving to the roof of her mouth, she followed Miss Pope into the tiny office where interviews were carried out and forms filled in.

Miss Pope had a kindly face, pink cheeks and rust-coloured hair turning grey at the roots. She didn't resemble her niece in any way whatsoever. Seeing as Jane's sewing wasn't that brilliant, Marcie had no doubt that Miss Pope was being kind giving the girl a job. Just like me being kind to Garth, she decided. With a sudden pang of guilt she reminded herself that she hadn't seen poor Garth for ages and neither had she sought him out. But I will do, she told herself, and at that moment in time, she really meant it.

Miss Pope was watering a spider plant when Marcie entered. She didn't look up.

'Sit down, Miss Brooks.'

89

Marcie nervously obeyed, rehearsing in her mind what she would say in her defence for dunking Jane like a biscuit.

She could still see Jane spluttering soapy water and wanted to laugh out loud at the thought of it.

The little watering can Miss Pope was holding so delicately between finger and thumb made a tinny noise as she placed it on top of a metal filing cabinet. She cleared her throat and folded her thick tweed skirt beneath her as she seated herself in the wooden swivel chair behind the desk. Her overall, Marcie had noticed, was hung up behind the door.

A buff-coloured folder sat on the blotting pad in front of her. A notepad sat on top of that. Something was noted on it; Jane's claim to be an innocent victim no doubt.

Believing herself to be in the right, Marcie decided to come clean and explain what had happened before being accused of anything.

'I can explain what happened. It wasn't my fault,' she blurted.

Miss Pope jerked her head up to face her. She looked quite stunned.

'Miss Brooks! It really does not matter who is to blame for your position. That really is nothing to do with either me or the hospital board. The plain fact of the matter is that it is not our policy to employ women with children in this department. The fact that you are not married is neither here nor there as far as I am concerned. However, there are some elements on the hospital board to whom it does matter – it matters a lot. It is best for everyone here that you leave now before you are asked to leave. Your wages and all other monies due will be paid forthwith. I've asked the wages department to see to it straight away.'

Marcie sat stunned. This was not at all what she'd been expecting. Her pink lips stayed parted as she took it in. She'd been sacked! Not because of anything Jane had reported, but because someone – perhaps someone in the sewing room – had found out about her and passed the information on.

This was not the first time Miss Pope had had to let a girl go because she was pregnant, getting married or, like Marcie, unmarried with a child. If she had the choice she'd keep the girls on. But it wasn't up to her. Some people on the board who held great sway with the decision making were very narrow minded.

She could see that Marcie was shocked.

Sighing, she clasped her hands before her, her shoulders relaxing as she leaned slightly forwards, her heart aching because of what the poor girl was going through.

'Are you alright?'

Marcie's face was very pale.

'Would you like a cup of water?'

Marcie nodded. She felt devastated and betrayed. OK, she wasn't keen on the work here. Hemming hundreds of bed sheets was mind numbing, but the pay was regular.

Strangely enough she was quite calm about leaving, about not having to come back here to work. She'd made no friends here, only worked to survive. There was only one question she badly wanted answered before she left.

Raising her eyes to meet those of Miss Pope, she asked, 'How did you find out?'

'We had a letter.'

Marcie knew it wouldn't be answered, but she asked the obvious question. 'Who was it from?'

Miss Pope shook her head. 'I'm not allowed to say. Do you deny the letter's contents?'

Looking down at her tangled fingers, Marcie shook her head. Her fingers seemed to untangle by themselves, an after-effect of a great burden having been lifted. The truth was out.

'Johnnie – my fiancé – got killed. He was riding a motorcycle. A lorry turned across his path.' She shrugged. 'We were going to get married.'

There was a moment of silence, the only sound the ticking of the blue plastic clock on the wall. It had gold-coloured hands that quivered as it marked off each second.

'I'm sorry. I realise you're a willing girl and in our judgement – mine and Miss Gardner's – your work was exemplary.'

'Unfortunately that's not the sort of judgement that seems to matter here!'

She made no attempt not to snap or be polite. This woman was not to blame, but the hypocrisy of people! How did they expect her to live? Granted she had her sideline with Angie Babbington, but they weren't to know that. Luckily Angie didn't seem to care what Marcie got up to as long as the dresses kept coming.

Miss Pope sighed and looked away. 'No wonder some girls end up on the streets. Who can blame them if they haven't got a job?'

The legs of the chair scraped the tarnished brown linoleum as Marcie leaped to her feet.

'Never mind, Miss Pope. Don't you worry about me,' she exclaimed, her head high, her tone strident. 'Bugger the hospital! Bugger the bloody job! And bugger all them bloody sheets!'

## Chapter Eleven

Rosa Brooks waited until Marcie had gone to bed before talking to her husband. Her family knew she talked to him on occasion, but she did so only in private. She did not speak to him when the family was around. After all, they were still man and wife despite the fact that he'd crossed over into the spirit world years ago.

Her mouth never opened and closed when she spoke to him. Neither did any sound escape her lips. The words were in her head – or were they in her heart? Wherever they were, it didn't really matter. She knew when Cyril was near. She heard him when he spoke to her.

Cyril had been serving in the Royal Navy when she'd met him. He'd been stationed on Malta, his ship anchored in Dockyard Creek close to the Royal Navy bakery and the treasury next door.

She'd been standing on the waterfront close to Victoria Gate staring at the water when he'd first set eyes on her. He'd been coming down in the lift from the city of Valletta which towered overhead. He'd obviously been drinking somewhere along The Gut with his seafaring mates. They'd been singing and shouting and swearing like drunken sailors do.

It was after midnight, a time when no respectable girl would normally be out. So, of course, the drunken sailors presumed she was not respectable.

For her part she'd barely heard their comments. Her eyes were misty and salt tears were running down her face to join the gentle waves lapping against the crumbling steps. One step and she would be in the water. The water was black and peppered with the odd orange light from the city above. It looked welcoming, so much more so than this life she was presently leading.

She had been about to jump when one of the sailors had put his arm around her.

'Come away from that water.'

Cyril had been very persuasive. In all their married life he'd never asked her why she'd been standing at the water's edge that night. And she'd never imparted the information. But he knew now he was on the other side. He knew everything now.

'God bless our granddaughter,' she whispered at the same time crossing her chest in the time-honoured way. 'She will do great things. We will be proud of her,' she said softly. She said it convincingly because she knew it was the truth. No matter what her family did, she would always be proud of them.

Marcie lay awake for a long time thinking of what her grandmother had said to her. 'When one door closes, another opens.'

Rosa Brooks hadn't reacted to the news of her being sacked in the way she thought she would.

'Everything happens for a reason.'

She was reeling them off one after another – useless sayings that might or might not be true. They were probably invented to make people feel better, thought Marcie. Useless, stupid sayings. They weren't really working, but then they didn't need to. She'd left the hospital feeling surprisingly elated. She'd worried about meeting the orders when Angie Babbington had ordered extra dresses. She hadn't counted on her designs getting this successful this quickly. It was like reaching a fork in the road. Should she opt for the security afforded by a regular job and a weekly wage, or jump off into the unknown and go into business for herself? As long as the proper job was there she would have held on to it. But she hadn't held on to it. She'd lost it. There was no longer a choice – or rather, there was only one choice. Whoever had sent that letter had done her a favour. But who had sent it? Perhaps she would never know.

## Chapter Twelve

Monday morning was a good day to deliver the black and white dresses to the shop. The day was bright – the sun was doing its best to break through the low-lying cloud – though judging by the wind direction it would rain later.

Although having recently lost her job, Marcie was feeling good. Making up the dresses had taken most of the weekend. It had been hard work but she consoled herself with the fact that now she was home it would no longer be such a chore. She'd finished pressing them that very morning using an iron heated on the gas ring and two or three damp cloths.

The dresses were enclosed in a polythene cover that her grandmother had acquired from a friend at the dry cleaner's. The package was bulky, bouncing over the side of her arm, but her shoes had low chunky heels so she managed fine.

There was not the same crush of shoppers as there was on a Saturday so she made good time, getting there by one o'clock.

The door bell jangled merrily above her head as she entered. She bobbed her head above the racks of clothes.

Angie saw her. 'Marcie! More frocks,' she said excitedly.

'More frocks! Two frocks,' Marcie said.

They both laughed because they'd used Tony's word for dresses. Using the word themselves had become something of a light-hearted joke.

Something – or rather someone – moved just behind Angie's shoulder. It was Rita Taylor.

Rita's small blue eyes went straight to the two dresses. Angie had removed their covering and hung them up high enough for her to inspect before accepting them – though that's what she would most definitely do.

It had been some time since Marcie had seen Rita; in fact she'd purposely kept out of her way.

There were three reasons. The first was that as a new mother they really wouldn't have much in common. Rita was still footloose and fancy free. Secondly her generosity in supplying her with birth pills had been an outright sham. It was partly her fault that Marcie had got pregnant. The third reason was that Rita's father had done her a lot of harm. OK, he'd fetched her from the home for unmarried mothers, but she couldn't forget that he'd raped her. She knew that wasn't anything to do with Rita but even so. In her heart forgiveness towards either of the Taylors would be a long time coming.

Rita's eyes were narrowed. Her small mouth was pursed like a squashed rosebud.

Marcie managed to say hello, though it was guarded, not at all like the exuberant greeting of the past before everything had changed.

Rita returned the greeting, but that was it. She moved in on the dresses, contemptuously fingering the hems.

'New stock?'

Unaware of the bad vibes flowing between these two, Angie answered exuberantly, 'They are indeed! And very sought after. Miss Brooks designs and makes them for us. Would you like to order one for yourself?'

Marcie knew instinctively what would happen next.

Rita turned up her nose. 'Humph! I don't think so. Luckily I've got the money to purchase better quality gear from proper designers and boutiques in the King's Road. Sorry.'

She attempted to brush past, leaving Angie

with her mouth hanging open.

Marcie stopped her. She smiled sweetly as she eyed Rita up and down from her blonde bob to her short skirt and plump legs. 'I don't think I could accommodate Miss Taylor anyway. I haven't enough material to make something in that large a size!'

It wasn't in her nature to be so cutting about anyone's shape, but this girl had done her so much harm. She couldn't help it.

A puce-coloured blush spread from Rita's cheeks all the way down her neck. Marcie almost expected steam to come rushing down her nostrils. Luckily the moment when they might have fallen into a cat fight passed without incident – except for the doorbell. Rita slammed the door so hard that it fell from its spring and hit the floor, rolling over and over, its clapper clanging all the while.

It suddenly came to her that she might have done the wrong thing in upsetting Rita. After, all she was a customer of Angie's.

'Angie, I do apologise. She's a friend of mine. Correction, a former friend of mine.'

Angie gave her a direct look. 'I'm glad you said former friend. If she'd been a true friend I'd have advised you that you had no need of enemies. And think nothing of it. I can do without customers like her.'

Talk of fashion and future orders took their minds off the incident. Angie wanted more of Marcie's designs. 'Could you manage to make three a week? I'd prefer four, but I know it's a lot when you're holding down a job as well...'

'It's fine,' Marcie said brightly. 'I gave up the job. I've decided to work for myself so four should be no problem.'

Angie's eyes lit up. 'That is absolutely great. I was wondering if you wouldn't mind me showing these to a London friend of mine. She's got a boutique in Chelsea ... would you mind?'

Marcie could hardly believe her ears. Would she mind? Of course she wouldn't mind! In fact she almost cried with joy, and also with laughter. Angie asked her what she was laughing about and she just had to tell her what was going through her mind. There was Rita, cow that she was, boasting that she bought all her clothes in the King's Road. Well, watch out for me, Rita Taylor. You might well be buying one of my dresses anyway.

'It's very likely,' said Angie and burst into laughter. 'You have to admit it, things happen in Sheppey. It's not quite the backwater people think it is.'

Marcie was coy about answering. Things did happen in Sheppey but she had to wonder at the rest of the world. London was like a single brilliant star luring her to explore, to come, to stay. Not everyone could be content living on a small island surrounded by water and perched like a lost gannet staring out at the North Sea.

For the moment she was relatively happy with her lot. She had Joanna, but would Sheerness and Sheppey be all she ever wanted? Her father kept going backwards and forwards to London. Perhaps she really was a chip off the old block. She had to believe that because she couldn't remember her mother.

Shaking the thoughts from her mind, she got the

bus home. The bright lights of London were forgotten on her journey. Rain was smacking like birch rods against the windows. She shuddered. Home was definitely the place she wanted to be on a day like this. The warmth of her grandmother's kitchen would be fragrant with the smell of baking cakes and soups rich with tomatoes and herbs.

The rain had stopped by the time she got off the bus and a huge rainbow seemed to arch from Sheerness to Southend. She made for the front door, put her key in the lock and turned. Nothing happened. The door appeared to be locked.

Thinking her grandmother might be having a quiet snooze she didn't knock but walked to the end of the street and the entrance to the back lane.

The lane was muddy and wet grass fronds flicked at her knees. The back gate to number ten was open. Frowning she headed up the garden path for the back door and pushed it open.

Her grandmother was not alone. She was bouncing Joanna up and down in her arms.

'Gran, the front door's locked.'

'I wanted you to come round the back. We have a visitor. He came round the back too.'

Her grandmother seemed relieved to see her, but it was neither her nor her daughter that drew Marcie's attention. A scruffy, pathetic figure sat huddled in an armchair to one side of the kitchen fireplace.

'Garth?'

A row of twisted teeth showed when Garth smiled. His pale eyes were big and as innocent as a child. The basic fact was that he still was a child.

'Hello, Marcie.'

A coughing fit immediately followed.

She quickly took her coat off and took Joanna from her grandmother. Their eyes locked and said things as eloquently as spoken words.

Garth was in a bad way. His cheeks were sunken and there were dark circles beneath his eyes. His hands, as dirty as his face, clutched a mug of beef tea.

'I found him outside the back door,' said her grandmother. 'He's been sleeping rough and has not eaten for days.'

Another look passed swiftly between Rosa and her granddaughter. Rosa read Marcie's look and answered as though she'd spoken her question out loud.

'The men who threw him out of his mother's home said that he had to be locked up away from normal people. He thought they meant a prison so he ran away.'

Marcie looked with pity in her eyes at a human being who knew nothing about lying; nothing about jealousy, hate or any of the other negative emotions that afflicted mankind. Garth Davies was not like other human beings.

'I found him curled up by the bush where the hen house used to be. I fear his mind is not as clear as it was. He thought the hen house would still be there. His memories are not keen.'

'But he remembered me. You remembered me, didn't you, Garth?'

Garth smiled over what was left of his steaming mug. 'Marcie. You're Marcie.'

Marcie nodded. 'That's right, Garth.'

101

Jiggling Joanna up and down in her arms, she went closer to her grandmother.

'What are we going to do with him?'

Her grandmother's look was forthright. 'He has to stay here. He has nowhere else to go.'

After they'd eaten dinner, Marcie had put Joanna to bed and Garth had fallen asleep on the small settee in the living room. Marcie followed her grandmother up into the attic where the boys used to sleep. Babs had taken the two single beds when she and the family had moved into the council house. Rosa had never wanted Babs or the children to leave, but eventually she'd come round to the idea – especially once she'd heard that Marcie was expecting a baby.

Luckily there was an old mattress and two old feather pillows still up there. Clean sheets were fetched plus half a dozen grey army blankets. 'Your grandfather brought many of these here when he came home on leave,' her grandmother told her.

Well, that explained a lot, thought Marcie. The blankets had obviously been army issue and had come marching home with him – just like a large number of things that didn't belong to him came marching home with her father. Now he really *was* a chip off the old block, she thought as she pummelled a pillow into shape.

When she looked back at her grandmother she paused for breath. Her grandmother's face was buried in one of the blankets. She knew she was sniffing it, searching for some last vestige of the man she had spent her life with.

'Have they been washed?' Marcie asked.

Her grandmother's face emerged from the blanket. 'Of course.'

Marcie found herself saddened by the way her grandmother answered and the way she had looked. Even though her grandfather had long passed over, her grandmother sensed his presence and could even smell some remnant of his existence, even if his bedding only smelled now of carbolic.

She found herself wishing she could do the same with Johnnie, but that could never be. It saddened her to think that she would never see him again, never smell him again and never touch him again. And yet she did have a remnant of Johnnie. She had Joanna.

## Chapter Thirteen

The last thing they'd allowed for was Garth creeping out in the middle of the night.

The first days of the week went fine, but having been living outside for a while, he'd got used to the cold. Usually they'd find him the next morning curled up in his favourite spot where the chicken shed used to be. On Thursday he was found on the beach and on Friday at the back of a shop in the High Street. The police brought him back on each occasion because Rosa Brooks had had the good sense to suggest that Marcie sew his name and address inside his coat.

'He's a bit mental. If he gets too much for you

I'd have him put away if I were you,' the policeman suggested.

'In Dover House?' said Rosa. Dover House was
an asylum for the mentally insane.

Marcie was horrified. 'You can't put him there!'

'It may come to it should he get into any mischief,' said the police constable. He was young
and spotty and had a superior air.

Marcie cringed in response to the way he kept
looking at her.

'That your baby?' he asked.

She felt Joanna dribbling onto her shoulder.
'Yes.'

His sly eyes dropped to her ring finger. She'd
left off wearing the fake wedding ring because it
was turning her finger green. She felt herself
reddening under the intensity of his gaze.

'I see.'

It was like some kind of condemnation, as
though she'd committed perjury and had been
found out. But she hadn't lied and the young
policeman had guessed the truth.

There were four dresses to be finished that week
and Marcie found herself looking forward to
Monday. Finishing four dresses all of the same
design wasn't so bad and she was pleased with
the results.

Her father came home that weekend and asked
if she wanted to go out with him and Babs.

'No need for us to bring the kids round for
Mother to look after. Our Archie's old enough to
do that. And next door will keep an ear out for
them.'

The dresses were finished. She had no reason for declining her father's invitation unless her grandmother refused to babysit. As it turned out her grandmother bid her go.

'You have not been on a night out for a very long time.'

It seemed strange putting on one of the dresses she'd designed herself. This one was a new creation made of lilac Crimplene, a new fabric that never creased and was easy to work with. A long zip ran from its mandarin collar to just below her navel. It was straight up and down; no darts to worry about except from armpit to bosom, and therefore easy to run up.

The night had turned warm, but she still pulled on her favourite pair of white stretchy boots. Her legs looked very brown against the white and her skirt was very short.

Hair washed and brushed and hanging half way down her back, she didn't look so young and vulnerable as she used to do. As she eyed herself in the mirror she found herself wondering what her mother would think of her. Would she look even more like her as she got older? She thought of her mother often, especially now that she had a daughter of her own. Marcie knew that whatever happened she would always do her best for Joanna. Nothing in the world would make her walk out on her like her mother was said to have done. She recalled the fleeting looks she sometimes saw in her father's eyes. And where was her mother? Nobody had any answers to that question, though in her heart all roads led to London and perhaps her mother's path had led there too.

Saturday night was music night at the Lord Nelson and the pub was bursting at the seams. A girl with black hair and a hooked nose was singing 'Anyone Who Had a Heart' in as Cilla Black a style as she could muster. The band, especially the drummer, wasn't helping the poor girl. They were too loud and almost drowning her out, but trooper as she was, she carried on. It was a bit like a battle between instruments and songstress. Fortunately the singer had the microphone.

'Hello, Marcie, love. How are you?'

She was asked again and again how she was and always gave the same answer.

Obviously a lot of people did know about Joanna. Most assumed she really had been married and tonight, despite her green finger, she'd thought to wear the ring.

The music changed to 'Not Fade Away' by the Rolling Stones. The group bashed it out, a guy taking over the microphone. A few people began dancing around just in front of where the group were, trying their best to move in the little space available.

'Can I have a dance, love?'

She recognised a bloke she'd known at school. It was just a dance. What did it matter?

Crowded as it was, Marcie lost herself in the music. She was almost herself again, young and carefree, though of course she was not. On the other hand, things were certainly looking up. The job at the hospital had been dull. Making really fashionable dresses and getting paid for them was something else. She was a success! And not yet eighteen. How fab was that?

There weren't that many dancers among the clientele of the Lord Nelson. The fact was that most blokes were there to drink and had two left feet. Some, like her dad, were there with their wives.

When she got back to where they were standing – her father never sat down in a pub – they were arguing.

'You're showing your tits. Cover them up.'

Babs dared to answer him back. 'Don't be so bloody stupid.' As she reached for her drink, his hand smacked down on hers.

'No wife of mine is going around with her tits out. Cover yourself up.' He'd downed three pints already and was halfway through the fourth.

Babs pouted her pale-pink lips. The colour and the pout were copied from a magazine picture of Brigitte Bardot. Her stepmother was even wearing a pink gingham dress similar to the one the French starlet had been wearing. The hair was blonde too of course, but the figure was overblown. Babs was much more brassy than Bardot.

The dress hadn't been so bad earlier in the evening. The fact was that Babs had undone a top button.

Young as she was, it occurred to Marcie that Babs liked winding her dad up. She liked to make him jealous. That was what this was all about. But her father could turn ugly – a fact that made Marcie nervous. Her father had mellowed a little, but he still had a temper. Tony Brooks was likely to add a deeper colour to his wife's pearly blue eye shadow and black mascara if she didn't watch out. It wouldn't be the first time she'd sported a black eye, and possibly wouldn't be the last.

This was the first night out Marcie had had for ages and though the Lord Nelson was no great shakes, she wasn't going to have it ruined by a domestic fight.

She moved quickly, leaning close to her step-mother. 'Let me button it up for you.'

Her father's second wife was in no position to argue. She was pressed up against the bar and Marcie was pressed up against her.

'Don't do that.' Red-painted finger nails attempted to claw Marcie's fingers away.

The whole evening might have ended with Babs getting a black eye, except that someone else intervened.

'Marcie! I want you to dance with me.'

Marcie felt as though someone had poured iced water over her. The last person she wanted to see was Alan Taylor.

Marcie pushed him away, though in that crush it wasn't easy.

'Let me just hold you,' he said, caressing her hair as he held her close.

Marcie found it impossible to move away. The crowds pressed too close and set her heart racing.

Alan's breath stunk of booze. He couldn't possibly smell that bad after just an hour or two. He'd had to have been boozing all day.

She saw her father's face contorted with rage, his anger now directed at his one-time friend, Alan Taylor.

A pair of hands came over her head clutching two pint mugs.

'Two pints of best,' the man was shouting.

Shielded by the crush of people trying to get to the bar, she didn't see who landed the first blow. The first she knew that her father and Alan were fighting was when the crowd thinned out, circling the two men who had fallen on the floor.

Her father was on top of Alan, his hands around his throat and he was shouting.

'Keep away from her, you fucking nonce! Keep away from her or I'll swing fer you!'

'Get off him, you silly sod. Get off him, Tony!'

It was Babs shouting and Babs who was kicking her husband in the stomach with the toe of her winkle-picker high-heeled shoes.

'Babs! You'll kill him!' shouted Marcie who was sweating with fear.

'Better that and get him to stop rather than him ending up in the nick!' Babs retorted.

The whole thing would have been funny if it hadn't been so serious. Her stepmother's Brigitte Bardot getup was seriously awry. Her bouffant blonde hair had flopped and was falling over her eyes, and her pouting pink mouth was shouting all the worst expletives under the sun – words that would never pass the lips of the French film star.

There was something primitively exciting about what she was seeing, but also something fearful, something best avoided. Marcie could smell the excitement and see the bloodlust in the eyes of those watching.

Suddenly there was a gap in the crowd on the opposite side of the ring of spectators. A familiar figure wearing a plum-coloured suede cap and a haunch-high mini skirt waded into view. Rita

109

Taylor was screaming at the top of her voice.

'Get off my effing dad, Tony Brooks. Get off my effing dad!'

She kicked into Tony's guts with far more force than Babs had used.

'Get off! Get off! Get off!'

Marcie saw her father look up at Rita. At first he looked surprised. Then he began to laugh.

'It's your girl, Alan,' he said, his angry scowl gone in an instant. He began to chuckle as though something was very funny indeed. 'Bloody hell, Alan. Have you seen that stupid hat she's wearing? It looks like a pimple on a rock!'

Rita was squatting down beside her father, her face now the same colour as her cap.

Marcie's dad got to his feet while Rita cradled her dad's head. Blood was streaming from Alan's nostrils and he was coughing as he tried to catch his breath. Tony had almost strangled him.

'You Brooks! You're all fucking animals,' shouted Rita. Initially her eyes were fixed on Marcie's father. Then she saw Marcie. 'Just like you, Marcie Brooks,' she snarled, her face set like a livid wax mask. 'I know what you did. My dad told me so. You're a tramp! Nothing but a tramp and the sooner you leave Sheppey the better. And take your brat with you,' she shouted as Babs and her father herded Marcie to the door.

'What was she on about?' Babs asked once they were outside.

'Nothing to concern you. She's as thick as her old man,' said Marcie's father. He rubbed his stomach. 'Christ, she packs the kick of a mule.'

Neither woman mentioned that Babs had sunk

a few kicks into her husband's guts. He'd had enough beer to safely forget that fact.

'Come on. Let's get home. I'll drop you off our Marcie.'

Marcie didn't argue with that.

Not being in on Marcie's big secret, Babs was puzzled. 'What did you do to upset your old friend Rita, then?'

Her father began to mumble an explanation. 'Well, it's like this...'

Marcie got there first. 'He used to treat me like a daughter. She got jealous.'

She was sitting in the front passenger seat so saw him glance at her. Babs was riding in the back as though she were the Queen or at least the lady mayoress.

What was that?

Marcie jerked upright in that semi-state between sleeping and waking, when the line is thin between what is real and what is not.

One glance at the curtains billowing into the room and the open window swinging on its hinges and reality reasserted itself. The nightmare was broken, though the shadowy figure she half recognised still lingered somewhere at the back of her mind.

Satisfied she was definitely in the real world she got out of bed and crossed the room. The bedroom lino was cold beneath her feet and the breeze from the window pleasantly crisped the film of sweat that covered her body.

Once the window was closed and she'd checked that Joanna was still sleeping, she got back into bed. Pulling the green satin eiderdown up to her chin she gazed at the lampshade and the black shadow it threw across the ceiling and asked herself a simple question. Why now? What was the significance of her worst nightmare returning after all this time?

Turning onto her side she heaved the eiderdown even higher, closed her eyes and wished.

*Everything will be alright in the morning. Get to sleep.*

She tried to convince herself that Johnnie was close by, if only in spirit, supporting her no matter what. She fell asleep though slept fitfully, semi-alert in case the dream returned.

In the morning she had butterflies. She eyed her reflection in the bathroom mirror, alarmed to see that her expression confirmed what she felt. The fine brows were arched and the blue eyes were luminous – a little excited, a little afraid. She told herself that the nightmare would not return and half convinced herself that it was so. In the nightmare she'd been once again in the Taylors' bungalow. Alan Taylor's face had loomed over her.

In the morning she recounted her dream to her grandmother.

'I know it's not real, but just a bad memory left over from what he did to me.'

When her grandmother eyed her it was as though she could see into her mind, into her very soul. 'The nightmare will open a door.'

Marcie frowned but made no comment. She knew – or rather – she *felt* that her grandmother would enlighten her.

'The nightmare is left over from an unhappy experience, but in time will develop into something more, an intuition that is always right and always frightening.'

'But is it real?' she asked, aware that she was knotting her fingers, not because she was scared, but purely because she was feeling so confused. 'And I feel so apprehensive, yet I don't know why.'

'Approach it with an open mind. Believe like a child that something will happen and it will,' said her grandmother. After having said it, she went off out into the back garden to tend to the herbs.

Marcie sat very still, not sure exactly what was being said.

*You're a woman now, not a child. Think logically.*

She was halfway through tacking the last dress ordered by Angie when the bad news came.

First there was the sound of her father's car pulling up outside. Then there was Babs, her face flushed and her breath racing.

'Angie's is gone,' she said, shouting the news straight into Marcie's face.

Marcie could see by her stepmother's face that this was no time for silly quips. Something bad had happened.

'Went up in flames,' exclaimed her father who had rushed in behind his wife.

The kids had come too. The two boys rushed straight through the cottage and out into the garden. Annie wandered over to where Joanna was sitting on a blanket eating a Farleys' Rusk. Annie espied a dropped piece, picked it up and shoved it in her mouth.

Marcie stared. 'Angie?'

Her father shook his head. 'Poor girl. She was led away by the police crying her eyes out.'

Stepdaughter and stepmother had never got on very well, but on this occasion Babs was on her side.

'Marcie, I'm so sorry, love. First you lost the job at the hospital and now this. It's just not fair.'

Marcie flopped down into a chair, her mind reeling. Now what? The sound of her grandmother's footsteps, the old down-at-heel shoes tapping on the kitchen floor, made her look up.

'One door closes, another opens,' her grandmother repeated softly.

Marcie prayed she was right.

## Chapter Fourteen

Marcie went along with her grandmother to see the still smouldering shop that had been Angie's Boutique. The best news about it was that Angie had not been inside at the time. She'd gone away to Brighton for the weekend to visit her sister. News came also that having seen the damage for herself she wouldn't be coming back. She was too upset.

Joanna was sitting in her pushchair. Marcie rocked her backwards and forwards on the pavement outside the remains of the shop. All that was left were blackened timbers and moulded lumps of plastic that had once been mannequins and shop fittings.

The most fashionable dress shop in Sheerness – in fact in the whole island – had come to an ignominious end. A lot of people said they were devastated by it. For Marcie it was more than that. She was gutted. All her hopes and dreams for her designs were now no more than cinders. The question was what was she going to do now? She had no wage from a job and no income from the shop. On top of that she was concerned about her reputation. Rita had had evil in her eyes. Marcie was convinced that her name was about to be dragged through the mud. The thing was she could cope with her name being dirt. As usual these days, it was Joanna she was concerned about.

A cloud of ash whirred on the breeze and cold cinders made a pitter-pattering sound as they were blown out onto the pavement. Some of them scattered around Marcie's feet. She looked down at them.

'I feel like Cinderella,' she said wistfully.

Her grandmother, Rosa Brooks, a woman famed for her psychic powers, was strangely quiet.

Marcie looked at her.

'Garth has gone missing,' she said simply.

The rest of the day seemed to pass in a dream. Joanna still laughed and played and had to be changed and fed. Rosa Brooks went about her chores silently and looked as though her mind was far away.

Once Joanna was put down for her afternoon nap, Marcie resumed work on the last of three dresses earmarked for Angie's Boutique. The dresses were no longer wanted, but Marcie found it impossible not to finish them. Being creative was like giving birth; come hell and high water, there had to be a birth, a complete article at the end of all the hard work.

Her father came calling at around tea time. He'd been out looking for Garth.

'He is not dead,' said Rosa.

Father and daughter exchanged knowing looks. They both knew better than to argue with her.

'So,' said her father, 'what's that you're making? Another of your fancy frocks?'

Marcie smiled until she recalled that she and Angie had laughed about her father and his old-fashioned phrases. Still, at least Angie was alive.

'No one wants it now. There's no boutique in Sheppey now,' she said angrily. 'Great! No job. No boutique. What the bloody hell am I going to do?'

She threw the garment onto the floor. She didn't care that her language had caused her grandmother to glare disapprovingly. Everything in her life was turning sour.

'You'll be fine in a day or two,' said her father.

His attempt at joviality only served to anger her more. What did he know about it?

'Dad! I will not be fine! I have no job, no husband and no prospects of anything good ever happening to me again. And I've a baby to support! So don't say that. Just do not say that!'

He looked surprised at her show of temper suddenly recognising that there was a great deal of himself in his daughter. Strange he'd never noticed it before, he thought, and wondered why. The truth was that he'd only seen her mother in his daughter's features, but he wasn't ready to face up

116

to that. Not yet.

Much to his merit, he tried again to show sympathy, resting his big rough hands on her shoulders, then taking them off again when he saw how incongruous they looked, how ugly and rough compared to her.

'Look, love, something will turn up. It always does you know.'

Her temper had not calmed that much.

'Not in Sheppey!' She gulped a lungful of air before continuing. 'There's nothing here. It's got nothing except mangy sheep and mangy people! I want a career in fashion, but not here. I need to be in London. That's where I need to be. London!'

Tony sucked in his bottom lip. He didn't often feel helpless but on this occasion he did. He felt a desperate urge to sort something out.

'I've got contacts,' he said suddenly.

Marcie had met some of her father's contacts. 'Don't tell me! One of them owns a boutique.'

He looked hurt. 'As a matter of fact, yeah. Yeah, he does.'

She didn't say outright that she thought he was talking a load of flannel, but that was exactly what she was thinking. Her father would say anything to make her feel good because making her feel good would make him feel good. Whether he was telling the truth or not had nothing to do with it.

'You wait,' he said, less jovial now, more serious. 'I'll fix you up with something in London. Just you wait and see.'

## Chapter Fifteen

It was Father Justin who found Garth Davies and brought him round to Endeavour Terrace.

'He insisted he lived here,' he said to Marcie's grandmother.

'He does now.'

Rosa Brooks asked no questions but pressed Garth to sit himself at the table. Two doorsteps of white bread were set in front of him followed by a spoon. A pot of lamb stew was simmering on the stove. Rosa dipped a ladle into the thick, aromatic potage and poured a generous portion into a white china bowl. Garth fell on it, devouring the bread in great gob-stopping mouthfuls between spoonfuls of soup.

The sight of Garth alarmed her; his face was smudged with what looked like soot and his hairstyle – not that he'd ever had much of a hairstyle – was oddly truncated at the front. On close inspection it looked singed. His smell alarmed her more than anything. He smelled of smoke and that worried her.

Unwilling to cast aspersions, Rosa Brooks turned to the priest. 'Can I tempt you, Father?' She knew a salivating set of lips when she saw them.

'Indeed,' said the black-robed priest, 'though not quite so large a bowl if you don't mind. Gluttony is one of the seven deadly sins after all, though in Garth's case I don't think he's eaten for days.'

Rosa had known Father Justin for a long time and understood what he really meant. He wanted to be tempted. He wanted a large portion and being a good Catholic she had to appear generous – especially to a priest.

The priest thanked her and, although he didn't gulp his food like Garth, he certainly paid it great concentration. When they more or less finished together, she poured tea for them both.

Joanna chose that moment to wake up. Her cry carried down through the plasterwork ceiling, demanding attention. Marcie had gone to the Labour Exchange with the hope of finding a job in one of the local factories. She hadn't really relished the prospect but had thought that a larger firm might be more forgiving of a girl in her circumstances.

While Rosa went to attend to the child, Father Justin finished his food, pushed his bowl away and turned his attention to Garth. The boy – for he couldn't help thinking of Garth as a boy despite the fact that he was fully grown – was reaching for more bread, dunking it into the morass of vegetables and gulping it down.

Garth didn't see the look of disgust on the priest's face. Father Justin was as susceptible to the baser responses of humanity despite his holy cloth.

'I think I will have a word with the Sisters at St Saviour's,' he said out loud. 'That's where you should be, Garth, my boy, with the rest of the loonies.'

Father Justin was the pillar of priestly

behaviour when he had an audience, even if only one parishioner. Out of earshot of anyone who might be appalled, he said what he was thinking, becoming baser and fouler mouthed than any of his parishioners could ever dream of.

Garth didn't understand what he was talking about anyway and he would have carried on, enjoying kicking over the traces and saying what he liked.

He didn't get chance to say any more. Marcie came breezing through the door. Initially, her look seemed one of surprise, though he could never be sure with Marcie. She had a habit of turning away from him he noticed. A suspicion that she might be gifted – or in the church's opinion – cursed with the same affliction as her grandmother had crossed his mind. He'd heard rumours about Rosa, had touched upon the matter with her, though Rosa had blanked him out.

His smile was broad. 'Why, Marcie. You're looking flushed my girl. Have you been rushing now?'

'No,' said Marcie, taking off her scarf. 'Not really.'

Her flush was surprise at him being there. As usual she tried not to look into his eyes. Her smile was for Garth and her pleasure at seeing him was obvious.

'Garth, where have you been?'

'Hello, Marcie. I'm eating stew.' It was as though he had not been missing at all, but had merely popped out to the shops for five minutes. Marcie knew from experience that Garth had no concept of time.

'So I see,' said Marcie. 'It looks as though you're

enjoying it.'

'You're a fine-looking woman, Marcie Brooks,' said Father Justin getting to his feet. 'Let me help you off with that coat, now.'

Marcie tensed, surprised at the speed with which he came behind her, his fingers brushing her shoulder as he helped her out of her coat. He hung it up at the back of the door. She suppressed a shiver when he looked her up and down with far more familiarity than a priest should ever use.

'My, but you're a lovely girl, Marcie. And strong too. These arms seem strong.'

He ran his hands down her arms, patting them as though she were a horse, thumbs caressing.

'You know I have a vacancy for a cleaner at the presbytery. Would a few hours a week be useful to you?'

For the first time ever Marcie stared into his eyes and what she saw there scared her. It certainly wasn't cleaning he wanted. Father Justin had sin in mind and she was the object of that sin. In his eyes she read his desires, his need to satisfy the lust he felt for her. All she wanted was for him to leave.

'No thank you! I'm going to London.'

He looked deflated. 'Are you now? I didn't know that.'

Rosa came down with Joanna who gurgled with delight on seeing her mother.

Rosa did not ask her granddaughter whether she'd had any luck getting a job. She just knew she had not. An unspoken message passed swiftly between them. Neither would mention where she had been until Father Justin was gone. Although the priest was formally welcomed when he came to visit, he wasn't liked and neither was he trusted.

'Where was he?' She directed the question at her grandmother taking Joanna into her arms.

'Father Justin says he was sleeping rough in a yard at the back of the shops in Sheerness.'

The statement seemed to reverberate between them and again there was that meeting of eyes and of minds. Marcie felt confused but gained something from her grandmother's fearless look. It was as if she were telling her not to be afraid at what she was seeing because she was seeing it too. They were both worried about Garth and both wary of the priest.

'Do you not think that young Garth here might be better off at St Saviour's with the good sisters there,' said Father Justin.

Marcie frowned. She'd never heard of the place. Her grandmother on the other hand had.

'Garth needs a home, not an asylum.' Marcie was horrified. This time grandmother and granddaughter did not look at each other, though they shared a single thought: something bad was about to happen. They both knew it.

## Chapter Sixteen

The police came for Garth on Tuesday morning.

'We have reason to believe the said person was seen at the back of the shops. A witness states he was sleeping there.'

A sergeant had come this time accompanied by the same young constable Marcie had met before.

'That doesn't mean to say he did anything wrong,' Marcie pointed out hotly.

'My granddaughter is right,' said Rosa. 'And we know he did not do anything.'

The sergeant almost laughed in her face. 'What are you, psychic or something?'

The wrinkles around Rosa's mouth intensified as she clamped her, lips tightly together.

'Anyway,' the sergeant went on. 'He is known as being not all there so it stands to reason that he's not the sort to be left unsupervised with a box of matches.'

Marcie's jaw dropped. Her grandmother laid into them before she had chance to.

'His mother was careless with the men she went with, but was never careless with matches. And neither is Garth. He is just a poor soul injured when he was born. That is all.'

The sergeant was having none of it. When he took a deep breath he seemed to swell within his uniform, as though emphasising his authority in these matters.

'You cannot trust the lad to do things normally, madam, like other people do. Surely you've noticed that?'

'He's slow, but there's not a nasty bone in his body,' Marcie interjected, refusing to believe that Garth was responsible for destroying the future she'd planned for herself. 'He wouldn't do anything like that.'

She could see by their faces they were not convinced.

'Tell me who this witness is,' she demanded, fixing the sergeant with a disdainful glare and a defiant stance, arms folded, shoulders square.

'Young lady...' began the sergeant in a condescending tone.

She half wondered whether Father Justin had had a hand in this. Wasn't he keen to see Garth carted off to the asylum?

'I'm not at liberty to say at this moment in time. Not until we've asked this young man some questions and had him positively identified. But the person concerned does live above a shop in that rank.'

It was useless. Everything has become so difficult, thought Marcie. It was as though the life she'd always known in the place she'd always known was falling down around her like a house of cards. A tap on one card and the whole lot fell down.

'When will he be home?' asked Rosa Brooks.

The sergeant was hesitant. It was obviously a question he had no wish to answer. 'The evidence will be assessed and so will he. He may be brought back here on bail, or he may be detained in a safe place – a suitable place for somebody like him – for his sort of person – if you know what I mean.'

'No, sergeant. I do not know what you mean,' snapped Marcie, her eyes blazing. Why was it people could not accept Garth for what he was? Just a poor creature in need of human kindness.

The thought brought her up short. That's exactly what my grandmother used to say to me, she told herself. Funny how alike we're becoming.

The two policemen prepared to leave. At least they weren't using handcuffs. As they said, Garth wasn't the sort to run away and couldn't run very fast anyway.

'We'll be off then,' said the sergeant. 'Unless there's any tea on offer,' he added hopefully.

'No!' Marcie was livid. 'This way to the front door.'

All she wanted was them off the premises even though poor Garth had to go with them. She held it open for them.

The sergeant nodded a silent 'thank you', not daring to look her in the face.

The young constable gave her a quick smile at the same time as letting his eyes drop to her bosom. His look was blatant. His hand brushed against her belly as he passed.

'Keep your hands to yourself!' she snapped.

'It was just an accident,' he replied. The smug look on his face said otherwise.

'We'll be down to see you,' she shouted after Garth. Garth was all smiles when he waved back, excited because he was going for a ride in a police car.

The old house shook when she slammed the door.

Perhaps Marcie would never have left Sheppey and pursued her dream if it hadn't been for Alan Taylor.

Following another fruitless search for employment at the Labour Exchange, she'd wandered off along the beach at Sheerness, the sea breeze crisping her skin and sending her hair into thick tendrils behind her.

She looked out to the grey horizon trying to look further into her future. Would she always stay in this place? One half of her would always be here, she realised suddenly. This was where her roots were. The other half of her would always be out there searching for a better future and also to reclaim something of her past.

The breeze was brisk, the halcyon days of summer not yet here – if they would ever chance the east coast of England at all.

But at least it cleared her head and revitalised her flagging energy which in turn helped to lift her depression. Her grandmother said that things always came in threes and it was true in her case. First she'd lost her job, then the boutique – her only other source of income had burned down – and now Garth had been carted away by the police. Perish the thought that he should end up in an asylum. She didn't care about Father Justin's reassurances; the place had to be hell on earth.

For a moment she thought she heard somebody calling her, but didn't bother to look round. The old fear that she was being followed and that someone was about to jump out on her had disappeared, obliterated by her current problems.

'Marcie!'

A hand jerked at her shoulder bringing her to a stop.

Somewhat dishevelled but still possessing a dapper confidence, Alan Taylor looked inordinately pleased with himself.

'Didn't you hear me call you? You trying to

avoid me, Marcie?'

Of course she was.

She shoved her hands deeper into her pockets and eyed him grimly. 'What do you want, Alan?'

She was deliberately surly, though he didn't seem to notice.

'Marcie! My beautiful Marcie. You know we've got a lot to talk about, darling. Ain't that right, sweetheart?'

'No. I don't think so.' She tried to brush past, but he blocked her path.

'Get out of my way, Alan.'

He shook his head. 'I will not. I want to speak to you.'

Marcie narrowed her eyes. How could she ever have thought that this man was a better father to her than her real one? He'd betrayed her trust. He'd taken advantage of her – of her body when she'd been at her most vulnerable. Her shoulders stiffened and her jaw was like iron. 'Well, I don't want to speak to you.'

She shook off the hand gripping her arm. He grabbed her again. The breeze got up and tangled her hair over her eyes. In the skirmish she slipped on the wet pebbles and he went down with her.

For one dreadful moment he was on top of her, his slippery lips on her face, covering and sucking at her mouth and nose until she could barely breathe. He was suffocating her and didn't even know it, too engrossed in ripping at her blouse, groping for her breasts! He was drunk and wouldn't listen to her pleas for him to stop. She had to do something. And fast.

Gasping for air, she managed to turn her head

away. His head dipped lower, his lips sucking at a bared breast.

Desperate to escape, her hand scrabbled amongst the cold pebbles, her fingers clawing for something, anything she could use as a weapon.

It was not a pebble but a thick piece of wood, a piece of driftwood most likely fallen from a passing ship on its way to Rotterdam or London. It was light enough for her to lift and heavy enough to make a clumping sound against his head.

He gave a strange, strangulated sound deep in his throat. The piece of wood remained sticking at an angle at the back of his head, as though it had stuck there, caught on his collar. One hand reached hesitantly back to remove it, his eyes bulging with surprise.

His fingers never reached the wood. His hand fell limply. His body slumped against her, no longer groping, no longer kissing; no longer moving.

Marcie struggled to wriggle out from beneath the weight of his body thinking she had merely knocked him senseless.

It was only when her body was free of him and she saw the blood soaking into the back of his hair that she realised he was dead.

The piece of wood was stuck at a right angle across the back of his neck. Now that she could see it more clearly, she realised that it had been part of a packing case but had been wrenched free. It was probably only two-thirds of its original length, the end she had grasped broken and splintered. The bare ends of huge nails stuck out from the intact end that had connected with

Alan's head. Four inches of an exposed nail was embedded in the nape of his neck. Blood oozed from the wound onto the beach beneath him.

She'd killed him! She hadn't meant to do it... She'd been so determined that he not rape her again that she'd lashed out with the first thing that came to hand. It had been an accident, but it was still wrong, a mortal sin. She'd killed a man! Even if it had been the only way to stop him.

She thought of the two policemen who had collected poor Garth. Would they believe that it had been self-defence? Would they care about whether she was telling the truth about Alan attacking her?

She could almost hear their comments, already:

*Girls like you always say that.*

*You've lost your job. Got no other means of support so I hear.*

*And you have a baby but no husband. You're not married. You haven't been telling the truth. So how do we know you're telling the truth now?*

A sense of terror overcame her. Her first instinct was to run away. No way was she going to own up to this. She'd made up her mind about that. The trouble was had anyone seen her? Had anyone seen Alan following her?

Eyes wide with fear, she scanned the beach in one direction and then the other. She even looked towards the sea wall then back at the sea, as though anyone was likely to be out there on such a blustery day as this.

The wind was cold, the beach deserted. Even the candy-floss booth where she'd once worked when first leaving school was shuttered up against the cold wind and the promise of rain.

Feeling sick at what she'd done, she took one more glance at the dead man lying there. The tide was easing itself further up the beach, clotted fronds of spume hissing into the pebbles.

She ran to the sea wall, not daring to stop until she was hidden from anyone who might be chancing a walk along the promenade. Lights were coming on in houses beyond the promenade as twilight and a rising mist took hold.

It was an accident!

That's what she told herself. Once she'd caught her breath, she slowed her pace. Nobody but a fool would rush from the scene of a crime. Anyone seeing them would wonder and point the finger. She didn't want the finger of suspicion pointed at her. She wanted to get on with her life, but she had to tell someone about this, someone who could help her.

Her grandmother guessed of course. She saw that Marcie's buttons were not properly done up; she saw the wildness of her hair and the hunted look in her eyes.

'Something bad has happened. Tell me about it.'

So Marcie told.

Rosa too knew who could best help her granddaughter in a situation like this. With methodical intent and without a trace of panic, she put on her coat, the black one with the fur collar that she used for weekdays. 'I am going to the phone box. I am going to ring your father.'

Marcie sat waiting, fearful lest the police come calling before her grandmother came back.

Fearful lest she should end up in prison and lose everything that mattered in her life, especially her daughter, her beautiful baby girl.

## Chapter Seventeen

London! The rows of houses in green suburbs gave way to terraces and shops and corner pubs, narrow pavements and big red buses.

Although this wasn't exactly her first visit to London, Marcie felt as though she had entered a foreign country. The move had been so abrupt, the leaving prompt and leaving no time for reflection.

Already she was missing the flatter landscape of Kent and the Isle of Sheppey. The air here was different too, laden with soot and traffic fumes, not fresh and tangy with salt and the smoke from the Isle of Grain. Most of all she was missing her daughter, Joanna.

Her father had appeared as if by magic in response to his mother's phone call.

He insisted she'd done the right thing in calling him. 'The bastard got what he deserved,' he pronounced once he was sure Rosa Brooks was out of earshot.

It was all very well saying that, but in Marcie's opinion, it would have been better if it had not happened in the first place.

The police did come to the house and had questioned her father about what had happened.

Rumours about riffs and quarrels within and between families were always going the round on the island, so it was obvious that news of her father having a set-to with Alan Taylor would get to the ears of the police.

Once they'd asked for his alibi and the details checked out, they left looking dissatisfied but contrite. News later went round that Alan had stunk of booze and had likely fallen on the piece of wood accidentally.

'Had ruddy great nails in it,' so Babs had said in her mother-in-law's kitchen, totally oblivious to the fact that Rosa and Marcie knew everything about it.

What with having no job and Alan Taylor's sudden demise, it was thought that the time was ripe for Marcie to move to London. Perhaps she would have had second thoughts if her father hadn't already done the groundwork. He knew people who could help her. He'd told her that before and she hadn't believed him. Following Rosa Brooks putting on her second best coat and heading for the phone box, everything was now in place. The wife of a friend of her father's owned an upmarket boutique on the King's Road, Chelsea. They also had a sewing room above it and, although they bought in 'frocks' as her father insisted on calling them, they also designed and made up their own range. Marcie was being taken on to fill a gap left by a girl who had left to pursue a different career. It seemed to Marcie too good an opportunity to miss and everyone told her so. The only big drawback was that Joanna couldn't go with her. Marcie made the heartbreaking deci-

132

sion to go home at weekends, her grandmother taking care of the child during the week.

Coping without Joanna was never going to be easy. If it hadn't been for her daughter she would never had given a second thought to leaving the Isle of Sheppey – not under the circumstances. Alan Taylor had done her no favours. The only person who would really miss him was Rita, his daughter. It amazed Marcie now to think they had ever been close friends. Rita had showed her selfishness over and over again. She was not nice, though you can hardly call yourself that, Marcie thought. You brained her father. You shed his blood. Strangely, she could not feel any great remorse. She looked at her father; saw the tough features, the darting eyes always looking for the best opportunity. Was she so different from him? She decided that perhaps she was not, that the mother she resembled was on the outside only, that inside she was very much her father's daughter.

He sensed her looking and smiled at her. 'No need to be nervous, our Marcie. What's done is done.' He patted her hand. 'Old Alan got what was coming to him. I couldn't have done a better job meself.'

It occurred to her that he was talking to her as though she were Archie or Arnold, the two young sons who he expected to be just like him. She surmised he'd seen something of himself in her and she didn't want to disappoint him.

'I don't regret what I did, though I didn't mean to kill him. I had to protect myself, didn't I? I wasn't going to let him do that to me again. I was within my rights to defend myself.'

'Of course you were, darling. Just don't mention this little do to Victor's wife will you. Gabriella is just an old-fashioned girl with a rich husband who tells her he's just a businessman. If she knew half what him and his associates got up to, she'd have a bleeding fit. Know what I mean?'

Marcie smiled and said, yes, she knew what he meant, and yes, she would mind her Ps and Qs. What made her smile most was her father referring to Victor Camilleri and himself as business associates. Her father's frequent prison sentences made it all too obvious that the businesses he was associated with were rarely legal. If her father's profession was far from legal, then it stood to reason that Victor Camilleri's profession was much the same.

'Once you've settled in, I'll show you around. We'll have a night out together. I'll introduce you to a few people that are useful to know. I don't want you feeling lonely. After all there's no bugger you know up here is there?'

'I'll tell Gran you said that,' she said with a mischievous sidelong look.

Her father burst out laughing. He knew exactly what she meant. His language was moderated back in his mother's house in Endeavour Terrace. The closer they got to London the less moderate it became.

'You're right! The old woman would have a head fit!'

Old woman! He wouldn't dare use that terminology back in Sheppey!

Her father wasn't entirely right about her being lonely in London. She'd brought the letter from

Allegra. Up until now she'd avoided replying to it, thinking there was no point. Their time in Pilemarsh had been fleeting and, besides, they had nothing whatsoever in common. Allegra was from a different class to her. It was like comparing a sleek, pedigree feline with a moggy from the alley. That's how Marcie felt about it, though things could change. Gabriella Camilleri sounded as though she were out of the same box as Allegra, all rounded accent and beautifully groomed. The Camilleris lived in Chelsea. Allegra lived near Regent's Park. She didn't know how distant Regent's Park was from Chelsea. In time, once she'd settled in and got her bearings, she might very well seek her out.

I don't feel afraid, Marcie thought as she looked up at the façade of the building in front of her. The Camilleri family lived in a luxury apartment overlooking a park. The building was built of red brick with white-framed windows and fancy stonework above windows and around the door. A commissionaire opened it for them.

'Good morning, Mr Brooks,' said the man. His fingers lightly brushed the brim of his hat in an unusually formal salute. 'Shall I deal with the suitcase, sir?'

He was referring to Marcie's small suitcase which her father was carrying.

'Good morning, Forester,' said her father. 'No need. I can manage it, old son.'

The elderly doorman's accent was a world away from her father's, sounding more Harrow than Hackney. The contrast was so funny that if it were anyone else and on any other occasion, she would have laughed out loud.

They got into the lift.

'What's so funny?' her father asked on seeing her expression.

Still smiling, she shook her head. 'I was just thinking.'

'What?' He looked peeved, sensing the joke was on him.

She wouldn't hurt him. 'I was wondering how a girl from the sticks is ever going to fit in. Will I, or won't I?'

'You'll be fine,' he stated, lighting up a cigarette.

She sensed he was thinking too, ready to retaliate when she said what she said next – but she said it anyway.

'Why can't I stay with you?'

He fidgeted from one foot to the other. 'Nah! You wouldn't want to stay at my drum. It ain't nowhere near as good as this. Only the best for my girl! You're getting a nice room here. And this place overlooks the park. Victor thought that was best because you'll be near the frock shop and don't need to catch a bus.'

Marcie eyed her father knowingly. Outwardly she'd pretend to believe all the spiel he was giving her. Inside she knew he didn't want her living in too close a proximity. There were most likely two reasons for this: the first was that he didn't want her to get mixed up in the criminality he himself was mixed up in; the second was that he was probably living with another woman. As regards the former, she herself wasn't keen to be too close to the gangster world her father was a part

136

of. As regards the latter it was better she did not meet this other woman. That way she could not lie if asked, she could only plead ignorance.

## Chapter Eighteen

Eight pounds a week! Marcie could hardly believe she was being paid eight pounds a week to do what she loved doing. Nothing was taken from her wages for bed and board; Gabriella, a lovely Italian woman with warm brown eyes and brandy-coloured hair, insisted that she live as one of the family.

At first she'd been bashful about encroaching on the family life of people she did not know, but despite standing only five feet two inches in stockinged feet, Gabriella Camilleri was not the sort of woman who took no for an answer.

'You are too young to be on your own in the city. There are many big bad wolves around,' she said while shaking a warning finger. Then she laughed and said that seeing as she was Tony Brooks' daughter, she might very well be able to take care of herself.

Marcie immediately perceived from that particular observation that Gabriella Camilleri knew a little more about her husband's business associates than either her husband or Tony Brooks gave her credit for.

On first entering her room, Marcie felt a great sense of having been somewhere similar before.

The double sash windows overlooked the trees in the park, just as the attic room at Johnnie's parents' house had overlooked trees.

The room was furnished with a single bed, a bedroom suite with a wardrobe far too big for the few clothes she'd brought with her, plus a small writing desk and a chair. Luxury of luxuries, she even had her own little electric kettle, a teapot and crockery. A small coffee jar sat beside a small tea caddy, a cup and saucer. A jug of fresh milk was provided daily. She even had her own biscuit tin.

A green satin counterpane covered the bed; she'd seen similar in Hollywood movies covering the likes of Bette Davis and Audrey Hepburn. The whole ambience of the room was far and above what she'd been used to back at Endeavour Terrace. Even so just thinking of the little room she had shared with her baby had brought tears to her eyes.

'I will make you tea,' Gabriella had decided, presuming that Marcie was feeling homesick.

'No need. Honestly,' she protested.

'You must be missing your family, your grandmother in particular?'

Her father hadn't said a word to the Camilleris about her circumstances. They'd agreed that it was best if they thought Marcie was just a girl looking for a break in the big city. As far as they were concerned her returning home every weekend would be to keep an eye on her elderly grandmother rather than to visit her baby.

At their first meeting, a smiling Victor Camilleri had limped across the palatial living room to shake her hand.

'Tony's girl! So sad to hear of your predicament,' he said in a heavily accented voice. 'A lovely young girl like you should have had more time with her man, more time to make babies.'

He patted her hand as he said it, his voice oozing sympathy though his smile was slightly odd exposing large, yellowing teeth. Despite the kind words she felt like Red Riding Hood.

'My husband is not home very much,' Mrs Camilleri explained. 'He has many business interests that take him away at all hours.'

I bet, thought Marcie. Her father had always been involved with the seedier side of London life and nightclubs in particular. Tony Brooks had explained that he worked for Victor Camilleri looking after his various properties. She took it as read that one of these was a nightclub.

Marcie learned that there was no swaying Gabriella once she'd decided on what was going to happen. She found that out in the sewing room once she'd seen Marcie in the black and white quartered mini dress originally intended for the Isle of Sheppey's one and only boutique.

'Stand up,' she'd said on sight of Marcie wearing the dress.

Marcie had done as ordered.

'Is that a Mary Quant?' Gabriella had asked, her eyes moist with admiration, her breath slightly hushed as though she were in church and afraid that God might hear her.

Beaming with pleasure, Marcie shook her head, 'No. It's a Marcie Brooks.'

'Really?'

Praise coming from someone as elegant and knowing as Gabriella was really welcome. She had such an eye for fashion, such a way with the clothes she wore. Marcie found herself wondering how come she'd ended up marrying a man with one leg shorter than the other. He has money, she countered. You shouldn't forget that.

It didn't take long for Gabriella to get her designing and making dresses like the one she was wearing and the others she'd made for Angela Babbington.

The design studio and sewing room were immediately above the boutique on the King's Road. The boutique was called Daisy Chain. A huge plastic daisy hung over the door.

Marcie loved the place. Being here had lifted her spirits. She could forget the awful things about her home on the Isle of Sheppey, though she would never forget the good things.

Each weekend she went home. As the train or her father's car neared Sheerness, her hunger to see her daughter increased. Leaving first thing on Monday morning was hard, but once she was nearing London her spirits lifted again. There are things to look forward to, she told herself – things in London and things on Sheppey.

There were some things about living with the Camilleri family that reminded Marcie of home.

Gabriella Camilleri insisted on saying grace before dinner. She also attended mass twice a week.

Her husband, Victor, did not go to mass. He tolerated grace with thin-lipped disdain, his eyes always open, studying the light fitting, the view from the window or the food he was waiting to devour. Sometimes he caught her peeping from beneath fluttering eyelids and grinned.

She couldn't help but grin back.

Because both her and Mrs Camilleri worked the same hours in the sewing room and the shop, it wasn't often she was alone in the flat when Mr Camilleri was there. But one day she'd had a headache after days of close work on lace collars that had to be carefully attached to Crimplene dresses.

On hearing the door shut, Mr Camilleri limped out of his study. Marcie knew now that one of his legs was shorter than the other following contracting polio in his childhood. His shoes were specially made, the bottom of his right shoe built up to help compensate his lack of inches in that leg.

Apart from that he was always well dressed in silk handmade suits, the trouser edges razor sharp, the jackets sitting like a second skin on his shoulders.

He had dark eyes that seemed to be continually on the move as though he were gathering information from his surroundings and storing it for future use. His swarthiness betrayed his Sicilian roots.

A younger man came out behind him holding an open file with both hands. He was wearing black-rimmed spectacles. In an instant she was reminded of Clark Kent, Superman's alter ego. He seemed to stiffen when he saw her and didn't smile. He stared.

'Shall we attend to it later, Michael?' Victor said to him over his shoulder. 'Carry on where we left off while I take care of this young lady.'

141

The young man's stare was broken. He glanced at the older man before disappearing back into Victor's study.

Victor smiled at her. 'Marcie. You are home early?'

Most of his statements sounded like questions, deserving of an answer when sometimes there was no answer.

She ran her hand across her forehead.

'I've been doing a lot of close work recently. It's given me a headache.'

'Ah,' he said nodding his overlarge head. 'Then you should rest, Marcie. Go to your bed right now. I will bring you a glass of water and some aspirin. Yes. Aspirin will take away the pain. A little sleep and I guarantee you will be as right as rain.'

Her head was throbbing so she didn't argue but went to her room and lay down on her bed.

As promised he came to her with a glass of water and two aspirin.

'Take these. You will feel better then. Drink.'

He waited and watched as she popped the aspirins into her mouth and swilled it down with water. It wasn't until they were well on the way to her stomach that she remembered that other time when a man had bid her drink. Was Victor Camilleri using the same trick as Alan Taylor?

She pinched herself. Everything seemed fine – except for her throbbing headache.

Mr Camilleri smiled. 'There. That is better. Now cover yourself. Sleep.'

He pulled the half of the satin eiderdown she wasn't lying on over her and patted it flat.

When she closed her eyes she felt the coolness

of his palm on her brow.

'Sleep.' The way he said it was incredibly hypnotic – and soothing – very soothing.

His fingers stroked her hair back from her face. She felt like a child again. Victor Camilleri was treating her as if she were his own daughter. The Camilleris didn't have a daughter; they had a son. He had a flat in Primrose Hill. He was following in his father's footsteps, Mrs Camilleri had told her. That was why she hadn't met him yet. His name was Nicholas.

'That feel good?'

'Yes. It does.'

'Can I make you laugh?'

She couldn't believe he had any chance of doing that. Her head was aching too badly, but she acquiesced.

'My family originally intended that I should become a priest.'

Marcie's eyes snapped open.

Victor was smiling in a Dennis the Menace fashion, cheekily but with wicked intent.

'So I made love to every girl I came across and waited to see where my seed took root. Gabriella saved my life. We had to get married.'

Despite her headache Marcie laughed. Gabriella Camilleri insisted on saying grace and going to mass and was much more the stuff Catholic priests are made of. Victor was not.

'I wish you were my daughter,' he said and seemed to mean it. 'You must meet my son.'

The way he said it was odd – as though if she couldn't be his daughter perhaps she could be something else. And he wanted her to meet his son. If what Gabriella had told her was anything to go by, he was the best and handsomest son who'd ever lived. Perhaps it was true.

When Victor went back into his study, Michael was sitting behind his big mahogany desk perusing the file. He looked up when Victor came in and took off his glasses.

'So that's the girl.'

'That's the girl.'

'She's very young.'

'Good. The younger the better,' returned Victor lighting up one of his big Havana cigars. 'A wife should be young so that she looks to her husband for learning about life.'

Michael lowered his eyes. 'That should please Roberto.'

Roberto was the name by which Nicholas Roberto Camilleri was known. He preferred it that way. Michael was his half-brother, the resultant fruit of one of Victor's many liaisons. Gabriella turned her eye to his indiscretions – just as Marcie would be expected to do.

## Chapter Nineteen

Marcie was excited. Her father was keeping his promise to take her out on the town. It would be her first night out since coming to London.

Excitedly she scoured the shops on the King's Road for the right shoes and ended up buying a pair of burgundy patent ones with thin ankle straps – similar to the ones she'd seen gracing Angie Babbington's feet. The dress she bought to go with it was made of fine flecked pink wool, had a Peter Pan collar and buttons down the front. She chose burgundy tights to match.

She showed her purchases to Mrs Camilleri, who silently picked the items over, her eyes scrutinising each little button, her fingers probing into each odd-shaped buttonhole.

'Don't you like it?' Marcie asked, a little disappointed at Gabriella Camilleri's face.

Mrs Camilleri turned her dark eyes onto Marcie and explained softly, 'Marcie, I do not think you understand. You are going to hit the bright lights of London. This dress is very nice, but it is more suitable for going to mass or for an interview for an office job. You should have bought something far more glamorous and trendy.'

Marcie sighed as she fingered the soft pink wool from which the dress was made. 'I didn't realise that.' She shrugged. 'It will have to do.'

'And before you ask,' said Mrs Camilleri, 'the shoes are far too prim and proper for a nightclub.'

A nightclub! She hadn't even realised that she was going out to a nightclub. Her father had said a night on the town. Back in Sheerness that mean a few pub visits then fish and chips on the way home. Quite frankly the outfit she'd bought would be considered overdressing back there. But here in the King's Road...?

'Not even the shoes?'

Mrs Camilleri shook her head. 'They are nice

shoes, but not suitable for a nightclub. Night-clubs are sexy, you know. No matter whether they are dancing on stage or sitting with their spouses, women in nightclubs are on display. We have to look as desirable as the dancers there.'

Feeling disappointed, Marcie shrugged again. 'It's all I have that's suitable.'

Mrs Camilleri eyed her thoughtfully, a merry twinkle in her eyes. 'Something will come up,' she said at last.

Earlier when she'd been out shopping, Marcie had ruefully eyed the window displays in Daisy Chain, wishing she had the money to buy the well-made products she saw there. Daisy Chain was one of the most expensive in the whole street, catering for the Chelsea girl who usually had an indulgent father with a large bank account.

It was sheer luck that on the same day she was going out with her father she was asked to help serve in the shop. One of their regular assistants was sick. She felt no apprehension at the prospect, only a bubbling excitement. It was great to design and make clothes, but it was also interesting to meet the people likely to wear them.

It was Friday so the shop was busy though not so busy as it was on a Saturday. She got quickly in the swim of things and found herself gaining more and more confidence as she talked fashion and held her own when the customers asked questions. Time flew to midday when she and the two girls working there arranged the rota for lunch breaks. Carol was a whip of a girl with pert breasts and the longest, loveliest legs Marcie had ever seen. April was fresh faced and pretty, her

146

hair cut short like Julie Driscoll.

The customers were interesting and so were the tales told her by the other two assistants. They could pick out what a girl would buy just by looking at her.

For her part, Marcie envied the sleek blondes with their crisp outfits and voices to match. She found herself wanting to be like them, be able to buy whatever she wanted without a second thought.

Carol and April giggled when she said that, declaring that it wasn't always fathers fuelling these girls' bank accounts. Sometimes the boyfriends themselves came in to choose gifts for their girls. They were usually much older so they told her, and she'd have to keep a straight face when they told her they were buying for their nieces.

'They've got it right,' said Carol, a sly knowing look in her catlike eyes. 'They're earning money just for being pretty. Beats working in a shop any day.'

'Beats working,' added April.

The two girls laughed. Marcie laughed with them. After all, they were only joking weren't they?

Carol had gone out to buy something from the chemist. April was incarcerated in the ladies' cloakroom with a packet of cigarettes and a little pink pill that even an innocent like Marcie knew was not a Smartie.

A man came in. At first she saw feathers – two very long feathers waving from the brim of a black, broad-brimmed hat. His head was bent. When he straightened she could see he was wearing dark glasses. And he was tall. Tall, dramatic and quite, quite mesmerising. She'd never seen a man like him before as he moved like an athlete between the clothes rails.

His appearance close up almost took her breath away. The collar and pocket flaps of his plum-coloured velvet jacket were edged in black braid. The silver and pink cravat at his throat gave contrast to his purple shirt and his hair was dark and shoulder length. His boots had two-inch Cuban heels. A diamond flashed in his earlobe. She'd never seen a man wearing an earring. She couldn't stop staring at him, taking in other small things that she hadn't noticed before. He was so wildly different – just as Johnnie had been she reminded herself.

She decided that he had to be a member of a rock group, or failing that a disc jockey from one of the pop radio stations. She'd heard they were wacky. Heard they were wild.

'Can I help you?' she asked brightly. He wasn't anything like the middle-aged men who bought for their girlfriends, but she sensed he was just as wealthy and just as demanding.

He turned at the sound of her voice, looked her up and down then straightened and pronounced what he wanted.

'I think you could. I think I would like to buy a black dress for a girl I intend taking out on a date.'

The resonance of his voice took her by surprise. It wasn't that it was loud, only commanding; a deep rasp that made her toes curl up.

'Right,' she said, determined to make a good impression on this wildly rugged-looking man.

He took off his sunglasses. His eyes were dark brown. 'These look nice,' he said turning his attention to a rack of simple but well-cut dresses on the rack closest to him.

'This one in particular,' he said holding it aloft.

'That one's really lovely. Simple but beautifully cut. Do you know your girlfriend's size?'

His eyes raked her from top to toe, perhaps a little too intimately but she excused him that.

'About your size. Can you hold it up against you so I can see how it looks?'

'Of course.' She did as he said, holding a plain black dress up against her. The dress was truly lovely, fully lined black linen with a square neckline and a scalloped edging around the hem.

Throwing her hip to one side, she pointed her toe, one foot in front of the other.

'You see,' she said, smiling and tilting her head to one side like the models she'd seen in the magazines.

'I think it looks lovely. Do you think you could try it on – just to make sure?'

It wasn't usual for the staff to be that obliging, but she couldn't think of any reason for refusing.

'OK. Just give me a minute.'

The changing cubicle was empty. It was shielded from the shop by a thick curtain that didn't always close that well.

Marcie didn't give it any thought. She slid out of her own clothes and into the dress.

When she emerged he folded his arms across his chest and nodded; the peacock feathers in his hat flashed blue and green beneath the spot-lights.

149

'I love the dress. Love you in it too, darling. You've got a good figure. Nice legs too.'

These comments were not quite what she'd expected. She felt her face warming but focused on the sale.

'And the dress?'

His hooded eyes strayed momentarily to the dress, though not for long. She felt as though he was not just stripping the dress from her body, but the flesh from her bones. It was as though he wanted to see what she was made of – like licking off the chocolate in order to see whether it was an orange cream or a nougat centre.

'The dress is lovely. You're right there, darling. No comparison to the lovely thing it's covering though.'

The blush was threatening again, but she held it off. The shop assistants got ten per cent commission on everything they sold. This dress was expensive – very expensive – and Joanna needed a new winter coat.

'Do you think it's right for your date?' she asked him courteously.

He rubbed at his chin with thumb and forefinger and tilted his head this way and that as he circled her. She attempted to turn round with him, but once he was behind her he placed his hands on her shoulders. It was obvious he wanted her to stand still.

'Oh, I think so.'

What was he waiting for? He liked the dress and it seemed it was the right size for his girlfriend. Marcie found herself getting nervous.

'Would you like me to wrap it up for you?'

He opened his mouth to answer when the shop door opened and someone else entered. She glimpsed another young man, though this one was not so dramatically dressed. Her first impression was of someone ordinary and slightly scruffy in Levis and brown suede jacket. He looked vaguely familiar, but her glance didn't linger.

Her customer was reaching for a pair of white boots – Marcie's favourite items. She'd once had a cheap pair herself but they'd worn out ages ago. These were far more expensive, made in France and what was more, they looked it.

'I think these to go with it,' he said placing the boots against the dress. 'What size are you?'

'Five.'

'Try them on.'

Marcie's blonde hair swung forwards hiding her face as she sat down and pulled them on. She became aware that the second young man had joined the one with the peacock feathers in his hat.

'Will you stop messing around here? We've got things to do.' The young man who had only just entered sounded surly and impatient.

The wearer of the black hat with peacock feathers kept his eyes firmly on Marcie. 'Stay cool. I'm not messing about. I think I'm in love.'

The second young man seemed a little familiar but she couldn't quite place him. She saw him toss his head. 'Christ! That's the fourth this week.'

The man with the feathers in his hat prevented her from studying the newcomer.

'I hope I haven't been too much bother, darling, you know, having you try stuff on and all that.'

'Not at all,' she said. She blushed. She couldn't

hold it in any longer. 'You've made my day. We never see men who dress as fashionably as women. I think you're what they used to call a dandy.'

'Yeah,' grumbled the new arrival. 'Straight out of a bloody comic strip.'

'Excuse my mate,' said the first man. 'He's got a complex.'

'Oh!' Marcie didn't care about their banter. She had Joanna's new coat to consider.

The man with the feathers in his hat flapped a hand as though he were batting a ball.

'I think the boots and the dress go well together. Wrap them up will you?'

She went back into the cubicle and changed back into her own clothes. In her head she was counting how much commission she'd made – certainly enough to buy Joanna a new winter coat and perhaps even new shoes.

'That's seventy-five pounds altogether,' she told him feeling very happy with herself.

'That's fine.' He nodded but did not attempt to pay her.

She decided that was OK. She would wrap the merchandise and then he would pay her.

'Great,' he said when she tried to hand him the large carrier bag containing the dress and the box containing the boots.

'Right. That's seventy-five pounds,' she restated.

'Great.'

He made no move to give her any money. She was beginning to get nervous.

'Look,' she said, 'I know it's a lot of money, but I'm sure your date will be really pleased with what you've bought her.'

'Would you be?'

His tone and the look in his eyes took her off guard. While wearing the dress and boots she'd felt envious of the girl they were being bought for.

'If I was her, I would be pleased,' she responded.

'Then take them. They're yours, but on one condition.'

She was young and new to the city, but she guessed where this was going even before he propositioned her.

'Go on,' she said, apprehensive at what he was going to suggest.

'You can be my date. Seven thirty. I'll pick you up.'

'For Christ's sake! We have to go. The old man will be waiting for us.'

In the heat of the moment she'd almost forgotten the other young man. He'd been pacing up and down between the rails with a sour look on his face.

Marcie held out her hand.

'The money,' she said, in response to his quizzical grin.

'No,' he said, shaking his head. 'I don't need to pay.'

An awkward customer! This was certainly something Marcie did not need. She fervently wished for Carol to come back from the chemist's and April to come back from the cloakroom.

'If you don't pay I'll call the police,' she said, jutting her chin out and holding her head slightly to one side. 'I mean it,' she added.

He rested his elbows on the countertop and looked at her.

'I do not believe that a sweet little girl like you would have me arrested.'

'Well, I will,' she retorted, unable now to stop her face from reddening.

'For Christ's sake! Put the girl out of her misery. She just bloody works here.' The other young man sounded impatient.

'That's right. I just work here,' she said in a very precise manner. 'No money. No goods.' She swung the carrier bag behind her back, holding it there with one hand while holding out the other hand for payment.

The customer used two fingers to jab the rim of his hat sending it back a little on his head. A mischievous smile played around an expressive mouth that promised to be velvet against bare flesh. She found herself wondering how often those lips kissed and how many girls they'd kissed. Hundreds. Perhaps thousands. Girls followed pop groups in droves. And were willing to give up more than kisses she reminded herself. She blushed at the thought of them kissing her own lips.

'I'm not paying,' he said in the same precise manner she'd used, though she detected a twinkle in his eyes. He was making fun of her. The illusion of somebody different had turned sour. She wasn't having anyone making fun of her.

She shrugged. 'Fine. I'll put these things back into stock.'

'There's no need.'

The door jangled open just as she began carrying out her threat. April was back from having a fag and popping a pill.

Marcie stated her case. 'This gentleman doesn't want to pay. He's being a nuisance. I think we should call for the police.'

At first she didn't cotton on to the expression on April's face – until she blurted, 'Roberto! Darling! Fab to see you! Love the gear! Especially the feathers!'

After tweaking the feathers, she ran her hands down the front of his plum-coloured velvet jacket. She was all over him.

'Roberto! Darling, this jacket is F.A.B. Did you get it at Sergeant Pepper's?'

Marcie didn't hear his reply. Face red with embarrassment she was too busy looking from one young man to the other, trying to work out exactly what was going on here. She'd certainly seen the second young man before, though not the first, except...

She recalled Gabriella's collection of silver-framed photographs and instantly knew.

'The young lady doesn't understand,' said Roberto. 'She doesn't know who I am and that it's compulsory that she comes out on a date with me. I chose the clothes for her. I think she'll look great in them. Don't you?'

'If Marcie doesn't want to go with you, I will,' said April.

'Sorry, darling.' Roberto tickled her chin as though she were a silly child. 'Well, Marcie *is* going out with me tonight.'

He was smiling at her in a self-assured way that was both annoying and alluring.

'I've heard all about you, Marcie Brooks. I

heard you were a right little corker. Your father told me so. We can put the date on hold. I know you can't make it tonight because your old man's taking you out. The truth is, my little sparrow, that my mother said you needed some decent clothes to go out in. She suggested I chose for you. My mother knows I have very good taste.'

Marcie's jaw dropped. She eyed the carrier bag and the box she'd placed within it. The string handles of the carrier bit into her fingers. 'These are for me?'

'Your father would want you to look fab to the power of four.'

She decided his terminology matched his outfit; it was way out, modern and meant to impress.

'You are Nicholas Roberto Camilleri?' She felt embarrassed that she sounded so awestruck, but she couldn't help it.

He nodded. 'Yep!'

He had a straight nose, high cheekbones and an arrogant set to his chin. This was a man who was sure of himself, sure of his allure and not likely to take no for an answer.

'We're all off out tonight. Call it the firm's party,' Roberto said to her. 'So in a way it is a date; except that we'll all be there along with your old man. Great stuff, huh?'

He smelled good, a subtle mixture of fresh maleness, expensive aftershave and a hint of the outside freshening the inside.

'Roberto! Time we were off.'

The guy in the brown suede coat was leaning on a clothes rail and looking totally disinterested. *The young man in glasses.*

There was no time to say anything to the young man she'd seen in Victor Camilleri's apartment.

Roberto tilted her chin slightly and kissed her lips.

'*Ciao!*' he said on his way out and waved. The young man named Michael never said a word.

Marcie stood staring long after the door was closed. It was as though they'd been visited by a whirlwind that had rushed through, done its damage and passed on to pastures new.

'Wow,' said April. Her blue eyes were wide with outright envy, 'Wow! Aren't you the lucky one! The Camilleris footing the bill for new togs. And Roberto Camilleri doing the choosing. Wow! If that doesn't beat it all!'

Her eyes reflected Marcie's own amazement.

'That's three wows,' said Marcie, determined to play it down, opening the bag and peering in. Should she accept the gifts or not?

'You're not going to refuse a date with him, are you?'

'You heard him. It's a family thing. My father invited me.'

'That's tonight. What about tomorrow night?'

'Is he in a pop group?'

April shook her head. 'Not that I know of.'

'But he does work for a living – sorry – no need to answer that. He obviously must if that plum-coloured jacket is anything to go by.'

April popped a sliver of Wrigley's chewing gum into her mouth. 'He works for his father of course,' she explained as she started to chew. 'The Camilleris all stick together. It's a family business. Remember?'

The shop had gone quiet. The two girls went behind the counter where the till was and the tube of Smarties that really were Smarties – a little sugar-coated chocolate to keep up their energy. Marcie took the carrier bag behind the counter, placing it down next to her leg. She couldn't help staring at it. These were expensive clothes, the most expensive she'd ever owned.

'It was kind of him.'

'Lucky you!' April pouted her baby-pink lips. 'Wish he'd invited me out. So? Will you go?'

Marcie smiled. It was a long time since she'd gone out on a date. Johnnie had been her last date, the one and only boy she'd ever properly dated.

'I suppose I will. He seems nice enough.' The truth was that she was bubbling with excitement.

'Nice? I don't know about nice,' warned April. 'Give him an inch and he'll take a mile, his hand up your skirt before you'd even noticed it was on your knee!'

'How do you know?'

April shrugged nonchalantly. 'How do you think I know? A girl has only one asset to make her way with in this world. The Camilleris can open doors for me. It pays to keep on the right side of them.'

'He'll take us to nightclubs and introduce us to people. I'll tell you this, Marcie, it's better to be an old man's darling than a young man's slave.'

Marcie could have been struck dumb. She could have blurted out that they were nothing short of prostitutes – that's if she was getting the right drift on what they were saying. The last thing she wanted to do was to upset anyone, so she steered the conversation elsewhere.

'I thought their son was named Nicholas?'

'Nicholas Roberto. Still, what's in a name? You've struck gold there, girl. Enjoy it while it lasts and get what you can off him.'

Carol asked what they were laughing about when she came back from the cloakroom. The two girls told her. Like April, Carol issued a warning.

'Don't get involved with Roberto. He eats women for breakfast.'

'And Michael?'

April made a face. 'He's got a chip on his shoulder a mile wide. That's what comes of being the second son.'

Marcie frowned. 'I thought the Camilleris had only one son?'

'They have,' said April. 'But two different mothers. Victor Camilleri likes to play the field. That's where his son gets it from.' She sighed. 'I suppose I shall just have to wait my turn.'

'Me too,' said Carol. 'Whatever he wanted me to do I would do.'

April agreed with her. 'That's the only way a girl can get the good things in life. We all know that.'

Marcie laughed. She presumed they were joking – until she saw their serious expressions. Her laughter was brought up short.

'You'd do anything for a fur coat or a pair of shoes?'

April laughed.

Carol handed her a chocolate caramel.

Marcie looked at the caramel and accusingly at Carol. 'I thought you went out to buy something in the chemist's?'

Carol winked. 'I needed a pick-me-up. The sweet shop was nearer.'

Flowers arrived the next day. They were sitting in a vase on her table in the sewing room. They had a heady scent.

Marcie asked Meg, the old girl who did the cleaning, who'd put them there.

'Dunno,' said Meg, a half-smoked cigarette hanging from the corner of her mouth.

Marcie smiled. It had to be Roberto.

There was another bouquet waiting for her in her room, though bigger and looking more shop bought than the pretty posy in the sewing room.

'They're from Roberto,' beamed Mrs Gabriella Camilleri. She stood on tiptoe so she could whisper into Marcie's ear. 'I think you are the girl of his dreams.'

Marcie didn't know what to say. No one had ever sent her a bouquet before.

'Two bouquets!' Marcie exclaimed. 'Sweet peas and these.'

Mrs Camilleri looked puzzled. 'Did he? I did not know that.'

## Chapter Twenty

Marcie eyed her reflection in the full-length mirror fastened to the back of the bedroom door. She was wearing the black linen dress and white boots. Her hair was piled on top her head and fastened with pins. A few tendrils had escaped and hung down like pieces of torn silk around her face. A thick silver bangle, triangular silver earrings and a purple feather boa completed the picture. Her eyes were emphasised with black eyeliner and mascara. Her lips were as beige as the rest of her face though they blossomed like a rose at its centre. She was seeing a trendy modern girl with things to do; places to go and handsome guys to see. Roberto was handsome. He'd be there tonight when she went out with her father. Her stomach churned with excitement. London had been good to her so far. Her only real bugbear was that she had not made any friends here – not real friends of her own age. She'd dismissed Carol and April as being work colleagues, not friends as such.

Mrs Camilleri stood behind her, eyeing the same reflection. 'Your father will be very proud of you. You are very beautiful, just like...' She paused.

'Like what?' Marcie asked.

For a brief moment Mrs Camilleri seemed stuck for words. 'Just like a daughter should be.'

The words came out in a rush. Marcie was quick minded enough to suspect that something was unsaid as much as said with those words. She decided not to push it. Tonight she was going out with her father and Mrs Camilleri was right. She looked beautiful.

Tony Brooks looked at his watch. He was running late. Mrs Reynolds had made him a cup of tea. She looked cleaner and less harassed than she used to. This had nothing to do with her husband having followed up the job Tony had put his way. The bastard had done a runner back to Jamaica, though not before knocking Ella about and getting her up the spout.

One of the kids had been put to bed. The other was playing with a set of wooden bricks that Tony had bought for her.

He'd never much liked this debt collection lark, but Camilleri paid him well for his trouble. Blokes on their own swinging the lead he could cope with. Young families looking cold and miserable in a city they'd been told was paved with gold were becoming the norm in Victor Camilleri's miserable Victorian tenements. The rental business was booming on account of the flood of immigrants arriving from the West Indies. The properties were sub standard and the rent was high. Victor Camilleri had his fingers in a lot of pies; renting to an influx of black people was one of them. Some other geezer called Rachman had been running the same racket as Victor, cramming newly arrived immigrants – blacks, Irish and Poles – into cramped accommodation where the roofs leaked and fungus grew out of the walls. Ella had one of the better drums, but it was no palace. The windows shook when a train went by down on the adjacent railway line. The wallpaper was peeling and the tired old three-piece looked as though it was pre-war and had barely survived a direct hit from the Luftwaffe.

Ella slumped down in the armchair opposite him. After bashing the chair arm back into place after it had sloped sideways, she ran her hands over her growing stomach.

'I cannot have this baby.'

He hated the way she said it, her face screwed up and whining as though she were choking on the words. She looked down at her stomach. 'I cannot afford to.' Her eyes were big and brown. He couldn't help feeling as though he were falling into them. He wanted to do more to her than that.

Tony leaned forwards, jamming his elbows between his knees, his hands clasped tightly together. His chin jerked up and down in a stiff nod as though he understood and sympathised. He could afford to do the former, but God help him with the second. Three weeks rent was owed when he'd first come calling here. He hadn't meant to fall for her and couldn't quite understand why. He lay awake at night thinking that one over. He usually went for blondes. Ella was dark skinned, spoke with a West Indian accent and had wiry hair kept in place by a brightly coloured bandana. Her breasts were high, firm and round. Her hips were ample and her backside was a joy to behold.

While his hormones danced in one direction, his conscience reminded him that he had a wife; a blonde wife. Babs had been a ringer for Brigitte Bardot when she was younger. Things had changed. Getting blowsier year on year, her figure had ballooned; as good a reason as any to fall for Ella, he told himself.

Disregarding the ache in his loins wasn't easy, but he was here on business. 'Look, love, this has to be the last time. You've got to keep a better check on your money – stop the old man taking from you for a start. I can't keep paying it for you. You know what will happen if it don't get paid, don't ya?'

She nodded. She knew alright. Some of the blokes who worked for Victor would have smashed everything up – Ella too probably. She'd seen it happen to neighbours.

Tony sighed and thought what a prat he was getting to be. In the past he'd been paid to put on the pressure, but he'd been younger then. Must be getting old, old son, he thought to himself. He couldn't bring himself to slap a woman, especially not when there were kids about. He still had to get the money out of her, but a few kind words cost nothing.

'I know what you mean, girl. The National Assistance only spreads so far, love, but so does my dosh. I'm paying your rent, love, but you do have to pay me back sometime.'

'I wouldn't ask you for any more,' she protested. 'You've been so kind to me. I told you before I knew I was pot bellied that I was going to get a job. I was going to pay you back. But with this...' She spread her hands helplessly.

When she looked at him with those big brown eyes, Tony was as soft as chocolate, but the edge of reason still nudged its way forwards. 'You can get rid of it,' he suggested. Good Catholic boy that he was, he knew what the Church thought about abortion. However, he also understood how desperate a woman could get without a steady income. Despite dictates of Church or society, the practicalities of life had to be addressed. If Ella did pop another kid into the world, she'd be hard pressed to make ends meet. Desperation could

164

lead to prostitution; he knew plenty of slappers who used to be good girls until a smooth tongue and a wandering dick had got them into trouble. Single mothers with kids to support were particularly vulnerable. Part of him wondered if he cared about Ella's predicament purely because she reminded him of his daughter. Marcie could so easily have not come home. But he knew that his feelings for Ella were far from fatherly.

The windows rattled as another train went by heading towards Piccadilly. Neither of them spoke – neither of them could speak – until the rattling had ceased and the train had disappeared into a tunnel.

Ella looked down at the scuffed lino where the edge of a ragged mat was unravelling as surely as her life. It looked to him as though she were considering his suggestion. He knew that if he asked around a name was bound to pop up. Old biddies in crummy tenements down near the docks and other places were still going strong despite the relaxation in the abortion law.

But Ella had already been asking around. 'I have heard of a woman...' she began, her black eyelashes fluttering across her high cheekbones. 'She charges a lot of money. Her name is Mrs Smith.'

'I bet it is,' Tony said with a sardonic smile and a toss of his head.

'Do you not believe me?' she said with wide-eyed innocence.

Laughing, he reached across and patted her hand. 'They're always called Mrs Smith, though you might get the odd Mrs Jones thrown in for good measure.'

She looked puzzled.

He enlightened her. 'Smith and Jones are common names. Harder for the law to track down. Know what I mean?'

She nodded.

Tony was already digging into his pocket. He brought out a wad of one pound notes.

'I'm not sure what the going rate is for sorting you out. Here. Thirty pounds tops – that should do it.'

He reached to offer her the money. She looked at it. He wasn't sure how to read the look in her eyes. There was fear, that much was for sure. But fear of what? The money? The operation itself or the condemnation of her own conscience?

Perhaps she was afraid of feeling obliged to him, which was quite understandable. To his surprise he felt a great urge to touch her dark glossy skin. Slowly her fingers curled around the fan-shaped fistful of pound notes. She looked down at them scrunched in her hand.

Tony studied her reaction, wanting her to look up at him with gratitude but knowing she never would. Ella, he'd found out, was fiercely independent. He could only guess at how desperate she was feeling to accept his money. It was all about the kids of course. She'd do anything for them, he thought. If he asked her, she'd go to bed with him. He'd like that. Should he ask...

A pang of conscience he didn't know he had swept over him.

'Everything will be alright,' he said for no reason other than to hear something, even the sound of his own voice.

She was slow thanking him. Was she thinking there might be a catch? he wondered. The prospect was tempting. He wouldn't make the first move. He'd leave it to her, and if she did, then he wouldn't refuse.

Slowly and silently, she got to her feet and went out to the kitchen. He heard the grating of a tin lid and guessed she was putting the money in the safest place she knew. She probably kept the tea or sugar in the same tin. It seemed a totally naive thing to do; if anyone did break in they'd make straight for those tins. He smiled and shook his head. Women were so predictable.

The toddler began yawning and crying for her bottle. Ella gave it to him, picked him up and snuggled him down beside the other child in the double bed that dominated the room.

Tony put his teacup on the table and prepared to get up from his chair. Tonight he was taking Marcie out on the town. Boy, was she going to love it! Not a smoky old pub or third-grade dance hall in Sheerness. This was London and the bright lights would still be shining in the early hours of the morning. She was young, the city was swinging and she would love it!

Pressing his hands down on the chair arms, he was about to get up when Ella came and stood in front of him, legs braced, fingers already unbuttoning her blouse.

He said the first thing that came into his head. 'Ella. There's no need for this.' But that wasn't what he was thinking. His dream was coming true.

She gave him a 'happy face' smile, the sort that

photographers insist on before they click the shutter; a smile that's not real but just pasted on for the moment.

Her blouse parted to expose firm, glossy breasts with large areolae and nut-brown nipples. Despite his best intentions, his passion rose in his pants.

He tried clearing his throat. 'Ella, love. I don't want anything in return. Honest I don't.' Like hell! He wanted her like crazy!

She smiled sadly and shook her head. 'Of course you do. All men want something in return for their money. But this is me wanting this, Tony. I want to feel that I have given you something in return for all that money – for the sake of my children if nothing else. It is a matter of pride. I do not want charity. I do not want anything from any man for free.'

He could smell the musky scent of her body. It came over him in a soft wave as she dropped her skirt and let her blouse and her underwear fall down on top of it.

She gleamed in the muted light coming in from the window. Her belly was taut. Her breasts were firm and her hips flared out from a narrow waist.

He wanted her. He desperately wanted her, but some segment of the scruples he'd once known stayed his hand and cooled his ardour.

'I can't do this,' he said shaking his head and attempting once again to get to his feet.

'I want you to,' she murmured in a soft hush of a voice, her long fingers entwining at the nape of his neck, pulling his head towards her, his lips closer to one of her breasts.

'You cannot do me any more harm than Joe has done me already.'

The fact that she was pregnant was not that noticeable just yet. Her belly was rounded but it was early days. She could still get away with it.

He thought of what his family would say if they found out. He thought about what his mates would say and tried not to smile. His mates would crow at his triumph. He'd had a black piece, though that in itself wasn't that unusual nowadays. What was unusual was that this woman already had kids and precious little else.

Babs wouldn't find out of course. She was miles away with the kids living in a council house on the Isle of Sheppey. Was he crazy or what? Quite probably. But he couldn't help himself. He was drawn to her. He was drawn to the prominent nipple with his eyes and his mouth.

The bed was occupied, so they did it on the floor. The carpet was thin and the lino was cold. Her body was warm.

Ella mewed like a cat during their coupling and purred like one once it was over, her buttocks sitting in the curve of his groin, his arm around her as he nuzzled her neck.

'You were gentle,' she said and sounded surprised. 'And you waited for me.'

'You could tell that?'

'Yes. Not many men wait for a woman to be fulfilled.'

Now it was his turn to be surprised. He couldn't recall ever waiting for a woman to climax before he did. Something must have happened to him. Her name was Ella.

He cleaned himself and kissed her on the lips, rearranged his clothes and checked his appearance in the cracked mirror of an ancient sideboard – the big Victorian sort that Scouts burned on bonfires on Guy Fawkes Night.

'You look very smart,' she said to him.

'Thank you.'

Timing what he had to do, he'd decided to put on his whistle and flute so he could go straight from Ella's to pick up Marcie.

He felt her eyes on him. 'Are you going somewhere nice?'

He stood by the door, hand poised on the old-fashioned Victorian doorknob.

'Out on the town.'

'With a woman?'

He caught a hint of jealousy in her voice but nodded anyway. 'Yes.'

He didn't elaborate and neither did he linger. He was already late for picking up his eldest daughter. The car was parked against the kerb and had attracted attention from a gang of small kids intent on ripping off his wing mirrors.

They scattered on seeing him, regrouping around a lamppost where an impromptu swing hung from an overhead bracket. Funny, he thought, how kids all over the country congregated around swings hung from lampposts.

He smiled as he got into the car. Before driving off he ducked down so he could better see the front window of Ella's ground-floor flat. He saw the thin muslin curtain pulled back a matter of inches. Her face was like a shadow surrounded by the darkness of the old-fashioned interior.

He raised a hand in farewell. She raised hers only briefly. The curtain fell back into place. She was gone.

## Chapter Twenty-one

'Bellissima!'

Gabrielle Camilleri's luminous brown eyes seemed to fill with tears. 'My Roberto has such good taste.' Her ample bosom heaved with pride. 'And, of course, he is so excitingly handsome. Did you not think so?'

Marcie found the flattery a little overblown, but Mrs Camilleri had been kind to her.

'He's very good-looking,' said Marcie. 'He takes after you I think?'

Blushing like a girl, Mrs Camilleri clasped her hands together, her face full of adoration for her one and only son.

'Roberto is my pride and joy. Whoever he marries will be his princess.'

She looked tellingly at Marcie, who for her part had been impressed by Roberto's way-out app-earance. Roberto was indeed the stuff of legends, but she couldn't help holding back. Johnnie was dead but the thought of going out with anyone else didn't seem right. She had to counter what Gabriella was hinting at.

'I also met Michael,' said Marcie.

The moment the words were out of her mouth, she realised she'd said the wrong thing. Mrs

Camilleri's expression soured at mention of Victor's illegitimate son.

'He is not like Roberto. Not like him in any way at all,' she pronounced.

The bitterness was obvious. Marcie said goodbye and left.

Tony Brooks was knocked sideways when he first set eyes on his eldest daughter coming out of the apartment block where his boss lived. There were two reasons for this. Number one was she looked absolutely stunning. Number two she reminded him so much of her mother.

'You look a right bloody knockout,' he managed to say. 'Like a bleeding film star. You're better looking than Marilyn Monroe any day of the week.'

'I would do. She's dead and you're late.'

'Sorry, love. Got caught up in some business and then in the traffic.'

The car was black and shiny, though had acquired a dent on one wing. Her father wasn't that brilliant a driver. Perhaps it was because he'd never passed a driving test.

'You're supposed to pass a driving test,' she'd once said to him.

'Not me, darling. I can drive and nobody can stop me.'

'The police might.'

'Nah! Not at my age. I look too distinguished.'

He was kidding himself about looking distinguished, she thought, but he was incorrigible and had never quite grown up; he just didn't think the law of the land applied to him.

Marcie shook her head. 'Is it far?'

'Nah! Be there in a jiffy.'

She took that with a pinch of salt. The older she got the more convinced she was becoming that men were unreliable – except for Johnnie of course. One thing she would always believe was that Johnnie would always be the great love of her life. No one would ever replace him, of that she was certain.

'So you're liking your job?' said her father while squeezing the car between a bus and a taxi coming in the other direction.

The taxi blew its horn. The people on the bus bounced as the driver slammed on the brakes.

'Yes,' she replied.

She closed her eyes and forced herself to dwell on other things. Yes, she liked her job but her heart was heavy. Joanna was miles away. She was missing her.

The wages at Daisy Chain weren't bad, but they were not enough to bring up a child. She had to do something that would bring in more money.

'Just you wait till we get to the club,' said her father. 'All the young studs there will be after you, so just you stick with yer old dad. No matter what they ask, say no.'

She laughed at that. 'I'm old enough to take care of myself, Dad.'

'Course you are, but stick with me anyway. Right?'

'I met Roberto Camilleri today. He came into the shop.'

'Did he now?'

'You didn't say that the Camilleris would be there too at this club.'

'Who told you that?' he said, looking straight at her while aiming the car at the road ahead.

'Dad! Keep your eyes on the road.'

He turned his attention back to the road just in time to brake at a zebra crossing. Two young studs in leather jackets gave him two-fingered salutes and shouted abuse.

He wound down the window.

'Wanna make something of it, you...'

'Dad! Let it be. Think of your driving licence,' she added cheekily.

He blinked at her. 'Oh, yeah.'

Marcie took a deep breath and watched the people thronging along the pavement. It was Friday night. People milled in and out of pubs. London had a buzz that the place she'd grown up in could never match. She couldn't help feeling both excited and apprehensive about this evening. Roberto had made an impression on her and much as she tried to push him out of her mind, his charm and flamboyant appearance wouldn't go away.

'He's a bit of a lad, young Roberto. Watch yerself. I wouldn't want him breaking my little girl's heart.'

She fancied that he might have chuckled if it hadn't been for her. Men admired the stud in the pack, didn't they?

'No one can ever break my heart again.' Her jaw ached when she said it. Johnnie's death had broken her heart. Sometimes he never seemed that far away. She wondered if she would ever see him in the same way that her grandmother saw her grandfather.

'You still think of that lad – Joanna's father?'

Amazing! Her father had hit the nail on the head.

'How did you know I was thinking of Johnnie?' She eyed the mane of dark hair that showed little sign of grey.

Her father smiled and tipped her the wink. 'You get that same funny look in your eyes that your gran gets when she's in tune with me dad.'

'P'raps I'm doing more than thinking of him. P'raps I'm seeing him – just like Gran sees granddad.'

'Very likely, my girl. It runs in the family. My mother's mother was also that way inclined, if you know what I mean. Back in Malta that was. She's no longer with us, of course. She's crossed over as your gran would say. Had a bomb drop on her during the war. They got a lot of bombing out there. They was out there at the time you know – your gran and your grandfather. Me too, though I don't remember much about it. But your gran went through a lot. You want to ask her sometime.'

'It's a wonder Gran and Great-gran didn't get burnt as witches, what with the Catholic Church and all that.'

Her father laughed. 'Too bloody true! I can just imagine my old mother flying through the air on a bleedin' broomstick!'

The city lights flashed past on both sides of them. Every so often Marcie felt little glances of pride come her way as though he couldn't quite believe that this beauty sitting by his side was

175

really his daughter.

She caught him looking. 'Keep your eyes on the road.'

'I'm a good driver!' he exclaimed. 'So how do you like Victor and his family?'

It was just like him to change the subject. Marcie remembered having a headache and what Victor had said to her. 'He's different.'

Her father laughed. 'He's bloody mental! That's what he is.'

She didn't know what he meant. 'He's Sicilian,' she countered.

Her father laughed even harder, throwing his head back so the veins stood out like twigs in his neck. 'That too! Too right he's bloody that!'

Her comments seemed to amuse him a lot, though she couldn't fathom why. Obviously something about them had tickled his funny bone. Done with talking of the past, she changed the subject.

'Where is this place we're going?'

'Cleopatra's Bath Tub.'

'What?' Marcie giggled at the name. 'Why is it called that?'

Her father shrugged. 'I don't know. I think the boss just liked the name.'

'The boss?'

'Victor Camilleri. He owns it. He owns a few others as well, though some of them are not quite so upmarket as this little lot. This is where the real glitz and glamour is, Marcie. You just wait till you see it in here.'

The building housing Cleopatra's Bath Tub turned out to be something of a disappointment.

Books not being judged by their covers came to Marcie's mind as she looked up at the plain brick façade. There was a sign saying Cleopatra's Bath Tub Club above a plain green door. The door was narrow and had a small aperture at head height. When her father knocked, the aperture opened. Whoever was behind the door took one look, saw who it was and opened the door for them.

'Good evening, Mr Brooks.'

The man behind the door had the chubby face of a child and the body of an all-in wrestler.

'Arthur! How the devil are you, my man?' The two men shook hands.

'Fine and dandy, Mr Brooks. Fine and dandy.'

A ten shilling note passed from her father's big hand into the meatier shovel of the doorman.

'You're a gentleman, Mr Brooks.'

'Call me Tony,' said her father, squeezing the doorman's elbow in a friendly manner. 'All my mates call me Tony.'

Cleopatra's Bath Tub Club was dark and smoky. Egyptian-style tomb tableaux decorated most of the walls and the waitresses were dressed in white tunics with gold belts, fake gold necklaces and Egyptian-style multicoloured headbands. Some of the girls smiled sweetly at her father, reserving less welcoming looks for the statuesque blonde who had come in with him.

'My daughter,' he said to one of them.

'Yeah,' said the gum-chewing waitress. 'They all say that.'

Something in Marcie Brooks snapped. She'd had enough of being labelled a tart because she

177

had a kid, so she wasn't taking this. The girl flinched when she grabbed her wrist.

'You're hurting me,' she whined.

'Yes, and I'll hurt you some more,' said Marcie squeezing the girl's wrist a little more tightly. 'He's telling the truth. He is my dad,' said Marcie. 'I'm unique in that I know who my dad is but not my mother.'

The words were out before she could stop them.

'Leave it out, Marcie.' Tony seemed embarrassed.

Alarm flashed in her father's eyes – or was it anger? Sod it! She didn't care.

'Because I mentioned my mother?'

She'd hit on the truth. She could see it in his eyes.

'Nah! Because you're cutting off the waitress's blood supply.'

It was a lie. She knew it was a lie, but she let go of the girl anyway.

She found that she didn't regret saying what she'd said even though her dad got dead shirty when her mother was mentioned. Well, she was growing up, so he was going to have to get used to it.

The waitress knew when to eat humble pie. She gave a curt nod and managed a weak smile. 'Oh yeah. There is a likeness. I can see it now. Do you have a table booked?'

'Are you new, girl?' her father said, his expression and mood soured.

The girl nodded. 'Yeah. Four days, three hours...'

'You won't make another hour if you don't sort

yourself out and get to know who's who around here. I'm Tony Brooks. I'm with Mr Camilleri.'

'Oh!'

The cocky manner had died a death and was swiftly replaced with courtesy. 'This way, sir.'

By this time they had reached the table where Victor Camilleri was sitting with his sons.

Victor shook Tony Brooks' hand, 'Tony. Good to see you, my old friend.'

He beamed at Marcie. 'And you're showing London at night to your beautiful daughter. And so you should, Tony. She has hardly left her room since coming to London. I think it is time she went out and enjoyed herself more.'

Victor Camilleri had dextrous eyes. They saw her but they saw everyone and everything else as well. He was a man who observed and took note of what was going on around him. He owned this club. He owned these people who worked for him.

He ordered champagne. It wasn't long coming.

'I believe you have already met my sons.'

She said that she had.

Michael, the illegitimate one, smiled tightly as though to smile any wider would crack his face. She read hostility in the grey-green eyes. It felt as though this hostility was directed at her though she could not comprehend any reason for it. Perhaps he always looks like that, she decided.

Roberto was his opposite; he greeted her as though they hadn't seen each other for years. His appearance was not quite so outrageous as earlier in the day. She surmised that he was less so when in his father's company. All the same, he wore a yellow evening shirt with frills down the front and on the cuffs. His suit was of indigo velvet and matched his bow tie. His hair was brushed forwards to hide the earring.

'The outfit!' he exclaimed, indicating the black dress and feather boa with extravagant gestures of his hands. 'Was my mother right or was she right? I have good taste, yes?'

She wanted to giggle because he sounded so much like his father, making statements as though they were questions. But she didn't giggle. She merely agreed that yes, his mother was right and he was right. She also saw what her mother saw in him. He was a prince among men, confident and full of himself. He couldn't fail in whatever he chose to do in life.

'All I need are enough nights out to justify the price,' she said laughingly.

'You didn't pay for it,' Michael interjected. 'You couldn't afford to pay for it on your wages.'

She stared at the morose expression. It was hard to believe that Michael was Roberto's brother. If his comment was designed to make her feel like a pauper, he'd certainly hit the target.

She felt her face colouring up. 'I didn't ask for charity,' she hotly declared.

Roberto's square jaw stiffened as he glared at his half-brother. 'Michael, your comment was uncalled for. My mother ordered and I obeyed.'

'As we all must,' Victor added. 'I know nothing about fashion myself, but I know my wife. What she does not know about fashion is not worth knowing.'

Victor's comment was measured and well timed.

His busy eyes flashed onto Michael's face before moving onto Marcie. 'You are a credit to your father, Marcie Brooks. The dress is lovely and you are lovely. Why, if I was twenty years younger – and single of course... I would take you out myself.'

Marcie flashed Roberto a grateful smile.

'That honour falls to me I think, my father. I will take Marcie out, though I would point out that it's going to take more than one night before that dress is worn out. And then you might have to buy a new one and start all over again.'

The offer was obvious. Marcie felt herself blushing down to her roots. Would she ignore the warnings and go out with Roberto anyway? You bet she would!

Victor ordered more champagne. 'The good stuff.'

The men asked Marcie if she minded them smoking. Being asked made her feel important. She said she did not mind so they went ahead and lit their cigars.

'This is something of a celebration,' said Victor. 'It is not often that I employ a man who carries out my orders to the letter and with such astonishing efficiency. If I didn't know better, I would think that Tony here is paying my tenants' rent for them.'

There was more laughter. Marcie wasn't sure about the joke. She'd presumed that Victor's business centred on nightclubs. Now he was speaking of tenants and rents.

'You own property?' She directed her question directly at Victor.

'Ye ... sss,' Victor said slowly. The way he looked

at her was difficult to interpret; there was appraisal, but there was also a feline wariness as though he would leap at her throat if he had to.

'I didn't know that.' She smiled benignly, feeling she owed him a great deal.

Michael chipped in, 'Mr Camilleri owns a lot of property. He has a lot of tenants,' he said bitterly.

There was accusation in Michael's tone.

Victor perceived it just as Marcie had. He turned threatening eyes on his son.

'I'm warning you, Michael. You are testing my tolerance. My breaking point is getting ever nearer. Beware, Michael. And bear in mind that I take in the people other landlords refuse to take. Blacks, coloureds, Irish even...'

She could tell by Victor's blazing eyes that Michael was supposed to back down. He didn't.

'They're strangers here in a strange land. And they're still human. They deserve a decent place to live, not—' His tone was bitter as he met his father's angry glare.

'Michael!' Victor's dark brows furrowed in warning. 'That is a matter of opinion.'

Marcie felt herself turning cold. The tension between Victor and his bastard son was palpable. The subject matter was disturbing and Victor's response most disturbing of all. Was that really his attitude towards foreigners or just towards black people? On Sheppey it was still rare to see people of colour but since being in London, Marcie had become aware that the city was full of different nationalities and races. It was part of what she loved about being in London – it was so lively, cosmopolitan and different, and there was room for people from all over the world.

She wanted to point out to Mr Camilleri that he too had been an immigrant once. He was not British by birth and yet he had found a home here, just as her grandmother had done. But fear of this man stayed her tongue. Up until now she hadn't much liked Michael. Now she found herself siding with his point of view. Not that she would come out with it. Not here, not with her father and Victor Camilleri sitting at the table.

Her father would probably be OK about her views, but she feared Victor Camilleri. Despite having witnessed his charming side, she knew he was clearly not a man to cross.

'How about you, Marcie? Do you think black people are lesser creatures than white?'

It was Michael who asked. She started, blushing at the thought that he must have seen a sign of discomfort on her face.

'That reminds me... I'm showing Marcie the sights tonight, so if you don't mind me not being around for the rest of the evening...'

There was a jovial intensity in her father's face and demeanour – almost as though he hadn't caught the gist of the conversation at all. In fact he couldn't possibly have missed it.

Victor patted him on the back. 'Regretful as I am not to have your company for the rest of the evening, I bow to the needs of a beautiful young lady, Antonio. You must show London to Marcie. She is young and will enjoy it.'

There was no doubt in Marcie's mind that her father's intervention was perfectly timed and purposeful. The subject of race was dropped and everyone was suggesting where her father should take her first that evening.

'First things first, we will eat,' Victor said. In the blink of an eye, his expression and tone had switched from mean to magnanimous.

The food was glorious and the champagne flowed.

Victor's views on race and foreigners were not exactly forgotten, only pushed to one side. Perhaps it was the champagne, but Marcie felt confident enough to joke and talk with these men as though she'd known them for ages.

Roberto smiled at her across the table. Michael threw her a look she could not quite interpret and stalked off to the bar where he leaned brooding, every so often throwing more looks in her direction.

She decided to ignore him. Roberto was paying her a great deal of attention and she was enjoying it.

Roberto had classic good looks, a wide mouth, one half of which seemed perpetually to be smiling. His clothes were a riot of modern fashion fads. He still reminded her of a disc jockey she'd heard of from Radio Caroline. He too wore purple velvet jackets and wide-brimmed hats. So different. So exciting.

His eyes continually met hers across the detritus of empty champagne bottles. In the past she would have blushed, but not tonight. Perhaps it was the champagne that made her bold. She held his gaze.

Her father leaned close. 'This party's for you, doll.'

184

Somehow his comment amused her. 'Why?'

'Because you're my daughter and you're gorgeous!'

Studying her father's face as she smiled at him, she read his expression. What she saw there convinced her that either he was lying or he didn't have a clue. Yes, she'd been welcomed in the Camilleri household, though she couldn't really understand why. It seemed as though Victor thought highly of her father and she knew that Mrs Camilleri thought highly of her dress designs. But there was something else, something she couldn't quite put her finger on. A little push might help bring whatever it was into the light of day.

Making an instant decision, she got to her feet, champagne glass in hand.

'Here's to Mr and Mrs Camilleri. My grateful thanks for giving me a foothold on the ladder to fashion success. It's what I've always wanted to do – design my own collection, and one day I might do just that. Cheers everyone.'

'Fashion! Oh yeah,' said Roberto laughingly raising his glass too. 'You're here to be a fashion queen.'

He kept on laughing.

'Of course,' said Victor Camilleri throwing his laughing son a look of disapproval. 'You will be successful in whatever you decide to do, Marcie Brooks. I, Victor Camilleri, will make sure of that.'

Despite the champagne Marcie found it difficult to relax. She didn't actually do so until they were sitting in the back of a taxi.

'Dad, your timing was spot on. I didn't know

185

what to say when Michael asked me that question. Or rather I did but didn't think Mr Camilleri would like it much.'

He patted her hand and sighed heavily. 'You were right not to say anything. Old Victor's a bit racist when it comes to black people. Did I ever tell you he used to be a count? That was back in Sicily of course. All behind him now.'

She squeezed his hand. 'Thanks anyway, Dad. Now are you sure he's OK about you taking me out and about?'

'No problem at all, sweetheart. All they're going to do tonight is visit a few pubs and clubs that they operate in and have a good time. They don't need me tonight.'

Tony Brooks settled back against the black leather seat. Everything was well with the world as far as he was concerned. He'd heard Ella had fallen behind with the rent again. He was going to have to go round there and have a word. 'I'll do it tomorrow,' he'd said to Victor. 'That alright with you?'

Victor had snake eyes; they stared at you unblinking while he sorted out his thoughts. He also had a snake smile. 'I don't like my tenants taking the piss, Antonio. Know what I mean?'

Tony had taken that as meaning that everything would be OK. He'd go round Ella's tomorrow and sort things out. Victor trusted him. He failed to ask the other question – whether he trusted Victor. And that was something he should have done.

## Chapter Twenty-two

Two a.m. The cobbled street led to derelict buildings that had been bombed during the Blitz and were scheduled for redevelopment. There was only one street light remaining. The muted light from its ancient gas mantle flickered to reveal where corrugated iron replaced a gap in what remained of the old brick wall.

Before the bomb had dropped, the street had once been lined on each side with five-storey tenements. Only three remained standing, their end walls crumbling into the bombed-out shells at the end of the street. Moss covered areas of brickwork as a result of water spewing from broken guttering. Windows were ill fitting. The stone steps leading up to the front door were cracked and iron railings above basement entrances bent outwards threatening to skewer passers-by. Not that many people frequented the narrow pavements except for those who lived here. And those that lived here could not afford to live anywhere else.

Roberto was sitting beside his father in the rear seat of his handsome black Bentley. A piece of muscle called Bog was in the driving seat. They were parked behind another car, a dark-green Ford Zodiac driven by two more of their operatives: mean types, the shock troops of their letting operation.

At present the car in front of them was empty.

Father and son's eyes were turned towards the first of the towering houses that had once been home to merchants in the days when Great Britain was becoming an empire. After that they'd been boarding houses. Now they were crammed with immigrants seeking a new life in a country they were supposed to regard as 'the Motherland'.

Not a word passed between them. They were stiff with expectation, waiting for the fun to start.

A chair came flying out of an upstairs window. A woman screamed. A child cried. At the same time a man was flung out of the door. He was tall and stringy and almost naked. The woman came screaming out after him, two children clinging to her thin nightdress.

Bog noticed, 'Blimey! That'll make her nipples stand out!'

Roberto gave him a playful slap on the shoulder. 'You're a pervert, Bogsy. You know that, don't you?'

Victor's employees flung out a bed, a mattress and other furniture. The woman screamed for the police. The black man got up and tried to stop Victor's men throwing them out. Their fists landed on his chin. Their feet kicked his stomach once he was on the ground. Heads appeared in upstairs windows. They disappeared just as quickly. Nobody wanted to get involved. They'd come here to make good. They knew better than to make trouble.

Roberto got out of the car and crossed the street as though he owned the earth, not just the crummy tenements. He bent down so that he could see into the frightened eyes of the man lying on the ground.

'I want my rent.'

Blood trickled from the corner of the black man's mouth. His look was more defiant than Roberto had expected.

The bloke's wife came running over. 'Here! Here!' She was tugging at her wedding ring. It eventually came off. She held it out to him.

'Twenty-two carat. It was my mother's and my grandmother's before her. It is Victorian. I swear ... I swear!'

Roberto let the ring lie in his palm. The weight was good. In this light it wasn't possible to see the hallmark, but he guessed it was there. Still, no point in being too compliant. He had a business to run. This bitch had to understand that.

Grabbing the back of her head he wagged a warning finger just inches from her nose. 'You'd better be telling the truth, bitch. If this is brass I'll bring it back and shove it down your fucking throat. Have you got that?'

She nodded silently, her eyes round with fear.

Roberto let go of her hair. All would have ended then and there if the bloke on the ground hadn't protested.

'No, Bessie! Not your ring.'

As he attempted to get up, his feet flailed in a dirty puddle. Some of the black foetid water splashed onto the hem of Roberto's trousers.

He surveyed the meagre specks – and exploded.

'You fucking...'

He buried his foot in the man's guts. The man

curled up with the force of it.

The woman screamed. 'Please!'

She grabbed at his arm, attempting to pull him back. The two sides of beef employed by his father stood back leaving Roberto to call the shots.

Flinging out his arm, the woman spun off, falling to the ground just in front of her two children who were clinging to each other, frightened and helpless.

'This is all that's standing between your old man getting a good walloping,' he said to her. The meagre light of the gas lamp was enough to make the thick band gleam. It was gold alright. A red ruby flashed in the centre of it.

'Let them back in,' he called over his shoulder.

Victor and his son settled back against the smooth leather of the custom-built seats, smoking cigars.

'This has been a good night's work,' said Victor. He exhaled a plume of smoke in a satisfied sigh. While Victor employed men like Tony Brooks to do his dirty work for him when it came to collecting the rent, he liked to keep his hand in from time to time. Roberto never needed to be asked twice to join a collection. Both men derived a vicious satisfaction from getting their hands dirty.

Roberto was thoughtful. 'What's the plan for Brooksey's girl?'

Victor took a moment to reply. At last he said, 'She's quite something, isn't she? In time she'll be no different than any other woman. They all want the pretty things of life.'

'I suppose you're right,' Roberto said somewhat gloomily. The promise to look after her would probably be broken. Supplying upper-class tarts – most on long contract terms – had become a lucrative and interesting sideline. The Camilleris were getting involved in legit operations. Politicians, company bosses and bankers ended up beholden to the family. Christine Keeler and Mandy Rice-Davies had brought down a government. They were building an empire with theirs.

But Marcie was different. There was sex and there was more than that – possession. He'd rarely wanted to possess a woman. He guessed it had something to do with the fact that Tony Brooks had asked for his father to look after Marcie for one very specific reason. 'She's not used to London,' he'd said. 'She's a bit green in the way of the world. Know what I mean?'

Roberto had been struck by the statement. He'd gone out of his way to find out more about her. His father had said she was lovely. But it wasn't just her looks. It was clear she was an innocent. No one else had touched her. And no one else would. She was clean. She was pure.

'She's not going to be one of the girls,' Victor had said to his son. 'She's a good Catholic girl. Gotta lot of respect for family. She's going to go home every weekend to look after her grandmother. I've promised to look after her and look after her I will. After all, Antonio's grandfather was from Palermo. Did you know that?'

Roberto had not known that but he understood that looking after this girl was a matter of honour – of family, in fact. Because of this she really was here to help his mother and he decided, with an amused smile, she was also brought here to provide him with a bride. That was how his parents' – especially his mother's – minds worked. He could mess about with any girl at all but he was expected to marry an untouched Catholic girl. And Marcie would suit him fine.

He fingered the ring in his pocket. At the same time he fought to control his basic instinct. 'I want her,' he said.

His father exhaled a plume of cigar smoke. 'Then have her.'

Behind them another family was picking up their meagre belongings and returning to the crummy two rooms they called home.

## Chapter Twenty-three

After three days the sweet peas sitting on Marcie's work table wilted. The bigger bouquet still blossomed. On arriving at her table on the fourth day Marcie found fresh sweet peas had replaced those that had wilted. They released their heady perfume when she touched them. She chose to believe that Roberto was responsible but resolved not to mention it. He would have to mention it first.

Tonight was to be their first date. Marcie dressed in the black linen dress, feather boa and white boots. The dress was short and the boots delectably long. Tan-coloured tights emphasised the whiteness of her boots. She regarded herself with some apprehension. Did she look like a girl with a secret?

It was hard finding the courage to tell Roberto that she was an unmarried mother. Not yet, she thought to herself. The eyes shining back from her reflection flashed with a sudden fear. She couldn't tell him yet, not until she was sure of his reaction.

'Roberto is here for you,' said Mrs Camilleri.

She looks more excited than I do, thought Marcie on eyeing the bright face and incredibly doleful eyes.

'Do I look good?' She did a little twirl.

'Fab!' Gabriella exclaimed, her hands clasped tightly together as though in saintly prayer. Unlike a saint her fingernails were polished and shocking pink.

'Forgive me, Johnnie,' Marcie whispered as she collected her bag from her bedroom.

As she made her way out, Michael came out of the study wearing his spectacles, just as he'd done on the first occasion she'd seen him.

It was difficult to read his expression but she couldn't help thinking he looked sad.

He tugged his forelock as she passed before silently retreating into the study that seemed almost to be his prime domain.

According to Carol, Michael had trained as an accountant, though his studies had been curtailed when Victor had insisted he entered the family business.

She glanced over her shoulder at the closed door. The fact that Michael and Roberto were half-brothers was difficult to accept. Heads turned when Roberto entered the room. Everyone seemed to know him and want to be with him, especially the girls. Michael on the other hand kept a lower profile, at home with his books and his balance sheets. But there was something about him that was compelling. She didn't quite know what.

Roberto was waiting in the hall and smiled at the sight of her. 'I have good taste,' he said.

'Are you referring to me or the dress?'

He smiled. 'Both.'

He took her to a small Italian restaurant off Marylebone High Street. A frieze of Italian street scenes glanced through painted arches decorated the walls. A coffee machine hissed like a sleeping dragon on the countertop where a waiter in tight-fitting pants plucked languorously at an ancient mandolin.

The air was filled with the smell of strong coffee, tomatoes and herbs.

A bottle of white wine helped oil their conversation.

He talked a lot about himself. She didn't mind that. She didn't want to betray too much about herself.

Roberto was explaining his taste in clothes. 'I like to stand out from the crowd. Getting involved in pirate radio made me that way.'

'I knew it!' she exclaimed, clapping her hands.

He'd actually been a disc jockey on Radio England, a pirate radio ship previous to Radio Caroline.

'Tell me all about it.'

Later she wondered perhaps if he wasn't just a bit too full of himself. But he was funny and she needed to laugh. He told her how lovely she was and how glad he was that she was staying at his mother's.

'My mother will make sure you are chaperoned as a young girl should be.'

Marcie laughingly looked around her. 'But she isn't here! What shall I do sitting here alone with a man, a lovely meal and a bottle of Italian wine?'

'Not tonight,' he said, casually shaking his finger in front of her face. 'You're with me. You belong with me. I think she realises that. I think you realise that too.'

He was paying her an enormous compliment. She felt a fool to blush like a lovesick young girl, but that was exactly what she did. How come this man is having such an effect on you? she asked herself. No answer came. That's when she realised she hadn't thought of Johnnie tonight. Not once.

The night air finally dispersed the flush of excitement and wine consumption from her cheeks.

Roberto put his arm around her. 'Do you do it on the first night?' he asked her.

The question wiped the smile from her face. Up until that moment she'd felt fresh and new, as though she were sixteen again and just out of school. When he said that she wondered exactly what he might have heard. The spectre of being an unmarried mother was difficult to bear. People whispered. People gossiped and news travelled fast. There was also the fact that she went home each and every weekend. So far he hadn't questioned why. Perhaps it was something to do with his background. Italians and Sicilians were possessive of their women and maintained close family ties. To them it was good that she went home to see her family.

'What do you mean?'

'I only asked if you kissed on the first date. I didn't mean to upset you.'

Her whole body seemed to sigh with relief. She only hoped that he hadn't noticed.

'Oh!' she managed to say. 'Well ... I do ... sometimes.'

He stood regarding her with his hands in his pockets, head thrown to one side. And then he laughed and shook his head.

'Marcie! Oh, my beautiful Marcie! You are such an innocent. And I love it!'

He'd endowed her with a description she did not deserve and it felt wonderful. She was swept off her feet. With one word he had turned back the clock. It was crazy to go ahead and play the part, but play it she did.

'I prefer not to kiss – just yet,' she said hesitantly while looking up at him through a veil of blonde hair. Just to add the right touch of authenticity, she bit her bottom lip. 'Perhaps another time – when I know you better – if you don't mind...'

She lowered her head and her eyes. She felt his hand curving along the side of her head and knew he was hooked.

*You're lying!*

The voice was back in her head. Was it only her conscience, or was it Johnnie?

Nicholas Roberto Camilleri took her back to his parents' house in a red Maserati.

'I want to see you again. Tuesday suits me.'

He didn't ask whether it suited her or not, but

she didn't mind. Tuesdays were nights in just like any other night. Thursday night was the only one earmarked for going out. Carol and April had asked her out with them. She explained that to him and was surprised on seeing his face cloud over.

'I'd rather you did not go out with them.'

She studied his face, seeking the reason for his sudden change of mood.

'I'm only going out with girls. No boys. We were going dancing at some club they know...'

She jumped when he cupped her face in his hands. He'd done it so quickly and, although it didn't hurt, he was holding her very firmly and gazing intensely into her eyes.

'Those girls are no good. They will lead you into bad ways. Trust me on this. My concern is for you, Marcie. It will always be for you.'

His words took her breath away. So did the kiss that landed gently and sweetly on her mouth.

'I didn't say you could kiss me,' she murmured.

'Yes you did.'

'I did?' She sounded incredulous.

He smiled. 'With your eyes.'

Three nights that week they did the same thing. Three nights of the next he took her dancing, to the cinema and to an upmarket restaurant in Mayfair.

The waiters were not so familiar with him as at the Italian restaurant, but they were very professional, attentively spreading linen napkins on their laps and frequently asking whether everything was alright.

197

Marcie took it all in. London had a fizz like nowhere else in the world. The Isle of Sheppey seemed remote and dull in comparison. It had no upmarket restaurants with white-gloved door-men; no influx of people from every continent, every country. She frequently had to remind herself that her child was back there. Joanna pricked her conscience. If it hadn't been for her daughter she knew that she would stay here in London and never go home again.

The sweet bouquets of hand-picked flowers arrived dewy fresh on Mondays and Wednesdays. Daisy Chain was busiest at the end of the week. Those were the days when Marcie helped out. Both Carol and April looked at her expectantly for updates on her exciting love life.

'You're still going out with him?' April asked incredulously.

'I am.'

'Two weeks? You're the longest ever,' Carol added.

She burst out laughing, 'You cannot be serious!'

Carol coloured in the details. 'Nobody lasts longer than three dates with Nicholas Roberto Camilleri. It all depends on what the sex is like. If a girl doesn't come over, then he dumps her. If she's good in bed he sees her more than once.'

She couldn't believe they were telling the truth. Roberto had not demanded what every man demanded sooner or later. The truth of the matter was that he did nothing more than kiss her good-night, though sometimes it was obvious he wanted to go further.

Her own need for sexual fulfilment surprised her. She was young. Seventeen, going on eighteen years of age. She'd enjoyed making love with Johnnie but since then there'd been nobody. She refused to dwell on Alan Taylor's vicious attacks. Roberto had reawakened her, made her realise she missed having someone to hold, someone to kiss. Of course she wanted sex, though no more babies. Or at least, not yet. Not until she was married.

She talked to Carol and April about contraception.

'The pill,' stated Carol.

'The pill,' April echoed.

'But then–'

Marcie stopped in her tracks. She had been about to say that taking the pill meant she would end up throwing caution to the wind. Getting to sleep with someone was easy, but how about if having sex became just that? Easy. How about if it was the sex she wanted not the person she was having sex with?

At least next time she knew enough to ensure any pill came directly from a doctor. Much as she loved her daughter she did not wish to make the same mistake twice.

'Partnerships and marriages could become obsolete in no time if you go on thinking like this,' she stated.

'So we all save ourselves for marriage! How dull.' Carol's tone was mocking. 'Unless it's Roberto Camilleri. I'd certainly wait to be wedded and bedded by him!'

Marcie was glad of the laughter that followed. It stopped the moment from becoming too serious. Afterwards she thought of how pompous she sounded. After all, it wasn't as if she was a virgin. She was an unmarried mother. Even so, she knew she'd never be as casual over relationships as the other shop girls. I should be more careful, she thought to herself as she sat with her arms resting over a sewing machine.

*He's saving you for marriage.*

The voice was right. Carol and April had said the same thing. Thinking like a true Sicilian or Italian.

Roberto intended marrying a virgin. And she was it. Why hadn't she realised before?

He'd hinted at getting engaged.

'I will buy you a ring with a ruby the size of a crow's egg encircled with diamonds.'

'That sounds very flash,' she'd responded.

'Very Italian,' he'd countered.

She hadn't said yes or no. She knew enough about her grandmother's culture to know that Italians, Sicilians and even Maltese were very much the same. Nice girls were for marrying. As far as Roberto was concerned, she was a nice girl. My God, she thought, closing her eyes, what am I going to do? When do I tell him – if at all?

It was at times like these that she badly missed having someone of her own age to talk to. The girls at Daisy Chain were fine, but April's pills had got the better of her. Mrs Camilleri said she'd been transferred to another job where the stress would not weigh her down.

Marcie remarked that she'd thought April had enjoyed her job. 'She didn't seem stressed,' she added.

'Nevertheless...' said Mrs Camilleri, with a casual wave of her beautiful hands. 'It was for the best.'

It was difficult to read the look on Gabriella's face, but Marcie detected a worried frown.

'Is everything alright, Mrs Camilleri?'

Gabriella Camilleri was fiddling with bits of pattern, shuffling the pieces over a length of dark-purple material. She wasn't actually achieving anything by the process, leading Marcie to believe that her thoughts were elsewhere.

'None of your business,' snapped Mrs Camilleri.

Carol had also left. She'd confided in Marcie that she wanted a job in a nightclub. 'Roberto pulled strings,' she told Marcie with undisguised glee. 'I'm going to be a showgirl.'

So now she had nobody of her own age around. Her weekly leisure time was spent with Roberto; her weekends at home with Joanna and her grandmother. The loneliness lingered and Roberto was questioning why she insisted on going home at the weekends. Surely her grandmother didn't need that many visits...?

She'd brought a few precious things from home, most notably a walnut jewellery box in which she kept objects that were precious to her: a knitted bootee, worn by Joanna when she was only a month or so old; a pressed flower she'd put between the pages of a book. There was also an earring she'd found buried close to where the old chicken coop used to be. She liked to think it had once belonged to her mother. She didn't ask anyone if they recognised it. She didn't want to be disappointed.

This was also where she kept precious letters. One of them was from Allegra, one of the two girls she'd met at the home for unmarried mothers. Enclosed with that letter was the address of Sally, the other girl who she'd shared a room with. She couldn't be certain that they would answer her letter, but she lived in hope that they would.

There was a new addition to her treasure box; Roberto had bought her a ring. 'For you,' he'd said, kissing her on the forehead while sliding the ring onto her middle finger.

She'd stared at it in wonder, knowing it was gold and that the red stone had to be a ruby.

'Is it real?'

He'd told her that it was.

'But not an engagement ring,' he'd added and smiled. 'Not yet.'

Normally it was her father who came home with her or failing that she'd catch the train. It was on a Friday morning and she'd arranged to meet him for a coffee when he told her he couldn't make it.

'I've got business to attend to,' he said in his boyish, shifty manner.

'Dad, you've never played poker have you?'

Tony Brooks looked at his daughter as though she'd sworn on the Sabbath.

'I don't like cards. Not even Snap. You should know that, Marcie. As a kid you used to ask me to–'

'Shut up, Dad.'

At one time she would never have dreamed of

telling him to shut up. That was when she was just his daughter. Now she was the mother of his grandchild his attitude had changed. More often now he looked at her for a lead – as though she knew more than him. With a pang of regret she wondered whether he'd looked at her mother in the same way.

It was becoming noticeable that her father's visits home were becoming less frequent. Each time Marcie arrived home without him Babs would be waiting at Endeavour Terrace, sometimes with the kids, just as often without. She'd never been one for dragging the kids around behind her; never been that much of a one for kids at all for that matter.

She recalled her last weekend home. Babs had been there and the obvious had been stated.

'He's got another woman! That's it! Well? Is it?'

Babs screeched the accusation and even Rosa Brooks assuring her that his family would always come first to her darling Antonio began to pale.

The truth was that Marcie didn't know whether her father was having a fling or not. Nobody had seen him with another woman. There were no rumours that he was seeing another woman. But on the third week in a row of not wanting to go home to Sheppey, Marcie had to admit to herself that there was no smoke without fire. He had someone, though who the hell it was, she didn't have a bloody clue!

So here he was sitting across the table from her in a run-of-the-mill Wimpy Bar where the wet weather outside and the warmth within caused condensation to mist the windows.

Marcie went straight for the jugular. 'Have you got another woman?'

He stared at her at first, almost as though she'd just stepped on his toe with a spike-heeled shoe.

He recovered quickly and was suitably indignant. 'Course not!'

'I don't believe you.'

He raised his voice. 'Now steady on...'

'Babs misses you. So do the kids.'

Mention of the kids brought a more positive response, though not enough to make him promise to come home.

It occurred to her that her father was involved in something shady that he couldn't talk about. What did he actually do for Victor Camilleri? How beholden was he to the Sicilian, who had a way with words and eyes as sharp as a fish eagle? She asked him outright.

'What kind of hold has Mr Camilleri got over you?'

For a moment he looked at her with his mouth open. 'Nothing. Nothing at all.'

Judging by his expression, he was telling the truth, the whole truth and nothing but the truth. Still, it was a well-known fact that Tony Brooks could lie to the devil and be believed if he had to. And it could very well be the truth. Perhaps it's just me, she decided.

The fact of the matter was that Mrs Camilleri was indeed a very good judge of fashion and loved almost everything Marcie designed. But that was the moot point as far as Marcie was concerned. Her coming to live at the delectable flat in Chelsea had been Victor's idea, not that of his wife.

Victor was not likely to elaborate on the matter. For the moment she had to take everything at face value. Mrs Camilleri valued her creativity and for now that would have to suffice.

'You don't need to get the train.'

Marcie tuned in to what her father was saying.

'I can't borrow the car, Dad. I don't have a driving licence.'

Her father guffawed with laughter. 'Neither do I.'

'That's hardly the point.'

'No need to worry,' he said chirpily while patting her hand. 'I persuaded Roberto to give you a lift.'

Marcie's blood drained from her face.

'Bloody hell!'

Her father looked surprised at her exclamation. 'You ungrateful little cow.'

Marcie fixed him with a hard stare, her teeth grating with the effort of keeping calm – just a little calm.

'Dad! Remember he doesn't know about Joanna. In fact, he thinks I'm the next best thing to the Virgin Mary. All the family does. Do you get what I'm saying, Dad? These are Sicilians. Wives are expected to be untouched virgins on their wedding night. That's what he thinks I am.'

'Shit!' Tony Brooks buried his head in his hands. 'I didn't think. I only did what I thought was best for you.'

Marcie shook her head. 'Have you any idea of what you've done? Roberto has set me up on a bloody high pedestal and when I fall, which surely I will, there's going to be some explaining to do –

thanks to you! Trust my dad to muck up my life.'

His eyes flashed. 'Marcie! How did I ever do that?'

'My mother for a start,' she said grimly, not caring now where this conversation might be heading. 'I would have liked to know her. I would have liked to have had some contact with her. But you would never discuss her. You blanked me out every time I mentioned her. So where is she, Dad? Where can I find my mother?'

He got up. 'Sod it! Do you know what? You're becoming a right little cow. Hard as nails. You'll end up just like her. Just like your mother!'

'Dad! What do you mean by that?'

He was angry and she'd overstepped the mark. That's what she put that comment down to. He was just trying to hurt her.

She watched him go, hands buried in his pockets, shoulders hunched against the rain.

Roberto refused to listen to her reasons why he shouldn't give her a lift home that weekend. Even when she said she wouldn't bother to go, he insisted that she did.

'Your grandmother will wish to see you. And there is no need to concern yourself with regard to my behaviour. Michael is coming along as chaperone.'

'Michael?'

He laughed. Chaperones were usually women. 'My mother hates driving fast. Michael offered to come. He is in love with you. Did you know that?'

She shook her head dumbly.

Roberto laughed. 'He'll hate doing the job, but

I thought it would be fun.'

Yes. You would, she thought.

Michael did nothing except hand her a single flower. A carnation.

'I think somebody dropped it,' he said, then looked away.

Michael coming along upset her plan to tell Roberto that she was an unmarried mother, yet purely on instinct, she found his presence reassuring.

'Did you like the flowers I sent you?'

Roberto's question jolted her from thinking of Michael.

She beamed at him. 'I don't know how you sneak into the sewing room without me seeing you. And it looks as though you picked them yourself.'

She saw his eyelids flicker. 'Darling, I bought them in that posh flower shop at the end of the King's Road. Roses and stuff. That's what I asked her for. I thought that was them my mother was taking to the tap in the kitchen.'

Marcie suddenly realised her mistake. Roberto was referring to the bouquet she'd initially placed in her bedroom.

So who was responsible for the sweet peas, carnations and other common garden flowers placed on her work table each day?

She sniffed the carnation. Michael. It had to be Michael. Roberto was right. Michael was in love with her.

Eventually Roberto's shiny Maserati turned into Endeavour Terrace on Friday evening. The street lights were just coming on and a bank of grey cloud was rolling in from the sea.

'Just here. Number ten.'

He rolled to a stop where she told him too. She glanced through the narrow gate and the equally narrow path leading to the front door of number ten.

She felt a great urge to apologise. 'I'm sorry I can't ask you both to stay, but it's only a tiny cottage.'

Roberto shrugged. 'You want to see your family alone. It's understandable. You want to explain me to them before they meet me.' He spread his arms. His sunglasses had pinkish lenses so it was hard to read whatever was in his eyes. 'The clothes too – you'll sure as hell want to explain the duds, won't you?'

His reference to the yellow shirt and black velvet jacket brought a smile to her face. He was wearing an oversized tartan cap – the sort favoured by street urchins a century ago, though his wasn't ragged, of course, merely stylish.

She thought again how much he resembled his father in that he sometimes made statements as though they were questions. That was fine in itself, though she was beginning to suspect that there was really only one answer she could give – the one he wanted to hear.

'I'll see you tomorrow – once you've explained that you've fallen in love with a flash bloke with a good wedge in his pocket and a matching flash car.'

She raised a quizzical eyebrow. 'Who said I'd fallen in love with him?'

He ran his fingers down the side of her face, cupped her chin and shook his head. 'I did. I'm irresistible. Didn't you know that?'

Before she had chance to get out of the car, there was a banging on the window.

'Marcie Brooks! You fucking cow!'

The last person she'd expected to see was Rita Taylor bashing the car window with her fist.

Roberto too was taken by surprise. 'Who the hell's that?'

Marcie gave no answer. Her insides were turning to marshmallow.

Roberto got out of the car and went round to the passenger door. Michael got out from the back.

'Hey. Hey. Easy now.'

Michael grabbed hold of the flailing fists, pulling Rita away from the car. Marcie seized the opportunity to open the car door.

The girl who had once been her closest friend – a fact that Marcie had lived to regret – struggled against the strong arms that held her.

'Now, now,' Michael was saying while effortlessly holding Rita's arms to her chest.

Rita would not be calmed. Her face was contorted with rage. She looked so much bigger than Marcie remembered. The girl that had been prettily chubby was now obese.

An oblong of light fell out of the cottage and onto the garden path.

'What is going on here?'

Rosa Brooks was standing in the cottage doorway with Joanna in her arms. Marcie was filled with alarm. She hadn't told Roberto yet. It would be such a shock.

Rita's rage was firmly directed at Marcie. She was calling her all the bad names under the sun and mostly referring to her morals. Between rants she turned her angry face upwards to Roberto.

'I shouldn't have nothing to do with her if I was you, mate. She's a tramp that one. Led my dad on she did, then done him in. They say she didn't, that he got into a fight. But I don't believe that. She killed him. That fucking tramp killed him.'

Other doors were opening and other lights were turning on in bedroom windows.

'Marcie Brooks is a fucking slut,' Rita shouted to those who'd chanced putting their head out of the window.

'Let her go,' Marcie said to Michael.

'Are you sure?'

Marcie nodded. 'She lost her dad. He used to take the two of us around together. She's gone a bit loopy since he died.'

In her mind she could see Alan Taylor lying on the beach. She'd been very good at keeping the vision at bay, continually telling herself it was an accident. That's how she coped.

Rita lunged again. This time Roberto caught her and kept a firm grip on Rita's arms. His cheek was pressed against hers and he was trying to calm her down.

'Come on now. You've had a bit to drink, girl. Calm it down. Right?' He looked over at Marcie. 'She smells as though she's supped a brewery.'

'The stupid cow!'

Suddenly Marcie didn't care what came out. She was ready for whatever Rita had in mind and if she mentioned her dad again, she'd tell it as it was. That he was a rapist. That he liked young girls. Goodness knows what Roberto might think, but it couldn't be helped.

She braced herself for whatever happened.

'Go on then, Rita. Hit me. That's what you want to do, isn't it? Hit me. If you dare.'

Roberto let go of Rita's arms. She charged again, shrieking like a banshee as she lumbered forwards.

Marcie sidestepped, grabbed Rita's hair as she went by and swung her off balance.

Rita howled and came for her again.

Marcie clenched then raised her fist. This time when Rita charged she held her podgy hands out in front of her, her sharp nails gleaming with red varnish.

As the clawed hands raked into Marcie's shoulders she brought her fist up. There was a sickening crunch as her knuckles made contact with Rita's chin. Rita's bottom teeth crashed against her top ones and her head went back. She tottered to one side, grabbing the hedge before crumpling to her knees.

The people of Endeavour Terrace weren't the sort to go calling the police for every little problem. To their minds it looked as though the matter had been settled to everybody's satisfaction. Rita had come huffing and puffing with vengeful intent and had been soundly despatched.

Marcie met Roberto's eyes. He looked surprised.

'She's mad.' It was all she could think of to say. 'I'm sorry though. I'm not violent. I'm not like that.'

At first he beheld her silently. Then he smiled. 'You could have fooled me, babe.'

'That's her car,' someone said, pointing to a Mini Cooper 'S'.

Roberto took charge of the situation. 'Michael. Deal with the car. If someone points me in the right direction, I'll take her home; you follow on behind.'

Marcie heard Michael mutter, 'As always.'

Two or three neighbours were helping Rita to her feet. She was quiet now, her head wobbling on her shoulders.

Michael put his arm around her and guided her into the front seat of the Maserati.

Roberto looked on, hands resting on slim hips. 'She'll revive enough to show me where she lives.'

He kissed Marcie on the cheek. 'Take care, darling, and have a nice weekend. Perhaps it's better if I see you back in London on Monday.'

A sudden panic made her look towards the cottage gate. Her grandmother was still standing there with Joanna. The little girl was holding out her arms.

'Mummy!'

Roberto didn't notice. But Michael did. She saw the look of surprise on his face, his quick glance at her, another at his half-brother.

The last thing she wanted was for Roberto to find out about Joanna – before she had time to explain it to him herself.

Michael was looking at her. It was barely susceptible, but he shook his head before looking away.

It was a joy to be home. 'This is so wonderful,'

she crooned between kissing her daughter's head and hearing the new words the toddler had learned in the small space of a week. 'I'm glad you kept her up for me.'

Her grandmother was watching her with quick, quizzical eyes.

'Even if I hadn't, she would have been woken up by all the noise.' Her eyes narrowed. 'The young man – he is Sicilian?'

Marcie wondered how she could possibly know that, but countered that there wasn't much her grandmother didn't know. One look at a person and she had them categorised so she might as well explain.

'Victor Camilleri's son. His parents came originally from Sicily I believe, though they've lived in this country for some time. The other boy is his half-brother.'

'Do they go to church?'

'Mrs Camilleri goes to confession and mass three times a week. More sometimes I think.'

Heat was emanating from the old kitchen range. Rosa Brooks nodded herself asleep.

Joanna was sitting on her mother's lap. Marcie hadn't had the heart to put her to bed just yet. She'd missed her so and couldn't bear the thought of letting her go.

She was playing with the white bow at the front of her mother's navy-blue dress, chuckling and talking baby talk to herself.

The knock at the cottage door was muffled as though whoever was knocking was in two minds whether they really needed to or not.

Marcie glanced at her grandmother who was

peacefully sleeping.

'We'll answer the door, shall we?'

Her daughter's eyes sparkled at the whispered suggestion. Even if she couldn't understand what was being said, her mother's secretive tone sounded fun.

The last person she'd expected to see on the doorstep was Michael.

'I got lost,' he explained and looked sheepish. He was wearing his glasses.

Marcie stared. Joanna cooed.

'I won't say anything. I thought I should come back and say that.'

Marcie felt as though her tongue had stuck to the roof of her mouth. It was hard to swallow.

'I take it she is yours,' he added in response to her silence. 'Yes. She must be,' he said when she didn't answer. 'I heard her say "mummy".' He shook his head. 'Don't worry. Roberto didn't hear. Do you want me to tell him for you?'

She stared more blindly and shook her head.

'No,' he said, also shaking his head. 'I figured that.'

The way he looked at her was very worrying. She saw concern in his eyes and knew it was for her. She explained how to get to Rita's house so he could drop off her car and find Roberto. A few moments passed in silence.

'Marcie, you need to tread carefully.' His voice was husky, even guarded.

'He'll understand,' she blurted.

For a moment neither of them said anything. Then Michael managed a weak smile. 'Of course he will.'

## Chapter Twenty-four

Roberto had sat Rita in the passenger seat with her head lolling backwards and her eyes rolling in her head. By the time they were nearing the place he'd been told she lived, her head was resting heavily on his shoulder and she was snoring.

He lost Michael at some traffic lights. Easy to do seeing as he was driving a Maserati and Michael was driving a Mini Cooper 'S'.

Bringing the car to a halt, he nudged at Rita's head with his shoulder.

'Hey! Wake up.'

Groggily she opened her bleary eyes then groaned and touched her jaw.

Roberto could see that she still wasn't quite with it. My, but Marcie had landed her one hell of a punch. Marcie wasn't to know but the sight of her lashing out like that was strangely arousing. He loved fiery women, women who would fight back if a bloke gave her a bit of a slap. Oh yeah, he liked that alright. A virgin at first, then a firebrand; yes, Marcie Brooks could suit him fine. He'd marry her of course. She'd belong to him. He'd still indulge his huge passion here and there with one of the girls he came across in his business. That was the name of the game so to speak; make them feel as though they were the only girl in the world. Reel them in like a fish until they were well and truly hooked. Then have

215

them working on their backs. Not streetwalkers of course, but high-class girls with clean bodies and bright minds. Give them a bank account and a clothes allowance, and they would do anything he wanted. But not Marcie. Marcie was a virgin. His virgin and the girl he would make his wife. He hadn't asked her officially yet, but in time he would.

He clasped the nape of Rita's neck so that she could at least keep her head still. If she kept her head still she should be able to focus better.

'Hey! Is this your place?'

He swivelled her head to face the bungalow he'd been told she lived in.

Rita groaned. It sounded like yes, but he couldn't be sure.

'Did you say, yes?'

Her head lolled back and her eyes rolled again. Roberto swore. 'Oh, for fuck's sake!'

Her head whipped from side to side as he slapped one cheek then the other.

'Come on, you stupid bitch! Talk to me.'

The slapping he'd given her seemed to work. Her eyes fluttered open then narrowed as her sight began to clear.

'Who are you?' She winced, gingerly touching her jaw. 'Ouch.'

'I'm the mug who gave you a lift home. Is this where you live?'

He jerked his chin at the bungalow. The place was in darkness. He decided that even when it was lit up it was an ugly place, flash but tasteless, the sort of place where the Rita Taylors of this world would live.

216

'Come on. Let's get you indoors. You got a key?'

She nodded and the pain from her jaw kicked in. 'Ouch! I think I've got a loose tooth.'

'I'm not surprised,' said Roberto as he helped her out of the car. 'You took a big one right on the chin.'

She stood on the pavement and frowned at him. 'Marcie Brooks?'

'Marcie Brooks. Come on. Let's get you indoors.'

The thought of Marcie landing that ace of a punch made him ache with desire for her. He'd ached with desire for her from the first moment he'd seen her; who wouldn't? She was a stunner with her blonde hair and peaches and cream complexion. As for her figure – well – she certainly had curves in all the right places, thank God! One thing he could admit to for sure and that was that he wasn't a Twiggy man. No straight up and down girls for him. He liked a girl with hips and a bosom. At least with a bosom you could tell the front from the back. Not like Twiggy. Skinny cow!

The interior of the bungalow was exactly as he'd expected it to be. Flash carpet, flash furniture and even a padded cocktail bar in one corner. How crap was that?

It stunk of neglect and there was litter everywhere. He could see that Rita wasn't one for housework. Slummy cow!

Rita slumped down onto a stack of orange cushions jammed at one end of a brown settee.

Pinning her elbows to her knees, she leaned forwards, head in hands and moaned.

217

'That cow! She used to be my best friend.'

Roberto paused by the door. He had been meaning to go once he'd made sure she was OK. He'd half considered trying it on with her, but her curves had long since turned into layers of fat and were now too much even for him to handle.

He'd had no idea that Rita and Marcie used to be best friends, but the idea intrigued him. They were best friends who'd fallen out. When Roberto Camilleri fell for a girl, she had to be his and his alone. To that end he wished to know everything there was about her. Like his father he was of the old school that believed a woman's place was in the home and that she should live for her husband and her children alone, never for herself. Even his mother's dress shop had been at his father's instigation. Victor Camilleri knew his wife well enough to see when she was restless and might be tempted to kick over the traces and even upset his life if she were given half a chance. And so he'd ordained that she design and make dresses to sell in a shop, her shop, or rather his father's, because everything in women's lives was owned by men. Women were not capable of owning and should not be encouraged to do so.

And so because Rita had told him that Marcie and she had been best friends, he'd decided to stay at least until Michael caught up with him. That way he could find out about Marcie's past in order to design her future.

'Have you got any brandy?' he asked the dumb girl with the heavy thighs.

She shook her head. 'I don't want any.'

'It wasn't you I was thinking of.'

The cocktail cabinet was the obvious place and she didn't tell him otherwise when he went there.

He pulled out two glasses, held one up and looked enquiringly at her.

Rita nodded. 'OK.'

She didn't usually drink brandy. The half-bottle of Martell was part of her father's old stash. He'd drunk anything come the last so it came as something of a surprise that there was that much left.

She peered through bleary eyes at the bloke who'd brought her home. Even though she was still the worse for wear, he seemed like a dish.

'My bedroom's upstairs.'

'Is that so.'

'You can take me up there if you like. You can stay if you like.'

'Sorry, love. I'll have to pass on that. Perhaps another time.'

Roberto added a splash of soda to each glass, sure of the fact that another time would never come for him and her. He passed her one of the drinks and pulled up a chair so he was sitting opposite her.

She took a sip and grimaced.

'Work it around your jaw. It'll help with the pain.'

Rita's face was crumpled like a piece of squashed dough just before the baker got at it. The anger was still there; he could see it smouldering beneath the surface.

She took his advice and swilled the brandy around in her mouth.

Roberto took a sip from his own glass and chose his moment. 'So. You and Marcie used to be friends. What went wrong?'

Rita screwed her face up even more. 'I'll tell you what went wrong. I'll tell you everything. Then you'll see what a slut she is!'

'I'm all ears,' said Roberto, and waited.

## Chapter Twenty-five

The weekend at Endeavour Terrace came to an end all too quickly. Joanna had been perfect and to Marcie that was all that mattered. Marcie tried not to dwell on Roberto finding out about her status as an unmarried mother. Even if he did, if he loved her it wouldn't matter. That's what she told herself and although it calmed her at first, the fears came back, flowing over her with as much force as a North Sea wave.

Babs had visited with the kids in tow, bumping Annie down the path in her pushchair.

'That bloody bus conductor was downright ignorant,' she declared before turning her bad temper on Marcie. 'Well? Where is he?'

Marcie knew she was referring to her father. 'He said to tell you he had some business to deal with. Nightclubs get busy on weekends.'

Babs had smoked, drank and pursued men and affairs for most of her life. Her face and figure were beginning to show the ravages of time and the pubs and chip shops she'd often frequented. The dark crescents beneath her eyes looked as though they'd been drawn on with an eye pencil.

There were wrinkles around her lips from constantly drawing in and puffing on cigarettes. Her dark roots were showing in her hair and her tight skirt was straining over her belly.

'You tell that bastard that I'll cut his fucking balls off if I find out he's knocking around with a London tart! You just tell him that!'

Bundling Annie back into the pushchair, Babs left in a flurry of stale sweat and unwashed clothes. She was hardly the blonde bombshell she'd always tried to be and now that she didn't go out to work any longer, she didn't seem to give a damn about her appearance.

A disapproving Rosa Brooks shook her head. 'Such language.'

The two boys loitered. Their grandmother gave half a crown to each of them. 'Your father told me to give this to you.'

Marcie knew it wasn't true. Her father was lingering in London and not even his own mother had heard much from him in the past few weeks.

Archie pulled on Marcie's sleeve. 'When you see me dad, will you ask him why he doesn't love us any more?'

Marcie felt her heart lurch in her chest at the sight of the big doleful eyes, eyes as brown as his father. 'Of course he still loves you, he's just ... busy.'

'Can you ask him to come see us?'

What could she say except yes, of course she would ask him.

'Promise?'

'Archie, you can depend on it!'

She watched the two brothers dash after their

mother, leaving the garden gate slamming back against the hedge. Her father had put himself out for her of late, but he was doing nothing much for his other children. OK, she could almost – *almost* – forgive him for not wanting to be with his wife. The woman was going swiftly to the dogs. But his children? She looked at it from her own point of view as a parent. Never, ever could she miss a weekend home with Joanna.

'I'm sorry that Rita and I fell out,' Marcie said to her grandmother when they were discussing things after Joanna had gone to bed.

'Cheap meat.'

Marcie almost choked on her tea. Rosa Brooks certainly had a way with words when it came to describing people.

'That girl was not your friend. She was her own friend. Always her own friend.'

A silence fell between them. There were two subjects Marcie was trying to avoid. One of them was Garth, the other was Babs. She was scared to ask about Garth and still didn't believe he'd had anything to do with the fire that had destroyed the only boutique on the Isle of Sheppey.

'Garth is well,' her grandmother said suddenly as though she'd read her thoughts. 'The staff there treat him very well.'

She sounded surprised that anyone beside herself could treat him anything but very badly. All the same her face was drawn and anxious. She'd always had a hand in caring for Garth.

'I don't believe he set fire to Angie's place,' said Marcie.

'No.' Her grandmother's face clouded. 'The man who lives in the flat next door said he saw him sleeping there. Yet Garth says he enjoyed the smell of the shop. I think he meant the fish and chip shop. Garth *would* like the smell of that.'

A wan smile played around Marcie's lips. Her grandmother had a point. Garth's belly followed his nose. A clothes shop would have no attraction for him at all. He dressed like a scarecrow. A fish and chip shop on the other hand...

'What if Rita knew that man...?'

Her grandmother's eyes met hers. Neither woman spoke until Marcie shook her head.

'I don't know where that came from,' she said, clutching her teacup with both hands. She shook her head. 'I was just thinking aloud...'

'The thought popped into your head.'

Her grandmother's eyes held hers, yet it seemed in that moment that Marcie was seeing features in the wrinkled face that she'd never seen before.

She licked her lips and shook her head, tucking a stray tress behind her ear.

'Where did the thought come from?'

'Someone put the thought in there. Someone who crossed over. Either that or you see it yourself. Adding two and two, or just knowing ... just knowing runs in our family.'

'My mother or Johnnie?'

'Johnnie loved you.'

Marcie was startled. 'And my mother did not?'

Whereas before her grandmother's expression had seemed open and all her thoughts easily accessible, it now seemed that a door had closed.

'I did not say that. But I know Johnnie loved you.'

She got up and took the empty teacup from Marcie's hand, leaving her granddaughter with her mouth hanging open and a questioning look in her eyes.

Her grandmother took both cups to the sink where she proceeded to run them beneath the cold water tap. Marcie followed her. 'Have you spoken to Johnnie?'

Her grandmother stopped swilling the cups and looked at her. 'Sometimes it's the living that tell us things.'

'Is my mother still alive?'

Her grandmother's wrinkled hand wrenched the old brass tap shut as though it needed that extra strength. The truth was that it shut off easily, the washers worn with the years.

'I cannot say.' She turned suddenly and looked into her granddaughter's face. 'You will be well off without her.'

The need to know prodded at Marcie's heart. 'Why did you disapprove of her?'

Rosa Brooks looked startled. 'Disapprove? I never disapproved! Not until she ran off leaving her child crying in the night.'

Her words brought back faint memories of not understanding why her mother did not come when she called. As a child she would have been heartbroken. She instantly recognised it as the reason her grandmother could not forgive.

'So she's still alive,' said Marcie.

Rosa Brooks said nothing. Her silence said it all.

Marcie turned over and nuzzled into the pillow. She closed her eyes and thought about her mother. If she was alive she had to be living in London. She was sure of that. And in time she might meet up with her – if she knew where to look. Perhaps her newfound instinct might lead her to that elusive woman. She sincerely hoped so.

## Chapter Twenty-six

The Pussy Cat Club was not exactly one of Tony Brooks' favourite haunts, but nobody he knew of any consequence went there so he judged it was just the place to take Ella.

He didn't know how it had happened, this attraction between them, though he had to concede the blame lay heavily with him. Her old man was a waster, she had no money to pay the rent Victor demanded for the crummy rooms she lived in, and he'd felt sorry for her.

He'd paid one of Ella's neighbours to look after her kids and given her some dosh for a new dress. Victor paid him well. He had no quibbles about that!

'How do you like this, honey?' she said in that fruity voice of hers. She did him a kind of half-twirl to one side then the other. The dress was red and covered in sequins and clung in all the right places. Someone else might have looked a right tart in it. Against Ella's conker-brown skin it looked a treat. Unlike a lot of the West Indian women that rented rooms with their families in the grim tenements Victor owned, she wasn't overblown. Her breasts were pert and he was pushed to cover each buttock with his hand – not that he was complaining.

Gold hoops jangled in her ears each time she moved her head – and she was moving her head a lot.

'Do they play music?' she asked excitedly as they squeezed themselves beside a small round table.

'Sometimes.'

He hadn't told her this was a strip club and the only dancing of note would be done by the 'exotic dancers' getting their kit off on the brightly lit stage.

'Drink?' he asked.

'Rum. With pineapple juice.'

He thought the drink an odd combination and the barman was of the same opinion. Besides, his stock didn't stretch to pineapple juice.

'Most people prefer rum and black.'

Tony looked at Ella. She wrinkled her nose at first before caving in. 'OK. I have to become English. Not Jamaican.'

As she looked around her, he studied the profile of her face, the nape of her neck. She seemed to stand out against the club's dark ambience, as though someone had traced round her with a contrasting colour. He couldn't tell what colour.

The bulbs in the table lamps dimly lit the faces of those smoking and drinking. Smoke from cigarettes and cigars drifted upwards, moving and twirling like something living.

Nobody looked in their direction. Thankfully there was no one here that he knew who would see him with his coloured girl. He didn't think of her as though she were a lesser mortal because of her skin colour, but there were plenty that did. God help them if they deferred to her with anything but respect. He'd give them a good clumping if they did.

There was nothing to worry about. The punters' faces were turned towards the stage. They'd come to see the strippers. The entrance fee was exorbitant, but the show was good.

She jerked her head round and smiled when Tony covered her hand with his own.

'Enjoying yourself, darling?'

She smiled broadly. 'You bet.'

It had been a long time since he'd gone gooey over a girl. At his age! What was he, nearly twice her age? He tried not to think of what his mates would think of him. Not that they'd say it to his face. To them he was the hard man, but every so often his heart ruled his head. It didn't happen often but when it did there was nothing he could do about it. Until the infatuation wore off – which it would in the end.

Ella made him feel like a kid again in the days when he'd first met Marcie's mother. Mary! She still came back to him and thoughts of her still hurt, though not so much since he'd met Ella.

'Can we dance?' she asked him suddenly.

'We'll see.'

He lit a cigar that Victor had given him. At the same time he wondered whether the Pussy Cat actually had a dance floor. He couldn't recall seeing one. Dancing was confined to the stage and nowhere else as far he knew.

Ella's face was a beautiful silhouette against the backlit stage. She clapped when everyone else clapped. The first dancer had made her entrance.

The dancer was billed as Little Lily. She wore her hair in pigtails and was dressed in a see-through baby-doll nightie. She was carrying a teddy bear. The aim was to make her look a lot younger than she was. Tony Brooks frowned. He might have spent some time in prison but that was for straightforward criminality – if being a criminal could be called straightforward. It certainly wasn't going anywhere near straight that was for sure.

The fact of the matter was that he had two daughters – or one, he reminded himself, still unsure whether he was Annie's father or not. He didn't like to see women in kiddie costumes and not because it wasn't to his taste. Some blokes got dark thoughts seeing that. He wouldn't want them close to his girls.

The girl on stage had small breasts and slim hips. Her legs seemed to go on forever, though the white cotton socks and pink flat shoes put him off taking her seriously.

She took her time removing the gauzy night-dress that barely skimmed her thighs. As she did so, she cuddled her teddy bear to her breasts and did other things with it that no teddy should ever do.

Eventually she stripped down to a G-string but that came off too.

There were hoots and catcalls, though not from

Tony. He'd seen it all before, but what he hadn't been prepared for was Ella being so engrossed in what was happening.

When the club crowd applauded, she joined them, smacking her hands together like a pair of cymbals.

Face shining with delight, Ella faced Tony. 'That was fantastic!'

He tried not to show his surprise. 'Not as good as you, darling.'

She batted her eyes sheepishly and flicked her fingers at his chest in mock rebuke. 'A private performance. Just for you and no one else, Tony.'

Her flattery made him swell with pride. Since he'd first started paying her rent, the attraction between them had intensified. Ella was no longer pregnant. Mrs Smith or whatever her real name had been had seen to that and luckily she hadn't seem to suffer too many ill effects from her ordeal. She seemed happier now than when he'd first met her and he couldn't help but hope that it was his influence on her. Tony also couldn't help comparing her to Babs. Babs had been a sexy bird when she was younger, but now... Christ, she was fast going to seed. Much as he loved his kids he was becoming more and more reluctant to the thought of going home to the noisy, messy council house. He told himself that she had the home she wanted and he paid all the bills. What more could he do? She should be satisfied with that.

His attention was suddenly diverted to an elegant woman with olive skin and dark eyes that flashed in his direction. She smiled at him and gave him a little wave. For a moment it seemed that she might come over. Then her eyes settled on Ella. She winked at him, as though she completely understood what he was up to.

Ella had noticed. 'Do you know her?'

Frowning, he shook his head. 'No.' But he did. She was Victor's girlfriend. He didn't want to introduce Ella to her. Though he loved Ella he knew there were people who wouldn't understand the attraction – black and white. And his boss was one of them. One day people might think differently about things, but not now. Not yet!

'Let's go.'

Ella looked surprised, seeing as they hadn't long arrived, but he wasn't giving excuses. Ali, Victor's girlfriend had arrived. That meant Victor wouldn't be far behind. The Pussy Cat Club was where married people met people they were not married to. He didn't want Victor to see him with Ella and know how she was now paying her rent on time. He didn't want that. She was his secret and he wanted to keep it that way.

'I must be nuts,' he muttered to himself as they regained the street and the falling drizzle.

'It's only rain,' said Ella.

'Yeah. Sure.'

She wasn't to know that he hadn't been referring to that. London had a buzz and it had Ella. Sheerness and the Isle of Sheppey was a different world, a world through which he passed but no longer stayed.

## Chapter Twenty-seven

Tony Brooks peered around the door of the sewing room. Marcie and the girls were packing up following a busy day of cutting and sewing and poring over new designs with Mrs Camilleri. Marcie spotted him.

'Hello, stranger. Where were you at the weekend?'

'Busy, darling.'

He slid into the room and parked himself on a work table while she packed up what was left to pack up.

She eyed him sidelong while slamming a sewing machine lid shut.

'A lot of people missed you.'

The comment was meant to make him feel guilty and judging by his flickering eyelids, that's exactly how he was feeling.

'Well,' he said shrugging his shoulders and thrusting his hands in his pockets. 'You know how it is. When old Victor shouts that he wants something done, then I've got to jump to it. Know what I mean?'

Marcie stopped what she was doing. Placing one hand on her hip, she narrowed her eyes and looked at him.

'Is there anything you want to say?'

He took on the same old vacant look that she'd experienced all her life. Her dear old dad wouldn't admit to anything, but there again he didn't need to. It was there in his eyes – a tower of guilt some twenty feet high.

'I don't know what you mean, darling.'

Without taking her eyes off him, Marcie picked up the three pairs of scissors left on top of the next sewing machine along. She liked to leave the sewing room tidy.

'Babs thinks you've got another woman.'

'What?' The word was long drawn out and the expression was believable enough. But Marcie knew her father well enough not to be fooled.

'Have you got somebody, Dad?'

His jowls wobbled as he shook his head. 'Noooo! Of course not.'

Marcie didn't believe him. Her father's face was like a map and if you hit the right place at the right time the wrinkles lessened or increased depending on whether he was lying or not.

Marcie decided he was lying. Folding her arms, she eyed him accusingly. 'Dad, I don't like Babs. I think you know that, don't you? But I do love the boys and little Annie. You love the boys too. I know you do. And Annie's a little sweetie.'

'Blimey! You sound like my old mother!'

'Good.'

He went all soft featured. 'My kids are every-thing to me,' he protested. 'Everything in the world.'

'Then listen to this,' she said, raising her voice and stabbing his chest – her father's chest – with a newly manicured fingernail. 'The boys were upset that you didn't come home. Archie asked me if you loved him any more and if parents forget what kids look like once they're grown up. And before long Annie won't know who you are if she doesn't get to see more of you.'

She fully realised that Archie hadn't said the bit about parents forgetting what kids look like, but the words had slid easily off her tongue. It seemed the right thing to say, the thing that would elicit the right response or action. A little white lie never hurt anyone.

'Your sons love you,' she added, her face as stern as some of the teachers she'd known in her schooldays.

His brows knitted as he thought things through and shuffled from side to side in brown suede shoes.

He sighed in exasperation. 'OK. I'll go home this weekend.' He didn't sound over enthusiastic, but she had to give him the benefit of the doubt. 'Are you coming with me?'

She paused before answering. 'I don't know.'

He looked as surprised as she was. Roberto had told her he couldn't see her during the week but only at the weekend. Up until now she'd looked forward to going home every weekend. The weeks had seemed too long and the weekends not long enough. It would be the first weekend she'd missed going home to see Joanna, but she couldn't help it. Her heart was in the grip of a man who intrigued her. He was so fashionable, so colourful, so outrageous. Just this once, she said to herself.

Roberto, however, was surly following their visit to the Isle of Sheppey. Although the feeling was faint so far, Marcie began to have reservations

233

about their relationship. Roberto had placed her on a high pedestal and she knew it was inevitable that she would fall off.

She was brushing her hair when the words seemed to come whispering into her ear. Looking over her shoulder proved that there was no one there.

*Don't go with him.*

Her unease vanished when he arrived to take her for a drive in the country. 'It's Saturday morning and before you tell me you have work to do, I've already got permission from the governor – I mean my mother,' he added with a winning smile.

All reservations about their relationship melted away. You were just tired, she told herself.

Her mood brightened, her eyes sparkling. 'Where are we going?'

'To the country,' he said, wrapping an arm around her waist and pulling her to him. 'We'll find a little country pub. Have a ploughman's lunch. Cheese, fresh bread and lashings of butter and all washed down with a pint of bitter. How does that sound to you?'

'Good. Very good.'

Dressed as casually as he knew how – light-blue jeans, white cotton shirt and shaggy sheepskin waistcoat, he stood with head cocked, finger on chin and eyes looking skywards. 'Let's call it a mystery trip shall we?'

Marcie laughed. Mystery trips were what old folk went on, piling onto coaches starting their journey in Sheerness and ending up at a pub in Minster. She knew Roberto's mystery trip wouldn't be like that. It would be exciting, just as he was exciting.

'Wonderful,' she squealed clapping her hands together. 'Oh my God! What shall I wear?'

'Come as you are.' His eyes scraped her from head to toe. She was wearing ice-blue jeans and a black polo-neck sweater – casual wear – and black ankle boots with elastic inserts to make pulling them on that much easier.

The Maserati roared out of London heading south.

'Is this the Brighton Road?' she asked, her throat full of laughter as she considered how lucky she was to have him.

'Do you want it to be the Brighton Road?'

'Yes. Why not?'

He didn't confirm one way or the other– not that it mattered that much. The sun was shining and Roberto was back to being his old self. He was pampering her and it made her feel good.

'Are you going home again next weekend?' It was the question she was dreading. She was torn and rightly so.

'I'd like to.'

'I would prefer you not to. I would like to take you away to a hotel.'

'Just the two of us?'

So far he'd not progressed from kissing her good-night. Going away together so suddenly was a total surprise.

'Of course just the two of us. Who else would be with us?'

Nervously she fingered the ring he'd given her. It weighed heavily on her finger just as her guilt weighed heavily on her mind.

'This is a bit sudden,' she said breathlessly. Despite her nervousness she managed a fleeting smile. 'Why now?'

The road was clear. The countryside was a vibrant green.

His hands were firm on the wheel. A road clear of traffic gave him the chance to look at her. 'I get the impression that there's someone else in your life, someone you love more than me. Am I guessing right?'

'Of course not! Whatever made you think that?'

She pretended that the passing scene – high hedges hiding the fields behind them – were in some way interesting. She didn't want him to see the look on her face. She wasn't that good at lying.

He shrugged. 'You're attractive. Perhaps I'm not passionate enough for you.'

'Whatever made you think that?'

'I only kiss you.'

'I thought that...'

Her voice trailed off. She didn't know what she thought. Yet again she'd got herself entangled with a man who she presumed respected her. Alan Taylor had been kind to her. She'd thought his attention fatherly. It had turned out to be far from the case.

'Never mind what you thought!'

Marcie fell into silence. The nervousness she'd felt earlier was coming back big time. There was something about his manner that made her feel uneasy. He was sitting stiffly, the knuckles of his fists white with the intensity of his grip on the steering wheel. Silently he stared straight ahead as he drove.

After a few more miles he spoke to her. 'Nice around here, don't you think? A bit secluded perhaps. We could get out and make love in the grass. I think we will.'

He swerved the car into a narrow side lane. The high hedges gave way to leafy glades, copses intersected by wooden stiles and tumbling stone walls.

He finally stopped where the road widened into mud and gravel.

'Roberto!' She was suddenly scared.

The car stalled and Roberto grabbed her.

He showed none of the affection she'd been used to, heaving himself onto her, tearing at her clothes as his mouth sought her lips, her neck and the swell of her bosom.

'Roberto—'

He clamped his hand over her mouth, his eyes staring wildly into hers.

'Silence! I don't want you to say anything. Right?' The hand across her mouth slowly loosened as she stared at him in round-eyed horror. Assuming she would remain silent, he removed his hand and kissed her hard and long. At the same time his hand travelled to her jeans, tearing at the brass stud at the waistband, then the zip, then forcing his hand down into her pants.

Suddenly he removed his lips from hers and she came up for air.

'No! Roberto!'

The slap stung. She touched her cheek with her hand thinking he might have broken her jaw or at least a tooth.

'Just shut the fuck up! Right?'

He held a warning finger in front of her face. His eyes were blazing.

Marcie was terrified. It was as though there was another being living inside him. Why had he changed?

He came round to her side of the car and dragged her out by her hair. She screamed.

'You're hurting me!'

'Dirty bitch!'

He hit her again. The force of the blow sent her falling into the muddied ruts where other cars had stopped. He fell on top of her, pressing her into it.

He reached into the mud and smeared it over her face. She shrieked with fear, closed her eyes and spit dirt from her mouth.

'Roberto! Stop!'

Muddy water seeped through her clothes the whole length of her body. Roberto tore her jumper out of her jeans and scooped her breasts out of her brassiere cups. He tore at her jeans that were now soaking and plastered with mud. Her bare flesh was now as filthy as her face.

Marcie bit her lip. She refused to cry. She would not scream. She couldn't quite believe this was happening to her again.

*Go outside yourself.*

Her eyes flickered open. There was no one else around. She hadn't expected there to be.

*Pretend you're not here.*

She closed her eyes and ceased struggling. She had one thought above all others in her head: she mustn't die. For Joanna's sake, she must not die! She would do as the voice told her, lying there like a log, letting him have her body though her mind was elsewhere. Not responding. Not giving him anything.

Roberto rutted into her, his mouth sucking cruelly at her nipples and all the time he revelled at the fact that she was lying in the mud, filthy and getting filthier with every thrust of his body.

Just for a moment she returned to her physical presence. 'Roberto, please stop.' She tried to reason with him. 'We're getting dirty.'

'It's where you should be. In the dirt.'

*Come with me.*

Her mind went back to where it had been, floating above the trees, smelling the spring buds, watching the birds feeding their young. Below her she could see herself, lying as though she were dead; Roberto might just as well have been screwing a log. She wasn't with him.

And then it was over.

She blinked and there he was standing there peeing into a puddle between her feet. Seeing her looking at him, he kicked at her foot.

'Cover yourself up. You look disgusting.'

She looked down at her bare body, somewhat surprised to find herself back in it. She covered herself up and looked at him.

He was leaning against the car, looking to where the sun threw dappled shadows among the trees.

On seeing she was dressed, he flicked a lighted cigarette into the grass.

'Get in!'

He jerked his chin at the car. He'd draped a tartan blanket over the passenger seat so she wouldn't muddy his seat.

Marcie sat in it mutely. She was numb. She was angry and considered insisting they go to the nearest police station, but she was also wary. Roberto's charm hid something darker and more dangerous and it was better to go floating above the trees than be buried beneath them.

What had changed to make him do this?

Her thoughts went back to that other time when she'd woken up at Alan Taylor's place. This time she was fully aware of what happened.

She was on the edge of hysteria, but would not give in.

*Get a grip.*

The command seemed to come from out of nowhere and yet it seemed so real, so relevant.

*You won't get pregnant.*

The voice was probably right. She wasn't yet on the pill but she'd only just finished her period. Her heart raced, her blood pounding in her head. But she held on to her self-control. She would not break down.

Deep in thought, she failed at first to notice the signposts or the fact that the road was familiar to her. Only once in her life had she taken this road. It was a road and surroundings that still sometimes surfaced in her dreams.

Roberto spoke. 'Recognise where you are?'

Her eyes alighted reluctantly on places she'd thought never to see again. The spread of fields as she remembered them was suddenly interrupted. A window frame factory graced one side of the

240

road, an alien presence of mauve brick and angular lines, a latecomer but a sign of things to come. The entrance to a quarry swept dustily away through iron posts on the other.

Pilemarsh Abbey came into view, unchanged and solid.

She had a great urge to pinch herself in case she was still asleep and dreaming of things past.

Roberto brought the car to a halt in the gateway that she sometimes saw in her dreams. The gates had been changed. In the past they'd been wooden like those of a prison. The inmates had not been able to see out and nobody had been able to see in unless the gates were open. The gates were now of wrought ironwork. She had an unobstructed view. Nothing else had changed; the pristine crispness of rustling poplars and the blank windows of the house beyond, the drive, the paths and the grass blown into waves by a brisk breeze.

Built by a wealthy merchant in some past century and bearing more than a passing resemblance to the factories he'd owned, the house had three main floors besides the attic accommodation in the roof. There were eighteen windows on the top floor, the same on the first floor, some square, some embellished with a gothic point formed of red and yellow bricks. A wide front door graced on either side with Dorian columns of shining white alabaster broke the line of windows on the ground floor.

Eighteen windows! She took a deep breath, trying hard to keep a grip on reality, to remain in the here and now and not to let the past take over. It was so easy to drift back and feel that the

241

time in between had never happened. Trivialities invaded her thoughts. Had she subconsciously arrived at that total of windows or had she counted them off on her fingers in the same way that a prisoner etches marks in stone?

The scene was little changed. A crocodile of coach-built Pedigree prams – probably the very same ones she and her friends had used – were ranged along the gravel path in front of the ground-floor windows. Just as in her time here they were caparisoned with cream-coloured canopies, their fringes fluttering with each breath of wind, and yet shabbier now. Some were lopsided, as though the metal spokes holding them up had broken or bent.

Her attention was drawn to a man sweeping fallen leaves from around the legs of the metal bench circling the trunk of an oak tree, raking them to him like a reaper gathering an abundant harvest. Yet it wasn't leaves she was seeing him gather; neither was it a harvest of oats, wheat or rye, but something else, something much more precious. They'd harvested children in this place; taken them from their natural mothers and passed them to adoptive parents.

The sound of her heartbeat thudded in her ears, drowning out whatever it was Roberto was saying to her. The tone of his voice was all she needed to hear to know he was not using sweet words but using the bad words that men use when they want to make a woman feel bad – feel like nothing.

The house, Sally and Allegra, the religious texts on the walls, the echo of girls' voices and babies' cries – like a railway station halfway through a journey, the girls lives going one way, their babies in another. Except for her. She'd been lucky in that respect. She had something to thank Alan Taylor for.

She saw the house as it was now and as it had been. The frowning façade had changed little; frozen in time, just as she was, just as she had been the time before and that first day at Pilemarsh Abbey and the days that came after.

The old memories lay like slate epaulettes on each shoulder, and so did the lies born of fear. Roberto was shaking her, shouting at her that she'd lied to him, that she'd had a baby out of wedlock and therefore she was a whore, a slut, a low-down tart.

She stared into the face of the man she'd thought she loved. Where there had been charm there was now only ugliness, but compared to his looks what he was saying was a lot uglier.

'OK, it seems I got the wrong end of the stick, thanks to your old man. But I'm willing to let bygones be bygones. Now here's the deal: you get rid of the kid and we're still in business. Right?'

She looked at him unblinking. He made no mention of the fact that he had just attacked her. He could not surely believe that she had consented to what he had done?

He shook her. 'Did you hear me? Get rid of the kid!'

The anger welled up inside her. Anger at his unwanted attentions but also at his cavalier attitude that everything could be forgotten as long as she did the unthinkable.

'She is not a puppy or an unwanted present.

She's my daughter! My little girl. Her father got killed before we were married. I'm not a tart or a whore. I really didn't know about your parents' plans – not at first – or I should have been more honest. But there it is. It's too late now.'

His expression was as hard as stone, his eyes cold as lead. 'It could still work if you don't visit her again. Leave her with your grandmother. She sounds capable enough.'

Marcie stared at him. 'No!'

'Not even for me?'

He sounded hurt, but she didn't care.

Dictated by her emotions, her words were delivered with a quiet but firm deliberation. 'I will not give up my child for you or anyone. It doesn't matter what you do to me. Rape me again and roll me in the mud all you like. Hit me or call me all the names you can think of, but it won't make a scrap of difference. Joanna comes first. And that's that!'

His dark eyes seemed to turn darker and she sensed rather than saw his jaw clench. Would he hit her again? She didn't know. She didn't care. She only knew that the job that had seemed so promising was now less so. She had to leave Daisy Chain. She had to move out from beneath the Camilleri's roof.

The journey back to London was more silent than the one to Pilemarsh.

Just as they entered the suburbs he said, 'You wanted it as much as me. You love me. You'll come round to the idea.' He sounded as though he'd made the decision for her.

Her jaw was aching, reminding her how violent

he could become if she didn't behave as he wanted her to. She didn't reply but pondered how well the day had started out and how badly it had ended. All the way back she sensed his anger simmering beneath the surface. She asked herself why she hadn't seen it before.

He dropped her at the entrance to the apartment block where his parents lived.

'Change your dirty clothes,' he said to her with an air of contempt. 'And fix your face. You look a mess.'

He drove off then. She knew without him telling her that he'd be in touch, picking up where they'd left off and presuming she'd fall in with his plans. Roberto was used to getting his own way.

She hurried past the commissionaire. 'We went walking in the country. I slipped and fell in the mud,' she added blithely.

He nodded and smiled but there lingered a look in his eye. *I'll believe you, millions wouldn't.*

She was only thankful that nobody would be at home. The Camilleris were away for the weekend visiting relatives. She wouldn't want them seeing her like this and to have to explain – or lie.

## Chapter Twenty-eight

Once inside the apartment, she lay her head back against the front door and closed her eyes. The mud was drying and her body ached, especially where Roberto had hit her.

She closed the door to the flat softly behind her not wishing to be heard.

She listened but heard only the sound of her own breathing.

'Bastard!' she exclaimed through gritted teeth. A shadow moved in a doorway. She heard the unmistakable sound of a footstep.

Michael came out of Victor's office with some paperwork in his hand. Michael had an intense way of looking at people. It was hard to hide behind a mask, harder still to look away.

'Are you OK? What happened?'

She used the same excuse she'd made to the commissionaire. 'I slipped and fell into some mud.'

'And hit your cheek?' His tone was as gentle as his expression.

She raised her hand to cover the redness, though the gesture in itself was useless; he'd already seen the damage, the red marks of palm and fingers imprinted on her cheek.

'I need to take a bath.'

She headed off past him and down the hallway, aware of her bedraggled appearance blinking back at her from the ornate Italian mirrors Gabriella had installed at regular intervals.

First she went to her bedroom to collect her robe and some fresh clothes. The penthouse apartment had two bathrooms; hers was the smaller one close to her room. She needed a hot bath to ease her aching body. And she was scared – dead scared. She didn't want to be pregnant. Was it true that a hot bath taken straight after sex would wash the sperm away?

Sinking into the hot water she closed her eyes. It had been a long time since she'd prayed, but she certainly did so now.

Michael had disappeared by the time she came out. The hallway was empty. Her moment of relief was short lived. Michael reappeared.

'I take it my half-brother has shown his true colours,' he said to her.

Marcie felt her face reddening. Lowering her eyes she tugged nervously at her hair.

'Your brother was under the wrong impression about me. I suppose you are too.' Her voice was soft.

Michael frowned. 'I hope not.'

She placed the coolness of her fingers onto her temples. Her head was beginning to ache. 'Perhaps.'

'I am not like Roberto,' he said on seeing the wary look in her eyes. 'You know you were brought here as a bride?'

'So I'm beginning to understand. How crazy.'

She stumbled a little. Michael caught her. Firmly but gently he took hold of her arm and guided her into the spacious drawing room. The chairs and settees were modern and unfussy. Pride of place went to a grand piano on which sat an array of silver-framed family photographs.

Michael sat her down and poured her a brandy. 'Drink this.'

She looked into the dark liquid and was immediately reminded of another time when drink had been offered by Alan Taylor.

'It's not drugged,' he said, as if reading her mind.

She detected the hint of a smile playing around his lips, though it was guarded. His grey eyes were serious though gentle. His whole manner was persuasive and not at all intimidating.

The fiery liquid burned at the back of her mouth but did nothing to lessen the clarity of her thinking.

'Roberto found out about my baby. It must have been Rita, I guess. It seems that my father – thinking it in my interests – gave your father and brother the impression that I was an untouched virgin. A submissive wife for their beloved son. How ridiculous is that!'

She swallowed more of the fiery liquid.

Michael gave a strained laugh. 'Ridiculous.'

'You think so?' He was saying she was not submissive. She liked that.

'Come on. This is the girl who threatened to call the police when she thought a bloke she didn't know refused to pay for a dress.' He was grinning. She guessed he was trying to cheer her up. And she certainly needed that.

Marcie laughed as she too recalled their first encounter.

'Roberto was so sure of himself.'

'And I was surly.'

'Any particular reason?'

'My brother – correction – my half-brother's behaviour. He gets me like that. And you.'

'My behaviour makes you surly?'

He looked down at his drink. 'I thought you were gorgeous. I also thought I didn't have a chance.'

'And the flowers? You picked them yourself.'

His expression turned sheepish. 'I stole them. From a garden just along from my flat. I put a pound note in the old dear's door though. I knew I shouldn't, especially with what my father had planned for you. But I couldn't resist making the gesture.'

The fact that he'd actually paid for the stolen flowers was not entirely surprising. Michael harboured an innate sense of right and wrong. It was touching, even endearing.

'I'm certainly learning who to trust in London. And on Sheppey for that matter.'

It was all becoming clear. Rita had told Roberto everything, had probably even insinuated that Joanna was Alan Taylor's child.

Michael sighed deeply and cupped his own drink with both hands as he sat down beside her.

'So let me guess, Roberto wanted you to forget about your kid if you wanted to continue the relationship with him.'

'Yes.'

Michael rested his head against the back of the sofa, his eyes closed.

'You were the lucky one. He thinks you should be grateful to be chosen by him. Not like the other girls. They're taken on for a totally different reason.'

Marcie frowned, 'You mean Carol and April.'

The veins on his neck blossomed like spring twigs when he jerked his head in a tight nod. 'Them. And others.'

'They're taken on to serve in the shop.'

He shook his head. 'No. Can you dance?'

Marcie shrugged. It seemed an odd question.

'Yes. I suppose so.'

'And you look good and people – men in particular – find you attractive. You don't speak badly either. Some girls have to have elocution lessons their accents are so bad.'

Marcie kept staring at the side of his head. 'Tell me.'

At long last he sighed and looked sidelong at her.

'The girls taken on in the sewing room and the shop are usually less than twenty years old with absent or negligent parents. And, as I've already told you, they're always beautiful. My father makes the rules and his wife, Gabriella, carries out his wishes. She's Sicilian. That's all she's required to do. After a while, once they've been assessed...'

Marcie felt a cold chill trickling down her back like melting ice. The girls were brought in to do more than sew. They were being groomed to entertain.

'First they dance in one of our strip clubs and then they are introduced to rich patrons. It's only unsullied girls they want, not cheap prostitutes. The girls don't do so badly I suppose. Their "sponsors" set them up in expensive apartments with plenty of money. But once you're in ... well ... it's difficult to get out. And in return for your good fortune, my father expects feedback. These rich geezers are in the know in business and banking. My father makes the most of the information. He likes to have a foot in both markets – legal and illegal. Get it?'

'So why are you telling me all this?'

He seemed to muse on that, his grey eyes looking straight into hers then down into his glass.

He raised his eyes again. His look was intense and totally unassuming. It was like being caressed without being touched.

'Because I'm not my father's son,' he said. 'I'm not like him at all. I can't change him or stop what he's doing – I've tried. So instead I've decided to go back to my studies and strike out on my own. Strictly legit. I'm going into commercial property – buying shops and letting them out. I only came here to collect my things. Take care, Marcie Brooks. If you want to take my advice, get out while you can. The bright lights of London aren't all they're cracked up to be.'

The next morning she smouldered with anger one minute and despair the next. What was it with men?

In the early hours of Sunday morning she was lying awake, staring into the darkness and numb with fear. By Sunday evening her fear had turned to a simmering anger which came to a head half-way through Monday morning. Ostensibly she was going out for doughnuts to have with their mid-morning coffee in the sewing room. Instead of finding herself queued up in the cake shop, she found herself standing in line at the local nick. The police sergeant behind the desk had slicked back grey hair and watery blue eyes. He also had a line of people waiting for attention. The queue gradually shuffled forwards but only slowly. When it came to the turn of the woman in front of her, she began to get cold feet.

'I've lost my Henry,' she said in a high-pitched voice, the sort that sounded as though she was perpetually hysterical.

'Right, madam,' said the sergeant after licking the end of his pencil. 'And your husband's full name?'

'My husband? Archibald Lester Framlingham.'

The sergeant turned his watery eyes on her. 'I thought you said his name's Henry.'

'Not my husband. My cat. Henry's my cat and he's gone missing. He ran out when the coalman came through the passage with a hundredweight of nutty slack on his back. Henry's not used to going out you see...'

Normally Marcie would have listened enthralled and amused for the next instalment, but her mind was elsewhere. She could still feel the wet mud soaking through her clothes, and still had the bruises on her inner thighs. Roberto had not been gentle. Far from it.

Her eyes darted around the gloomy police reception noting the curling corners of posters warning about thieves and fuzzy photos on wanted posters.

The door opened and let in the brighter light of day from outside. Suddenly she wanted to be out there and not telling some stranger what had happened to her.

'Yes, miss?' The sergeant with the watery blue eyes was looking straight at her, pencil impatiently poised, ready to write down details of her and her problem.

She felt as though her knees had turned to jelly

and that she wanted to stuff her hands even deeper into the big patch pockets of her Crombie jacket.

'I...'

'Yes?'

She swallowed. She couldn't do this – or could she? Roberto had raped her. The best place for him was prison – the louse, the rotten, snotty louse!

'Miss?'

She glanced over her shoulder. The queue had vaporised like morning mist. The only person in the waiting room was the old lady wanting the police to find her cat.

*You were raped.*

'A man ... he ... um...'

The sergeant eyed the long legs exposed by her ultra-short mini-skirt, made a swift assessment then sighed and put down his pencil. 'I don't have all day to waste on young women just popping in to kill time. Do you want to make a statement or what?'

His manner was brusque. She felt herself reddening.

'What will happen to him if I say he ... that a man took advantage of me?'

Wispy grey eyebrows rose towards his hairline and wrinkles as deep as a ploughed field waved across his forehead. He exhaled a blast of onion-scented breath as though he didn't really want to bother with this.

'The boyfriend was it? You were kissing and canoodling as young folk do. You gave him the come on signals and then cried wolf when he responded.'

'No! That isn't what happened at all.'

She was appalled, not least because the door to the outside had swung open a few times to admit more people, more customers for the sergeant to take note of and dismiss. The people were arguing amongst themselves and appeared to be making complaints against each other. They were also wearing carnations and looked as though they'd been to a wedding.

'She's been jilted,' a woman in a flowery dress shouted in the direction of the sergeant. The younger woman beside her exploded into floods of tears.

Marcie ogled the scene, finding something of amusement but also pathos and sympathy. The younger woman's dress strained over a five-month pregnancy.

She was pulled back to the task in hand by the sergeant behind the desk.

'Well,' he barked, 'are you going to make a complaint against your boyfriend or are you going to kiss and make up? In which case don't waste my time. I've got more important things to do than dealing with young girls who can't keep their knickers on! If you didn't wear such a short skirt these things wouldn't happen.'

Cheeks ablaze, Marcie fled.

Even the outside air wasn't enough to cool her hot face or dry the tears that stung her eyes. How could she have been so bloody stupid! No matter how she'd worded it, she would carry the can.

*You went for a drive in his car? Just the two of you? He'd found out that you had a child out of wedlock. Well, then what do you expect with a reputation like*

254

*you've got?*

She wanted to run away. She didn't want to go back to work. She didn't want to go back to living with the Camilleris or with her father.

What are the options, she asked herself. In her mind she ticked them off just like her grandmother ticked off the items on a shopping list.

First, the Isle of Sheppey. No. It wasn't possible, neither for herself nor for Joanna. Rita Taylor would not let it drop, shouting the odds with her foul mouth and her nasty accusations. The rotten cow would always be a nuisance both to herself and her daughter. She was also missing her baby. Joanna too must leave Sheppey, but where would they go? Finding accommodation that would take children in London was almost impossible, especially for someone who didn't know the city that well. So who did she know here who did know the city? The only people besides her father were the two girls she'd met at a home for unmarried mothers.

The rest of the afternoon in the sewing room felt hot and oppressive. Every so often she looked up at the battery-operated clock ticking away on the wall. The seconds passed like minutes, the minutes like hours.

Gabriella asked her what was wrong.

'Just a bit of a headache,' she said with a tight smile.

'I won't be home this evening,' Gabriella Camilleri said to her. 'Victor and I have a church function to attend. The bishop is visiting and we've been invited to meet him.'

Marcie was relieved that she would have the flat

255

to herself. She prayed that Roberto wouldn't come round once he knew his parents weren't there.

When the doorbell rang she jumped a mile. She opened it to find Michael was standing there.

'I won't come in. I only wanted to ask if you were OK.'

He looked thoughtful, almost plaintive, as though he was in some way responsible for what his half-brother had done to her.

'Roberto,' she said, her eyes flickering along the hallway behind him.

His smile was reassuring and warm. 'He's down at Limehouse as the guest of a Chinese gambling club. They want protection. He's arranging it.'

Marcie knew that the only protection the Chinese required was from the Camilleris. They paid, they got protected; in other words the Camilleris and their stooges didn't go in and break up the joint.

She sighed with relief and found herself saying, 'Look, I'm truly grateful for you being such a good friend, and I would invite you in, but not tonight. There's something I've got to do and besides, quite frankly I'd prefer to be alone.'

His smile wasn't so bright. 'A friend. Well, I suppose that's a start. But I'd like to be more than that – when you're ready. If you ever are ready that is.' He'd been leaning against the door jamb, but now he straightened up, resigned that he had to leave. 'So I'll leave you in peace.'

After he'd gone she recalled his sad smile but hardened her heart to it. He'd been kind to her and she had time for him. However, she wasn't

256

yet ready for anything else, even though it did occur to her to ask him to help her find accommodation and a job – one that paid well. He'd probably direct her towards a nightclub. Most of the girls who earned good money danced half naked in one of the Camilleris clubs.

It was tempting, but she didn't feel she wanted to do that. There had to be something else. So at least for now she'd pass on asking for his help. So that night she wrote once again to both Sally and Allegra and hoped and prayed that this time one of them would write back.


## Chapter Twenty-nine

Rosa Brooks clutched at her black patent handbag with both hands and took as shallow breaths as possible. She disliked hospitals at the best of times; there were good intentions in such places but also a certain emptiness like that left behind when souls have flown.

Rather than leave Joanna with Babs, who was becoming surlier and scruffier than ever nowadays, she'd left the toddler with her next-door neighbour, a grandmother who couldn't stop loving children.

No one else was likely to visit Garth Davies except her. He had no family, no home and no friends except the ones he'd made at number ten, Endeavour Terrace.

The strong smell of carbolic persisted from the

very moment she'd entered the front door of the mental hospital where Garth was incarcerated. Cared for was not the right word for it she'd decided even before she'd got here. Such institutions as this were little more than prisons with their heavy doors, their high ceilings and windows that were barred from the inside.

A nurse dressed in a dark-blue dress and a small white cap asked her if she was a relative. She lied and said she was his great-aunt, the only family he had left in the whole world.

The clumpy heels of her stout walking shoes thudded on polished brown floors and echoed off walls that were painted dark green to shoulder level then eau de nil the rest of the way.

The windows had wire-enforced panes so far up; the light came in but nobody could look out.

'Garth? You have a visitor.'

Garth's face lit up like a Christmas tree. 'Auntie Rosa!'

Rosa gasped. 'What's that he's wearing?'

The fact was she knew exactly what it was. Garth was wearing a thickly padded jacket with belts and buckles. His arms were pinned to his sides, hugging himself in an embrace it was impossible to escape.

'It's a straitjacket,' said the nurse, her plump hands folded in front of her.

'I know what it is,' snapped Rosa, fixing the ruddy-hued face with sharp, disproving eyes. 'Garth is not dangerous. Why is he wearing it?'

'It's for his own good.'

'Then you will explain to me *why* it is for his own good?'

The nurse took a deep breath and held it – almost as though she is trying to look bigger than what she is, Rosa thought to herself. Her sharp-eyed look was unrelenting. The nurse caved in and released Garth from the restraining jacket.

'He's escaped a number of times. We're afraid he may do himself an injury. Pull this if you need to,' said the nurse, pointing to an antiquated bell pull with a cast-iron handle.

Without more ado, the door was closed. Rosa took in the sparse details of the room. There were four chairs and a table. Garth was seated opposite her on the other side of the table. There were no pictures on the walls and no curtains at the one and only window. Luckily it appeared to face north so she did not have to suffer bright sunlight in her eyes. However, the room was cold. It almost made her envy Garth's warm jacket, but only to a point.

The only other thing to lighten their dour surroundings was someone humming the 'Londonderry Air' – 'Danny Boy'. Rosa found it soothing and it helped her concentrate.

'Garth, they tell me you've been trying to escape.' She kept her voice low, almost as though she were afraid that the walls might have ears. It felt that way: this place of cold surfaces and strange echoes.

Garth's eyes were as bright as ever. 'I didn't like it here, but I'm alright now. This jacket's warm. Do you like it?'

It wasn't often that Rosa Brooks was lost for words, but she most certainly was now. She had to remind herself that Garth was a simple soul who'd faced some pretty grim knocks in his short life. He'd been used to being neglected. Attention of any kind was a bonus as far as he was concerned.

'Have you been pretending to run away because you were cold, Garth?'

He nodded and giggled until he dribbled. Rosa leaned across and wiped at the drool with her handkerchief. She shivered and hugged her coat around herself.

'It is certainly very cold in here. I think I might do the same if I was here very long.'

Garth nodded vigorously. 'Pretend you're going to escape and you'll get a jacket too, Auntie Rosa.'

It was hard not to smile, but Garth's simple logic also saddened her.

'I do not think they want me to stay, Garth, otherwise I might very well do the same as you. That was a very good idea. I have brought you food.'

She smiled and took out the bag of food she'd brought with her: home-made pasties, pies and cakes.

'It wasn't my idea,' he said, drooling afresh as he set eyes on the home-cooked fare, his nose twitching like a hamster. 'It was Albert. He told me to do it.'

He took the pasty to his mouth then devoured it at a rapid rate so that crumbs flew everywhere.

'This Albert. Does he try to escape too?' she asked cautiously.

Garth shook his head, sending a shower of crumbs down the straitjacket, over her black coat and over the table. He chomped a while before he could answer properly and even then a shower of crumbs came with it. Garth's teeth were uneven, his upper jaw overshot so he couldn't help it.

'Albert's been here for ages. It's his home. He doesn't want to go. Not now after all this time. But he does know how to get out because he built this place. That's what he told me. He was a master builder.'

Rosa sighed as Garth recounted the tales of this Albert character who she presumed was another inmate. The poor soul might have been a builder but he'd have to be very old by now if he'd ever had a hand in building this place. The stone carving above the entrance said '1833'.

'Perhaps Albert would like to share this food with you,' offered Rosa.

Garth looked puzzled. 'I don't know.'

Rosa raised her eyebrows in pretend dismay. 'You mean he will not like my cooking?'

Garth's frown deepened. He turned suddenly and looked over his shoulder at the right-hand corner behind him. 'Albert, would you like a pie? My Auntie Rosa brought them for me, but you can have one if you like.'

During the half-minute Garth turned, his attention fixed on the right-hand corner of the room, the humming stopped. It resumed the moment Garth turned round again, his face wreathed in smiles.

'Albert says he doesn't need to eat anything any more. That means he don't need to go to the toilet either. That's good isn't it, Auntie Rosa – not having to eat and not having to go to the toilet?'

He laughed, not really knowing what he was saying, but having fun saying it. But Rosa knew, she heard the humming. Garth heard the humming, but not everyone did and not everyone would believe, she told herself – which could be catastrophic for this poor boy.

There was a chance Garth could be released once those in authority gave him leave. She'd offered him a home. Everything was in place, but if they thought he was hearing voices he could be in here for ever.

She leaned forwards, her dark eyes bright with intent, hypnotically gazing into his.

'Garth! Listen to me. You must not tell anyone here about Albert. Promise me. He must remain a secret. Only you and I must know that he's the one who told you to escape. I don't think you should pretend to do that again just so they give you a padded jacket. Here. Have my coat.'

It was her best coat and a woman's coat, but she'd decided Garth must never feel cold here. If he kept up this pretence of escaping they'd likely keep him in longer. She decided to have a word in the right ear on her way out.

'Tell no one?' he asked with childlike innocence.

'No one,' said Rosa. 'Do you promise?'

He nodded. 'I promise.'

The humming stopped once she was outside the door. It would still be there for Garth. Only the gifted could hear such a sweet sound. She'd hear it again herself on the next occasion she came to visit.

## Chapter Thirty

When Sally Saunders opened her eyes, she found herself face to face – or rather face to sparkle – with the latest present her lover had bought her: a cuff rather than a bracelet, two-inches thick and composed of top-quality diamonds. She knew they were top quality because Klaus was a Swiss banker of great wealth and taste. He never bought anything that wasn't top quality. 'Just like me,' she'd said to him, and he'd agreed. Neither of them were under any illusion that his wealth had bought her too.

Sally had classic good looks, her nose just a little too large and straight to call pretty. Her hair was fair, helped to a more glamorous blonde by the attentions of a skilled – and expensive – hairdresser.

Stretching out her arms to either side of her, she trailed her fingertips over the spot where the warmth of her lover's body remained and smiled. He was gone but the diamonds remained, as ever a girl's best friend. But he'd be back. He'd look after her. That was why she'd chosen him.

'Madam?'

As usual, Anne Marie had entered without knocking. A tall thin woman, she wore black with as much elegance as a mannequin wearing a Dior gown. She entered at the same time every morning and always used that same, questioning way of addressing her mistress as though she were querying whether the term was acceptable.

Out of habit, Sally adopted the same questioning tone back. 'Anne Marie? How do you always know when I am awake?'

Anne Marie's expression remained business-like. 'That is my job.'

She set the breakfast tray on the side table just as she did every morning. Fruit juice, coffee and a sliced apple with prunes, plus a single rose in a silver holder. It never varied and was always only picked at. Sally had no intention of letting the years eat into her figure too soon. She had made that mistake before – though not through food. Over a year had passed since she'd given away the baby boy she'd given birth to at Pilemarsh Abbey. She harboured a morbid fear of getting fat and unattractive. She'd been wooed, pampered and undressed by some of the wealthiest men in the world. There would be more in the future. There must always be a future.

'Your post, Madam.'

Anne Marie pulled back the curtains and fluffed up her pillows so her employer could sit up and deal with her mail.

Sally glanced at the letters. One of them had been sent on from her old address. Her sister wrote occasionally, but only when family commitments warranted a diversion from the norm. She had half a dozen children and they filled her life. Asking what her sister was up to was like dipping into a gossipy magazine – it brightened her days. But I'm sure I gave her my new address, she thought with an irritable frown.

Raising herself more comfortably against the puffed-up pillows, she peered sidelong at the handwriting. There was nothing familiar about it. She frowned and racked her brains, hoping it wasn't Klaus's wife finally waking up to the fact that her husband didn't take as many business trips as he told her and knew Soho better than he did Stuttgart or wherever else he was doing business.

'I will run your bath?' said Anne Marie without waiting for an answer. No reply was called for. Running the bath was a routine task.

The sound of water splashing into the brilliant white enamel came from the bathroom, Anne Marie becoming immersed in clouds of steam.

Sally ripped open the envelope and unfolded the letter within. As she began to read, she reached for her coffee cup and brought it halfway to her lips.

She paused...

The words danced before her eyes. She reached out to place the cup back on the tray without taking her eyes from the letter. The cup crashed to the floor as the address on the heading caught her eye.

Anne Marie, immersed in steam and the gushing of the bathwater, did not hear.

Sally fell back upon her pillows and stared into space before making a swift decision, swinging her legs out of bed and heading for the bathroom.

'Add some cold,' she ordered Anne Marie. 'I'm in a hurry. I need to make a phone call. And get me some writing paper.'

She picked up the diamond bracelet, twirling it

between her fingers and thumb before throwing it onto the bed. Did diamonds matter more than friends? On this occasion they did, but she couldn't *not* reply. She had no choice but to brush Marcie off – at least for now, until she'd spoken to Allegra.

*My dear Marcie,*

*It was a great surprise to receive your letter. I can't imagine how you got my address, but I was pleased to hear from you.*

*You know me, footloose and fancy free. The past is the past and although I'd like to strangle the rotter who got me in that state (please note how restrained I am with my language nowadays) I really feel it's all in the past and doesn't matter much – at least to me.*

*I'm having fun: men falling at my feet and drinking champagne out of my shoe. You know how it is. I am and for ever will be the blonde bombshell and realise now that I never was cut out to be a mother, so it's just as well that I never dedicated myself to the task.*

*Anyway, I must go. I've been invited to a friend's villa on the Riviera. We'll have a great time if past parties are anything to go by.*

*Toodle pip until we speak again,*
*Sally*

*PS. Please note the change of address.*

Marcie read the letter for a second time. Sally had told her to contact her and now she was brushing her off. Sally's response was very disappointing and not at all what she'd been led to believe from her first letter. But there, people change and perhaps Sally was now in a situation where it would be very detrimental if her past came to light.

'I know the feeling well,' she whispered to herself.

The other women in the sewing room were trickling into work. Two of them were new arrivals, closer to her age and pretty. They were both excited because they'd been told they were to receive training in the shop on the King's Road. They would be well-paid shop assistants, Mrs Camilleri had told them.

She'd carefully avoided looking at Marcie when she said this. There was a nervous fluttering to her hands, which disappeared once she was dealing with the older seamstresses: two ladies well into their forties who wore spectacles and kept pin cushions dangling from a ribbon around their necks.

Marcie knew she was being selfish, but her brush with Roberto was still raw so she didn't dare tell the two girls what she knew. She wanted to get out of here and she wanted a place to bring Joanna. The two girls would have to look out for themselves just as she would have to.

She was running up a seam in a royal-blue dress with long sleeves and a row of gilt buttons down the front when Mrs Camilleri approached her wearing a very tight expression on her face.

'Marcie, I have a favour to ask you. A valued client wishes someone to come around to alter a dress. As you know I usually attend to valued clients myself, but on this occasion I feel myself indisposed. This woman does not usually ask for a seamstress to come round to her and she has particularly asked for you.'

'Oh.' Marcie was flattered. She'd enjoyed working in the shop and meeting people. One of the customers had remembered her. 'I must have impressed somebody. Unless you would prefer to go,' she suggested knowing that Gabriella tended to take care of home visits.

'No,' said Gabriella Camilleri a little too sharply. 'You go. I do not wish to.'

The sharpness of her tone was unusually pronounced, almost as though she feared the client or at least was in awe of her.

It did cross Marcie's mind that she was being sent there for something other than an alteration. Was Roberto on the end of this, waiting for her in a private flat? He hadn't come looking for her. He hadn't phoned the shop to ask her out. A block of ice seemed to slither down her back. Roberto could make his mother do anything. It wouldn't surprise her if he was waiting at the address, ready to rape her again and to make her feel bad.

Marcie glanced pointedly in the direction of the two older women bent like rusty hairpins over their whirring sewing machines.

Mrs Camilleri saw her glance there. 'Mavis and Betty are very busy.'

There was something not right about this; Gabriella's lips were being sucked clean of apricot-coloured lipstick and overall she looked ill composed.

'This is the address.'

Marcie took the card, barely glancing at the address, but glad to be getting out.

On the way out she cut through the shop. Daisy Chain was busy, thronging with schoolgirls who'd skived off from school, young women with time on their hands, and dishy Chelsea girls who wouldn't dream of landing a job when they had rich fathers to indulge their whims and shower them with money.

'A Whiter Shade of Pale' by Procul Harum was playing over the music system. Pale pouting lips sang the odd lyrics as though they made total sense.

A supply of felt hats with big brims was getting rapt attention from leggy blondes and brunettes wearing hip-skimming skirts and knee-high boots. The hats came in only two colours: black or purple. A new line in sunglasses had also come in. Marcie tried a pair on. They half hid her face.

'Like bumble bees' eyes,' someone said to her.

She smiled at that.

'James Bond if you wear the hat with it,' said a girl called Sandy who'd taken Carol's place when she'd left.

The phone rang, startling Marcie from her thoughts. Sandy answered it, blushed into the receiver then put her hand over it. 'It's for you,' she said to Marcie. 'It's lover boy,' she whispered.

At first she was going to refuse to take the call. On reflection she decided it would be better if she did take it. If she didn't answer he might come round here after her. She didn't want that. She was making plans and wanted to be out of here before he came round.

She curled her fingernails into her palm before taking the call. 'Hello?'

'Miss me?'

He sounded as though nothing had happened. She couldn't believe his arrogance, but until things were sorted out she couldn't afford to face his anger again.

'What do you think?' she replied as cheerily as she could fake.

'You love me!'

'Not now,' she murmured, holding her hand over the receiver so he couldn't hear. 'What do you think?'

She heard him laugh. 'You couldn't survive without me, babe. We're a team. If we weren't I would have had that ring back off you by now.'

She fingered the ring. It had occurred to her to chuck it, but something stopped her.

'So where are you?'

'Round and about. Keeping my eye on you.'

The menace in his voice sent fresh shivers down her spine.

'Do you want these?' Sandy asked after she'd put down the receiver.

Marcie was still quaking with fear. Roberto could be anywhere, looking for her, watching to see what she was up to. She made a swift decision. 'I'll take them both. Can you put them on my account?'

Sandy said that of course she could. That was the other reason why working for Daisy Chain was a real plum of a job. There were so many wonderful perks. Nobody else paid like Daisy Chain. She knew now she should have questioned that. But it was too late and time was running out. She had to make plans – and fast.

The apartment was situated in an exclusive lot adjacent to an upmarket hotel. On showing the business card to the commissionaire, he directed her to the lift and told her that she wanted the third floor.

'Miss Montillado should be there. I've just showed up another visitor.'

He was cheery and put her at ease, so the name he mentioned didn't sink in at first. Not until she was standing in front of apartment number ninety-eight did the bells start ringing in her head. With a sudden start of realisation she glanced down at the card.

Miss Allegra Montillado.

'Allegra!'

The elegant young woman looked as ecstatic as she felt herself.

'Allegra?' she said again, just in case she was mistaken.

Allegra's eyes shone. Her hair gleamed and she wore pearls around her neck and in her ears. They looked expensive. Everything about Allegra was expensive.

'Marcie! It is you.'

Her smile was jaw-breakingly wide and her welcome was genuine. The two girls threw their arms around each other.

'You smell wonderful,' Marcie remarked on being first to break their embrace.

'French perfume,' said Allegra. A true thorough-bred, her skin gleamed like a well-groomed and well-cared-for horse. She opened the door a bit wider. 'I've given the maid the day off because I knew you were coming.'

Marcie was going to ask why, but the interior of the apartment was opulent enough to strike her dumb. Everything was white: the carpet, the curtains, the furniture – all except the cushions that were a soft shade of jade velvet. A large plate-glass window seemed to take up half of one wall. Through it she could see the roofs of Edwardian townhouses, apartment buildings and chimney tops stretching like a bumpy forest floor to a misted horizon. A grand piano obscured a portion of the view, though not too significantly.

A leopard-skin coat was draped over the back of the settee together with a black chiffon scarf.

Marcie remembered what the doorman had said about Allegra having had another visitor. She began to apologise for the intrusion. 'Look, I really need to talk to you, but if it's inconvenient I can come back another time. We could make a date, have coffee or something...'

Her words poured out like a mountain torrent. She just couldn't stop them. Meeting Allegra again made her so excited.

Allegra shook her head and ordered her to stop. 'There's no need for you to go.'

'Marcie!'

An internal door had opened. The woman standing there was blonde, curvy and very familiar.

'Sally!' Marcie stared then frowned. 'But I thought ... that bloody letter you sent me. You brushed me off.'

Allegra and Sally – two unlikely friends if their past association was anything to go by – exchanged looks.

'There were good reasons to do that,' said Sally. Marcie winced at the force with which Sally hugged her. 'Let's talk about it over the delicious refreshments Allie's provided.'

A bottle of champagne sat unopened on the teak coffee table. Next to it were three glasses and a box of chocolates from Harrods. Next to that a bowl of strawberries.

'I'll do the honours,' said Allegra, proceeding to open the bottle.

Marcie was speechless.

Sally winked. 'Beats gassing over a cup of tea any day!'

Marcie had to agree with her.

The three old friends toasted each other, Sally suggesting that they dunk a chocolate in their drink as a thoroughly unique way of toasting the pregnant – and rather fat – girls they had been. They were now sleek, upmarket young women. Nobody argued with that, although Marcie didn't regard herself as anything like upmarket. She was still as she was; her main residence the old cottage where her Maltese grandmother lived. The chocolates were gorgeous and so was the champagne.

Marcie was desperate to ask Sally why the negative letter, but Sally and Allegra were aching to ask something more important.

'So how's the nipper? Growing up as gorgeous as her mum is she?'

Sally said it so flippantly, with her face wreathed in smiles as though it really didn't matter to her

273

one way or another. Her eyes said otherwise. It *did* matter. It mattered very much.

Wary of rubbing an old wound raw, Marcie was careful with what she said.

'She's toddling now and knows a few words. It isn't easy being a single mum, but I manage.'

Alan Taylor had told the staff at Pilemarsh that he was her father, so at least she didn't have to explain anything about him – especially about the fact that he was dead. Or so she thought.

As they reminisced about Pilemarsh, discussing the staff and the surroundings rather than the sadness of giving their babies away, Marcie wondered at the change in herself and Sally. They were all well dressed, especially Allegra who always had had exquisite taste. Her dress was charcoal grey, the deep V neckline enhanced with a white collar. The dress had matching cuffs and her dark hair was cut into a fashionable shoulder-length bob. She was the most elegantly beautiful woman Marcie had ever met in her life.

Sally's appearance also shouted of money but differently. Her clothes clung to her curvaceous figure, the neckline cut to display a deep décolletage. What looked like real diamonds flashed in her ears and a single diamond sparkled from the gold collar around her neck.

She saw Marcie looking and grinned in her old wicked way. 'Would you believe me if I said it was from Woolworths?'

Marcie shook her head. 'No.'

Sally threw back her head and laughed, 'Too bloody right it isn't! Christian Dior would throw himself in the bloody Thames if you'd said that!'

Christian Dior! And solid gold by the looks of it.

'A friend bought it,' Sally said in a quieter voice.

Obviously a man, thought Marcie. It was difficult to read the look in her eyes, but she sensed that Sally was still touchy about her class and her morals.

'Good for you,' she said, raising her glass. 'Now perhaps you'll explain the letter.'

Again a look passed between the attractive young women sitting opposite her. She sensed there was some secret they were sharing.

'You tell her,' said Sally. 'It was your idea.'

Allegra cleared her throat. 'You're working for Daisy Chain and living under the Camilleri's roof. They're very good at helping young girls settle in London, but they don't do it entirely out of the goodness of their hearts. Gradually they take over the girls' lives and also take a great deal of their income. They also open your mail.'

'I've already been told that.'

'Blimey! Aren't you the cool one.' Sally poured herself another drink.

'Aren't you afraid?' asked Allegra.

Marcie had been looking into what remained of her champagne, twirling the stem between her finger and thumb. 'Only of Roberto Camilleri,' she said, raising her eyes.

'Ah!'

'I already know what goes on and that's why I wrote to you two. I need to get away from them, but I don't know where to go. I've no friends here. You're the only people I know in London

275

besides my dad – and I don't really want to live with him. Besides, I need to get Joanna away from the Isle of Sheppey.'

She didn't enlighten them with the list of reasons for all this, though she recounted them in her mind.

Number one, she had to get beyond Rita Taylor and her bad mouthing about Alan's death – just in case.

Number two, she had to get away from Roberto and from the future planned for her by the Camilleris.

Number three, she might very likely kill her father if she saw him. What the hell was he thinking of taking her to a place like that and telling them such a pack of lies? Just wait till he showed his face! But that was by the way. There were more important things to consider.

'I want to stay in London. I want to bring Joanna here, but I'll need a place to stay and a way of earning a living.' She looked from one old acquaintance to the other. 'Are there any openings in the jobs you two do?'

Sally burst out laughing. 'Our jobs! Now there's a thing.'

Allegra shifted in her seat, unfolding one elegant leg from across the other. It wasn't correct to think that Allegra looked slightly flustered but there was a hint of embarrassment.

'More champagne?' asked Allegra.

Marcie shook her head and brushed away a crease on her skirt.

'I like your outfit,' said Allegra, pointedly eyeing the royal-blue blouse and checked hipster mini-skirt Marcie was wearing. 'Whose design is it?'

'Mine. I designed it and made it. Daisy Chain took me on for my design and sewing skills – anyway, that's what they told me. Of course, I know better now.'

Allegra nodded. Her arms were folded on her knees. Her dark lashes swept her cheeks and she appeared to be contemplating the chocolates though Marcie noticed she'd only eaten one, nibbling at it like a mouse. Her fingers dipped into the strawberries.

'I was shocked when I saw the return address on the letterhead of the first letter and then the second,' Allegra said suddenly. 'I take it no one knew you wrote to me?'

Marcie thought she saw fear in her lovely eyes. Now what would someone like Allegra have to fear from the Camilleris?

Marcie shook her head. 'No. I posted the letters myself.'

Allegra seemed relieved.

'So that bloke who collected you from Pile-marsh – he wasn't your father, was he.'

Sally's statement – it certainly wasn't a question – came out of the blue.

Sally grinned. 'I can see by your face that you're surprised at what we know. But there, we're part of the city scene. We know what goes on. Anyway, we know that Tony Brooks is your old man – right-hand man to Victor Camilleri. Ain't that so, Allegra?'

For a split second Marcie thought she saw another flicker of embarrassment flush Allegra's serene expression.

'So I understand,' Allegra said hurriedly. 'Now let me get this straight,' she said, determinedly changing the subject. 'You want to move to London and bring your daughter with you.'

'That's right.' Marcie was resolute in her manner.

'And you don't want to earn a living lying flat on your back,' said Sally. One corner of her mouth upturned with amusement.

'No!'

'And you're good at what you do – designing and sewing.'

Allegra got up, folded her arms and began pacing the room as she put Marcie's requirements into some order.

'How would you like your own sewing room and designing certain items for a very...' She paused. Marcie waited. '...specialised market.'

'Specialised?'

Thoughts of making overalls for factories or hemming sheets for hospitals were the first things that crossed her mind. None of them appealed; she'd had enough of hemming sheets at the hospital.

'Look,' she said rising to her feet. 'Working for someone else isn't going to make me much money, certainly not enough to take care of Joanna. *And* I'm going to need a nanny to look after her if I'm working in a factory or hospital. Even then that depends on whether they'll have me. They're not keen on hiring married women with children let alone unmarried.'

'How about being your own boss?' Allegra's smile lit up the room.

Marcie frowned. 'What are you suggesting?'

The stunning, elegant woman who had amazed both Marcie and Sally with her manner and her wonderful wardrobe when they'd first met crossed the room, opened up a shiny radiogram and put on a record.

Marcie was puzzled. Placing fists on hips, she was about to ask what Allegra was playing at when Sally began to dance. Not rock and roll or the twist or the shake, but something sexy and languorous to the tune of 'The Stripper'!

She watched in amazement as Sally peeled off her dress, sliding a strap down her arm, teasingly bringing it back up again before peeling it down her bare arm.

At the same time she peeled the dress from her body then kicked it to one side.

Wearing only her underwear, she danced around the room, her hips swaying from side to side, her hands caressing her bare flesh.

She was wearing a lacy bra, scanty panties, a suspender belt and stockings rather than tights. Men preferred stockings. Roberto had told Marcie that in the days before he'd found out the truth about her.

The underwear was nothing like anything she'd ever seen; the colours vibrant, the materials lacy, silky and beautifully stitched.

She watched in amazement as Sally undulated to the music, acting coy one minute and wanton the next. Carefully, so as not to snag it with her long, lacquered fingernails, she slid one of her stockings down over her thigh, her knee then her calf until she finally pulled it over her painted toes.

Bump went one hip one way, and a second stocking was off. Hunching a shoulder, off came one bra strap. Hunching the other shoulder off came the other. Curving her hands over her breasts, fingers meeting, a quick flick, and her bra was off, twirled and went flying at the window.

Marcie gasped in amazement.

A silky tassel hung from each nipple.

'Twirl them,' shouted Allegra, clapping her hands in delight.

Sally did just that.

Marcie found herself shrieking with laughter. Like Allegra she began clapping in time with the music while Sally went on stripping.

Bump went her other hip in one direction and the strings holding her panties on that hip were untied. Bump went her hip in the other direction, and that set of strings was also undone.

Accompanied with a brazen shout of 'They're off,' Sally whipped off the two small triangles that made up her underwear and danced with them over her head. Only a slender sheath of silk remained and covered very little.

'Dah, dah, de dah dah, de dah, de dah, dah!'

They'd all joined in with the last line of the music, dancing around the room with her. They finally all fell into a heap on the settee, still laughing, enjoying the precious moment of being together again as much as they did the music.

It was Allegra, always the serious one, who caught her breath first.

'So,' she said, getting herself into a sitting position. 'Do you think you can make outfits for exotic dancers!'

Sally butted in looking very serious and pointing at herself. 'I should warn you before-hand that not all of us are as overdressed as this.'

Marcie knew when she was being wound up. 'I don't do birthday suits. I can never get the buttons to match – even though there's only one of them.'

Their laughter just wouldn't be held in.

At last they lay there, breathless and replete, warmly glad they were back in good company, three girls who'd been through difficult times together.

'So what did you mean when you said I should go self-employed?' Marcie asked.

Allegra sat up straight. 'We're basically talking theatrical costumes. They cost a fortune and a lot of work goes into them. I know it's not the stuff you see on the catwalk, but getting to be a designer in a fashion house can take for ever. And you have to have done an art school course.'

Allegra maintained a serious expression as she laid it on the line. Marcie knew very well that what she was saying made good sense. Unless she had some kind of qualification from a college she hadn't a cat in hell's chance of making her way in the world of fashion.

'This way, making the items that girls like Sally need, it means you would make money from the very start. They don't give a damn what qualifications you've got as long as you can do the job.'

Marcie's mind was racing. This was hardly the stuff she wanted to make, but if it meant that she and Joanna could live together what did it matter?

However, there were reservations. Nothing

could be that easy.

'How would I sell these things? I wouldn't have to have a shop would I? I mean, stuff like that isn't sold in shops, is it?'

Allegra bubbled with laughter and Sally guffawed like a trooper before attempting to explain.

'No need to worry about that! No, you won't need a shop. All you need are contacts, and we've got those. Isn't that right, Allie?'

Allegra nodded. 'Yes. We know an agent who acts for the girls and can give you the orders. You don't even have to go out looking for them yourself. All you have to do is design and make. The dancers will be put in touch with you and will tell you what they want. How good is that?'

Never in her wildest dreams had Marcie ever considered making what Allegra was talking about. Theatrical costumes! Yes, she was a dedicated follower of fashion, but what her old friend had just said made sense. She had to make a living – fast. Still, she had to make sure.

'Would I make enough to live on?'

'You bet, sweet child!' laughed Sally who was busily retrieving her clothes with gay abandon and unashamed nudity, the cheeks of her bottom tilted up and shiny.

Marcie felt a wave of excitement course through her veins.

'Where would I live?'

'We know just the premises. The shop on the ground floor is let out. You would have the work-room above that and the flat at the top of the building,' said Allegra. 'And Joanna wouldn't be neglected. You wouldn't be doing all the work yourself. You would employ some people. Besides, you have two willing nannies who would drop in when they could.'

She exchanged a bemused smile with Sally.

Bubbling with excitement Marcie shook her head in disbelief. She felt all warm and gooey inside. London had seemed a lonely place until she'd been reunited with these two – except for Roberto, but then that was at an end. It was just that Roberto wouldn't accept it as fact. But he had to, he really had to.

'If I didn't know better I would think you two have been planning this for some time,' she said brightly.

Their exchange of looks was surreptitious but undeniable.

'We talked about it before you arrived,' said Sally. 'You don't think I put on impromptu shows like that for just anybody do you?'

Marcie bit her lip as she thought of the most difficult task connected with their scheme. 'The only thing I'm worried about is taking Joanna away from my grandmother.'

'We didn't say it would be easy,' said Sally. 'But hell's bells, it's your kid first and last, ain't it?'

She had to concede that. Joanna came first and she wanted her child with her.

'A mother should be with her child,' she said softly and wondered if her mother would have stayed if things had been different, if she'd had good friends to help her out.

'This workroom and this flat above it. You seem very familiar with it, as though you've set everything up ready for me.'

The two of them beamed at her like a pair of Cheshire cats.

'Just say we're your fairy godmothers,' said Sally.

Everything seemed so wonderful and Marcie felt she was riding along to a better future – until an obvious question came to her.

'Wait a minute! Wait a minute! Landlords want some kind of bond up front for a workshop *or* a flat. I'm going to need both. Now excuse me right now, but I don't have that kind of money.'

'I do,' said Allegra.

'And I can help out,' added Sally. 'So no more arguments. You pack your things and get out.'

Marcie was wise enough to know there was no point in giving the Camilleris notice that she was leaving. In any case, she had to avoid Roberto. He wasn't taking no for an answer and he wouldn't want her leaving without his express permission. If he caught up with her she could get worse treatment than last time.

'OK,' she said, her stomach knotting with nerves as she nodded her head. 'Show me this place and we'll take it from there.'


## Chapter Thirty-one

Babs had dumped the kids on a neighbour and caught the morning train to London. She was livid. Never mind that her old man had sent her some dosh in the form of postal orders, she felt murderous. There was only one reason why he hadn't come home as far as she was concerned. He had a bit of stuff on the side!

Well, she'd sort him out good and proper! And his bit of stuff too. Probably some blonde tart with sparrow-like legs and tits the size of barrage balloons, she thought, as she marched to the station, her wobbly bits held in place with an armour-plated corset.

Her dark thoughts stayed with her all the way to London and kept her company as she hurried along the station platform, fists stuffed into her reefer jacket pockets. A pink plastic bag with multicoloured polka dots smacked like a satchel against her side.

First she'd go round to his place and if he wasn't there, she'd go round to see that bloke he was working for – Victor Camilleri. If she could get hold of his address that is.

The underground was packed but she put up with it, finally alighting in the heart of gangster-land.

The East End stunk of old bricks and stale beer with a touch of rotting vegetables thrown in. Oh, and the gas works. They were pretty grim too, but nothing, no smell, no hell and high water was going to prevent Mrs Barbara Brooks from giving her old man what for.

The swine hadn't been home for weeks and she'd had enough of his excuses. If she couldn't find him she'd find Marcie; yes, she thought to herself, me and Marcie are chums now, ain't we? Marcie will tell me what he's up to.

Her father wasn't around to come to her rescue and move her out. There was no one at home in the basic bedsit he lived in and the woman downstairs said he didn't always come home at night. It was no big surprise. Her father was easily led astray by lame dogs, blonde tarts and horses that never finished the Derby, let alone winning it.

She determined she'd do it alone and tell him when she caught up with him.

They say that lightning never strikes in the same place twice, but in her case it did. Once again she'd thought to sneak into her room and this time sneak out again with all her belongings. Once again there was Michael dealing with his father's paperwork.

Brown suitcase at her side, she leaned against the wall and purposely looked away from him then back again.

'Are you following me?' Her expression accused him.

He gave her a surprised and slightly amused look. 'Should I be?'

'I thought you were leaving here to work for yourself.'

'I am. I called into Daisy Chain to see you. I wanted to ask you to dinner. I didn't know you were leaving.'

'Don't tell anyone. Please.'

He was standing with his hands in the pockets of his Levi Strauss jeans, white shirt open at the neck, sleeves rolled up exposing tanned skin, and his head held to one side. He looked insulted but also quizzical.

'Of course I won't. I think it's the best thing

you can do. I'll give you a lift.'

He reached for her suitcase. She stared at him. She hadn't really given Michael that much attention in the past, perhaps because on the first occasion she'd seen him he'd been dwarfed by his half-brother's overpoweringly charming presence. On closer inspection she now saw there was gentleness in his eyes that his brother did not have. Neither did Michael show signs of Roberto's macho arrogance.

'Do you have a place to go to?' he asked.

She nodded, her lips seeming to be glued together. Just fear of course. She didn't want to jeopardise her plans.

'Do you need a lift there? I'm still offering. If you want one.'

She had been planning to get the bus. Her funds didn't stretch to a taxi. The plan was to move her things into the flat then catch the train to Sheppey to collect Joanna. She hadn't allowed for anyone discovering her here and she certainly hadn't intended leaving a forwarding address.

'I won't tell anyone where I dropped you,' he added when she still couldn't seem to find her tongue.

She raised fear-filled eyes to his face. 'Do you promise?'

He took hold of her case. 'You and me both. We're both finished here, I think.'

'Are you in a hurry to get there?' Michael asked her on the way to Balham.

She looked at him for clarification, determined that no man was ever going to lead her up the garden path again. She was getting older. She was getting tougher.

'Don't look at me like that. I am *not* the Big Bad Wolf! I just thought we could have a coffee perhaps in lieu of dinner. Would you?'

Michael was *asking* her rather than telling her like Roberto would have done. She decided to accept his invitation.

'Though I can't stay long. I have to catch a train.'

They stopped in a small Italian coffee house where each cup of coffee was percolated in a hissing, steaming machine with gleaming chrome handles.

They took a table by the window. Michael spooned two sugars into his coffee. Marcie abstained. They both sipped before speaking.

'Roberto is still phoning you?'

She nodded. 'I keep telling him I don't want to see him again, but he phones and when that doesn't get him anywhere he comes round to see his parents. He brings me flowers and insists I go out with him. I keep telling him no and he keeps telling me that I'll come round to his way of thinking. Just forget my daughter and everything will suit him fine. I tell him I cannot do that.'

Michael took another spoonful of sugar and stirred thoughtfully at his coffee. She wondered if he always took so much sugar, or was he thinking too deeply to notice he was repeating himself?

'He thinks you are like the rest of the girls; you all want a good-looking boyfriend and lots of money. Most of the girls are quite happy with him and even happy to be passed on to someone else.' His eyes flashed up from the coffee to her face. 'I have to tell you right now that your father did not plan for this. My father took you in as a favour, not for the same reasons as the other girls who work for him at all. I thought you should know that. I think you would be quite safe from that career – unless you particularly want to go in that direction.'

'No, I do not.'

So the Camilleris really had been doing her a big favour. She began to relax. Michael had most certainly eased her anger with her father, but she couldn't bear staying there. She had to slip away, purely to avoid Roberto.

They began talking of their families; he told her about his mother and that she too had been an unmarried mother. 'Her parents, my grand-parents, threatened to have her put into an asylum if she didn't have me adopted. But she stuck to her guns. Luckily Victor supplied the maintenance. Her parents never forgave her and never spoke to her again.'

Marcie told him about Joanna and Johnnie. She also told him about her grandmother and how special she was.

'She knows things before they happen,' she told him. 'She says it's my grandfather telling her these things. My grandfather is dead, but she still talks to him. Do you think that's mad?'

He shrugged. 'Why should it be? We pray in church and believe someone dead is listening to us, so what's the difference?'

She could see his point, though such a state-ment would probably turn Father Justin's face deep purple.

'You're smiling,' he said to her. 'It's nice to see you smile. You don't smile often enough.'

'Don't I?'

She couldn't help being surprised, but on further reflection she realised he was right. Back at home in Sheppey she smiled a lot more than she did in London. The only exception was when she'd renewed her acquaintance with Sally and Allegra. She hadn't laughed so much for ages.

'You must miss your baby a lot.'

She trailed her spoon around the circumference of the coffee, making peaks of the foamy surface.

'I do. I think that's why I don't smile too much.'

'You're bringing her to London?'

'How did you guess?'

'There's a sparkle in your eyes as though you're looking forward to something very special.'

Marcie found herself relaxing in his company. Michael Jones – Jones was his mother's name; he'd never accepted the name Camilleri – was easy to confide in. She found herself telling him a lot of things including the fact that her father hadn't been home to see her stepmother and her half-brothers and half-sister for weeks.

'He sends her money but that's hardly the same. She's certain he's got another woman.'

Michael frowned. 'I hadn't heard as such, but there, if a bloke wants to keep a bird a secret from his wife, it's best he keeps her a secret from everyone.'

She told him he was probably right

'Look,' he said after a moment of thoughtful

introspection, 'how about you let me take you down to collect your kid and bring you back again? You're going to have a lot of stuff to bring with you. Am I right or am I right?'

She told him he was right but that she didn't have a problem with that. 'A girlfriend is giving me a lift.'

She didn't say who that girlfriend was and that she took her clothes off for a living.

The flat was above a shop in Balham. The shop sold cheap trophies for darts leagues and Sunday football leagues. Marcie was being rented a room at the back.

'It's wonderful,' she said, head back in order to better see the Victorian cornice running all round the room.

'I thought it would suit,' said a smug-looking Allegra.

'Suit? You bet it does.'

Marcie was over the moon. The flat had two bedrooms, a living room, a kitchen and its own bathroom. Recently refurbished, the walls were painted in fashionable magnolia and the carpet was equally fashionable and brown. It wasn't large but it was hers and it was smart.

She presumed Allegra owned it. 'How can I ever repay you?' she said to her.

'Think nothing of it,' returned Allegra.

It was left to Marcie and Sally to deal with the furnishings: curtains of a geometric mustard and brown design, a G-Plan three-piece suite, plus matching sideboard. There was a double bed and two wardrobes for the bedroom and a small dining set for the kitchen with metal legs and a Formica top.

'Great! I'll make the tea,' said Marcie as they both paused to take a breath.

'I'll make the toast,' said Sally.

'I haven't got a toaster.'

'Never mind. I'll use the gas grill.'

Over tea and toast Marcie asked Sally how she'd become an exotic dancer.

'Carla,' she said before biting into a second piece of toast.

'Is she one of the Camilleris?' asked Marcie, eyeing Sally warily.

Sally laughed throatily, testament to her forty-a-day cigarette habit.

'Not bloody likely. They don't cross our Carla I can tell you.'

Marcie found it hard to imagine that the Sicilian men might be afraid of a woman. 'How come?'

'She's a hard nut is our Carla and clever with it. She's been known to supply good acts for night-clubs. She's the one they send for when their class acts don't turn out so classy. She furnishes them with top-quality girls who know how to move it around. Know what I mean?'

Marcie said that she thought she did. She noticed that Sally's eyes were sparkling, that she wanted to say more about this Carla person.

Sally winked. 'Don't think that men get all their own way when it comes to shady women and shady deals. Carla's boss can knock spots off some of them – so I've heard.'

'And she's a woman?'

'Oh yes, and I tell you what...'

Information regarding Carla and her boss had come pouring out of Sally's mouth. Now she clammed up, as though suddenly realising that she had said too much.

'Never mind all that,' she said cheerily. 'Tell me all about your baby again. Joanna? That's her name, isn't it?'

That night Marcie lay in her bed in the new home she would share with her daughter. Her life was seemingly dividing into two sections: there was her first home on the Isle of Sheppey and this home, the new home she would share with Joanna.

Her whole being tingled at the thought of bringing Joanna to live with her; Sheerness was home but London was exciting. She'd made good friends here and found a good career.

She giggled at the thought of what she would be making. Who would have thought it? She'd already decided to tell her grandmother that she was designing and making the same things she'd always made. Declaring the truth was not on.

## Chapter Thirty-two

Marcie wasn't willing to share the truth of what had happened and what she was up to – even with her father. She sensed he was going to have a go at her about leaving the place and position he'd found her.

'I'm working things so that I can have Joanna with me. If you see Gran before I do you can explain. Are you going home this weekend?'

Mentioning going home put a stop to questioning her reasons for leaving Daisy Chain, which led her to the inevitable conclusion that Babs was right: her father had another woman. There was nothing for it but to ask him outright.

'Who is she?'

Her sudden question took him unawares. He turned defensive.

'Don't you speak to your father like that, young lady! Show some respect.'

'Like you do for your wife?'

'Sod this,' he said and took off, slamming the door behind him. He came back in on realising that he was walking out of his own bedsit. Marcie had gone to visit him.

She looked around the squalid room, searching for evidence of what he was up to. The place was usually a tip, though it looked as though he'd at least made an effort to improve matters. His clothes were hanging over the back of a chair rather than in a wardrobe, but even that was an improvement. They were usually strewn across the floor.

He was in a foul mood.

'Get out of here.' He did the pointing at the door thing, as though she were the fallen woman being turned out into the snow. She almost laughed at the comparison. Where was that stuff coming from?

'I'm going.'

'Ungrateful little cow. That's what you are. I got you a decent job and this is all the thanks I get.'

Marcie paused. She was about to say that he'd made things difficult for her but the Camilleris and Roberto were hopefully in the past. Whoever asked in the future she would tell the truth. She was a single mother working hard to make a place for her kid in a difficult world. If it wasn't for her grandmother, she didn't know what she'd do.

Thinking of kids made her think of her half brothers and sister. She felt sorry for them, but her stepmother was not her favourite person. Babs wasn't exactly wicked in a *Snow White and the Seven Dwarfs* kind of way, but not that likeable either.

Reminding her father about his commitments and his family on the Isle of Sheppey didn't do her ego much good either. She was missing Joanna and feeling guilty about not having her in London. Two weekends had passed without a visit. She couldn't hold it off for much longer, but she was desperate to get her business off the ground and was working night and day to get things going. She had so much to prove – both to herself, to those that loved her and to those that doubted her.

As her grandmother didn't have a telephone and the phone box on the corner was often occupied, Marcie phoned Father Justin O'Flanagan at the presbytery, which did have a telephone. He promised faithfully to take a message to her grandmother.

'But I will be home next weekend,' she added enthusiastically. 'So much has happened. I've got so much news.'

'I'm sure she'll be glad to know that, my child. Your grandmother has been worried about you and I'm sure your daughter misses you; mother and child should never be parted. And old folk should never be left on their own no matter if they do have the solace of our Blessed Virgin to keep them company.'

Marcie caught the condemnation in his voice and knew he was doing it purposely. He wanted her to feel bad about it. But she didn't feel bad. Was she selfish because she didn't feel bad? She was young and alive and had places to go in her life. The city she had not wished to come to had a buzz she could not get from her cold, damp home sitting on the edge of the North Sea.

'I'll be home soon.'

'I'll be up in London myself next week. Perhaps I could call in on you.'

'No.' Her mind worked frantically. The last thing she wanted was for Father Justin to see the outrageous garments being sewn up on her wonderful professional sewing machines. The machines had cost a fortune; she kept repeating this fact over and over to Allegra who merely brushed it aside saying that she would get her money back eventually. 'I shan't be around. I'm doing some research on current fashion. It helps me focus on what I should be designing.'

'Ah!' He sounded disappointed. 'Then I won't be bothering you. Shame though. I wouldn't have minded a chat over a cup of tea.'

Having to see his eyes over the rim of her tea-cup was something Marcie had every intention of avoiding.

Before he had a chance to try to persuade her, she pretended that she was in a phone box and her money was running out.

'I've got no more pennies, Father. I'd better go now before the pips sound. Tell my grandmother that I love her – and that I'll be down shortly.'

She brought her fingers down on the telephone cradle. Allegra had thought it a good idea for Marcie to have a phone in her flat. As far as business was concerned, it was. As far as phoning her family was concerned it was a dead loss; none of them had a phone.

'Look at this, Marcie, you've done me proud.'

Marcie had forgotten that one of her clients was trying on her new stage outfit. Eileen Palmer, whose stage name happened to be Madam Medusa, worked with a fifteen-foot python named Monty. She'd ordered a slinky outfit in silver lurex, the legs cut so high that the crotch looked likely to cut her loins in half.

'I look just like one of them Amazon warrior women,' she exclaimed in a thick Bermondsey accent as she twirled and posed in front of a full-length mirror.

Eileen's breasts swelled over cutaway bra cups as she stretched herself to full height on four-inch stiletto-heeled shoes. Her nipples peeped over the top of the low-cut cups like pink-eyed fledglings peering out of their nests.

'The blokes love it when my nipples poke out,' she said, eyeing them with outright satisfaction.

It occurred to Marcie that Eileen could only just about glimpse her areolae over the immense swell of her breasts.

'I bet the audience love that,' laughed Marcie.

'Bet your life they do, darling. They love to see Monty flicking his forked tongue over them. They think he's injecting a bit of poison and I'm going to fall down in naked agony.'

Marcie held in her amusement, until her eyes met Eileen's.

'Silly buggers,' said Eileen.

The two of them burst out laughing.

Barbara Brooks sat across from her mother-in-law with a devilish look in her eyes. For years the old cow had looked down her nose at her thinking she wasn't good enough for her son. Well now she was sure as hell going to give some back!

'She's black!' She spat the information out as though the taste of it was bitter on her tongue. 'Black!'

Not a flicker of resentment, shock or even disdain crossed her mother-in-law's face. Rosa Brooks was unmoved.

'Well!' Babs sat up dead straight with her head held high behind a pall of cigarette smoke. 'What do you think of your beloved son messing around with a black tart?'

Rosa's expression was inscrutable. 'My son will do the honourable thing. He will never leave you. You are his wife – until death.'

'Yes! His bloody death if he don't sort 'imself out!' Babs snorted, her whole body bristling with the indignation of the wronged wife – though goodness knows she was hardly a saint herself.

'You did not see Antonio to speak to yourself?'

'No. I did not. I just met this woman, this Ella!

That bloke Tony works with gave me her address. She's got two kids and lives in a slum. That's all I can describe it as – a bloody slum!'

Everything Babs was saying was being delivered at the top of her voice. Rosa was glad the cottage had thick stone walls and that the windows were closed. What happened within the family should be kept within the family.

'So how do you know that the woman is telling the truth?'

'Of course she's telling the truth!'

'She may just want it to be the truth,' offered Rosa, taking the kettle off the gas stove and using a little water to warm the pot. 'She may have set her cap at my Antonio without him realising it. Women can be very devious when they want something.'

There was meaning in her voice and in the swift uplifting of her dark eyes.

Babs was only momentarily deflated. She knew where Rosa was coming from. She'd angled her particular cap at Tony, determined to get him even though he hadn't exactly been free at the time. Yes, Mary had gone missing, but that hadn't meant they wouldn't get back together. It had been she who had persuaded Tony to divorce her on the grounds of desertion.

'She's his woman. I'm sure of it. Someone needs to find him and speak to him. I thought Marcie could.'

Babs hadn't said she'd like a cup of tea, but Rosa poured one anyway.

'Yes. Marcie could. But I do not think it would do any good. She is his daughter. He still thinks

299

of her as a child even though she is a young woman and a mother.'

'How about if you go up and speak to him?' Babs leaned forwards, the look on her face leaving Rosa in no doubt that this was what she'd come here for in the first place. She wanted her mother-in-law to talk to her son and make him see sense. It would hurt Rosa's pride to do so and Babe knew that. Rosa saw little wrong in her son because he was her son – her only son.

'No.'

'Huh! Well, that's typical. And you, always the one for the family and all that!'

Again Rosa turned those dark eyes on her daughter-in-law, fixing her with a hard, fiery glare.

'I will not go. I have Joanna to look after. I will ask Father O'Flanagan to go and speak with your husband. I will also ask him to take Marcie with him. Your husband loves one and respects the other.'

Babs was satisfied. She left Endeavour Terrace with a gloating look on her face. Getting Rosa Brooks to admit that her son wasn't bloody Prince Charming was, to some extent, an act of revenge for all the crap she'd put up with over the years.

*Do not swear in my house, Barbara.*

*Do not smoke in my sitting room, Barbara.*

*Do not read trashy magazines at my kitchen table, Barbara.*

*Close the garden gate after you, Barbara, or next door's dog will get in and foul my garden.*

Well sod it! She purposely left the garden gate swinging on its hinges and with a toss of her head made for home.

In her warm cosy kitchen, Rosa sat thoughtfully in one of the overstuffed armchairs to the side of the fireplace. Closing her eyes she let her thoughts drift towards the ceiling while her tea went cold on the table.

She didn't need to speak to Cyril out loud. The words were silently thought and Cyril responded. Not all the time. Sometimes he just didn't seem to be there. Atmospherics used to affect the radio transmissions of fighter aircraft during the war. When Rosa didn't get any response from Cyril she put it down to the same thing.

She decided to speak to Father O'Flanagan anyway, but wouldn't send him to check on Marcie. She'd seen the look in his eyes. He couldn't help it of course. The church ordained that priests should be celibate. Nature decreed otherwise. She'd send him direct to her son to remind him of his marriage vows – even though there had been occasions when Babs had failed to remember hers.

Marcie too had not been home these last two weekends. Rosa was scared. Was it a case of like father, like daughter? She hoped not. This week-end Marcie had promised to be home to see her and Joanna. She'd tried to persuade her to visit Garth, but Marcie had refused. She'd seen the look in her eyes. Nobody liked to visit asylums – even if they cared for the person incarcerated there.

Marcie rang the phone box at the end of the

street. Somebody fetched her grandmother. They exchanged the usual greetings. Marcie finally plucked up courage to ask what was on her mind.

'Gran...? I was wondering...'

She was wondering whether Rita had been around making a nuisance of herself or whether she'd heard of any gossip spreading about her and the night she'd met Alan Taylor on the beach. In her darkest moments she still wondered what might happen to her if anyone found out the truth about that night. It wasn't that she felt consumed by guilt at what she had done, more she worried about what would happen to her daughter if she were ever arrested. What if she ended up in prison, just as she was finally building a better life for her and her child? She swallowed hard and shut her eyes, finding a strange comfort behind her closed lids.

'What is it?' asked Rosa Brooks.

Marcie had second thoughts about asking. It wasn't fair to burden her grandmother with any more of her troubles.

'It doesn't matter,' she said and severed the connection. Let sleeping dogs lie.

A sliver of light showed between the curtains to Bob Wilson's room. The light caught on the gold chain twinkling among Bob's chest hairs. He was lying in bed smoking. Rita was lying beside him seemingly dead to the world, one heavy leg draped across his groin.

He gave her a nudge. 'Hey! Sleeping Beauty!'

She didn't make a sound which was unusual for her. Usually after they'd done the usual, they had a bit of shut-eye and she'd be snoring like a good 'un.

Easing his leg across the bed, he reached over to pour himself the last of the whisky. No more than an inch trickled from bottle to glass. They'd sunk the rest the night before. Rita had taken a few pills with hers. She'd offered him some, but he'd declined. He dealt with the stuff, made a packet from it, but he didn't indulge. Give him booze any day. Bob Wilson was no prat. He knew what was good for him. Whisky was good. Pills were something you took for a headache.

He tried again. 'Hey! You fat cow!'

Usually if he called her that she'd turn round and catch him a blinder around the kisser. But she didn't.

Her face was very still and very white. He touched her face. She felt like ice.

His blood turned cold. His face paled.

'What the fuck...?'

He looked closer and tried the procedures he'd seen on *Doctor Kildare* on the telly. No pulse. No breathing. It didn't take a doctor to know that she was dead.

Being a canny sort of guy, he knew what he had to do. He had to prepare some kind of defence. The cops would question the pills in her body so he had to come up with a reason for them being there, and he had a corker.

## Chapter Thirty-three

Just before going down to Sheppey to bring Joanna to London, Marcie nipped along to the King's Road to do some window-shopping. The exotic costume business had gone off with a bang, but she still had a yen to design dresses. Going along to the King's Road, gazing in the windows and fingering the rows of blouses, skirts, dresses and accessories were fodder for her own designs.

There was a risk in doing this, of course, though she reasoned that since she'd left Daisy Chain and the Camilleris, Roberto had no reason to visit his parents quite so much.

Even so she kept a sharp lookout and hid her features behind dark glasses and the broad-brimmed felt hat that she'd bought the last time she'd been in Daisy Chain. Her new dress was of a psychedelic design, swirls of purples and mauves diffusing into strawberry pink and pistachio green.

'Marcie? Is that you?'

The voice was familiar and took her by surprise. She presumed the worst. My God! Roberto?

She didn't wait to find out. Without looking back she hightailed it in the direction she'd come. *I'm not looking back!*

What good would it do if she did? A second less speed could make all the difference.

Out of breath and flustered, she caught a taxi for home. It occurred to her that he would follow.

304

His car was fast. The taxi did well to press its way through the midday traffic. On arriving home, she dashed up the metal stairs at the rear of the shop, pushed the key in the lock and fell through.

Once the door was closed, she lay against it, still panting but feeling safer.

*But you didn't actually see anyone.*

You didn't see anyone; you just heard him and set off like a frightened rabbit. Now how stupid was that?

Feeling silly now, she began to giggle. Running away because someone called to you! Silly cow!

Gradually her breathing abated, her panic subsided.

The footsteps were faint at first, no more than a slight clinking of leather on metal. Someone was outside. Someone was climbing the metal steps to her door.

Her breath caught in her throat. One metallic step followed another. She began to shiver at first.

*No! Stand up to him! It won't be the first bully you've stood up to.*

The voice was back again. The words seemed to come out of nowhere. They didn't seem to be inside her head. It was more as though someone or something unseen was whispering into her ear.

*It won't be the first bully you've stood up to.*

She remembered Bully Price threatening to torture Garth's pet cat if he didn't steal for him. And how she had finally dealt with Alan Taylor's unwanted advances.

The clanking of heavy shoes against metal was getting higher, coming closer.

*The best form of defence is attack.*

That whisper again. Was she hearing voices like her grandmother did? Whose voice? Her grandfather's? Her mother's? Or perhaps Johnnie's?

The idea that her mother was dead and helping her face Roberto caused Marcie to grit her teeth and swallow her fear.

She grabbed a heavy onyx vase from the table and raised her arm, ready to bring it down on Roberto's head.

Before he had chance to knock, she swung the door open.

She gasped. 'My God!'

Father Justin O'Flanagan flinched. 'No. Just his earthly representative. My word, Marcie. Am I that unwelcome?'

Marcie lowered the arm wielding the vase. Her grandmother would offer tea, so Marcie did the same.

'Your father hasn't been home much. His wife is irked to say the least.'

Marcie pulled a face. 'I bet she is.'

Barbara would be hell to deal with. She'd been bad enough the last time she'd seen her.

'I thought I'd go round and have a talk to him – man to man. Your stepmother seems to think he's got a lady friend – a black lady friend. I think she's one of these immigrants coming over from the West Indies. There's been hordes of them in the last twenty years since the end of the war. Barbara is very put out.'

Marcie almost smiled. She liked the thought of Barbara being put out. The smile didn't break through. If Barbara was put out, how must the boys be feeling? They worshipped their father.

They must be missing him and hurting bad inside.

The eyes that Marcie had likened to addled egg yolks scrutinised the living room of the flat.

'This is a very nice place you have here, Marcie. I went to the address your grandmother gave me, but they said you'd moved on. It was sheer chance that I happened to spot you and follow your cab.' His slack lips spread into a self-satisfied smirk. 'The hat and glasses threw me for a moment, but I still recognised you. It's about body shape you see. Everyone has a definite body shape; once I commit that body shape to memory I never fail to remember its basic structure.'

The words were slightly shocking coming from a priest but she gave away nothing of what she was thinking; she clenched her jaw and put up with it. The way he kept looking at her was making it very difficult not to wrap her arms around herself as though she were suddenly naked. But she didn't. Working and living in the city had made her harder. She could cope with the old devil and was even able to look into his yellow, devilish eyes.

It was Saturday afternoon so there was no sound from the sewing machines. The girls didn't work on Saturday afternoons. Thank God for that, thought Marcie. If Father Justin had heard machines he would have wanted to inspect the workshop. Even without the holy water to hand he would have resorted to tap water in order to give her venture a blessing. His eyes would pop out of his head when he saw the tiny G-strings and the exotic outfits she made. The last thing she wanted was him poking his nose around in there!

'So you run up these mini-dresses that all the young girls are wearing, do you not?'

'That's right,' she lied. 'I'm doing very well.'

'I would love to inspect them,' he said. 'To see your working operation so to speak.'

*I bet he would!*

The last thing she wanted was Father Justin inspecting a replica Victorian corset or a lustrous pair of panties with a narrow crotch and a spray of ostrich plumes sprouting out the back. He'd probably blow a fuse, or at least turn the colour of a turkey gizzard.

She was suitably apologetic. 'I'm sorry. I can't do that. One of the girls has gone home with the keys by mistake. I can't let you in there.'

His eyes dropped to the saucer and his fingers resting on its rim. He'd turned thoughtful, his mind going elsewhere.

'You know that Garth has been let out of the institution where he's been spending these last merry months? The police have dropped all charges.'

Marcie gasped. 'That's wonderful news! What happened?'

'The police found the real arsonist.'

'They did?' Marcie had to know more. 'So who did set fire to the shop? Do the police know who it was?'

There was something ominous about the way Father Justin O'Flanagan leaned forwards, almost as though the information he wished to impart was straight out of a James Bond novel, like Doctor No. She'd been to see the film. The shooting and chasing was all very well, but best of all she'd loved the bikini Ursula Andress had been wearing.

Father Justin took his time answering, supping the last of the tea before raising his eyes, and this he did only very slowly.

'Apparently the witness changed his story. He'd been lying to save his girlfriend, and didn't she get what she grossly deserved!' He crossed his broad chest. 'Mother of God forgive me. One shouldn't speak ill of the dead, but...' He shook his head and tutted like an old woman. 'I heard this only second hand, but it seems this girl wanted revenge on someone so set fire to the shop, and it might also be that she killed someone. Her father as it happens. Now isn't that a cruel and dreadful thing?'

Marcie sat very still, as though a frost had suddenly encapsulated her whole body and if she moved she would surely break. Father Justin did not need to state the name of the female perpetrator. Marcie knew it. Rita had set fire to Angie's Boutique. She'd lied to save her own skin, and what was that Father Justin had said?

*One should not speak ill of the dead. Rita was dead?*

'How did she die?' Her voice seemed far away, just like the past that she and Rita had shared.

'Drugs. Some kind of pills she was taking at the same time as drinking alcohol. That's what I heard. But terrible don't you think that she murdered her own father? That's what the witness states. Terrible,' he went on shaking his head. 'Just terrible.'

Marcie shook off the numbness she was feeling and asked the Catholic priest if he would like another cup of tea and a piece of fruitcake. As he'd already devoured two pieces of cake plus two cups of tea, he declined.

'Must think of the waistline,' he said jovially.

She considered it too late for that but did not say so. Father Justin O'Flanagan, she noticed, smelled of fruitcake on account of eating so much of it on his parish rounds. His belly was as round and firm as a fruitcake just fetched from the oven.

'So what have you come here for?' she asked him.

She noticed that her sudden enquiry seemed to throw him off balance. His mouth, which had opened merely to laugh or utter some inane comment, hung open before he regained his power of speech.

'Ah well. Time I was leaving. I'm off to see your father don't you know.'

Marcie nodded. 'Ah yes. My father hasn't been going home to see his lady wife. I wonder why? But there it's a man's world and a woman is not supposed to question either her husband or her father.'

Her sarcastic tone was not wasted on the priest.

'Now, now, Marcie. A little Christian charity if you please. Your stepmother has a point. Husband and wife. Those whom God have joined together let no man put asunder.'

*Or a motorcycle on the North Circular.*

Marcie wasn't sure whether the thought was her own or she was hearing things again. Too much work, she decided. At least having Joanna here will stop me from designing and sewing all the time. We can have some time to ourselves.

'Do I mention to your father that I found you?' he asked.

She thought about it. When she was younger and with fewer responsibilities she would have stuck to that first inclination. Now she felt more sure of herself, more able to cope with whatever-her father's opinion might be.

'Tell him,' she said. 'Tell him if he needs someone to talk to, I'm here. Tell him that.'

When Father Justin O'Flanagan got to his feet, he pressed one hand onto her shoulder, his fingers tightening in an ambiguous action that Marcie couldn't be sure of.

'You're a good daughter, Marcie Brooks. A good daughter to your father and a good daughter of Mother Church.'

'Thank you, Father.'

There was that hesitation again. 'I was wondering...' His hand resettled on her shoulder like a homing pigeon that didn't wish to leave.

'I was wondering if I could stay here for the night? I do have a bed booked at St Anne's with an old friend, but...'

Horrified at the thought of the old lecher sleeping close by, she tilted her head back and beamed up at him. 'I'm sorry, Father. I've got a date tonight. He's coming back here to sleep. With me.'

She got quickly to her feet. His hand dropped from her shoulder. His jaw dropped. She'd meant her comment to pull him up short and it had. A good girl would never admit to a priest that she was sleeping with someone. A good girl would hang on his every word and do everything he wanted her to do. There again, a good priest wouldn't touch a girl like he did or look at her the way he did.

The message was loud and clear. She was neither available nor malleable. The little girl she'd once been was growing up.

After he'd gone she bolted the door and didn't open it again until Michael came to take her to dinner.

Over a grilled steak accompanied with a bottle of Beaujolais, she told him what she'd said to the priest.

'That's my gate to heaven locked and bolted,' he said with a grin. 'Thanks to you I've got a black mark against my name for something I haven't done yet.'

She looked at him, her black lashes forming a frame around her blue eyes.

This message was loud and clear and had to be said. She missed being close to a man. Part of her also wanted to blot out her recent bad experience with Roberto too; she wanted to make love with a man because she wanted to not because he forced himself upon her. On Sally's advice she'd been to the clinic and had been furnished with a supply of birth control pills. At first she'd been hesitant. Life with her grandmother had moulded her into what she was, or at least what she had been.

Sally was more worldly wise.

'The Brook Clinic supplies so you don't have to keep your legs crossed,' she'd said in that flippant way of hers.

Perhaps wanting a physical relationship was

312

also part of growing up, though it had to be with someone she trusted. She'd thought of it all week and now, she judged, was the time to say it.

Placing her cutlery neatly on her plate, she said, 'It needn't be a lie, Michael. We could make it *not* be a lie.'

She kept her gaze lowered to her plate and the wine glass she reached for.

Michael sat silently across the other side of the table, hardly daring to breathe and fearing he'd misheard.

'You're asking me to sleep with you tonight?'

'Yes. The priest wouldn't approve of course...'

He laughed. 'OK. Let's go to hell together.'

Marcie shook her head. 'No. Heaven. That's where we'll be going. Let's go to heaven.'

## Chapter Thirty-four

Joanna settled in nicely and Marcie was glad that her grandmother would not be alone. Garth was with her.

She'd had a funny feeling on that visit that there were colourful auras surrounding the pair of them. It was an odd thing to see and the colours didn't always seem to be the same. Sometimes they seemed to blend in together, as though they were two sides of the same penny.

Roberto had not found out where she was and even if he did it seemed that Michael would be there to protect her. 'He doesn't bother to ask me. I don't count,' Michael told her.

Michael was always there for her. He wasn't the hip guy wearing the right clothes, the right hairstyle and driving the right sports car. Neither was he so brash and keen to project a 'look at me' impression the moment he stepped into a room.

Roberto's half-brother was more reserved, more thoughtful. She took him down to Sheerness and introduced him to her grandmother.

Marcie had watched her grandmother's reaction, noticing the searching black eyes that seemed to look directly into a person's soul.

'He too is Sicilian,' she said later, at a time when there was just the two of them.

Marcie had nodded. 'Yes.'

'He has kind eyes.'

It was all Marcie needed to hear to know her grandmother approved. And she wasn't often wrong. Michael cared for her. He cared for Joanna too. She could tell that by the way he joined in any game Joanna wanted to play.

The child was particularly keen on puzzles depicting animals and the alphabet. A is for ant and B is for bear was the usual mantra heard when Michael came visiting, the child having persuaded him to join her down on the floor, the puzzle spread out before them.

Word regarding the new designer and maker of exotic costume had spread like wildfire. Marcie had enough work in her order book to last for months. Most of the orders came through the mysterious Carla.

'She adds a bit on, of course,' Sally stated.

Marcie stayed up all night getting her portfolio

together. Sally had hovered over her shoulder like a critical parrot, advising her on what girls preferred and what the punters – the men who frequented the clubs – liked to see them wearing. Not much by the sound of it.

'Your fame's spread far and wide. Arbroath has heard of you and is coming to place an order,' Sally said.

'That's a funny name,' said Marcie.

Sally's face was wreathed in smiles and she looked to be on the verge of a giggling fit. 'Funny person,' she chuckled.

Arbroath turned out to be a man. He was at least six feet tall and had smooth gingery hair brushed back from his high forehead.

'I've brought the wig, hen, so we can see the full effect. Sally tells me you have a few samples that can be adjusted to suit individual requirements.'

The accent of the Gorbals in Glasgow had come south with him. The wig was a mass of shoulder-length curls.

Some people might have stood there with a shocked expression on their face, their jaw dropping onto their chest. Marcie didn't do that. This was her first male customer and although surprised, she made the effort to be polite.

She showed him a mauve lurex outfit that he instantly fell in love with. He came out of the changing room preening like a peacock, hands on hips and mannish feet shoved into purple satin stilettos.

'I *love* lurex!' he exclaimed in a sudden and surprising falsetto voice. The voice had been adopted the moment his wig went on. 'Just one point, hen – could you give me a bit more room in the jockstrap area?' The request was accompanied with a pat on the crotch.

'I'm here to please,' Marcie responded.

'You didn't bat an eyelid,' Sally said to her afterwards.

'Did you expect me to?'

Sally laughed.

Between drawings and sticking samples of materials on stiff cardboard, she tended her daughter, who was teething again.

The girls who made a living taking their clothes off turned out to be a mixed bunch. A lot of them were bold and brash like Sally Saunders. Some were gorgeous to look at but gave their origins away the minute they opened their mouths.

'Bleedin' 'ell. Look at these tits. If they gets much bleedin' bigger I can chuck the mink stole and put these over me shoulders instead!'

Her name was Dorothy Lambert and her boobs were her fortune. She stood just five feet two inches in her bare feet. Her hips were as slim as a boy and her waistline was tiny. Her breasts on the other hand were huge and the reason for her success.

'So you wouldn't ever have them cut off,' Marcie asked her.

'Sometimes I would – when me back's aching like nobody's business, but then I lie down on me back and think of money.'

She cackled like a laying hen at her joke.

The incident with Roberto was hard to forget, but her new line of business and her new company certainly raised her spirits. She'd also had a period since Roberto's onslaught and was thankful she wasn't pregnant. Now she was safely on the pill and safe to make love with Michael any time she chose. She was putting the past behind her as best she could.

It was on a Wednesday morning that the famous Carla came calling. Close to six feet tall, her presence seemed to fill the workroom the moment she came in the door. She had dyed honey-blonde hair pulled back into a French pleat, oozed perfume and a trashy glamour, the latter emphasised by virtue of the oversized leopard-skin coat she was wearing. It had a huge collar flopping like a cape onto her shoulders and swung from a central shoulder yoke into a swirling circle at knee level. Obviously no slave to current fashion where chunky heels and square toes were currently the norm, her shoes were still old-style winkle-pickers with four-inch stiletto heels; in the right hands they looked capable of stabbing somebody and were safer staying on her feet.

'My name's Carla Casey,' she said extending a black-gloved hand. 'You've got me to thank for putting business your way.' Her voice grated like iron dragged against gravel, no doubt the result of smoking sixty plus per day.

'In that case, thank you.' Marcie shook the offered gloved hand.

The gloved hand held hers. She noticed a bracelet worn over the elbow-length glove. A pair of striking grey eyes looked her up and down. She was smoking via an ebony cigarette holder. 'Sally said you were quite a beauty.'

317

The voice was intrusive, like grit being thrown against the windowpane close to the ear.

'Did she?' Marcie felt momentarily flattered.

'Sally isn't always right,' Carla proclaimed dismissively.

Marcie felt deflated.

Carla appeared not to notice. 'Now. Perhaps you could show me around. Fifi La Mare tells me she's very pleased with the outfits you're running up for her girls.'

Fifi La Mare was the doyenne of a troupe of dancing girls with a vaguely horsey connotation. They carried long riding crops and wore tight-fitting outfits that exposed far more than they covered: little waistcoats, tiny briefs and long black riding boots with spurs and spiked heels. The expanse of thigh between boot top and knicker leg was covered in fishnet tights.

Marcie had been along to see their act with Michael. Eva, one of her freelance seamstresses, came in to look after Joanna. It had been Sally's night off and Allegra had come too though had left early with the excuse that she had a business appointment. It seemed an odd time of night for a business appointment, but Allegra led an odd life, being available more often during the day than she was at night.

'I saw their act,' Marcie informed her.

Again her comment did not draw a response.

The woman sauntered around the workroom as though she owned it, inspecting the garments hanging from rails and the items being run through a machine.

'Are you confident of always delivering work on

time?' Again she used an imperious tone.

'Subject to fitting. Some of the girls put weight on between ordering and fitting,' said Marcie.

Carla looked at her without a trace of a smile. 'It concerns me that your measurements are that inaccurate.'

'They're not. One or two got pregnant.'

'Ah!'

Carla unsnapped the clasp on her handbag, placed one ebony holder back in her bag and got out a fresh one. Marcie watched, fascinated, as she lit up. She'd only seen film stars with cigarette holders, never in real life. But never two.

'So,' said Carla, chancing the hint of a smile. 'Are you going to offer me some refreshment?'

Marcie nodded. 'Come this way.'

There was something almost laughable about Carla's attitude, not that she would dare laugh out loud. This woman had brokered a lot of business.

Marcie had left Joanna taking her midday nap in her cot in the other room. After checking with Carla, she made tea, thought about offering biscuits, but decided she didn't want the woman to linger that long, so put the tin back on the shelf.

When she went back into the living room, Carla was nowhere to be seen. Marcie frowned. There was no way she could have left. She would have heard the door. So where was she?

Setting the tray down on the coffee table, she went looking for her. First she pressed her ear against the bathroom door but the door squeaked open.

Then there were sounds. She stood mesmerised at those sounds. Not words, not quite, but

319

cooing sounds, sounds a woman makes to a baby or young child.

Marcie immediately knew where she was. She found her standing with her hands on the side of Joanna's cot gazing down at the sleeping child and murmuring all the silly things that mothers croon to their children. At first unaware of Marcie's presence, her face seemed transformed from the bitch of a woman who had come in demanding, ordering and specifying. Her mouth was open as though she'd just gasped with wonder. The hard bitch face was no more, her features softened as she reached down and touched the child's fingers.

'You are such a beautiful little girl,' she said softly.

Suddenly aware that she wasn't alone, she looked up.

'I was looking for the bathroom,' she whispered.

She made no attempt to move away from the cot. Her gaze went back to Joanna.

'What a lovely little kid.' Her tone had turned noticeably harsher.

Marcie frowned. There was no way this woman had been looking for the bathroom. It was easily found, being the first door on the right while the bedroom was the second. She could not allay the suspicion that Carla had purposely gone to this room.

'What are you up to?'

Carla's expression froze. Marcie could tell she was about to deny she was up to anything and keep to the bathroom thing, but she was having none of it.

'Don't lie to me. What are you doing in here?'

'Nothing.' Carla shook her head and gave a light little laugh.

Alarm bells rang in Marcie's head. Being a mother had made her extremely protective of her child. 'Did Roberto put you up to this?'

'Roberto?' Carla was almost laughing. 'You have to be bloody joking, darling!'

Marcie could not get rid of her feeling of unease. 'You look like my little brother Archie after he's raided the biscuit barrel and ate the bloody lot. Go on. Get out of my flat.'

Carla was full of indignation, drawing herself up to her full height. 'You can't speak to me like that!'

'Yes I can. You invited yourself in here. The tea's on the table. Drink it, use my bathroom if you must, but keep away from my child. No one has access to my child without my say so. Is that clear?'

Carla's face drained of colour, her pallor emphasised by her blood-red lips and the two spots of rouge remaining on her cheekbones. She walked stiffly from the bedroom and back into the living room. She paused by the coffee table, glancing down at the waiting tray as though she were trying to decide something. Then she smiled as though nothing untoward had happened at all.

'I do have a busy schedule today, so I won't stop for tea. I'm quite satisfied placing more business with you. Good day.'

'No need to go through the shop. You can go out this way,' said Marcie, opening the private door that led out onto the metal stairway. 'Out the back way. Tradesmen's entrance.'

She used the same stiff unsmiling fashion as Carla was using with her.

'There's a car waiting for me out front and you can't expect me to get down those steps in one piece wearing these heels! Be fair!'

Marcie closed the door. Carla had a point and she certainly didn't want to force her down a set of dangerous steps. After all, her referrals constituted a considerable portion of her business. She had to be balanced about this.

'This way.'

She accompanied her through the workshop and along the passage, past the trophy shop to the front door. The door shuddered as she tugged it open.

Carla gave a little nod of her head by way of goodbye. Her heels stabbed at the pavement before digging into the tarmac as she crossed the road.

The leopard-skin coat swirled around the tall figure making for the sleek black limousine parked on the other side. The driver got out and opened the rear passenger door. During the brief period the door was open, it appeared there was another person sitting on the back seat, huddled into the far corner. It occurred to her that perhaps the other person did not want to be seen. Not Roberto hopefully!

Standing behind the door for what must have been at least three minutes, she swallowed the fear that had risen like bile to her throat. It could not have been Roberto sitting in the limousine. Why should it have been?

She reminded herself of what Sally had told her

about the nightclub scene, that they were all hand in glove, nightclub owners feeding like louse on the other people involved. Women formed the backbone of the entertainment and in more ways than one.

But it was Roberto that Marcie feared. The main horror of any mother is for a child to go missing and her imagination was running riot. What if he had sent Carla to kidnap Joanna in order to force her to go back to him? What if he refused to give her back unless she did? What if...

*How do you know it was a man?*

There was that whisper again. It was like having a bucket of cold water thrown over her. She clutched at her heart and felt its beating returning to normal.

The voice was right. She couldn't be sure the backseat passenger hadn't been a woman. Did she see trouser legs? No. She had not.

Just in case they were lingering, just in case her first suspicion – crazy as it might be – was right, she tugged the door open.

The car was gone. A paper boy was hanging over his bicycle while fixing a pair of bicycle clips around the ankles of his baggy trousers. The rest of the street was clear. Nobody threatening, nobody looking in her direction.

## Chapter Thirty-five

Ella wouldn't let Tony Brooks have a key to her place, which is why he found himself outside and hammering on the door.

She took her time coming to open it which was just as well. He was fuming, his hands buried deep in his pockets, his hairy black brows beetled like a thatched roof over his eyes. Bloody priest! What the hell was his mother thinking of telling Father Justin O'Flanagan where he lived?

He'd still been in bed when the old sod had arrived; that's what comes of working for a bloke who owned the best nightclubs in East London. Like Count bleedin' Dracula, he thought to himself. I works at night and I sleeps all day.

So the priest had caught him in. Even though it was only just after lunch, Father Justin had licked his lips and asked for a drink and he didn't mean water!

'I've had a long journey,' Father Justin had said, his eyes sliding to where Tony had left the whisky bottle from the night before.

Brought up a good Catholic boy, Tony made overtures to pour out a measure, but even before he lifted the bottle, curiosity – and bad temper – got the better of him.

'Why are you here, Father?'

He knew the answer. Of course he knew the bloody answer even before the words were preached at him.

'You know your mother worries about you, and your wife – although she may be a second wife and not exactly exalted in the eyes of the Church – she is the mother of your children and thus is justifiably worried about you. You haven't been coming home, Antonio. Why is that?'

When Tony didn't answer, the priest's eyes fell back to the whisky bottle.

'Your wife seems to think you may have fallen into sinful ways – with a child of Ham.'

'Ham?'

Tony's face screwed up in consternation. He couldn't believe the priest knew anything about Ella's parentage, so what the hell was old Custard Eyes, as he called him, on about?

'Who's this Ham when he's at home?' he asked again.

'The darker children of Africa.'

Tony jerked his chin defiantly. 'Ella isn't from Africa. She's Jamaican and a Christian. She's also a very good person.'

'How can she be if she is liaising with you, and how can you be if you are demeaning yourself...'

Tony held the rest of the scene at bay. He was ashamed he'd hit the priest, but there was no excuse for speaking of Ella with such contempt. Anyway, what did the seedy old sod know of Ella and her life or that of her kids? Nobody knew her or her situation better than he did. She'd needed help and he'd helped her. That was all there was to it – except for the sex of course, but there, she'd needed solace, he'd needed solace.

The door to Ella's flat was still firmly closed in

his face so he gave it another hammering.

A door further along the hallway opened. He saw the whites of somebody's eyes peering at him.

'Have you seen Ella?' he asked, desperately trying to keep the urgency from his voice and failing miserably.

The eyes watched him approach, looking up at him like a lost spaniel once he was standing over them. The woman had woolly brown hair and a pockmarked skin. No raving beauty.

'She is gone, man.' Her voice was hushed, like a brush sweeping a carpet.

Tony frowned. Ella hadn't told her she was going anywhere.

He gave it the old confident shrug of the shoulders trick. It always made people feel that he meant business. 'What do you mean by gone, love?'

The woman shrugged her narrow shoulders. 'Gone away. Her ole man come for her and the kids. They gone home.'

Jamaica! They'd gone home to Jamaica.

'They flied yesterday,' said the woman, as though she'd read his thoughts.

The door slowly closed on Tony's shocked expression and his pain. He stood there for what seemed like an age, staring at the closed door.

The door opened again – just an inch or two. Seeing he was still there, the woman closed the door again.

'She must think I'm a bloody nutcase,' he said to himself. He wasn't sure whether he was referring to the pock-marked neighbour or to Ella. The former must think his behaviour odd. The latter had taken him for a ride – or so it seemed.

Turning back towards the door to Ella's flat he let the truth sink in. Ella had used him to pay the rent. Her husband might very well have had a hand in it. Not wanting a job on the buses, he had got the money from somewhere for the return ticket home. London, England and the crap weather and conditions couldn't compete with a sun-drenched island. Island in the Sun, he thought. A touch of the Harry Belafontes.

A stain on the wall beside the door to Ella's flat caught his attention. It looked enough like a face for Tony to bunch his fist and strike out. A shower of crumbling plaster fell from the wall in the brown-painted hallway. Tony told himself it was teeth and it made him feel better.

He stalked to the door, hunching his shoulders inside his big camel overcoat.

'Forget it,' he muttered to himself. 'Bloody forget it.'

So he marched off and thought about seeking some way of raising his spirits. It was too early for the club, so he thought he might head for Marcie's place. She'd told him about the flat above a darts trophy shop over Balham way. He'd head there and get himself a nice cup of tea and a bit of sympathy. And he could see his granddaughter while he was there. Marcie had told him she'd brought her up from Sheppey. Perhaps next weekend he'd go down there himself. Yes, he decided, it's time to go down and see me old mum. Besides, Babs could do with a bit of attention. OK, she'd be in a bit of a mood at first, but once he got her into bed without her nightdress on, she'd forget being moody. That's one thing he could count on with Babs: she never said no.

With that thought in his head he began to whistle. Ella was gone, but nothing was lost – except that Victor wouldn't be getting any rent from Ella this week and he wouldn't be paying it for her.

He'd only visited Marcie's new place once before and, although he hadn't made comment, he'd much admired her feisty spirit.

Rather than take the door from the street he braved the narrow passageway running beside the shop selling darts trophies, went up the metal staircase at the rear, taking the steps two at a time.

'Hi, doll,' he exclaimed as Marcie let him in.

His attention was briefly taken by someone halfway through the other door that led down the front stairs and out onto the street.

Michael Jones!

'Hey, pal. What you doing here?'

Marcie interceded. 'He's a friend. Michael's welcome here.'

'Fine by me,' Tony said, as if it would make any difference if it wasn't. 'I'm off home the weekend,' he said to Marcie. 'Care to join me?'

Marcie hesitated. He saw the pair of them exchange a look and suddenly felt old and no longer Tony the Charmer, the Isle of Sheppey's answer to Tony Curtis.

'I see. You've got other plans.' Lines deepened around his eyes when he smiled.

Marcie nodded. 'Yes. That's it. We've made other plans. Michael's taking me and Joanna down to Sheppey. He's offered to collect us too. Gran's promised to give him a Sunday roast he'll never forget.'

'Looking forward to it,' said Michael.

They exchanged smiles. They seemed to do everything at the same time: look at each other, smile at each other and say the same things almost at the same time.

'He don't need to bother. I could take you and bring you back.' Even as he said it, Tony Brooks knew that it was no use. His daughter was grown up. She didn't need a dad. She needed a man and it looked as though that man was Michael Jones.

'OK,' he said holding up his hands in surrender. 'Your old dad knows when he's not wanted.'

The big bruiser called Malcolm had a glossy black skull and a ring through his nose. Even without the ring he would have still got the nickname the Black Bull. Like the animal that had given him his nickname, Malcolm was built like one. Tony knew him well. Heavy meat meant Malcolm didn't move that fast so when Tony decided he was going to borrow Victor's E Type for the weekend, there was sweet FA the Black Bull could do about it.

'Hey, Tony!'

Tony couldn't hear what Malcolm shouted as the nearside wing of the car grazed the Black Bull's kneecaps, though he could guess. What the hell! He was practically family now with Victor – even if it was via Michael rather than Roberto. At least that's what he told himself as he wound down the window and sniffed the fresh air. Sod it! He'd run the missus around in it this weekend and the whole family would have a whale of a time. What happened when he got back to London would be another matter. And he'd have to go back. His life might depend on it.

## Chapter Thirty-six

It was good to be back in Sheppey. The salty properties in the air were not described as bracing for no reason and, despite bad memories, Marcie felt childishly excited the closer she got to home.

'I can't believe that I still think of this as home,' she said to Michael. 'Funny how I can't quite get it out of my mind that I'm coming home even though I live in London.'

'Home is where the heart is – and the people you love most,' said Michael.

Rather than phoning the presbytery and dragging Father Justin away from sinking cupfuls of tea and gobbling wedges of home-made cake, Marcie had sent a telegram.

Her grandmother was waiting at the gate when she arrived. Marcie sucked in her breath at the sight of Rosa Brooks. When had she grown so old? The figure in black seemed even smaller than on the last occasion she'd see her. She's shrinking with age, she thought and was saddened.

Rosa Brooks had insisted she understood why Marcie was taking her daughter to London. 'You have your own life to lead,' she'd said plaintively. 'Besides, this is England, not Malta.'

The sight of her grandmother now made Marcie feel guilty at taking her daughter away. She knew without asking that her grandmother was hurting, though wasn't sure what she could do about it.

Garth came out of the cottage, pushing past Rosa Brooks while skipping up and down like a five-year-old.

'Marcie! You're back!'

He continued to skip, his arms flapping at his sides like a pair of dodo's wings. His clothes were cleaner than when he'd lived with his mother and he smelled of fresh soap and had his hair neatly cut and combed.

It seemed to Marcie that his stay in the institution hadn't traumatised him in any way.

'How are you, Garth? Glad to be home?'

'Yeah! Me and Arthur like it here.'

Marcie mouthed the word Arthur questioningly to her grandmother.

'His friend.'

Marcie nodded. The look in her grandmother's eyes explained everything. Garth had an invisible friend.

Rosa's deepest wrinkles were around her mouth and her eyes, so that when she smiled they seemed to spread over her face.

Her smiles were all for her granddaughter and her great-granddaughter. Joanna gurgled with delight on seeing her great-grandmother and went willingly into her arms.

While dallying with the child, Rosa raked

331

Michael with her deep dark eyes, taking in everything about him. He received a smile which accompanied a questioning look in her eyes.

'Do you require a bed for the night?'

The question took both Marcie and Michael by surprise. Michael declined saying that he had business to attend to in London.

He'd been buying up vacant shop lots and letting them out for weekly rents. According to him nobody seemed that interested in commercial letting. 'It may take a few years, but eventually I'll clean up,' he said, the light of enthusiasm shining in his eyes. 'Come on. There's a lot of demolition and rebuilding going to go on in London. Once I'd explained how it was, the financial backing came easy.'

'The banks must love you,' Marcie had said.

'Them and others,' he'd answered. He'd been cagey about his financial backer, the sleeping partner he sometimes referred to, though he insisted it was all above board. 'My backer likes to keep a low profile. In fact I haven't even met him yet. I was contacted via a solicitor.'

Aware of his manner, Marcie didn't pry. She was glad he was doing so well without the assistance of Victor Camilleri.

Fluffy white clouds were sprinting across a lake of blue sky. Spring was flowing into summer and the holidaymakers were returning to the beaches at Sheerness and Leysdown. Families were out in force buying candy floss and sticky rock from the ramshackle booths along the seafront in Sheerness. In Leysdown the young crowd would be gathering outside the cafés and amusement arcades, boys leaning against motorcycles or scooters swigging Pepsi or Coca-Cola. Girls wearing short skirts giggling together whilst trying not to look interested in the boys.

Thoughts of Leysdown brought a lump to Marcie's throat. Leysdown was where she'd met Johnnie. It seemed a lifetime ago now. So much had happened, including his death. Sometimes she awoke in the middle of the night after dreaming that it had never happened, that he was still alive. This usually happened when a motorcycle was revving up in the street outside, though when she looked she could never see one.

Johnnie was still alive in her mind though he'd been buried nearly two years ago. Things had changed so drastically in such a short time. Alan Taylor was gone and so was his daughter. And Michael had come along.

No longer afraid that Rita would pounce out on her and call her names, Marcie went for a stroll along the seafront the next morning. Lulled by the warm sun and the fresh air, Joanna fell asleep. Garth came to keep her company. There was something oddly oppressive about his presence. It may have been something to do with him being the catalyst with regard to Rita, her father and the burning down of the boutique.

'The lady in red is watching over you,' he said suddenly, his mouth full of candy floss.

Marcie stopped pushing the pushchair.

'The woman who used to sit under the tree in my grandmother's garden?'

He nodded before once again immersing his

face in a cloud of cotton candy.

It wasn't the first time that Garth had mentioned the woman she now accepted was her mother.

Marcie resumed her walk. 'Who said so?'

'Albert.'

Albert seemed to be responsible for a lot of things. Garth was a little clumsy and sometimes knocked things over or spilt food and drink He always blamed Albert for doing so. Marcie wasn't so sure he was acting dumb. He always said it with a twinkle in his eyes.

The crowds along the prom were a happy band; mums and dads, kids, toddlers, babies and dogs, all tripping along the prom and glad the sun was back.

She glimpsed the faces of young mothers like herself. Kids were a big responsibility and could make your heart or break it. If her mother was still alive she wondered whether she ever thought of her. If she was dead, she wondered if she had regretted leaving. Either way she hoped she'd been loved and, if her mother was dead, hoped she was looking down on her. She too would look down on her child should anything dreadful happen.

'I'm really glad the lady in red is watching over me,' she said after some thought. 'It's nice to think that even when you're dead you can still protect those you leave behind.'

'And before,' said Garth. 'Mothers look after you before you're dead.'

'Of course. Mothers always look after their children.'

Halfway home it suddenly struck her. He'd said that mothers look after you before you're dead.

How did he know that the vision he'd seen was her mother? She racked her brain, trying to remember if she'd ever suggested the woman was her mother. She had not. She was absolutely sure she had not. She then remembered what her grandmother had said. She said that if she ever found her mother she did not want to meet her again. She'd said it as though her mother was still alive.

The weekend was working out well though she couldn't help worrying about her grandmother. She seemed tired and on some occasions a little distant.

Marcie caught her sitting before the fire, her chin in her lap and her eyes closed. Her frail hands – skin as thin as rice paper and speckled with brown spots – hung lifelessly over the chair arms.

Marcie knelt at her grandmother's side. 'Gran?'

The hooded eyes flickered before fully opening. Her smile was vapid. Realisation dawned. Her grandmother was not well.

'Have you been to the doctor?'

Rosa Brooks shook her head and sighed listlessly. 'What for? I am suffering from old age. That is all.'

Her dark eyes held the blue ones of her grand-daughter. Something – perhaps a sudden thought – seemed to flash there. Marcie knew instinctively what the problem was. Rosa Brooks was feeling lonely.

'Have you spoken to grandfather lately?'

The old woman smiled. 'We speak every day. I tell him that I miss him and will be glad when we are together again.'

The forthright way her grandmother spoke of her dead husband touched a raw nerve. Even death had failed to sever the bond between her grandmother and her grandfather. Other marriages were far from convivial; her father's for a start.

On his first night back at home, Tony got thrown out by his wife so came round to stay with his mother. His mood was ugly.

'She locked me out! Can you believe that? The stupid bitch locked me out!'

'Antonio!'

Tony Brooks, the hard man of London's East End, apologised to his mother for his language. 'Sorry, Ma. But she winds me up something rotten,' he spouted as he paced the room.

His mother pointed to a chair. 'Sit down, Antonio. I will make you tea.'

'I don't want any.'

'Sit down anyway. You are wearing my carpet out.'

Tony obediently settled himself in one of the wide armchairs by the fire. His mother put the kettle on then went out into the back garden to cut herbs and a cabbage. Garth had taken to growing cabbages. It was the only thing he'd learned how to grow so that was all he grew. Unfortunately this meant that there were rather a lot of them. Cabbage had to be used in practically every meal and Rosa Brooks had started giving some away to the neighbours. Father Justin was also cajoled into taking one or two.

Marcie was sitting in the armchair on the other side of the fireplace giving Joanna her bottle. Her father's eyes dropped to the baby.

Marcie perceived his expression softening before her very eyes.

'She looks just like you when you were a nipper. Pretty. And pink.'

'Pink? You mean like Pinky and Perky?'

Tony chortled at the very idea of her looking like one of the wooden puppets from on the telly.

'No. You were beautiful. Just like her,' he said, nodding at his granddaughter. 'Christ,' he added shaking his head in disbelief. 'Me. A grandfather. How did I ever manage that?'

'You fell in love with her grandmother. Isn't that how it all started?'

He looked startled, like a tennis ball that's been firmly batted back to the sender. 'What? Well... It wasn't...'

He stumbled over the words and looked uncomfortable.

'Never mind,' she said. On several occasions she'd tried bringing her mother into a conversation. Her memories of the woman who'd given birth to her were less than sketchy – they were almost non-existent. There was just the feeling of warm arms hugging her close. She couldn't help wanting more, but nobody, not even her grandmother, was prepared to talk about her.

Rosa came in from the back yard, a cabbage tucked beneath one arm and a bunch of herbs in the other. She proceeded to make tea. It was an unspoken rule in this house that making tea was women's work; certainly as far as Marcie's father was concerned. He took the opportunity to ask her about Michael. 'I mean, are you and him on the level? Is it a kosher relationship?'

Marcie smiled at his ineffectiveness to get to what he really wanted to know. She was learning how to handle him better, just like she was beginning to know how to handle most men. Never demean them or demand, but suggest things that she might want but make it seem as though it was their idea all the time. On this occasion such subterfuge wasn't necessary.

'If you mean are we likely to walk down the aisle, the answer to that is I don't know.'

Michael was keen on her and she was keen on him and the sex was good and without complication thanks to the birth pills supplied by the Brook Clinic. However, being independent was better than she'd envisaged. It was never going to be easy raising a child on her own, but so far she was managing very nicely. Having a good income helped. She would always be grateful to Allegra for that. As for Michael...

Her father threw his hands into the air then brought them down to rest on his head. 'Blimey! Imagine my little girl being married to Victor Camilleri's son. Wrong side of the blanket of course, but still his son. You'd be a Camilleri, part of one of the most powerful families in the East End.'

Marcie bridled. 'I didn't say I would marry him, and, anyway, I'd be a Jones. His mother never married his father.'

Her father looked put out that such a trivial fact had not occurred to him. But Tony Brooks was not a man to be down for long.

'You're right, darlin',' he said patting her hand

affectionately. 'All the same,' he said, his expression brightening. 'He's a lad likely to go places. Not so high as his brother of course who *was* born on the right side of the blanket so stands to gain most when old Victor kicks the bucket. But all the same, a good bloke for my girl to end up with.'

Marcie eyed him ruefully. 'Not bad at all when you consider that I suspected my father had sold me into slavery.'

'What?' He looked dumbfounded.

'You walked right into it. *And* you practically told them I was a virgin. Innocent, stupid and good to look at; a sweet innocent wife for that psycho Roberto. How stupid was that?'

He looked quite distraught. 'It didn't occur to me. Honest it didn't. And they never said anything.'

'No. They wanted things to run naturally – just putting me in front of him and leaving it to him to pluck me like a flower. Only they didn't know that I was far from being untouched and had a kid. Can you imagine what Roberto was like after he found that out?'

'He ended it I suppose...?'

Marcie found herself unable to respond to the question. If only...

'Love,' said her father, his hands falling away from his newspaper, sending it collapsing into his lap. 'If I'd known that's what they were thinking, I wouldn't have done it – or at least told you. It's just, I wanted it clear that they weren't to think about you at all for their other side of the business. Look, I had nothing to do with that side of the business, but you know they run girls as well as property? I just wanted to protect you from that.' Tony Brooks always had a ready excuse, but that was the way he was, a man who functioned best in a man's world. As long as his girl was alright, he didn't care that much about the sex trade side of Victor Camilleri's business.

She didn't elaborate too much on her leaving Daisy Chain and living under the Camilleri's roof. She didn't tell him anything of her relationship with Roberto and what he had done to her. Sometimes in the night she woke up sweating into already soaking bedding because she'd been dreaming about it. He'd raped her. It was a criminal offence and the police should have done something, she thought to herself as she rinsed out some of Joanna's bibs beneath a running tap.

*The police rarely see the woman's point of view.*

'You can say that again,' she said out loud to herself.

Avoiding responsibilities had formed the backbone of Tony Brooks' life. If in doubt, keep your head down. He was doing that right now, his nose buried in a copy of the *Daily Mirror*. He peered over the top of it. 'What was that, love?'

'Nothing,' she said. 'Just talking to myself.'

Looking out of the kitchen window she could see Garth digging amongst the cabbages, flinging weeds in one direction and snails in another. His mouth was going all the time.

'He is speaking to Albert,' said her grandmother on coming to her side at the sink with yet another cabbage from the garden.

'Hmm,' Marcie responded.

'And Albert whispers in his ear just as my dear

dead husband whispers to me.'

It was odd the way Marcie became absorbed in what her grandmother was saying. That was why it came out the way it did.

'Someone whispers to me.'

She felt her grandmother's eyes on her but didn't meet the searching gaze; the question she knew would be there.

'I see. Is it a pleasant voice?'

Marcie tried to think. Was the voice pleasant? She nodded. 'Yes. I think so.'

In London she would not have admitted she was hearing voices. City people didn't hear the pulse of life beating just beneath the surface. They certainly wouldn't understand someone hearing voices of people who were not there. They would think she was mad. Here on the Isle of Sheppey was a different matter. Perhaps it was the air. Perhaps it was the people themselves that were different, the pace of life slower and minds more open to the basic rhythms of life.

Her grandmother didn't ask her who she thought the voice might belong to, but there was a sharp brightness – a knowingness as Marcie had come to interpret it. Either she knew that her granddaughter was becoming more like her, or she didn't need to ask who she thought the voice might belong to – because she already knew.

Archie and Arnold came round to lunch on Sunday bringing Annie with them in her push-chair. The little girl could walk perfectly well, but knew she could count on her brothers to push her over to see her grandmother and her aunt.

On seeing Marcie, she stretched out her arms. 'Big cuddle,' she lisped.

Marcie gave her that big cuddle, although the little girl's face was sticky with jam. Annie's mother, Babs, hadn't changed one iota.

Archie and Arnold told her that Bully Price was trying to persuade them to work for him.

'As what,' she asked, her mind already racing ahead of the question to the obvious answer.

'Nicking bikes,' proclaimed Archie.

'I somehow had a feeling it might be,' she muttered.

'And he reckons he's going to marry you because nobody else will have you,' Arnold added.

Marcie bristled with indignation. 'Oh does he now!' she said, her fists resting on her hips.

'But I told him you wouldn't marry him because you were married already.'

Marcie cocked an eyebrow. 'Go on. I can't wait to hear this. Who am I supposed to be married to?'

'Jesus!' said Archie with unbridled enthusiasm, his fine hair flopping like a horse's mane over his eyes.

Marcie tried to work out where this was coming from. Impossible.

'How do you work that one out?'

Archie laughed. 'Because you've had a baby and ain't got no husband. Just like the mother of Jesus. His father was in heaven just like Joanna's father. My mum said he'd gone to heaven but he probably wouldn't have married you anyway.'

Marcie mangled the dish cloth she was holding and wished it were her stepmother's neck. The cow! Even Babs, who couldn't keep her legs together even when she was married, was slinging slander her way.

Marcie watched as the two boys and Annie tucked into their roast beef, Yorkshire puddings and three different lots of vegetables. An enthralled Joanna looked on, spoon only halfway to her mouth. Michael arrived, his sunny disposition making it seem as though the freshness of the outside world had entered the house.

Marcie went outside the back door to get some fresh air. Michael followed her out, his arm creeping around her waist, his lips brushing her ear.

'What a world,' he said.

She thought she knew what he meant. There were no big problems here; no big money either. She thought both of them knew the value of that.

Silently they watched the simple things.

Cabbage butterflies fluttered over the heads of Garth's vegetable patch. The smell of Sunday lunch brought him running down the garden path.

'Roast beef, Yorkshire pudding, roast potatoes, carrots, parsnips and cabbage,' he said to her. 'Me and Albert are going to eat it all up.'

'You're still coming back to London?' Michael asked her.

'Yes,' she said because she knew she had to. That's where the work was. That's where her home was and, despite everything, she had good friends there, but also enemies, she reminded herself. You also have enemies.

343

On the Sunday afternoon before leaving for London, her grandmother handed her a letter.

'I did not like the feel of it. Garth did not like the feel of it either so I kept it back. I wanted this to be a nice weekend. A family weekend.'

Marcie tried to read her grandmother's face. She was famous for having the gift of second sight. Marcie mused that she'd never realised this might include having x-ray vision. How else could she perceive whether a letter was evil or not?

She tried to laugh off the sudden fear it generated. 'Gran, you should be doing a stage act.'

'It is not an act, Marcie.'

Marcie knew better than to continue with that particular approach. Without checking the handwriting, she ripped the envelope open, searching inside with hesitant fingers for a note that might bring joy, but could just as easily bring devastation.

Her worst fears were realised. There was no letter; nothing but a playing card – the Ace of Spades. It had to be Roberto. The Camilleris owned casinos as well as nightclubs. Sending her a death card would be easy for him to do.

As she crumpled the envelope and ripped the card in two, a cold shiver ran through her body like the first frost of winter. There was no need to check the handwriting at all. She knew who it was from and what it meant; Roberto had found out her home address. It was likely that her father had given him the information without a moment's thought. It was also likely that Roberto had given him a very plausible excuse for wanting it.

'You look pale. Do you wish to share this fear?'

She looked up into her grandmother's eyes. The eyes that looked back at her were coal black and yet they had incredible depth. It was like looking into a long tunnel, a place to run to when things were bad and she needed safety and shelter.

She shivered. 'I feel a bit cold.'

Her grandmother cupped her elbow and led her into the small front parlour where coal glowed in the hearth.

'Come on. Let's warm you up.'

Marcie threw the crumpled envelope and card into the fire where they curled into flames then blackness.

Her grandmother waited and watched with her as the flames devoured the card and the envelope. She did not pass comment. Marcie was grateful for that.

'Garth told me it was a death card. The Ace of Spades. I guessed.'

She told her grandmother about Roberto. 'He wanted me to give Joanna away. He said that if I didn't give her away it meant I didn't love him. So I ran.'

For a moment her grandmother's narrowed eyes seemed deep in thought. 'This is a man who is in love with himself, I think.'

Marcie nodded mutely. It seemed so obvious when she really thought about. Her grandmother carried on.

'If he had loved you enough he would have loved and accepted your child as Michael does.'

Marcie nodded, her blue eyes enlivened by the fire and reflecting its glow.

345

'Your father said that he is going back to London. He sets great faith in these Sicilians. He's told them that you are doing very well and that he is grateful they took you in and taught you your sewing. He says he's told them that you are now your own boss. He is proud of that.'

The flames threw shadows across her face.

'Oh no,' she whispered. 'That means he's told them.'

Her grandmother frowned. 'Told them what?'

She told her grandmother about Michael being the half-brother of the sender of the letter. She avoided telling her too much about Daisy Chain and how young girls, excited to be working in the King's Road, were enticed by clothes and money into a life far removed from selling clothes. She wouldn't do that because her father worked for Victor Camilleri. She didn't want to blatantly declare that her father was a small-time criminal who worked for bigger criminals. It would be too hurtful.

Michael had been helping Garth with his cabbages when she'd thrown the card into the fire, but she told him about it anyway.

'He'll find out my address in London. I know he will,' she exclaimed to Michael in alarm on the journey back to London. 'I should have made my father promise not to tell anyone. He trusts Victor. He trusts all the Camilleris.'

'And that,' said Michael grimly, 'is a serious mistake.'

## Chapter Thirty-seven

There was no one waiting for her back at her flat or lurking behind the sewing machines in her workroom. Two, then three, days passed and still there was no sign that Roberto had found out where she was living.

Michael told her not to worry. 'I am going to sort this out once and for all.'

'Don't get hurt!'

She knew he intended confronting his brother. The thought of them facing each other and fighting was terrifying. They were both proud and headstrong, though each in their own way. She didn't want Michael getting hurt.

Despite the ongoing concern, she did her best to make life as normal as possible. The business was doing well. The girls she sewed for were great fun; rich, brash and blatantly sexual.

Sally came round to keep her company. 'Klaus is on holiday with his family. I'm at a loose end.'

Marcie didn't condemn Sally for her relationship with a married man. Nothing was black and white any more in this modern world. What Sally got up to was her business.

It was on a Tuesday morning that she realised she was being watched. The rush-hour traffic had been and gone. Across the road from the trophy shop were a newsagent, a greengrocer's and a bakery.

Marcie was on her way to the bakery with Joanna in her arms. Sally was having a go on a sewing machine in her absence. Her skills were woeful but she'd taken it in her head that she couldn't be a showgirl for ever.

'I've got to think of what I'm going to do once my tits start heading south,' she said in her vulgar but funny manner.

The sewing machine whirred away and in the background an American group, The Monkees, belted out 'Daydream Believer'.

Sally's verdict on the manufactured group followed her down the stairs. 'Not as good as the Beach Boys.'

Marcie chuckled to herself. 'They're supposed to be like the American version of the Beatles, not the Beach Boys,' she said to her daughter.

Joanna chortled as though she understood. Marcie couldn't imagine life without her now.

'I wish your daddy was here to see you,' she said softly.

'Daddy,' said the toddler.

A sharp pain stabbed at Marcie's heart. If only… Her first thought was for Joanna not having her father. Her second was for herself – not having a mother. For the thousandth time in her life she wondered where she could be; whether she was alive or dead.

The heavy mood had to be lifted.

'Let's get a tube of Smarties for my favourite girl,' she said to her darling daughter.

A workman came out of the shop opposite opening a packet of Senior Service before getting into a van and driving off. The only other vehicle

348

parked there was a black limousine. Marcie glanced at it then glanced again. It looked like the same one that Carla had gone off in.

Just as she turned curious eyes in its direction, a puff of smoke came out of the exhaust and it pulled away.

A sickening fear stayed with Marcie even after it was out of sight. Were her worst fears justified? Was it possible that it was Roberto she'd seen in the car and he was awaiting his chance to pounce, to persuade, to intimidate her to bend to his will?

The old-fashioned bell jangled as she pushed the door open with her hand and her hip. Joanna was clapping her hands with delight, face upturned at the brass bell. Marcie put on a brave smile for her daughter's sake and told herself it was nothing. Roberto didn't have a car like that.

*Though his father might and Carla must know Roberto. They frequent the same world of exotic dancers and smoke-filled nightclubs.*

She stepped over the old coconut matting worn flat by thousands of feet over very many years.

The old woman who ran the shop had been there since the days when Stanley Baldwin had been prime minister and Edward VIII had been King for a year before popping off to marry his American divorcée.

Miriam Coffee claimed to know everyone for miles around. She was a small woman with dyed black hair and a pinched face. Her lipstick was always red and her eye shadow bright blue or aquamarine. She only wore glasses for checking her price lists. Everyone else she scrutinised with beady black eyes that didn't miss a trick. New faces were treated with curiosity and subject to being asked where they lived, where they worked and what they were doing in the area.

Marcie had been no exception and had replied that she was a widow, had just moved in over the road, sewed undergarments for a living and was settling in very nicely thank you.

Her forthright answers had made a friend of Miriam Coffee.

'Smarties!' Miriam exclaimed, shaking a tube in front of Joanna for her to take.

Joanna laughed as she gripped the tube with her plump little fingers.

Miriam's bright red lips stretched over her uneven teeth. A gold tooth flashed at the corner of her mouth.

Marcie wasn't completely severed from concern about the black limousine. All and sundry had crossed the coconut matting. Miriam knew from experience when something wasn't quite right.

'You alright, my love?' she asked.

'That black car that just pulled away – did they come in here?'

Miriam's sharp black eyes that were usually as beady as a curious rat, lit up.

'That's what I was going to tell you. I've seen that car a few times. It does the same thing every time – parks outside my shop. The nerve of it! Nobody ever gets out and comes in, so I went out to them. Bloody cheek! That's my piece of parking there. My piece of pavement!'

There was no point whatsoever in pointing out to Miriam that the local council owned the pavement and not just the bit in front of her shop. They owned the whole lot. But Miriam didn't see things that way. Every morning she put out her tin signs for Lyons Maid ice cream and Old Holborn tobacco. The signs took up half the pavement, but no one dared protest. Even the council had respect for a resident who had been here long before the Blitz and long before the local council representatives had been born.

'So I went out to them and asked them what they were up to. They could have been casing the joint,' she whispered in a conspiratorial manner, leaning across the counter. 'Cigarettes! That's what the thieves around here go after.'

Marcie didn't doubt that cigarettes were in high demand, though not by people who could afford a shiny black limousine.

'But they didn't want cigarettes. They wanted in-for-mat-ion!'

Miriam said the last word like a drum roll. 'They wanted to know about you.'

Marcie's insides felt as though she'd swallowed a whole ice lolly. 'What did they want to know?'

'That's what worried me,' said Miriam. Her smile was gone. Jet-black eyebrows beetled over jet-black eyes. 'They asked me about the child and how often you took her out and whether the child was well treated. They seemed to know it was a girl and was named Joanna. I'm glad you called in. If you hadn't I would have come over to tell you. Do you think they're something to do with the child's father?'

Miriam's face was a picture of worry and reflected Marcie's own feelings.

Marcie shook her head. 'Was it a man in the car?'

Her question brought a swift nod from the little woman behind the counter.

'Definitely a lady. And I mean a lady. She had money written all over her.'

If the situation hadn't been so worrying, Marcie would have chortled and commented that the woman in the flash leopard-skin coat was no lady – especially when she opened her mouth.

Miriam sighed and leaned across her worn countertop, her bony fingers flashing red nail polish clasped in front of her.

'A lady doesn't just dress well; it's the way they speak. Ever so nicely and not dropping their aitches.'

Why was Carla asking so many questions? She frowned. It just didn't make sense. None of this made sense. Carla was a business associate and although she had a high-handed manner she'd seemed quite happy for their business relationship to continue. So what was this all about?

'That woman drops more than her aitches,' Marcie exclaimed, no longer able to hold back her mirth. 'She swears like a trooper, though I think she can put it on when she has to.'

Miriam seemed quite hurt by Marcie's condemnation of her appraisal. 'I'm telling you, she spoke ever so nicely – just like Celia Johnson. If she wasn't the real thing, then she must have been on the stage. I know how a lady speaks – believe me. I've had some of the most ladylike in the land in this shop.'

Marcie accepted it was likely that Carla might have done a bit of acting in her time – one way or another. 'I'm sure you're right.'

She didn't like to say that the stage Carla had likely been on was in a smoky nightclub where she was taking off her clothes. Elocution didn't come into it!

## Chapter Thirty-eight

The Swan Dancer was Victor Camilleri's favourite nightclub and the most upmarket. The girls dancing on the stage were dressed as pink swans – if you can call a few strategically placed sequins and dyed pink ostrich feathers adorning their heads and their gloriously exposed buttocks being dressed.

People with money and power came to this club; men who were makers and shakers in the twin worlds of making money and politics. The two, he'd found in his experience, went together; as did their need to let their hair down when the opportunity presented itself. That's why so many frequented the Swan Dancer. Victor was on first-name terms with most of them and welcomed them with a slap on the back, a knowing nod or a handshake smothered in cigar smoke.

He enjoyed meeting these men and, even more so, he enjoyed being privy to their bad behaviour. They were unknowingly furnishing him with material he could make money from. They already gave him tips for the stock market and funds where he could make a fast buck. And he gave them girls, fresh young girls who would do most things for money. Powerful men had powerful urges. He knew that himself.

Allegra was dressed in a low-cut red dress with cutaway arms that exposed her creamy shoulders.

Victor Camilleri bent his head and kissed the one nearest him.

'That man over there,' he whispered, his free hand holding aloft a smoking King Edward so the smoke wouldn't fall over Allegra's face. 'He's in line to become a government minister. Guess what ministry he's hoping to get.'

Holding a glass of champagne in front of her face and wearing a serene smile, Allegra shook her head. 'No. I don't know. But no doubt you're going to tell me.'

His hand went from her shoulder to her knee. 'Minister of Education. That man wants to be responsible for the education of school children and young people at university. Is that not a joke?'

Allegra kept her eyes fixed on the corpulent man with the red face and sweaty complexion. He was at least sixty years old. His mistress was eighteen years old and set up in a flat in Pimlico. She was thin and childlike with urchin eyes and straight fair hair.

'His idea of education covers a broad canvas,' Allegra said casually, as though she were hardened to the predicament of other people. It wasn't true, but she'd got used to pretending.

Unlike the other girls set up with rich old men, she had not met Victor through the sewing room and Daisy Chain. Both the Camilleri and Montillado family attended mass at the Church of the

Holy Trinity in Bethnal Green. That's where Victor had first seen the beautiful young girl who had once had it in mind to become a nun. Victor saved her from that – to his way of thinking. He had gone out of his way to seduce her. Unfortunately someone else got there first.

'Father Bernard,' she'd said in the midst of a tempestuous argument with her parents. They had still been keen for her to become a nun and, seeing as the child had been adopted, they could see no barrier to her doing so. But Allegra had changed her mind. At Pilemarsh she'd met other girls of her age. She'd felt free but regretful that she'd given away her child. She also swore that she would never set foot in a church again.

The fact that the conception of her child had involved a young priest changed everything. Her relationship with her parents became strained, with her father in particular. He threw her out. It was difficult for a girl used to a lavish lifestyle and plenty of money. Despairingly she'd tried to make it up with her parents, but whilst her mother wanted to forgive her, her father was resolute. He considered they'd done enough merely by taking her to the home for unmarried mothers and arranging the adoption of her child – their grandchild.

It was Victor who had rescued her. He'd lavished affection on her and listened when she explained how she felt about the Church, about the child she had given away and the priest who had caused her predicament.

He did everything he could to make things up with her parents, but they'd remained unmoved.

Drowning in despair, she'd cut her wrists. It was Victor who had saved her from herself. He gave her an option – the only option she had. She became his mistress and began to realise something very amazing indeed. She'd grown to love him and that in itself was a miracle.

She thought of this now and her eyes began to water.

'You OK?' Victor asked.

She blamed the smoke. 'I'm also a little tired.'

His hand slid from her knee to her thigh. 'Tired? Come on, darling, I haven't been round that much just lately.'

'Perhaps that's the reason,' she said with a generous smile. If there was one thing she'd learned early on in life it was how to massage a man's ego. Make him feel that she couldn't function without him; that she was at her happiest when he was making love to her. And, of course, there was no one who could do it like he could, at least, that was the picture she painted.

Victor's attention and his plume of cigar smoke switched to his son, who was making his way through the crush of small, round tables.

Allegra gave him a nod of welcome in response to the one he gave her. Father and son embraced.

'A man should always have a son to carry on his name,' Victor trumpeted. 'My son is a fine figure of a man, yes?'

People sat at tables close by overheard and gave their approval in shouts of yes and the clapping of hands.

Allegra watched cold eyed and chilled to the bone. She was reminded of a stage actor taking his encores with easy disdain – as if Roberto deserved such acclaim.

All the same, she was frightened of him. Her jaw tightened at the thought of him. Like father, like son. The two men were both arrogant and easily offended. They were also devious and vicious in their revenge. This father/son relationship could so easily disintegrate if the father knew that his son had tried to seduce her. But Allegra would never tell him that; strange as it might seem to an outsider, she loved Victor. Their relationship suited her fine.

She sipped delicately at the very good champagne Victor kept at this club alone, listening to what was being said with increasing alarm.

'Brooksy is such a prat at times. He crowed to me about this little business of hers. Do you know what she's doing?'

Victor laughed when his son told him that Marcie had a business making theatrical costumes. 'So you want this girl back!'

Roberto's face darkened. 'She can't just run out on me like that. She needs to know that.'

Allegra was panic stricken. She had to phone Marcie and tell her to get out of there. There was a payphone out in the hallway by the entrance where people phoned for taxis. She had to get to it. The cloakrooms were there too.

'We're leaving,' said Victor, cupping her arm and rising so that she had to rise too.

'I need the ladies'...'

Victor frowned. 'Well get on with it. Fast.'

She headed in the general direction of the ladies' cloakroom but did a slight detour to the

357

two telephone kiosks situated immediately opposite the doorman's desk.

Fingers became all thumbs. Her hands shook
as she attempted to get her purse from out of her
red patent clutch bag. Her heart was racing.
Pennies fell to the floor. A helpful hand reached
into the cubicle and picked them up. She found
herself looking into Victor's angry countenance.

'This ain't the ladies' cloakroom,' he growled.
'What the hell do you think you're up to?'

Tony Brooks was drunk as a skunk and lying flat
on his back. It wasn't just the booze that had laid
him low. Roberto Camilleri had been round to
have a little word and had brought that animal,
Malcolm, with him. At Roberto's command the
Black Bull had buried his fist in Tony's gut. Malcolm's closed fist was roughly the size of a small
anvil and just as hard. Tony went down. Malcolm
stood over him while Roberto poured a bowl of
porridge onto his face. Luckily for Tony it had
cooled.

'That's for nicking the old man's car without
permission.'

'Just the porridge?' Tony knew he was much too
glib for his own good, but he couldn't help it. He
felt he'd had grounds for borrowing the car.

On Roberto's say so, Malcolm thudded into
Tony's ribs.

'You nicked my old man's motor, you nonce.
He wants an apology.'

Although his gut felt as though it had exploded
into his lungs, Tony shook his head. 'I don't owe
him any apology. He's got it all wrong.'

'You've been pocketing the rent. Ain't that right?'

He'd been angry that Ella had scooted. The money had fuelled a booze-filled night and two whores who worked for Victor. It was them who'd reported him.

Malcolm lifted his foot. Tony winced at the thought of his right ribs being rearranged to match his left.

'You can't do this, Roberto, After all, ain't we going to be related? My Marcie ... and Michael?'

At mention of Marcie and Michael Roberto's stance altered. His jaw shifted from side to side as though he were grinding his teeth.

'Marcie and Michael? Are you havin' me on?'

Hearing Roberto's tone, Tony immediately knew he'd made a grave mistake mentioning Michael.

'They're good friends.'

Roberto bent down, blowing smoke into Tony's face. The sight of his eyes sent a chill through Marcie's dad. This bloke wasn't just nasty, he was vicious, as vicious a piece of work as you'd ever get this side of the river.

'Is he screwing your little girl, Brooksy? Is he having *carnal* relations with her?'

Tony stared. A warning signal went off in his brain. Say nothing. Don't dig yourself a deeper pit than you've already done. I shouldn't have told him about her new place, he said to himself. At least he hadn't given Roberto her exact address, had he? He'd merely told him how well Marcie was doing in her new venture, and how she was living and setting up her business upstairs from a trophy shop in Balham. Christ, what the hell have

I done? he thought, they could find her.

Roberto's face wasn't far from his. The clean-cut features looked demonic in the half-light coming in from the street outside.

'You sound like a fucking pimp, do you know that, Bertie? Still, not surprising seeing as you're running a team from Daisy Chain. Does your mother know what's going on? Does she?'

Roberto stabbed the burning cigar onto his cheek.

'Don't call me Bertie! Right!'

'So what do I call you? Pimp?'

The lighted cigar again, this time for longer. Tony winced and gritted his teeth.

Roberto was snarling. 'Let's get this straight, Brooksy. None of these girls are forced into reaping the benefit of a lasting relationship with a rich and powerful geezer. It's just suggested to them as a way to get the things they want in life. Nothing like that was ever suggested to Marcie. Scouts honour,' he said, giving a two-fingered salute. 'And by the way, it ain't been Michael screwing your daughter. It was me. I screwed her something chronic and she groaned with pleasure like the fucking little slut she is!'

Tony rubbed at the ache in his ribs, but it was nothing compared to the anger he was feeling now.

Taking the car had been a spur of the moment thing. He'd been involved in London's under-world long enough to know what went on there. Live and let live, that was his motto, but losing Ella had upset him. And now this. He'd survive this ordeal. In fact he'd go out of his way to survive it. And then he'd go looking for Roberto and when he caught up with him...

'Get up.'

It was Roberto rather than Malcolm who helped him to his feet. Tony eyed the young Camilleri warily. Something was on here.

Roberto brushed at the shoulders of Tony's leather jacket then rested his hands there. He looked into his eyes as though they were the best of old friends, friends who had fallen out over a very small matter.

'So. Michael. You approve of this?'

Tony could eat humble pie if he had to and lie as though he were telling the truth. He did all that now. 'I told her to lose the bloke, but you know how girls are nowadays,' he said with a nervous smile while gripping his aching ribs. 'After all, he's not you is he? He's not a Camilleri.'

Roberto's smile was slow to cross his face but Tony was glad to see it.

Roberto's mouth curled into a cruel sneer. 'No, Brooksy. You are right. He is not a Camilleri.'

Tony knew better than to disagree with him. Revenge, as they say, is best eaten cold. And that's what he would do. He would wait and take his revenge cold. Bent almost double with the pain of his broken ribs, he waited until they were gone.

There was a payphone down in the hallway. Gripping the banister tightly, he struggled down the stairs, each step sending a stab of pain to his ribs.

By the time he made the hallway the sweat was dripping off him and his cheek felt on fire where the cigar had burned his flesh. Worse than that were his ribs. He could barely breathe.

'You alright, Mr Brooks?'

The old lady on the ground floor was peeping out through a six-inch gap in her door.

'Fine. I need to phone my daughter.'

He managed to get the piece of paper out of his pocket with her number on plus the necessary coins. It was an effort to put the lot onto the phone shelf and one or two coins fell onto the floor. He glanced at them briefly. There was no way he could bend down to pick them up.

'Do you mind?' he asked the old lady and pointed to the coins. 'It's a matter of life and death...'

The busy flock wallpaper closed in on him and the red patterns became black and then no pattern at all. The receiver was left swinging. Mrs Allen from the ground floor picked it up and called for an ambulance.

Victor Camilleri swung his arm. Allegra gave one loud cry as she fell sideways. She landed on top of the teak coffee table where recently she'd quaffed champagne with Marcie and Sally.

'Who were you phoning, you fucking whore? Your boyfriend? Are you screwing around behind my back?'

'No!'

She screamed as he brought his crippled leg back again. This time it slammed into the table leg. The wood splintered. The coffee table crumpled beneath her weight and both she and it hit the floor.

She shook her head, her hair, usually so glossy,

sticking in wet tendrils around her wet cheeks and crying eyes.

'There's no one. No one!'

He grabbed a handful of her hair. Her neck straightened. Her chin went higher as she tried to alleviate the pain of having her hair pulled out by the roots.

'You're lying, you slut! Do you think I don't know what girls like you want? A bit of fresh meat now and again! Yes? Is the old man getting too saggy for you? Too slow to come in the sack?'

Tears and snot mixed on her beautiful face as she shook her head vehemently, terrified as to what he would do next.

'I would never do that. I love you.'

'So who were you phoning? Who were you fucking phoning?'

'A friend. A girlfriend.'

'A girlfriend, huh! So what's her name, this girl-friend you wanted to phone.'

'Sally! Her name's Sally.'

When he hit her this time, she fell to the floor and didn't get up. It was safe on the floor. Safe and dark.


### Chapter Thirty-nine

Allegra had taken to calling into the workshop in Balham three times a week and usually arrived at around lunchtime, drifting in on a cloud of Chanel perfume and perfectly attired. From the first moment they'd met Marcie had envied her class and her money. She always seemed to lead a hectic social life and even hinted at a rich fiancé. It occurred to Marcie that the fiancé was unduly possessive. Allegra had hinted that he was a very jealous man.

'I expect your parents are excited about the wedding,' Marcie had said blithely.

A frozen pause had flitted across Allegra's beautiful face. 'Yes,' she blurted. She did not go into detail.

Marcie dismissed the fragile moment. She didn't question how Allegra could afford such an opulent lifestyle, presuming her family supported her. It wasn't until later on that she found out the truth.

Today was Wednesday. Allegra always came in on Wednesday, but today she was late.

Sally was lounging back in a chair, her feet up on a cutting table. Her arms were folded across ample bosoms thrusting rebelliously against a yellow sweater and she was yawning.

'I'll make the tea,' said Renee, one of the part-timers who bragged that she'd been one of the Windmill Girls. The Windmill Theatre had boasted of never closing down during the war. It also boasted semi-naked showgirls forming still-life tableaux – dancing was forbidden. Renee seemed a bit short to have been one of their show-girls but she was a whiz on a sewing machine.

Marcie tucked a blanket around Joanna who had fallen asleep in an old Victorian nursing chair. She glanced up at the clock.

'Allegra's late.'

Sally opened one eye. 'P'raps she's gone off to

364

the French Riviera with some toff she's picked up.'

Marcie laughed. 'I can't imagine Allegra running off with a toff.'

'I would,' Sally said gloomily. 'Pete's alright, but I can't even get him as far as Brighton. It's Southend or nothing with him. He told me he's a "Kiss me Quick" sort of bloke. I said to him how France might turn me into a sex kitten like that Brigitte Bardot.'

Pete, Sally's beau, was a policeman and a bit of a Steady Eddie. Marcie had been surprised to know that she had a second boyfriend, a reserve for when Klaus, her rich lover who paid all the bills, wasn't around.

'So what did Pete say?' Marcie asked while taking the pins out of a heart-shaped G-string.

Sally pulled a disgruntled face. 'I don't think he was listening. He said he didn't like cats.'

Marcie looked at her. 'Are you kidding me?'

Sally burst but laughing.

Marcie joined her before once again looking up at the clock.

'She'll ring if she can't get here,' said Sally who'd noticed her looking.

'It's not working. Mr Griffiths downstairs has contacted the Post Office.'

Sally reached for a pair of lilac ostrich feathers that she was considering having stitched into a headdress. 'I think the lilac,' she said after viewing herself in a mirror. 'Is the teeny-weeny ready? I think I'll try it on.'

The teeny-weeny was the G-string.

'Drink your tea first,' said Marcie. 'Otherwise

you might scald your assets.'

Out in the small kitchen where the hot water heater above the sink made gurgling noises like a drowning goldfish, Renee was humming to herself as she filled the kettle, put tea into a large brown pot and opened a packet of custard creams. The steam from the kettle dampened her iron-grey curls so that they clung like limpets to her forehead. Her cheeks turned ruddy from the hot steam and she felt warm and happy.

Heading fast towards fifty, she could still hold a tune but her looks were long gone. The hourglass figure she'd had in her youth had widened and thickened to the proportions of a cottage loaf. Instead of Paris fashion she wore a full-figure apron that crossed over at the breasts and tied up around the middle.

She was just pouring hot water from the kettle to the pot when the door from downstairs opened. Surprised to see a man up here, she presumed he'd lost his way.

'If you're wanting trophies for your darts league, it's downstairs,' she told him.

He took off a pair of sunglasses. She noticed they had pink lenses. His shirt was pink too. His expression was as dead as stone. 'What's your name?'

Realising she'd made a mistake, she stalled answering. This man wasn't dressed like a darts player.

'Renee,' she said and managed not to sound wobbly.

He put his arm around her. She flinched. His

366

arm was heavy on her shoulders, but only because he was bearing down on her. She tried not to feel frightened, but she was.

'Well, Renee, look at me. Do I look like someone involved in a pub darts league!'

Feeling a great need to head for the loo, she shook her head slowly.

'Quite correct, Renee. Now, tell me this, is Marcie in there?' He jerked his chin towards the door on the other side of the hallway.

Renee nodded.

'Right.'

He regarded the flowered cups and saucers sitting with the sugar, milk and shiny brown teapot. The tray was made of tin and decorated with a picture of the *Flying Scotsman* – the steam locomotive that held the speed record from London to Edinburgh.

'Finish making that tea, Renee, then take a seat. I'll do the honours.'

He pushed her towards a metal-legged chair once she'd finished and picked up the tray. She sat down as stiffly as a jointed marionette made of wood.

Renee felt that her heart was beating so loudly she could hear it echoing in her head.

'Let's give old Marcie a little surprise shall we?' he said.

Then he was gone. Where once she'd been warmed by the steam, Renee now felt cold. Her hands began to shake. She threw them over her face. She didn't want to see what would happen. But she knew it would be bad.

Sally was still musing about her current stage outfit and planning for future stage routines. 'I'm thinking that I'd like leopard skin for my next routine. Imagine if you will me strolling on stage with a real leopard on the end of a gold chain – or one of those other things – a cheetah and me in a matching skin hiding the bits that count. What do you think?'

Marcie stood like Lot's wife – as still and white as a pillar of salt. She was staring at the person who'd appeared in the open doorway.

'Tea for two,' Roberto exclaimed. He jerked his head at the door leading to the metal stairs at the back of the building 'You can get out,' he said to Sally. 'Two's company, three's a crowd.'

Sally didn't need to be introduced. She'd seen the Camilleris arrive in clubs they didn't own. Managers and owners alike knew who they were. So did the girls. Even if she hadn't known him, the look on Marcie's face was enough to tell her who this was.

'I'm stopping right here,' Sally said grimly.

Joanna, who had been sound asleep on the sofa, chose that moment to wake up and call for her mother.

'Take the kid with you,' Roberto added, looking irritable that Joanna had had the temerity to interrupt his dramatic entrance.

Marcie picked up her daughter and held her tightly to her chest. 'My child stays with me.'

She felt like a tigress protecting her cub. Whatever it took she would not give in to him.

'We've got some talking to do.'

'We've got nothing to talk about. I don't want

you. I don't want anything to do with you.' She cuddled Joanna closer.

Roberto's eyes darkened beneath the broad brim of his hat. He wasn't used to being given the brush off. He glanced again at Sally. 'I thought I told you to clear off.'

'Sally is my friend. She's staying.'

'She's your friend?' He pointed a disdainful finger. 'That old brass. She's a stripper. Do you know that?'

'Yes. What would the Camilleris do without strippers? She takes her clothes off and you make money from it.'

Sally butted in. 'Yeah! Nightclub owner, pimp – what's the bloody difference, mate?'

'You cow...!'

He flung the tea tray, but Sally was quicker. The chair she'd been sitting on steamed with hot tea and spilt milk. She stood by the door, still defiant and determined she would not leave her friend alone.

'Roberto!'

Marcie's voice pulled him up short. Sensing her mother's fear and disturbed by the shouting, Joanna began to cry.

'I want you to go, Roberto.'

Her heart was beating wildly, but she stood her ground even though she feared him.

'I don't think you do,' he said, shaking his head.

'I do. I don't want you. I don't want anything to do with you.'

He looked at her in disbelief. Sleek and shiny with money, he'd had all the advantages from the day he'd been born; such a contrast with Johnnie who hadn't even known who his real parents were.

'You little tart! Who the fuck do you think you are?'

'Someone who doesn't want you,' she said coldly, determined not to shout and further upset her child. Her eyes glittered with contempt and hatred. Inside she quivered like a straw in the wind.

'You'll regret this.'

She shook her head. 'No I won't.' Curling his bottom lip, he diverted his attention to the mauve outfit Sally had been musing over earlier.

'You've dropped a long way from King's Road fashion to making this kind of stuff.'

'Someone has to. It's very lucrative.'

'Making tassels and stick-on pasties for strippers?'

'Not just strippers. I also make outfits for showgirls and female impersonators. Some men like dressing up as women.'

'They're queer,' he sneered.

'On the contrary, they love women. It's you that doesn't like women, Roberto; neither you nor your father. That's why you use them like tins of corned beef.'

When he shook his head she realised he wasn't going to take no for an answer. He would be back time and time again because he didn't believe that women were capable of sustaining a single important decision.

'You'll change your mind.'

She shook her head, aware of the warmth of her child against her body.

'Never.'

Black eyebrows formed a deep V, meeting like the tip of an arrow over his nose. 'Does the landlord of this dump know you're making this stuff? Is it him downstairs? If so I'm off to put him straight. Then you'll be out. You'll have nowhere else to go.'

Marcie's smile was slow and triumphant. She dared to hope that he would go soon. He certainly couldn't intimidate the landlord. Allegra was far and above all that.

'My friend Allegra owns this property. There's nothing you can do. Nothing at all!'

At first she thought that his dropped jaw meant he was seriously disappointed, but then he began to laugh.

'Allegra? Allegra Montillado? She owns this dump?'

Marcie was immediately unnerved. She exchanged eye contact with Sally. Sally's eyelids fluttered nervously before she looked away. Something was wrong here and she had a terrible feeling that she'd walked into some kind of trap.

Roberto's laughter died but the crooked smile remained. 'Oh, yeah,' he said, nodding his head slowly and wearing that know-it-all smile. 'Allegra Montillado! She might own it alright, but my father owns her. She's his tart. His bit on the side! Didn't you know that Marcie, darling? Allegra Montillado is nothing more than a high-class whore – my father's high-class whore! My father pays the rent on her high-class drum. He pays for every bit of high-class rag on her back. Didn't you know that?'

The veins on his neck stood proud like fine

twigs as he threw back his head and laughed. His thick dark hair tickled the collar of his plum-coloured velvet jacket.

'What a turn up!' His laughter and his voice made her ears ache and made Joanna cry with more force than before.

Marcie felt as though June had turned to November. A cold chill trickled like iced water down her back. Allegra was Victor's mistress? She couldn't believe it. She suddenly realised that she was in instant danger of losing everything she'd worked for: her business, her flat and a gang of friends of whom she'd grown very fond.

Roberto stood like the Statue of Liberty, triumphant and empowered. He pointed a disdainful finger straight at her forehead. 'You're leaving here, Marcie. I'll make sure that you're leaving here. And there's nowhere for you to go except to me.'

She felt surprisingly calm. Her eyes were steady, her expression surprisingly serene. 'No. There is another place I can go.'

'Back to that crap place you came from? Marry some local yokel and spend your life banging out kids with never two farthings to scratch your backside?' His smirk was as wide as Chelsea Bridge. 'Don't make me laugh, doll.' He threw a card onto the coffee table. 'Ring me when you're ready. If you don't ring I'll be back at seven this evening.' He was halfway out of the door. 'Oh, you can send the kid to your old granny if you like. Send the kid to her with Fairy Lightfoot there. She can make herself look respectable for once – probably for the only time in her life.'

He went then.

A few seconds and the door opened again. Renee peered around the door. With flickering eyes she took in the mess Roberto had made. She shook her head. 'He's gone. I saw him go. Not a very nice man.'

Marcie made no comment. She was rocking the screaming Joanna while trying to piece this together. She didn't hear Sally offer to help Renee clear up. The hand caressing her daughter's head was soft. Her hatred for Roberto was hard and strong. What was even worse was that Allegra had deceived her. The refined young woman who seemed of impeccable breeding and excellent connections was a high-class whore. Marcie could have accepted that. What she couldn't accept was that Allegra had kept it a secret and seemed to have been spying on her.

'I can't believe it,' she said, shaking her head.

Sally too was mulling over it too. 'I feel quite respectable,' she said with a toss of her head. 'Seems like we're sisters under the skin.'

Considering all that had happened Sally's flippancy was irritating and oddly out of place. Marcie was reminded that the two of them had confronted her with the idea of taking on the flat and the workroom in the first place. Making stage costumes for nightclub dancers had been their idea. That's why the business had grown so quickly. They knew the dancers themselves – or at least, Sally did.

Cuddling the now placated Joanna to her breast, Marcie looked around at her home. It wasn't large, but she'd grown fond of it.

Somehow it now seemed ugly because of one particular thought that she couldn't get out of her head. Was it really Victor's money behind this? Was Allegra just the front instructed to report back to him?

And Sally had been in on it from the start.

She turned accusing eyes in her direction. 'You must have known. Hadn't you two been in contact before we met up again?'

Sally was too quick to shake her head. 'No, I didn't. I thought she was just rich. You might as well forget about her. Nightclub acts live all over the place so as long as you're a bit central, everything will be alright.'

Marcie eyed her sidelong. Something wasn't quite right here. Sally's eyes would not meet hers and if it hadn't been for Renee mopping up the mess Roberto had made, she would have asked some stiff questions. As it was Joanna began crying for her feed.

Sally was putting her coat on. 'Don't let him worry you. Right?'

'You're off?'

Sally glanced purposefully at her watch. 'Good grief. Look at the time. My dentist will be wondering where I've got to if I don't get a move on.'

Sally's watch strap was loose and the face kept falling around to the wrong side of her wrist. Marcie noticed that when she'd checked the time she'd been confronted with the strap not the face. So! Two friends were deceiving her and everything about her new-found life was tarnished because of it.

'Sally! I'm getting the distinct impression that

Allegra is not the only one with something to hide.'

Marcie's shout brought everyone to a standstill. The busy Renee picked up another piece of broken cutlery and took it and the tray out of the room. Sally paused by the door. She could still rush out on the pretext of the dental appointment – an appointment that hadn't been mentioned previously.

The false eyelashes fluttered as she fought to find the right words that would do for now. 'Look,' she said, having at last regained her old courage and flippant casual manner. 'I think it's time you knew the truth. But I don't think I'm the right person to tell you. Give me an hour and I'll bring someone round who can tell you everything.'

'Is that so? Well, we'll see about that. I feel I've been taken for a fool,' Marcie said. 'You two have been taking me for a fool.'

Even though Roberto hadn't been aware of Allegra's involvement in her business, she still suspected he might have been putting it on – just so the situation could continue and he could keep his eye on her. It would explain why she hadn't been getting any phone calls or visits from him. He'd been biding his time, perhaps laughing at the fact that she was ignorant of what was going on. She'd been stupid not to see things as they really were. She'd been making outfits for nightclub acts. The clubs owned by the Camilleris used a lot of nightclub acts. Sadly, everything was falling into place and she was angry, and not just angry. She was frightened.

Sally shook her head vehemently. She was still

poised for flight.

'Look,' she said, her pearl pink fingernails gripping the edge of the open door. 'Give me an hour. Everything will be sorted. You'll see.'

The door closed.

There was nothing Marcie could do to prevent her from leaving. One hour! How much could she pack in one hour? How far could she flee? She rang Michael's office, where he'd set up his commercial property business. The receptionist told her he was out at an auction.

'Tell him it's Marcie and I'm going home.'

Sheerness and the Isle of Sheppey and a simpler life beckoned. She would not be here when Sally got back.

## Chapter Forty

Marcie's stepmother, Babs, stood by the back door with her arms folded. Smoke rose from a lighted cigarette hanging between the index and middle fingers of her right hand. She was frowning at the ungainly figure digging the dark earth where the chicken coop used to be. Armed with dibbers, the boys were making the holes for the cabbage seedlings to go in.

'Can't he grow nothing other than cabbages?'

Her question was directed at her mother-in-law. Rosa Brooks was sitting by the back door shelling peas. She always kept a low stool outside the back door for this purpose.

'No,' she said as she popped a pod and plucked the green peas from within.

'And he's talking to himself,' said Babs and frowned. She'd taken to visiting Rosa more often since Marcie had left for London taking her kid with her. She had it in mind to get herself a job now she had a ready-made babysitter to hand. Rosa could look after Annie while she went to work. A bit of extra money would come in handy. She hadn't broached the subject yet. A bit of softening up was called for first. Get Rosa on a different subject before asking if she was up to looking after Annie.

Frowning, she licked a sliver of tobacco from her lip and flicked it into flight.

Garth was her present subject of choice. 'He's not right that one. I don't know whether I should let the boys play with him. He might be a bit queer – you know...'

'No. I do not know. Garth would not harm anyone. Of that I am sure.'

Babs watched Archie and Arnold, her two boys, put their dibbers to one side and pat Garth on the arm before taking their bicycles out through the back gate. They'd obviously had enough of gardening.

'See you later, Ma,' they both shouted.

Garth's mouth continued to move as though he were chewing something. His voice carried towards them. His words were jumbled and he certainly wasn't talking to the boys. He'd seen them go.

Babs decided to give it another try. 'He's still talking to himself.'

'No he is not.'

Babs pursed her lips. Rosa could be a right cow sometimes. But she had to try again. That bloke at the fishmonger's had promised her a job serving behind the counter. Who cares if she came home smelling of smoked haddock? The money wasn't bad and best of all she got to take home the fish that had been on display for a few days and hadn't sold. Especially on a weekend; fish on Sunday would make a change from a Sunday roast, she told herself. It would also taste extra special because it was free.

'Mum. There was something I wanted to ask you. I've been offered this job and what with Tony working away all the time...'

Rosa wasn't listening. She'd got up from her chair, her old, dark eyes filled with alarm.

Babs looked up the garden to where it seemed the field of ripe cabbages in front of the seedlings had suddenly come alive. Leaves and stalks were bending and trembling. Garth was nowhere to be seen.

Rosa got to him first. He was on the ground, his limbs twitching and his eyes rolling in his head.

'Call an ambulance,' ordered Rosa.

Babs didn't wait to be told twice. She knew a fit when she saw one and headed for the telephone box at the end of the street.

Rosa cupped her hand beneath Garth's head. 'Garth? Garth? Can you hear me? Can you hear me, Garth?'

No one had trained her to speak calmly and firmly. No one had trained her to hold his eyes with her own. She just *felt* that this was what she must do.

Some would say that look was hypnotic, though Rosa did not look at it that way. To her mind she was sharing her own strength and also her own experiences in order to allay Garth's worst fears.

'Relax. Breathe deeply.'

She showed him how, taking deep breaths directly from her diaphragm.

'Listen to me. Listen to me... Do you hear my voice, Garth?'

Even as she said the words, the frenzied twitching lost its momentum, his eyes stopped rolling and stayed fixed on hers. Only the dribble remained staining his shirt collar and pullover.

He nodded. 'Yes.'

'Did you go somewhere?'

'Yes. I couldn't breathe, Auntie Rosa. And I was all alone buried under dust and dirt and bits of old clothes.'

Rosa brushed away the dirt that had been flicked onto his face. 'Like a tomb.' Her voice shook slightly as she said it. She too knew what it was like to be buried in a tomb with dead people.

He nodded.

Babs came running back. 'The telephone wasn't working. How is he?'

'Fine,' said Rosa. She brushed Garth's hair back from his face. 'There's still some fruitcake left,' she said to him. 'Can you manage another slice? Fine. He will be fine, I think. So no ambulance is coming?'

'No. But I did see Father Justin pedalling by. He was on his way to see some dying woman so said hc would ring the place Garth was in before.

He was certain they'd come.'

'Barbara, you are the stupidest woman I have ever met. Do you not realise what you have done?' Rosa's face was like thunder.

Babs frowned. 'I got help. That was what I was supposed to do, wasn't it?'

Rosa shook her head. 'Father Justin treads a narrow path and his mind is no different. He sees Garth on the outside only. He does not know what lies beneath, and even if he did he would go out of his way to destroy it.'

Babs didn't have a clue what her mother-in-law was talking about, though it was bound to be about dead people and seeing things that other folk couldn't see. She couldn't see anything herself but she wanted to stay on the best side of her. She wanted her to look after her kids if – or rather when – she got another job.

'Stand out on the kerb and tell them it was all a mistake,' said Rosa. 'Tell them he tripped and hurt his head. That was all it was. He is quite alright now.'

Babs stared at Rosa Brooks. Her mind was working like a steam train going full pelt along a straight line. She had to keep reminding herself that Annie needed to be looked after when she returned to work and her boys needed to be fed when they got home from school. She wouldn't be home until later. They could make their own way home then...

'OK. I'll sort them,' she said.

'Your skirt is wriggling up,' Rosa pointed out. She looked disdainful.

Babs opened her mouth, a sharp retort on the

tip of her tongue, before reminding herself that she was here on a mission.

Tugging her short skirt down over dimpled thighs until she looked reasonably respectable, she shot out through the house. The ambulance emblazoned with the insignia of the mental home was chugging to a stop beside the kerb. Brushing aside the midges attracted by her cheap hairspray, she sauntered like Jayne Mansfield on three-inch heels, getting there just as the two men crew flung open the doors. One of them was carrying a straitjacket. The other had a clipboard tucked beneath his arm.

You haven't lost the old magic, she thought to herself as their eyes settled on her best bits before smiling at her and asking the whereabouts of the patient.

'False alarm,' she told them, putting on her sexiest pout, one hand resting a hip flung to one side. 'The poor chap only hit his head. In fact it seems as though he's had some sense knocked into him. He's come round quite normal in fact. Wouldn't surprise me if he gets a job as a brain surgeon next.'

One of the blokes tugged his attention away long enough to shove his cap back on his thinning hair and shake his head. 'Sorry, love, but once we've been called out on a job we've got to go back with somebody. I also have to say we don't look kindly on people who call us out on false pretences.'

His mate, whose waistline equalled his height, nodded and confirmed it was so in a high falsetto voice.

'Look, boys, I had to do something,' she said, thinking on her feet as she shrugged one well-shaped shoulder. 'That Father Justin is a right card. He might have taken a vow not to have anything to do with women, but you take it from me, give the old goat half a chance ... so when my brother fell and hurt his head and I got the call from my aunt, well, I had an excuse ... I told him that dear Garth had gone potty again and he called you boys.'

The two men looked at each other then back at her. 'Father Justin?' said the fat one. 'Are you saying the old geezer likes a bit of hanky-panky?'

Babs knew how to undulate from her head to her toes. It was as though her body flowed like water curving around bends in the riverbank.

'Well, you can see how I am. He can't resist me. Reckons he dreams about me at night and – well – I leave the rest to your imagination, boys. If he were nine years old I'd say it was a wet dream. Wouldn't you?'

The two men smirked and there was that look in their eyes that men have when they think they know it all and have done it all. Babs knew that look. Men had looked at her that way since she was fourteen years old. She'd won them over. She knew she had.

'We ... ll...'

There was no sign of either Rosa or Garth in the garden. Babs headed for the back door to find Rosa had Garth sat in one of the big armchairs of the pair that sat on either side of the fireplace. His scrawny neck and overlarge head sprouted out from within the folds of a rough grey blanket. His neck being so scrawny and the blanket so large, he reminded her of a tortoise emerging from its shell. He was holding three crayons in his hand. He'd obviously been drawing – his other favourite pastime besides planting cabbages. Rosa had bought Garth a sketch pad in Woolworths. She was holding it open and frowning at whatever it was he'd just drawn.

'He looks a lot better. Just as well that they've gone,' said Babs. 'Though Father Justin will not be pleased.'

'It has probably made things very awkward for him,' Rosa said softly.

Babs chortled. 'Not half as awkward as I have that's for bloody sure.'

Just for once Rosa didn't reprimand her use of bad language. Her eyes were on Garth. Normally, despite any eventuality, he was jabbering away like a clueless mynah bird. But not now. He was sitting silently, the glowing coals of the range sending his deep-set eyes into dark shadow, the contours of his face into dark almost demonic relief.

Rosa looked worried.

Babs felt uneasy. 'What is it? What's happened?'

'Garth came in from the garden and would not speak. I gave him a piece of paper and some crayons. Even though he cannot read and write he can draw pictures.'

Wordlessly, Rosa passed Babs the piece of paper on which Garth had drawn one of his pictures. On one occasion in the past he'd drawn two people buried beneath a pile of earth. The incident had actually occurred when one of the neighbours had been buried beneath a pile of earth. The neighbour had been digging a nuclear fallout shelter – he'd been obsessed about the Russians invading. The supports for the underground structure – dug in his own back garden – had fallen in on him. He'd been killed. Garth had been helping him and had survived.

Babs frowned at the drawing. She shrugged, not understanding. 'It looks like a couple of cowboys in a gunfight. Or at least one of them looks like a cowboy. He's wearing a cowboy hat.'

'And the body lying between them?'

Babs looked as directed. The rough drawing showed a female form with long blonde hair.

'Oh Christ,' she muttered. She'd recognised Marcie and according to the drawing she might already be dead.

## Chapter Forty-one

Tony Brooks had signed himself out of the hospital the moment he was bandaged up and headed back to his bedsit to lick his wounds. Today he would sort things out with Marcie and perhaps nail that jerk Roberto. So far he'd hardly managed to get out of bed even to go down to the phone. When he had managed to phone his daughter, there was no response. There was no answer from the phone box at the end of Endeavour Terrace either. Sod it! Give it a few days and he'd give them a ring then and tell them what had happened. He'd have it straight in his head by then.

He'd crawled back to bed. He needed to rest. The doctors had told him that. His ribs would take some time to heal.

He turned his pillow over to the cool side in an effort to ease the thudding in his head. If it had been a hangover it would have worked but today it didn't. The hammering continued.

Peering out from beneath the pillow he saw the sliver of daylight piercing the slim gap between the dark-pink curtains – hardly the right colour for a man's room, but hell, this was hardly home.

Blearily he peered at the cheap alarm clock sitting on the bedside table. Eleven thirty. Time to get up. And still the hammering, though now he realised that it wasn't in his head. Someone was hammering at the door.

Groggily, he eased his legs out from beneath the pile of tangled bedclothes and staggered across the dull brown lino to the front door. His ribs were still heavily bandaged.

The two Jamaicans had mean faces. Their pinstriped suits had padded shoulders. Either that or they really were wide enough to hold up a road bridge. At first he thought one of them might be Ella's husband but he realised that they were men he'd collected rent from in the past, though usually he had back-up muscle on hand, and in fact Victor himself had done the last collection as he recalled. Something about teaching Roberto the ropes. He wondered briefly how they had found his gaff before realising that it was time for a quick exit.

'We want the ring,' they shouted. 'That is all.'

He didn't have a clue what they were talking about and wasn't about to wait and find out. Broken ribs or not, he was out to break the four-minute mile.

The lock wouldn't hold for long, and there was no time to dress. Grabbing what he could, he climbed out of the window dressed only in his underpants.

A tousled head came out from the other side of the bedclothes.

'Tony?'

The girl was a nightclub hostess. They'd got drunk together the night before. God knows what else they'd done. He couldn't remember. Couldn't even remember what her name was though it might be Freda – or Frankie – something like that.

He was gone, out of the window and taking the long jump to the ground. Luckily he was only on the first floor. If he'd been on the second he'd have broken his leg. As it was his bones jarred, but he hit the ground running.

He wasn't stupid enough to stop. If he could jump out of that window so could his two visitors if they'd a mind to. Or they might not, he thought, as he ran, his bare feet slapping along the concrete of the back alley. They weren't as desperate as him. Either way he wasn't staying around to find out.

He stopped to put on some clothes at the rear exit to a transport café fronting the North Circular. It boasted a pair of wooden gates at the entrance and they were mostly kept closed. Tony slipped through.

The owner, who was also the cook, came out to tip some food waste into a bin. The stink of old grease came with him and smears of food decorated an apron that at some time had been pure white. A half-smoked cigarette hung from the corner of his mouth. Tony knew him as George, an old soldier with a beer belly and a rotten taste in food. Fry-ups were top on his list.

He didn't look surprised to see Tony in a state of undress – almost as though he was never surprised to see anything in his back yard. Rodents mostly.

'Alright, Tony. How you doing?'

'I'm in a bit of a rush.'

'You in some kind of training?' he asked in a desultory fashion.

'Too fucking right. I'm out to break the four-minute mile,' said Tony while glancing nervously at the ramshackle gates. So far so good. They stayed closed.

Tony fastened his trousers and shrugged himself into an Aran cable knit. He looked down at his feet. 'Got a pair of shoes I could borrow, George?'

'Have these.'

George slipped his feet out of the tartan slippers he was wearing. Tony looked down at them in dismay.

'Not exactly Italian leather are they, George? Though I suppose beggars can't be choosers.'

'Ten bob to you.'

'I only want to borrow them,' Tony protested. 'Anyway, I didn't bring any money with me. I came out in a bit of a rush if you know what I mean.'

Having come out of the army to unemploy-
ment, George had strayed into gangland. He
knew how rough it could be out there. 'You can
owe me.' He jerked his thumb at the kitchen
door. 'Wanna nip through?'

Tony was never one for looking a gift horse in
the mouth when there was trouble on his tail. He
took instant advantage of the offer. 'Ta, mate.'

The kitchen swam in grease. Each mouthful of
breath was greasy and the slippers stuck to the
grungy floor beneath his feet.

The café was stuffed with lorry drivers and
tradesmen scoffing their midday meals. Bubble
and squeak-topped with an egg was number one
on the menu. Tony grimaced at the thought of it.
Knowing George, some of the stuff in the mess of
vegetables beneath the egg had been simmering
on the hob for weeks. Still, the blokes who
frequented the place were used to grub like that.
Their old ladies probably cooked much the same
way: plenty of fry-ups and plenty of lard.

Halfway through he spotted two familiar figures
in pinstriped suits. They slowed outside the café
and peered in. Tony ducked into a spare seat
opposite two blokes big enough to form a barrier
between the black guys and him.

They looked at him then at each other. One of
them glanced briefly over his shoulder before
going on piling a fork with bubble and squeak
dripping with runny yolk.

Tony fingered the few pounds he had in his
pocket. He considered his lying to George justified as he'd need the price of a taxi.

The bloke opposite him was very round. The

braces of blue overalls strained over his shoulders. His cutlery clanged onto the plate.

Tony met the look in his eyes.

'Need a lift, mate?'

Well, that was something of a relief. Tony answered that he wouldn't mind. 'Where you going?'

'Isle of Sheppey. Got some sheet metal to deliver to an engineering works in Sheerness.'

'That'll do me fine,' said Tony, unable to hide his relief. 'I live there.'


Michael knew something really bad must have happened to make Marcie leave her flat and her business so suddenly.

'So!' he said to Sally. 'Where's she gone?'

Sally was dancing at the Jamboree Club that night. She had a resident spot there on a Friday night because she was that popular with the punters.

'Don't know,' she muttered, fastening her suspender onto one of her fishnet stockings.

She took time to straighten her seam, running her hands over stocking top and bare thigh. She did the same with the second stocking, seemingly too busy to bother with the likes of him.

Michael wasn't fooled. Sally might be blasé on the outside, but he could tell she was nervous.

'Your bloke in tonight?'

'Might be.'

'The German or the copper?'

'The copper. And Klaus is Swiss, not German.'

Sally's 'lesser lover', as she called him, was a copper, an inspector in the vice squad who had got into the habit of taking his work home with him. Sally was a fine piece of work alright. She was sassy, sexy and as bold as brass. She was also Marcie's friend.

Being purposely evasive to Michael's enquiries, his patience was wearing thin. He grabbed her upper arm. 'I want to know what happened to make her leave, Sally.'

'You're hurting.'

'You're struggling.'

'Damn you.'

'Tell me. I don't want to hurt her, Sally. I love her. Do you understand that?'

Her eyes had a brittle sparkle to them when she looked up at him. Her bottom lip curled in anger. 'You Camilleris...'

'I'm not like them. Anyway, my name is Jones.'

'Your blood's the same,' she spat.

'No. That's where you're wrong. Did you tell Roberto where she was?'

'Of course not.'

'You and him had a bit of a fling – don't think I don't know about it. Does Marcie know you had a fling with him? Well, Sally? Does she?'

She looked ashamed when she shook her head. Michael found himself feeling sorry for her. He let go of her arm. He sensed she was close to tears and also how upset she was.

'I didn't tell Roberto where she was. Honest I didn't.'

He believed her, but there was something else going on here, something he didn't quite understand. Normally he would have shoved off, but he didn't. It wasn't in his nature to intimidate women, but he decided to push her that bit more. He wanted to find Marcie. He wanted to know she was safe.

'Have you tried her father?'

He nodded. 'He's done a bunk too. Latest reports are that he's heading for home on account of messing around with someone's wife.'

'Oh!'

Sally swivelled round in her chair to face the mirror. It was surrounded with light bulbs just like the ones in Hollywood films. Her hand shook as she applied lipstick.

Seeing this, Michael rested his hands on her shoulders. He felt the shiver of fear that ran through her and knew it wasn't because of him.

'You have to tell me,' he said, his eyes meeting hers via the mirror. 'Who betrayed her?'

For the first time ever on a Friday night, Sexy Sally did not take off her clothes in front of a baying audience of horny men. She'd broken down and told Michael all he needed to know. She'd told him about Allegra being his father's mistress and Allegra's beautiful face being bruised and battered when she'd gone round to see her after Roberto's outburst. She told him about Carla and also about the person who was funding the whole operation. He was still numb when he crossed London to see his father, the only person who could stop Roberto in his tracks.

## Chapter Forty-two

The taxi driver helped Marcie alight from the taxi that had brought her from the railway station to Endeavour Terrace. He also helped her out with the luggage she'd managed to bring with her.

'I used to go to school with you. Remember?'

His name was Paul Smith. 'How could I forget?'

He was pleasant enough and didn't hesitate to help her carry her belongings up the garden path. Having heard a car draw up and the front gate squeak as it opened, her grandmother was standing at the door.

'You are here!'

She sounded both relieved and surprised, as though there might have been some reason why she shouldn't be. Marcie was apologetic.

'Sorry, Gran. I didn't have time to phone.'

Her grandmother stared for a split second. That was all it took for her to take in Marcie's flushed cheeks and breathlessness,

'This is home. There is always a place for you here whether you let me know you are coming or not. And you are well?'

Again that probing as though she might not be well.

Marcie smiled and was reassuring. 'Why shouldn't I be?'

'Of course.'

Once her grandmother had taken Joanna from her arms, she paid the taxi driver.

He winked at her and held her hand for a beat as she handed him the money.

'If ever you fancied a night out, I'm your man.'

'I'll bear that in mind if I'm that desperate,' she said with a tight smile, before slamming the door in his face.

Her grandmother paused in the hallway. 'Father Justin is here,' she said over her shoulder.

'Eating cake and drinking tea,' Marcie added sarcastically. The old priest spent most of the day eating and drinking. She sincerely doubted he kept a crumb of food in the presbytery, except perhaps a bottle or two of communion wine. He depended on charity in the shape of his parishioners for his daily bread.

Her grandmother threw her a look that warned her to be polite and respectable.

'Don't worry, Gran. I'll keep a civil tongue in my head.'

They went through to the kitchen where the priest was sitting in one of the fireside chairs. He was presently leaning across to the other chair where Garth was sitting silently, a vacant look in his eyes. He jerked back when they entered. On seeing Marcie his eyes lit up, the yellow streaks in the whites running into the pale pupils.

'Marcie!' He got to his feet, smothering her hand with both of his. 'How are you, my child?'

His eyes twinkled and like the taxi driver, his hands lingered too long on hers.

'I'm very well, Father. And yourself?' she said

while retracting her hand. She adopted a con-
genial expression though the effort to smile
almost broke her jaw.

He told her that he was fine and that he'd come
here to try to persuade her grandmother to let
Garth go into the care of some nuns at a Convent
in Essex.

'Your grandmother doesn't agree with my suggestion. I think she has something against Essex.
She couldn't possibly have anything against the
holy sisters can she now?'

The comment was delivered with good humour,
a thick Irish brogue and a light chuckle.

'And how does Garth feel about this?'

'He does not wish—'

Father Justin butted in. 'Now, now, Rosa. The
poor fool can't know his own mind. You know
that as well as I do.'

Ignoring the priest's ugly eyes, Marcie looked at
the poor creature sat huddled at the fire with a
blanket around him. The day was neither warm
nor cold, certainly not cold enough to warrant a
blanket.

Garth had not acknowledged her arrival. He was
sitting staring at the glowing coals of the old cast-
iron range. It wasn't usual for him to ignore her
and the fact that he was doing so troubled her.

'Is he ill?' she asked.

'He is tired,' said her grandmother. She passed
Joanna back into her mother's arms before
dealing with the priest. 'That is all the cake,
Father,' she said, taking the empty tea plate from
the priest's hands. She took the last piece remaining on the cake stand and gave it to Joanna.

Father Justin looked surprised. So was Marcie. Although Father Justin O'Flanagan was not the most likeable of people, her grandmother always deferred to his position and was courteous, never showing her true feelings towards him. A lot of that courtesy was extended through cake.

The priest got to his feet but was languorous in his movements. Marcie concluded that he was not inclined to leave too swiftly. Turning his back to the range, he stood with legs slightly apart. He held his black robe aloft at the rear and rubbed his rear with his hands.

'I've been telling your grandmother that she's done her Christian duty for Garth and she'll be rewarded in heaven. The sisters will look after him well. He'll be better off there.'

London had made Marcie a braver soul than she had been. She chanced looking into his pale eyes and saw nothing but conceit and gluttony staring back at her. And something else; her flesh crept when she realised she could also see lust there.

'I think that's a ridiculous statement,' she said hotly, folding her arms while staring steadily into those awful eyes. 'Do you have some reason of your own for wanting him to go there, Father O'Flanagan? Do they pay you on a commission basis for patients referred there? Is the Catholic Church that short of funds at the present time?'

She heard her grandmother gasp. She saw the priest's mouth slacken as the sickly smile fall from his face.

'Not at all,' he said after swift consideration. 'I'm just thinking of your grandmother dealing with a boy trapped in a man's body. He still plays with the kids in the street. You have to be careful of him doing things like that. He's got urges and what with young kids around...'

'Your insinuation appals me. Garth wouldn't hurt a fly, Father Justin O'Flanagan. And now I suggest you leave. I'd like to talk to my grandmother alone and besides I'm tired and my baby's tired. I would appreciate if you left now.'

His expression stiffened. She could tell he didn't like being put down like that. The lust had certainly gone from his eyes. Waddling and shuffling his feet, he wished Rosa Brooks a good night and made for the back door.

Once he was gone Garth Davies expressed a deep sigh. Both women looked at him in surprise. Garth smiled at Marcie. 'Hello, Marcie. I'm better now.'

He grinned in his usual lopsided fashion, his two front teeth large and uneven.

For the second time in the space of minutes, Rosa Brooks had something to gasp about.

'That is the first time he has spoken for days.' She looked at her granddaughter as though seeing her for the first time. 'You did this. You came home and did this, yet on his drawing...'

'He's still drawing?'

Marcie could tell by the look on her grandmother's face that this was indeed the case.

'I bought him a sketchbook,' said her grandmother. 'His mother only gave him bits of white meat paper that the butcher uses to wrap up a pound of chops. I thought he deserved a proper sketchbook. He did one of you before you came home. That is why I was so surprised to see you.

And so relieved.'

Marcie read the look on her grandmother's face. She was not nearly so gifted as Rosa Brooks, but she knew her grandmother well enough to read that she was unsettled.

Marcie picked up Garth's sketch pad and saw the drawing. The people it depicted were drawn in coloured crayon. She saw the three figures: one lying on the ground and the others standing over her. The figure on the ground wore a skirt and was obviously a woman. The other two were men and one of them was wearing a wide-brimmed hat. She didn't need her grandmother to interpret who they were. The man wearing the wide-brimmed hat was Roberto. The other was Michael. She saw what her grandmother had seen; these two men were fighting over her. She knew then that it wasn't over. Roberto had come for her once and he wouldn't give up that easily. If he went back to her flat and found it empty, he'd guess where she'd run to. It was only a matter of time before he came for her again.

## Chapter Forty-three

The blow landed on his father's chin and sent Victor Camilleri sprawling, his heavy built-up shoe landing like a hammer on his good leg. Blood trickled from his cut lip. He looked surprised.

'I'm warning you Michael, my son...' He raised an accusing finger.

'Warn me all you bloody like. And don't call me your son! You did sweet FA for me until I was of an age to be useful to your operation. Roberto's your son, not me.' Michael stood over him, barely able to control his anger.

'You have to understand...' Victor began. 'He bears my name...'

'And is just as malicious! Just as corrupt. I asked you to help stop him from hurting that girl. You're the only one he listens to. Well, if you're not going to stop him then I am!'

Boiling with an anger he could not swallow, Michael headed for Victor's private study where he'd so often been left to sort out his private paperwork.

'You're the only one I trust, my son,' he'd said to him. 'You're a bright boy. You'll go far in life.'

What Victor had meant was that he could make good use of a bright boy who had made university and got a degree in accountancy – a safe career his mother had wished him to follow. She hadn't wanted another criminal in her life, but Michael had seen things differently at the time. Following childhood with only his mother, he'd been flattered that his father had wanted him. But he'd just been used. Roberto would never be supplanted in his father's affections.

Michael knew exactly what to look for. As Victor's criminal empire had grown so had his need to keep records of his transactions; it was all here, his dealings with local politicians who had given him the nod when a decrepit property was available for peanuts prior to demolition. Lists of the people – mostly immigrants – renting those properties, crammed in like sardines, sometimes a hundred people in a house built to hold thirty.

Victor had managed meantime to struggle to his feet and tug an antique blunderbuss from the walls. He had a whole host of antique guns; some of them in working order, though not the blunderbuss. He swung it round his head like a club, roaring as he charged towards his bastard son.

Michael ducked towards the door, the gun barely grazing his shoulder.

Victor prepared to charge again. The door opened, the butt of the gun grazed the edge of the door, landing on the head of his wife. Gabriella Camilleri screamed and went down on her knees.

Michael didn't hang around. Gabriella hated him and for obvious reasons. Let the two of them stew. He had to stop Roberto. He knew he could do that. He also knew where to find him.

Pete Henderson had been dragged from bed – Sally's bed – to hear this. And he listened. The more he heard the more the bells of promotion rang inside his head.

Pete knew he played second fiddle in Sally's affections to an incredibly rich Swiss banker and accepted it. There were perks to their relationship. Number one she wasn't faithful to him alone so he didn't need to be faithful to her. That suited him fine. He liked a bit of variety in his sex life. Number two she mixed with the underworld in a way that he never could. They trusted a girl who took her clothes off in their nightclubs, which in their estimation meant she didn't have a brain. Boy, were they mistaken!

He devoured the information Michael had brought him and knew it was dynamite.

'There. Now will you do something about it?'

Sally was shrugging herself into a diaphanous dressing gown. Luckily she was wearing something else beneath it so Michael wasn't treated to a free view of her body.

Sally's question was directed at Pete Henderson. She'd gone to the police station to find him. He hadn't been there so she'd left a message. She'd also phoned Carla, who'd fallen silent as Sally told her what she intended to do.

'You might not dance again. You know that, don't you?'

Sally knew exactly what she was saying. If the Camilleris found out that she'd betrayed them to the police then her livelihood was in danger.

Carla's voice was its usually gravelly self, but Sally perceived an undercurrent that made her think she was hiding something.

Carla had been the one who'd suggested that she and Allegra approach Marcie with the business scheme. It was Carla who to all intents and purposes supplied the money. The suggestion had seemingly come out of the blue. What was Marcie to her?

Sally cast her mind back to a few days before her meeting with Marcie and Allegra. Klaus had been around. Smiling as though butter wouldn't melt in her mouth and dressing relatively conservatively in a little black dress with a boat neck – cleavage discreetly hidden – she'd accompanied him to an upmarket cocktail party in Kensington. It was there that she'd got into a conversation with the wife of a high court judge. They'd gossiped about friends, family and the London social scene and also social problems among the young, especially teenage pregnancy. The woman had been friendly but had excused herself when she'd mentioned her friend Marcie and how brilliant she was at dress designing. She remembered mentioning her name and where Marcie came from.

The woman's expression had paled and she'd excused herself. Sally had presumed that the woman – like a lot of those with money and husbands of position – only talked about social deprivation. The aspect of working-class girls getting knocked up when they were barely more than kids themselves had been too much for her. That was what Sally had thought at the time. In a way the woman excusing herself was just as well, before she blabbed about her own past and her own child. Carla had come calling shortly after that.

'Are you listening to me?' Carla had said. 'You will never work again if you cross that nest of vipers.'

Sally knew she was right.

In desperation she'd gone back to Marcie's place in the faint hope that she'd returned. Instead she'd found Michael.

'Leave it with me,' he'd said. 'I'll call round as soon as I can.'

'So, copper. Are you going to do something with this?'

Pete Henderson had sandy-coloured hair and the hint of a moustache on his top lip. His skin glistened. His smile was as slow and shadowy as a python about to gobble up its prey.

'Consider it done.'

## Chapter Forty-four

The last people Marcie had expected to see at her grandmother's front door were Sally and Carla. Michael was with them.

She must have looked astounded.

Sally did the talking. 'Don't look at us like that, Marcie. We've only come down from London, not bloody Mars. Can we come in?'

Rosa Brooks came out into the hallway. Her black eyebrows beetled above suspicious black eyes.

'Who is this woman using bad language in my house?'

'We're not in your house, Mrs Brooks. We're still out on the doorstep,' said Sally. 'I promise I won't swear if you put the kettle on and make us a cup of tea. There's a dear.'

'They're friends,' said Marcie.

Her grandmother was not the sort of woman who took kindly to any form of condescension. There was a fierce look in her eyes.

'They're very good friends, Gran. They helped me set up my business.'

She hadn't had the guts to tell her grandmother that she made scanty costumes for showgirls and strippers. There was no need as far as she was concerned. What she did for a living was her business, but she treasured her grandmother's approval. So she'd told her that she made nurses' uniforms. She did sometimes, though not the sort a real nurse was ever likely to wear on a ward.

Rosa Brooks scrutinised both women. Marcie could only surmise what she was thinking.

Carla was wearing her leopard-skin coat and skyscraper heels. Sally was neat and sassy in a shocking-pink suit with navy-blue trim. The jacket was boxy, the skirt was short.

Rosa Brooks went into the kitchen where Garth was sitting at the kitchen table drawing.

'They've come,' he said.

Rosa looked at him abruptly. 'Who has come?'

'The aunties.'

He spoke as though there were some great significance to them being here.

Rosa frowned. She fully accepted that Garth had a similar gift to hers. She also accepted that the pattern of his gift varied greatly from her own. He saw more than she did – in the living as well as the dead.

Marcie took Sally and Carla into the front parlour. Marcie bent down to switch on the electric fire. The room was mostly used at Christmas or when someone important called like the priest or the doctor.

'A bit parky in here,' said Sally rubbing her hands together. 'Never mind. It'll soon warm up.'

Carla made no comment but gathered her coat more closely about herself. She seemed distant and not so forthright as she'd been in the past.

Michael stood by the window with his back to

the room. Although his eyes had met hers he hadn't kissed her. Cool and collected as always, she sensed he was dwelling on something that might concern her or might not.

She returned here and felt safe, but thoughts of London had come with her. 'Have you seen Allegra?'

'She's OK now,' said Sally. 'Victor beat her up. She's alright but... He thought she was phoning another bloke. She was trying to phone you to warn you about Roberto.'

Marcie felt a great sense of relief. At least that particular bridge could be rebuilt. She frowned. 'So why have you come?' A sudden fear made her look to Michael. 'Is Roberto out to get me?'

He smiled at her over his shoulder and shook his head. 'No. Roberto won't be going anywhere for a long time.'

'My Pete...' Sally exploded into a drawn-out description of how her 'lesser lover' as she called him, had arrested the Camilleris for deception, fraud and goodness knows what else.

For Marcie this was very good news indeed. It was as though the weight of the world had suddenly fallen from her shoulders. She brightened up immediately.

'Joanna's having her midday nap. You have to stay long enough to see her when she wakes up.'

'We have to get back,' Carla snapped.

Marcie's smile diminished. 'Your choice.'

Her good feelings obviously had no place in Carla's life, yet the woman looked nervous. She kept fidgeting with her bag, her clothes and her eyes seemed to wander all over the place.

She studied the heavily made-up face, discovering lines that she hadn't seen there before. Carla, she realised, was a lot older than she'd thought on first meeting. Why the sudden rudeness? Did she think Marcie was going to throw her out again? She seemed very nervous this time.

'Why exactly have you come?'

'Because I was asked.'

'I didn't ask you.'

'Sod this!' Carla sprang to her feet. 'I know when I've outstayed my welcome.'

She bundled her coat around her more tightly and clutched her black patent handbag.

'Carla!'

It was Michael who intervened. 'Carla, you're here for a purpose. I think you should stay.'

Marcie was still smarting. 'She can go if she likes. I don't need her for my business. I can get along by myself...'

'Marcie.' Michael's voice was firmly persuasive and when she read his eyes she saw only affection and consideration for her. 'Marcie, I think you should listen to what Carla's got to say.'

There was a pause as Rosa brought in a tray of tea and biscuits. Without a word or a glance at any of them, she retreated back into the kitchen where Garth was drawing a sketch that both amazed and alarmed her.

'We lied,' said Carla, her gaze firmly fixed into her teacup. 'It wasn't Allegra who put up the money for your business. It was me.'

Marcie was suddenly racked by a strange sensation she couldn't quite understand. She felt a great urge to flee as though afraid of what she was about to hear. On the other hand her body felt heavy as though she'd been immersed in liquid marble.

*Stay.*

The voice she'd presumed to be her mother's had left her alone for some time now. To hear it again – even that single word – took her by surprise.

'You? Why?'

'I was doing it on behalf of someone else. I...' Carla didn't seem to know how to begin.

'Let me start the ball rolling,' said Sally. And she did. She told Marcie about the cocktail party and the wife of a high court judge. She told her of Carla contacting her just after. Even before Carla began recounting the life of a homeless girl who'd met a certain Antonio Brooks, she knew who they were talking about.

'My mother!'

Carla sighed. 'Your mother spent most of her life in an orphanage. When she left there was nothing much for her. She got in with a bad crowd and trouble came with it. She was a bit of a bad girl...' She smiled at the memory. 'That's why your dad was attracted to her. She did well for a girl from nowhere. Me and her...' Again she smiled at the memory. 'We were mates. Best mates. She had no mum and dad and I wished I didn't have any. My old man used to get pissed out of his head and knock the stuffing out of us – me and me mum. I left home and hitched up with Mary, your mother. And we did alright. We had a nice little business going and had it made. I may as well be honest with you – we both worked the streets. Then along came Antonio Brooks and swept her off her feet.'

She shook her head. 'Amazing. What a change in a girl! One minute she was a real hard case, and the next all she wanted from then on in life was to be a good mother and wife. Unfortunately things didn't quite work out that way.'

Marcie listened in horror as Carla retold the story that had been told to her.

'Your mother went up to London to buy you a special dress for your communion. It was to be a big surprise. She hadn't even told your father. A mate of his had offered to drive her up. Unfortunately that "mate"...' Carla spat the word contemptuously. 'Well, he had his own agenda. The last thing she remembers is waking up in hospital with her clothes dishevelled and covered in blood. She couldn't remember a thing. Not even her name. She had no option but to make a new life for herself. Not even having a name, she assumed the name of a dead child from off a grave stone.'

Marcie listened, with her heart feeling as though it were in her throat. She had an ugly suspicion who might have given her mother a lift to London. Alan Taylor had made a few offhand comments that made her suspect it was him. He'd been obsessed with her mother, just as he'd been obsessed with her.

However, he was dead and she wasn't inclined to mention his part in this. Instead she asked, 'The woman in the chauffeur-driven car. That was her?'

Carla nodded. 'She couldn't resist peeking at you and her granddaughter.'

'Why didn't she come herself?'

Carla's gaze was now fixed on her hands. 'Well! It was bit difficult. Her husband's very posh. He don't know nothing about her old life. It was only after marrying him that her memory began to come back. But she couldn't tell him the truth. He's old. Once he's dead and gone, it'll be a different matter.'

Not once had she met the frozen look on Marcie's face.

'Being curious, she'd already found out that Antonio had divorced her for desertion and remarried. But there was one thing she couldn't find out from bits of legal paper; she couldn't find out about you. She wanted to see you, but was afraid of how you'd be towards her. After all, she did desert you – in a manner of speaking.'

Marcie could barely control herself and certainly couldn't speak. There were so many emotions whizzing around in her head; so many questions; so many things she wanted to say. Sentences kept forming and falling apart. Engrossed in what Carla had been saying, she hadn't noticed Michael move away from the window. He was now standing behind her. She felt his hands resting reassuringly on her shoulders as if to say, I am here. Trust me.

One question, the most important question of all broke through all the others. 'When can I see her?'

Carla locked her fingers around the teacup. 'You can't.'

All the high hopes Marcie had suddenly been entertaining came crashing down around her head.

Michael squeezed her shoulders.

Carla rushed on with her excuse – which to Marcie's mind was all it ever could be. An excuse. Not a good reason.

'Look, love, like I just told you, her husband is very much older than her and no longer in good health. He hasn't got long to live. Look at it from her point of view: he's at death's door and she's telling him she's not who it says on the marriage certificate and that she was once a whore and married to a hood. Sorry, Marcie,' she said on seeing Marcie's wince, 'but your old man is a hood. A crim! There's no getting away from it. And she don't want to tell him about her past. The poor old judge would have an instant heart attack. He's been good to her. She can't repay him like that. So if you'll just wait a while...'

Somehow it didn't seem a good enough excuse. Marcie couldn't help thinking that Carla was a very good storyteller. This all seemed so far-fetched; she'd never imagined her mother as a whore and neither could she imagine her as a judge's wife.

'I don't believe you,' she snapped.

Carla's features froze. Her eyes, the lids heavily embellished with purple eye shadow, flickered like the dying flames of a fire.

Finally recovering, Carla leaped to her feet and wrapped her coat around her as though the weather had suddenly turned freezing.

At the station she slipped away from Sally and made a phone call. The voice on the other end was firm and strong.

'Did you tell her what I told you to tell her?'

'Course I did,' Carla answered. 'I said exactly what you told me to say, that Leo is a high court judge and about to kick the bucket.'

The woman on the other end of the phone sighed deeply. Leo Kendal was far from being a high court judge, though he'd been sent down by a few in his time. He was old and dying from cancer. He was also a jealous man. Waiting was hard, but she would stand it. The end result would be worth it.

Michael had driven Carla and Sally to the railway station but returned. Sally had made small talk. Carla had sat staring out of the window. She'd gone into the station ahead of Sally and he'd seen her entering a public phone box. He vaguely wondered who she'd phoned. There was no way of telling.

'Do you think she's telling the truth?' Marcie asked him.

He shrugged. 'I don't know. But leave it for now. Give it some time and we'll make a few enquiries. Who knows what we might find out?'

The evening was bright and clear. The sunset was salmon pink against a background of glowing furnaces on the Isle of Grain.

They went for a drink in a local pub once Joanna was asleep.

'Sorry, Michael. I'm not good company this evening.' She pushed away the vodka and tonic. She couldn't drink. She couldn't eat. She couldn't swallow.

'It's understandable. In that case I'll leave the

question I wanted to ask you till another time.'

She fingered the glass as she thought about all that she'd heard. Her mother had been beaten and raped by a friend of her father. She could guess who that was so would never ask. She clearly remembered the way Alan Taylor used to look at her. She also recalled him mentioning her mother in glowing terms. That hadn't been kindness glowing in his eyes. It had been lust. She'd never know for sure of course, unless she could ask her mother directly, but she had a feeling she was right.

Perhaps the evening would have stayed sombre if the door to the bar hadn't crashed open. All eyes turned that way.

'Marcie! Michael!'

Tony Brooks looked a right sight. His clothes were dishevelled; he had a two-day growth of stubble on his chin and a black eye fringed with purple and yellow.

He staggered over. He smelled musty, as though he'd been travelling or cooped up somewhere airless.

Michael got him a pint.

Tony rubbed at his chest.

Silently Marcie eyed the man who had taken a girl from the streets and married her. She had to admire him for that. He was hardly the most upright man on earth, but basically he had a kind heart. He could forgive the devil himself if he spun the right yarn.

He swigged deeply on the pint Michael had bought him.

Overcome with emotion, Marcie kissed him on

the cheek.

He looked at her in amazement. 'What was that for?'

She smiled. 'For being you.'

'That's quite a shiner you've got there, Tony. Anyone I know?'

Her father grinned. 'Not unless you've met my missus. Still, I gave as good as I got.'

Michael's eyebrows rose. 'You gave your missus a pasting?'

'Not so much her, but that bloody Father O'Flanagan. They're supposed to be celibate you know, being Catholic and all that. But I don't think he was taking her bloody confession in the nuddy!'

He went on swigging his beer as though it was an everyday incident to catch a wife having it away with a Catholic priest.

Marcie and Michael exchanged looks and couldn't help but burst out laughing.

Later as they walked home, Marcie in higher spirits than at the pub, Michael turned her round to face the stars shining over the sea. The moon was full. It was almost as though the stars were touchable and the moon could be pulled down and bitten into – just like the cheese some said it was made from.

'What are you up to?'

'I said I wanted to ask you a question. Are you ready for me to ask it?'

She thought she knew the question he was going to ask but couldn't understand why he had turned her to face the sea and the vast expanse of sky.

'That's eternity,' he said as if reading her thoughts. 'Did you know that the star pattern we see isn't current, it's from thousands of years ago?'

She laughed, still not understanding.

'I want you to become Mrs Jones.'

Today had been momentous. He couldn't possibly comprehend just how propitious the time for asking this question. All her life she'd felt motherless – and fatherless for much of the time. Tony Brooks had been in and out of prison her whole life. She had much to thank her grandmother for but she was determined that Joanna would never suffer like she had suffered. At least now she knew for sure her mother was alive. She ached to be able to see her but if that wasn't to happen in the immediate future at least she had hope that it might one day.

And now she had Michael. Did she love him? She thought she did, perhaps not in the reckless first love way that she'd felt for Johnnie, but she wanted to be with him. She cared about him deeply. She also knew that first and last he would make a good father. She was certain of that.

*It's the right thing to do.*

This time she knew who that voice belonged to. Like her grandmother she had lost the great love of her life, but he was still there, whispering in her ear and keeping watch over those he had loved.

She nodded. 'A little voice tells me that it's a good idea. So I'll go with that.'

Michael folded her to him. His chest was warm against her back. His arms were protective.

'Does this little voice also tell you that I love you?'

Marcie smiled. She didn't need Johnnie to tell her that. 'I love you too. You'll be taking on two women.'

'Yep.'

'And then there's my family.'

'Yep.'

'And Garth.'

'Him too.'

Arms entwined they made their way back to Endeavour Terrace where they found Rosa Brooks sitting with a grin on her face.

'I've made tea,' she told them. 'And a cake.'

'Like for a celebration,' added Garth, who'd already been cut a piece.

Michael looked surprised, but Marcie wasn't. Garth was something different inside than he was outside. Her grandmother assessed people and drew her own conclusions and Marcie was beginning to do the same thing.

Marcie had her own reasons for marrying Michael and hoped the signs were good for their future. He was a good man. No matter what happened she was a stronger person than she had been. Besides that, she was no longer alone. She had Michael and knew he would always be there for her. And somewhere out there she had a mother who was watching out for her.

The publishers hope that this book has given you enjoyable reading. Large Print Books are especially designed to be as easy to see and hold as possible. If you wish a complete list of our books please ask at your local library or write directly to:

**Magna Large Print Books**
Magna House, Long Preston,
Skipton, North Yorkshire.
BD23 4ND

This Large Print Book for the partially sighted, who cannot read normal print, is published under the auspices of

## THE ULVERSCROFT FOUNDATION

| BB | 8/10 |
| --- | --- |
| BP | 11/11 |
|  |  |
|  |  |
|  |  |
|  |  |
|  |  |
|  |  |
|  |  |

# ANYONE WHO HAD A HEART

*From a small town in Kent to London in the swinging sixties...*

Marcie Brooks has returned to her home town with a baby and a ring on her finger, but for all her grandmother's insistence that she's a young widow, the truth is the only boy Marcie has ever loved tragically died before he could make good his promise to wed her. When Marcie has to leave Sheppey in a hurry, the offer of a job in a smart boutique on the Kings Road, arranged via her dad's dodgy connections, seems an ideal escape. Then she begins to realise that her new Sicilian bosses have other interests that are far from legal...